DATE			

The Youngest Miss Ward

ALSO BY JOAN AIKEN

The Youngest
Miss Ward

Joan Aiken

St. Martin's Press ≋ New York

Library of Congress Cataloging-in-Publication Data

Aiken, Joan, 1924–
  The youngest Miss Ward / Joan Aiken.
    p. cm.
  Companion vol. to Mansfield Park, a novel by Jane Austen.
  ISBN 0-312-19375-0
  I. Austen, Jane, 1775–1817. Mansfield Park. II. Title.
PR6051.I35Y68   1998
823'.914—dc21   98-41687
                                                              CIP

First published in Great Britain by Victor Gollancz,
an imprint of the Cassell Group

First U.S. Edition: December 1998

10 9 8 7 6 5 4 3 2 1

Fic.

PART ONE

I

To Mr Henry Ward, a gentleman of very moderate means residing at Bythorn Lodge in the county of Huntingdon, it was a matter of some mortification that he had only seven thousand pounds to give his daughter Maria when she was so fortunate as to capture the affections of a baronet, Sir Thomas Bertram, possessor of a handsome estate not far off in the neighbouring county of Northamptonshire. Mr Ward's other daughters were, subsequently, to fare even worse: due to a diminution of her father's fortune, the eldest Miss Ward, Agnes, could take only two thousand with her when, six years after her sister's wedding, she was able to contract a respectable, if undistinguished, alliance with Mr Norris, a middle-aged clerical protégé of her brother-in-law. More grievous still, at a time when the family was in some distraction, the third sister, Miss Frances, made a runaway match with a lieutenant of marines in Portsmouth. For the rest of her life this daughter would therefore be referred to as 'poor Fanny' with a mixture of distaste and condemnation by her elder sisters – particularly by Mrs Norris. And, to cap it all, the youngest Miss Ward, Harriet, allowed her life to take such an un-looked-for and outrageous turn that she, among the family, was never referred to at any time (except of course by Mrs Norris).

It is an account of her history and misfortunes, with a rebuttal of all false assertions and calumnies that the present narrative sets out to provide.

The youngest Miss Ward, Harriet, or Hatty as she was most frequently referred to did not, at the age of twelve when this journal commences, seem destined for a career of infamy.

From the first, she had been her mother's favourite, and spent much time in Mrs Ward's boudoir with that lady (who became bed-ridden three years after Hatty's birth) reading her lessons, books, and poetry or singing in a soft but true little voice with a small compass.

Good looks had been very unevenly distributed by Providence among the Ward sisters. Two of them, Maria and Frances, resembled their handsome father: they were the fortunate possessors of dazzlingly fair complexions, large blue eyes, and fine, tall, well-formed figures; they were generally acknowledged to be among the finest young women in the county.

The other two sisters, Agnes and Hatty, took after their mother, who had brought breeding to the family, but neither money nor beauty; she had been a Miss Isabel Wisbech, a distant connection of the Duke of Dungeness, and although clever, kind-hearted and elegant, she was unimposing, short and slight in stature, dark-eyed and pale-skinned, with very little countenance; this, as well as her gentle manner and complete lack of animation, caused neighbourhood gossip to assert that she had not been happy in her marriage.

Agnes and Hatty had both inherited their mother's small stature and dark colouring, but not her lack of animation; Hatty in particular had inherited her mother's elegance, and a sweetness in her countenance that would always recommend her to the notice of discerning strangers. For Agnes, the eldest Miss Ward, had a sharp, bustling and overbearing nature, while Hatty, quick-witted, playful and original in her cast of mind, had always been obliged to provide her own amusements, since two of her elder sisters were too phlegmatic to comprehend her jokes and imaginings, while the third was too short-tempered.

Mr Ward, amid this household of women, had become a disappointed man. His chief and lifelong ambition was to be appointed Master of Foxhounds, for he was greatly addicted to the chase, and would have hunted every day of his life had such a pursuit been possible, and had dissipated the larger part of his fortune on high-bred hunters. At the time of his marriage he had hoped that a connection with Colonel Frederick Wisbech, his wife's second cousin, who was the younger son of the Duke of Dungeness, and reputed, furthermore, to

8

be a very shrewd investor in the City, would bring him both social and pecuniary advantage. But neither of these blessings had come about. Colonel Wisbech thought Mr Ward a dead bore, and kept his distance, while the foxhounds remained under the negligent care of the Duke's brother-in-law.

But Mr Ward's worst and grinding disappointment lay in regard to his estate, which was entailed in the male line and would, in default of an heir, pass to one of his brother Philip's sons. Mr Philip Ward was an attorney in Portsmouth, of no social consequence whatsoever in his brother's estimate; the two brothers rarely communicated and had met but once in the course of eighteen years. It was a continual vexation to Mr Ward that this unimportant family should have the right to inherit his property simply on account of some piece of legal barratry. And life for a man of small fortune, such as himself, who lived on the fringe, but never in the company of titled connections, could never be easy.

Four daughters had the unfortunate Mrs Ward brought into the world by the age of thirty-one, and after the fourth her medical attendant pronounced without the slightest hesitation that a fifth child would indubitably kill her. Mr Ward was outraged at this news. He had taken little notice of the first three daughters; the fourth one he utterly ignored. From the delivery of Hatty, after which she was stricken by a severe birth fever, Mrs Ward's health steadily declined, and by the time of Miss Maria's wedding she had been bed-ridden for eight or nine years.

Preparations for a sufficiently handsome nuptial celebration due to the future Lady Bertram were plainly going to be beyond her power to set in train.

'Why should we not invite my cousin Ursula Fowldes to help us?' she therefore hesitantly suggested to her husband. 'Ursula might, I believe, be prepared to come and stay here, for a few days before the wedding, and take care of all the details; I fancy there is no one so knowledgeable, so capable as she, when it comes to matters of that kind. She has had ample experience, as you may recall, with the weddings of two of her sisters. And, for the marriage of our dear Maria

9

to Sir Thomas Bertram, we would not wish anything to be done improperly or negligently.'

Mr Ward thought very well of this suggestion. Lady Ursula Fowldes, eldest daughter of the Duke's brother-in-law, the fox-hunting Earl of Elstow, had seen two of her younger sisters, the Lady Mary and the Lady Anne, suitably married off; she must by now be thoroughly acquainted with all the correct minutiae of etiquette and procedure. (Why Lady Ursula had never married was a subject of conjecture and rumour in the neighbourhood; there had been talk of a broken romance some years before.) At this time she was twenty-seven years of age, and, by now, hopes of her contracting a matrimonial alliance had, for numerous reasons, long been relinquished.

'I believe Cousin Ursula might be willing to come and advise us,' repeated Mrs Ward, 'although it is a long time since I have seen her. She and I had a great kindness for one another, when we were younger. If you will supply me with pen and paper, Hatty dear, I will write to her directly.'

Hatty obeyed, but she did so with a sigh as she brought the writing materials. Among the Ward girls, Cousin Ursula was by no means a favourite, for she cherished very high notions as to her own position in society and (perhaps as a legacy of that legendary romantic attachment) bore herself in a stiff, acidic, superior manner and maintained a ramrod-straight deportment which tended to cast a gloom over any social gathering in which she took part. Her nose, her chin, her eyebrows were perpetually elevated in astonished condemnation; no one was ever so speedy to depress vulgar pretensions or to snub upstart impertinence as Lady Ursula.

'Ay, ay, your cousin Lady Ursula will certainly be the properest person to oversea Maria's affair,' agreed Mr Ward, quite satisfied for once.

At this period of the family's fortunes, since Maria had been able to contract such a gratifyingly eligible alliance with Sir Thomas Bertram, Mr Ward's frame of mind concerning his future prospects still remained reasonably sanguine. It was to be supposed that Maria's future connections might well achieve satisfactory matches for the younger girls as well. And he was entirely pleased with the notion of persuading Lady Ursula to visit his modest residence, Bythorn Lodge. For up to now, despite the family connection, there had been but few dealings between the Ward family and that of Lord Elstow at Underwood Priors. 'Our cousins, the Fowldes', 'Our cousin, Lady Ursula' echoed pleasantly through the mind of Mr Ward; during the forthcoming wedding festivities, this, he felt, would make a most satisfactory counterbalance to the titled connections of the bridegroom, Sir Thomas.

Abandoning his customary disparaging, not to say surly, manner towards the generality of the female sex, Mr Ward, for the duration of the nuptial celebrations, was prepared to treat Lady Ursula with distinction, cordiality and even with an approach to gallantry which would amaze his daughters.

There were, however, various domestic problems to be overcome before the arrival of the wedding guests. An elderly aunt of Mr Ward, Mrs Winchilsea from Somerset, had been invited for the occasion, and Bythorn Lodge possessed only a single guest chamber. One of the four girls must, therefore, move out of her bedroom to accommodate Lady Ursula. Plainly Maria, the bride, could not be thus displaced; the obvious choice would be one of the two younger girls, Hatty or Frances; but their quarters were inferior.

'Agnes must give up her room,' decreed Mr Ward, when the matter came to his adjudication. 'Agnes has the largest room of the three, with a view over the meadow; it is by far the most suitable, the only chamber proper for Lady Ursula who is, after all, devoting time and solicitude to our affairs; we should neglect no attention that can contribute to her comfort. Agnes must move in with Frances.'

Agnes was by no means pleased with this decision. Further to inflame her sense of injury, Maria had selected her younger, not her elder sister as an escort on the forthcoming bridal tour to Bath and Wells. Frances, not Agnes, had been preferred for a travelling companion. This choice was not particularly surprising to anyone in the family, for Frances and Maria, resembling one another in nature as in looks, had always been each other's best friend, leaving Agnes, the eldest, and Hatty, the youngest – separated in age by thirteen years and in disposition by every possible incompatibility – to get along as best they could during the lack of any other companionship.

But Agnes now felt this exclusion most severely. It was in her nature to resent *all* such slights, whether real or fancied, and the present instance was in no way mitigated by Maria – soon to be Lady Bertram – remarking in her usual calm, languid tone, 'After all, sister, it is your plain duty to remain in the house and look after Mama, when Frances and I are gone off on my wedding journey with Sir Thomas. I have heard you say, I do not know how many times, that you are the only person in the family who is fit to take proper care of our mother, that Fanny is by far too feather-pated to be entrusted with the housekeeping, and Hatty, of course, too young. So everybody will be suited; and I think you had best move yourself into Hatty's bedroom, for there will be a great deal of confusion in Fanny's chamber while she packs up her things to come away with me. Fanny is so scatter-brained. When we are gone off, you know, you may take your pick between my room and Fanny's – if Lady Ursula remains – since I daresay Fanny may stop with me and Sir Thomas for a number of months, once we are settled at his house in Mansfield Park.'

All this was bitter as gall to the irritable spirit of Agnes, the more so since it was based on completely reasonable arguments and thoroughly incontrovertible facts. In the end Agnes did choose to move in with Hatty (much to the latter's dismay) for two reasons: first, because the room was closer to her own; and second, because Hatty, being the youngest, was most subject to her elder's jurisdiction and could be ordered to carry armfuls of garments and other articles from one chamber to the other.

From this minor household displacement followed a mishap which would have repercussions that continued for many years to come.

Maria's wedding was to take place in the month of June. That year the early weeks of summer had been peculiarly close and oppressive, with heavy grey skies and a continual threat of thunder. The invalid Mrs Ward had found the warm and airless atmosphere especially trying, and had begged for as many doors and windows as possible to be kept open at all times. It so happened, therefore, that the front door of Bythorn Lodge was standing wide open when the chaise-and-four arrived that brought Lady Ursula from Underwood Priors. This was several hours earlier than expected. Lady Ursula had never been known to consult the convenience of others in her comings and goings, and since she considered that she was conferring a signal favour by this visit, she felt not the least scruple in advancing the suggested arrival time by half a day.

The household was already in some confusion, with preparations for the other visitor and the nuptial festivities, and no footman chanced to be stationed in the hall at the moment when Lady Ursula, tall, grim and disapproving, stepped through the open front doorway. She rapped smartly with her cane on the flagged floor, looked around her, and called out loudly in her high, commanding voice: 'Hollo, there! Where is everybody? Let me be attended to, if you please!'

Fanny Ward, running down the steep stair with a bundle of household linen in her arms was almost petrified with alarm at the sight of this daunting apparition.

'Oh, my gracious! Cousin Ursula! I – I h-had no notion that you was expected quite so soon! I – I am afraid Papa is down at the s-stables—'

Down at the stables was where Mr Ward invariably spent the hours of daylight when there was no hunting to occupy him.

'That is not of the least consequence,' said Lady Ursula coldly. 'You will escort me to your mother, if you please. Frances, is it not?'

'Yes – yes, of course—' Desperately, Fanny tugged at a bell rope, and when the flustered housekeeper appeared, gave equally flustered directions. 'Direct Jenny and my sister Harriet to prepare Lady Ursula's room immediately!'

'Escort me, pray, to your mother,' repeated Lady Ursula, a lifting note in her voice suggesting that she was not in the habit of being obliged to repeat her requests.

'Of course, certainly, Cousin Ursula – if you will step this way – I am just not sure that Mama is – but if you will follow me – and if you will just—'

13

Lady Ursula's expression conveyed that she was not used to being left waiting in passage-ways. A small upstairs hall had an armchair beside a french window leading on to a balcony, but Fanny's hopeful gesture towards the armchair failed to have any effect on the visitor, who continued to follow close behind her nervous guide.

Mrs Ward's bedroom door, like the front entrance, stood wide and thus revealed the scene within, which, to most observers, would have been a pleasing and touching one.

To afford her as much relief as possible from the sultry and oppressive closeness of the atmosphere, the invalid lady was half-lying, half-seated in bed, reclined against a mass of pillows and swathed in layers of the lightest possible gauze and cambric. Slight and thin even in the best of health, Mrs Ward now looked frail as a cobweb. Her dark hair was piled on top of her head, for ease in the heat, and covered with a wisp of lace. To the startled eyes of Lady Ursula her face, small and pointed, and at this moment somewhat smoothed from its habitual lines of pain, looked exactly as it had twelve years before. And the face of the child, holding a book, curled beside the bed in a slipper-chair, was its precise replica. But the expressions of each were at wide variance. That of the child held nothing but dismay; that of the sick woman brightened into joy and recognition.

'Ursie! My dear, dear Ursie! This is such a pleasure! We had not expected you until dinner-time!'

'So I had apprehended from the lack of preparation,' glacially replied the visitor, but mitigated her reproof by approaching and momentarily resting her cheek alongside that of the sick woman. The child, meanwhile, had nervously, like some small wild creature, started away from the bedside.

Lady Ursula hardly glanced at her, but Mrs Ward said softly, stretching out an attenuated hand, 'Dearie, we will continue with our Shakespeare reading at a later time. Soon, I promise. For we had reached such an exciting point! Mind you do not cheat and read on by yourself – I put you on your honour! I trust you! Now, as you may guess, Cousin Ursula and I have many years of conversation to catch up – and you, I know, will help Fanny prepare Ursula and Aunt

Winchilsea's chambers – and pick each of them a sweet-scented posy from the garden. Hatty's posies are always the best,' Mrs Ward told her visitor, indicating the lavender, Southernwood and geranium nosegay on her bed-table with a quick, hopeful smile as the child came closer and brushed her cheek against the outstretched hand.

But Lady Ursula, with hardly a glance at her young cousin, gave brusque orders: 'Run along, child, do; you are not wanted here. Your mother and I have private matters to discuss – run away, make haste, go along with you. And shut the door behind you as you go.'

Mrs Ward opened her mouth to protest against this, but then closed it again. She said gently, 'Sit down, my dear Ursie. Find yourself a comfortable chair. It is so *good* to see you, after all this time. You must tell me all about your sisters' weddings. And your Mama. And your Papa – Uncle Owen – how is he?'

'Very ill,' replied Lady Ursula shortly. 'He is drunk more often than sober, when at home. And when in London – which is where he spends the greater part of his time – my mother prefers not to inquire too closely into his doings. And she – she is hardly in this world at all. We will not waste time talking about *them*, if you please.'

With an air of disgust she pushed away the slipper-chair from the bedside and, looking around, chose an upright one more suited to her habitual posture. Seating herself upon it, she glanced frowningly at her hostess and said, 'You should not allow that child to tire you so. One of her sisters could surely oversee her studies.'

'Oh, but my dear Ursie, we enjoy such happy hours together. She is now my only – one of my chief pleasures. Pray do not scold me, Ursie! I hope you have not come here to do that! I have hoped to see you for so long! Why did you stay away?'

Mrs Ward stretched out a caressing hand and took that of her visitor.

'Come! Let us pretend that we are back in the schoolroom at Underwood. How are Barbara and Drusilla? How is my cousin Fred Wisbech? And my uncle the Duke, is he well? And – and my cousin Harry?'

'I have not the least idea,' replied Lady Ursula in a cold, remote tone. 'Our paths do not cross. Nor is it at all desirable that they should.'

15

'Oh, *Ursie!*' Mrs Ward's tone was hardly above a sigh, but it held all the sorrow and sympathy in the world. Now she held the visitor's hand in both of hers and softly, condolingly, stroked it. 'Oh, my dear, dear Ursie! Why, why have you never come to see me before this?'

'What occasion was there to do so?'

Lady Ursula's tone was cold, and her expression forbidding, but she let her hand remain where it lay. She sat immobile, like a large armoured vessel, held at the dockside only by the very slightest of mooring cables.

Darkness fell early on that hot, oppressive day. The provision of a more elaborate dinner than usual, in honour of the arrival of Lady Ursula and Mrs Winchilsea, had overtaxed the resources of the inefficient household, and, at the fall of dark, Hatty and one of the servant-maids were still running to and fro upstairs with bundles of gowns, cloaks, petticoats and toilet utensils which were being transferred from one bedroom to another. The most direct route for them lay across the head of the main stairway which led down to the entrance hall.

As sometimes occurs at the commencement of a storm, a sudden terrific gust of wind swept across the garden to break the sultry calm of the evening. The front door, which still stood open, blew shut with a reverberating crash, and all the hall candles were extinguished in the draught. Hatty, who at that moment had been crossing the upstairs landing with a heavy trayload of pieces from her eldest sister's bureau, was so startled that she missed her footing in the unexpected dark and tumbled headlong down the stair, accompanied by a clatter of breaking chinaware and a strong waft of spilled lavender-water.

'Oh, *mercy* on us, Miss Hatty!' cried out Jenny the maid, who had been but a few paces behind her. 'Oh, my laws, are ye killed? Whatever's come to ye?'

Mr Ward heard the crash of the front door slamming, Hatty's downfall, and Jenny's subsequent outcry.

'What in the *world* is going on here?' he demanded irascibly, issuing from his study, candle in hand. 'Not so much noise, if you please! Remember your poor mistress, lying ill in her chamber.'

Indeed, faint requests for information could be heard emanating from Mrs Ward's chamber, while Agnes, Maria and Frances all made their way, bearing candles, to the scene of the accident, Agnes at a hasty pace, the others more leisurely.

'Careless, abominable girl!' exclaimed Agnes in a tone of strong reprobation. '*Look* what she has done to my things!'

Fragments of broken pottery, glass, ivory and lacquer lay widely strewn over the flagged hall floor.

'But Miss Hatty, Miss Hatty!' wailed Jenny. 'She's surely dead – she's killed!'

'Do not create such a foolish commotion, girl,' pronounced Mr Ward, in a voice of severe displeasure. 'You will unnecessarily alarm Mrs Ward. Of course the girl is not dead, she has merely knocked herself senseless.'

'But may she not have broken some bones, sir?' suggested the housekeeper, Mrs Ayling, a calm, sensible woman who now arrived upon the scene. 'Should not Mr Jones have a look at her?'

Mr Jones, Mrs Ward's physician, lived not far away and paid frequent visits to the house. Hastily summoned, he pronounced that Miss Hatty had no bones broke, but was suffering from a severe concussion and must remain in her bed for several days.

Due to these circumstances, Hatty was obliged to miss the wedding ceremony and attendance on her sister at the church, besides the various festivities. She also missed meeting most of the guests. Her state of mind for the first few days after the accident remained somewhat confused, so she felt no particular regret at her exclusion from the service.

Afterwards her chief memory of the occasion was to be a visit to her bedside paid by Lady Ursula. The immensely tall, thin figure glided into her chamber and stood looking down at the invalid, it seemed, from a terrifying height. Lady Ursula's face seemed to poor Hatty like that of some bird of prey, the nose aquiline, the mouth drooping in a disdainful curve, the eyes deeply hooded. The visitor's hair, pulled straight back beneath a black lace cap, already showed strands of grey. Her hands were long, bony and emphatic, as she shook an admonishing finger at Hatty.

'Tiresome child! You have caused great trouble, inconvenience and loss to your poor sister Agnes. What a ridiculous, unnecessary mishap! It was a thoroughly childish thing to do, and most unladylike, besides!'

'Indeed, Cousin Ursula, I could not help it. I missed my footing in the sudden dark,' pleaded Hatty faintly, staring up at the long, severe face. To her still feverish fancy it was like some piece of marble statuary that had come stalking in from the garden.

'Tush. Fiddle, child! A lady should always have complete control of her limbs. If you had learned such essential control, you would have stood *still* when the light blew out – not tumbled down in that clumsy maladroit hoydenish manner. Your poor sister Agnes has lost some of her most cherished possessions.'

'I know, I know it,' whispered Hatty forlornly. 'How can I possibly replace them? Her ivory mirror – her silver brooch—'

The catalogue of losses sustained by Agnes had been the first information fed into Hatty's unhappy mind as soon as she began to recover consciousness. Agnes, eldest of the Ward sisters, had been particularly proud of the treasures accumulated on her toilet table, the chief of these being an ivory brush, comb and hand-mirror bequeathed to her by old Mrs Wisbech, her maternal grandmother, when that lady died. They had the initial W engraved on the back which, of course, served for Ward as well as for Wisbech. And now the glass in the mirror was shattered, the comb broken in two, the hairbrush badly bent. Besides this, a cherished little lacquer box was irretrievably smashed, a Venetian vial cracked, so that it would no longer hold aromatic vinegar, and several other articles dented or bent beyond repair. Since her life had hitherto been barren of friends or lovers, Agnes set immense store by such possessions as she had contrived to acquire, and the loss of them was a bitter grievance, which she made no attempt to make light of or pass over. Hatty was obliged to hear the detailed tally of her bereavement several times a day.

Indeed this episode permanently impaired the relations between Hatty and her eldest sister, which had never, at best, been particularly warm or cordial; and it soon led on to the formation of a scheme that was to affect the whole of Hatty's subsequent career. Up to this

18

juncture Mrs Ward, though bed-ridden, had given Hatty all her lessons, since Mr Ward latterly begrudged the salary of Miss Tomkyns, the governess who had instructed Agnes, Maria and Fanny. Mother and daughter had both taken pleasure in the quiet reading of history, French, Latin, Greek and Italian, besides plays, essays and poetry; music continued to be taught by a master who came once a week and instructed the younger girls, since Mr Ward considered music a necessary female accomplishment if they were to catch husbands.

But it was becoming evident that, as Mrs Ward daily grew feebler, this regime could not long be continued; and Lady Ursula, with whom Mr Ward discussed the matter, was strongly of the opinion that Hatty should now be sent away from home to live with another family. This plan was also eagerly promoted by Agnes, who had never liked her youngest sister, and could think of a thousand good reasons why her departure was desirable.

'She makes too much noise about the house for my poor mother; she is not receiving the requisite education – for her fortune and expectations in life, coming as she does at the end of the family, cannot be high, she must look to be obliged to support herself, most probably as a governess; *I* have not the time to see after her, so occupied as I am with the housekeeping and care of Mama; as we have just seen, she is becoming most regrettably careless and uncontrollable; by residing with another family she will learn better deportment and greater respect for her elders.'

The other family in question was that of Mr Philip Ward, their uncle the attorney in Portsmouth.

Mr Ward favoured the plan for two additional reasons, neither of which did he divulge to his family; the first being that some fifteen years previously, when his own fortunes were in better trim and his brother was still a struggling attorney in the early stages of his profession, Mr Ward had lent Mr Philip Ward five hundred pounds. Their situations were now reversed and Mr Ward had reason to believe that his brother might without any great difficulty have returned the sum, but for one reason or another, it was never forthcoming. 'Obliged to wait until some rents were come in ... clients were very tardy in paying their fees ... shocking outgoings about the house – and Mrs Pauline Ward had many medical expenses connected with the birth of the twins.' At least, reflected Mr Ward to himself, if Hatty were sent to live with the Portsmouth family, taking into account the subtraction of her board and pin money from his own budget, in the course of five years or so an equal sum might be saved. Moreover, set down among her cousins, was it not at least possible that the girl – though at present she had no particular attractions that her unloving father could discern – might, after the lapse of time and through sheer proximity, capture the affections of one of the boys and so be the means of retrieving the lost estate? At the present time this seemed wholly unlikely, but such improbable things did occur; certainly no harm could ensue from sending her to live with her uncle's family.

Accordingly, letters were exchanged about the matter, an agreement was reached, and, half a year later, Mr Ward walked into his wife's boudoir one morning, where she and Hatty were peaceably reading *Twelfth Night* together, to announce: 'So, it is all arranged. Harriet leaves this house on Thursday next to make her home with my brother Philip and his family in Portsmouth. By great good fortune Mr and Mrs Laxton, the vicar's cousins, are to make the journey to Portsmouth by stage that day, and will be pleased to escort our daughter.'

Two paper-white faces, two open mouths, received this news. Mrs Ward, indeed, fainted dead away, but since she had suffered from a number of fainting-fits during recent weeks, this was considered nothing out of the common.

'When – when shall I come back from visiting my uncle Philip?' whispered Hatty, through trembling lips, after her mother had been revived with aromatic vinegar and smelling salts.

'Why, not until you are grown up, child. If then. But it can make no difference to you. You are sure of a comfortable home in either place. And you will have your cousins for company.'

Mr Philip Ward's family, at this time, consisted of three sons – Sydney, Thomas and Edward – and a pair of twin girls, Eliza and Sophy, who were considerably younger.

Hatty absolutely dared not ask her mother if she approved of the plan; she could see that even discussing it would be too taxing for Mrs Ward's enfeebled state. And, in any case, discussion would be useless: Mr Ward, Lady Ursula and Agnes had firm hold of the matter. Opposition would be vain.

By means of a mental and moral struggle far beyond what might have been expected of her years, Hatty managed to accept the dictum without argument or protest.

'If – if Mama were to grow w-worse – if she should express a wish to see me – you would send for me, you would allow me to come home *then*, Papa?' she ventured, with imploring, tear-filled eyes.

Agnes broke out indignantly, 'Why, what use in the world would *you* be, if my mother should take a turn for the worse? All these years she has taken such pains with you – it will be a great relief to her, and a great rest, let me tell you, when she no longer has the burden of your instruction. Most likely she will improve in health when you are gone from here. And you must not be thinking that Papa can afford to pay your fare on the stage in order that you may come home for any trifling pretext – no, indeed! Is it not so, sir?'

'No, of course not,' he said impatiently. 'Do not ask foolish questions, child.'

'Can I take Simcox – can I take my cat with me?' Hatty asked forlornly.

But that evidently went under the heading of foolish questions; her father left the room without making any reply. And Agnes said sharply, 'Certainly not! Your cousins will for sure not want another animal in the house. Besides, cats cannot be transferred from one house to another – they always make their way back to where they have come from. Now you had better go and begin packing up your things. You can take a pot of my damson preserve to our Aunt Polly; it kept so well that we have several pots left from last year which are hardly mouldy at all. I daresay she has nothing .ar so good. And you may as well write farewell notes to Fanny and Maria, since you will not be seeing them until who knows when; Mr Challis is going to Bath soon and has promised to take messages from us to Sir Thomas and your sisters.'

Hatty crept away to her chamber – Agnes had moved back into her own room as soon as Lady Ursula returned to Underwood Priors – but she made no immediate attempt to begin packing. She sat motionless on the floor, with her head resting against the bed.

Grieving words filled her mind, but she brushed them away.

Not now. Another time.

II

BYTHORN LODGE, MR Henry Ward's home, was not a large house, but could be held to merit the status of a comfortable gentleman's residence, standing apart, as it did, from the village of Bythorn, in its own tolerably extensive pleasure-grounds, with lawn, shrubbery, carriage-sweep, and a vista of woods and meadows on every side.

His brother Mr Philip Ward's abode, in Lombard Street, Portsmouth, might also be considered handsome enough, for a town residence; it had two bow windows, on either side of the porch, was protected by substantial white posts and chains, and approached by three wide stone steps leading up to a handsome front door. It boasted also a substantial plot of garden-land at the rear, abutting on to a disused graveyard, besides stables, outbuildings, and a large and somewhat ramshackle conservatory.

Mr Ward had removed to Portsmouth from London several years earlier. Ostensibly the family migration had been for the sake of his wife's health, she having been somewhat thrown down by the birth of the twins. At the time, Mr Ward's business associates considered this move to be a grave sacrifice of professional connections, but in fact one of his chief clients, the Duke of Dungeness, and the Duke's eldest son, Lord Camber, both owned large tracts of land in Hampshire. The transfer had brought Mr Ward a great deal more of their affairs to manage, besides that of their acquaintance and connections in the country round about, and, as a result of the move, he had gained far more business than he had lost. Mrs Ward's health benefited from the Portsmouth sea-breezes, and the boys lost no time in finding their way on to the ramparts and into the Dockyard. They thought the change of dwelling a vast improvement on High Holborn.

But to Hatty, fresh from the silent green woods and meadows of Huntingdonshire, a transfer to Portsmouth must be a very different matter. Lombard Street, where Mr Ward's house stood, was a busy thoroughfare. Instead of green peace and country silence, she had to hear and endure the constant rattle and clatter of carts, horses, drays and carriages racketing over the cobbles, the shouts of market men and nightwatchmen, the chime of clocks, near and far, and, in the distance, the shrieks of seagulls and the staccato whirr and echo of musket practice. Although the house was a large one, as town houses go, Hatty found it almost unbearably cramped, close and noisy, compared with the rural silence to which she had been used hitherto. At night the din of traffic and the shouts of the watch disturbed her sleep; by day, outside of school hours, her boy cousins were continually racing up and down the four flights of stairs, slamming doors, and shouting to one another from top to bottom of the house (Mr Ward, who would soon have put a stop to this, being absent for a large part of the day at his attorney's office). While the youngest members of the family, the twins, Eliza and Sophy, were so sickly, pale, whiney and cantankerous that their peevish voices were to be heard, day and night, raised in perpetual complaint. Hatty could not conceive how so lugubrious a pair could ever have been born to a fat, merry high-coloured woman like her aunt Polly.

'It was that excessively wet, dismal summer of seventy-eight,' Mrs Philip Ward explained cheerfully as they sat hemming shirts. 'Or was it seventy-nine? Bless me! I remember it so clearly. There was not a decent strawberry to be had in the whole of London, though Mr Ward, your uncle Philip, sent as far afield as Blackheath and Barnet – since, my dear, when I am increasing I entertain such a craving for strawberries as you cannot imagine. La! I should not be talking to you in this way, but I can see that you are such a sage, sensible little creature – most unlike some of my pupils in the past, I can tell you! Lady Susan and Lady Louisa Wisbech – now there were a pair! Tease, tease and up to their tricks all day long – though, mind you, not a whisker of harm in either of them, dear girls, and both well settled now, I am happy to say. And as for their cousins the Fowldes – but we will not speak of them. Now you, my dear, I can see that you are old beyond your experience, and have been your Mama's comfort, I know, these any number of years. There, there! Do not cry, child! Life for us females is a continuous succession of hard, hard trials, and the quicker we settle down and accept that fact, the better we are able to come to terms with it. Lord save us! The trouble I have had with those twins. It is a wonder to all my acquaintance that I have succeeded in rearing them up to this day, and if it were not for Burnaby and her lotions and potions, I do not for one moment believe that I could have done so, and if you, my dear Hatty, can devise any means of rendering them less excitable and sulky, I shall be for ever in your debt!'

'I shall be happy to, ma'am – if Burnaby will permit it . . .'

'Ay, 'tis true, Burnaby's temper is not the easiest in the world – and it will not do to set her back up, for I depend on her very completely in the management of those twins . . . you must set about it little by little, Hatty my love, inch your way in slowly so she won't take a pet; I am sure you will know how to manage her. (For your sister Agnes is just such another, is she not? Fond of her own way and quick to take offence if she feels that her position is being assailed.)'

'Yes, that is so, ma'am. Well, I will try to make friends with the twins, if – if Burnaby will at least let me into the nursery.'

'*Do*, child. For, to tell truth, the thought of their future has me quite in a worry. I am half-ashamed to admit it, but I cannot find the way to reach their comprehension. My former pupils were so easy in comparison! Dear, sweet-tempered little things. But – in short – those twins put me out of all patience. I begin to suffer from such severe heartburn, such tremblings and hot flushes and palpitations if I am in their company for more than ten minutes, that your uncle has positively forbidden me to fatigue myself with them any more, but tells me to leave them quite entirely in Burnaby's care. Is not that singular? The dear boys never taxed me so, no matter how naughty and high-spirited.

Ay, ay, Hatty my dear, I think it a fine thing that you have come to live among us, for your uncle Mr Ward dislikes your father as heartily as one brother can hate another, thinks Henry so puffed-up in his pretensions that my husband would never willingly have paid off that five-hundred-pound debt, though nowadays, to be sure, it would be the easiest matter in the world for him to do so, prospering and thriving as he does, with half the nobility and peerage on his books; whereas your unfortunate Pa, by all that's heard, has hardly a feather to fly with; but – one way and another – I dare swear you will be better away from your poor dear mother in her last months. Lord! My dear, I know you do not think so now, but, just the same, it is kindest you are spared some such painful memories as would doubtless torment you lifelong; and since, as I hear, the household is now under the rule of your sister Agnes and her crony, Lady Ursula Fowldes – a pair of gorgons if ever the name was deserved – and Lady Ursula, moreover, set to fix her talons on your Papa, the very instant you are all out of your blacks, if what I hear from Cousin Letty Pentecost is to be trusted—'

A tide of ice seemed to run backward through Hatty's veins.

'What, ma'am? What *can* you mean? Mama is not going to *die?*'

'Ah, my love, there's no good blinking facts when they stare you in the face like bulldogs. The wonder is that the poor lady has endured as long as she has to this present. And as for that Lady Ursula, who used to be your Mama's great, great friend, we all know that your Pa will do anything that lies within his power to keep the entail of Bythorn Lodge away from our poor boy Sydney (though Sydney is as sweet and smart a lad as ever tied a cravat – if he does not end up as Lord Chancellor I'll be mighty surprised) – and, with Lady Ursula ready and eager to have your father, besides having been at her last prayers these five years, you may lay the knot will be tied between 'em so soon as it is decent to do so. Philip – your uncle – is wild angry about it, but there's no way he can see to throw an impediment in their path; wasn't your Papa doing the pretty to Lady Ursula as hard as he could lay it on at your sister Maria's wedding to Sir Thomas? Cousin Letty told me his civilities at that time were marked by many (your Pa not being, in the common way, over free with his gallantries and compliments to ladies). Though – mind what I say – whether such a union as that would *take* would be quite another kettle of eels. I'd not wager my Sunday bonnet on any issue from *that* pair excepting, perhaps, another girl-child; for that Fowldes stock seem all bred out – five skinny daughters, poor Lady Elstow bore (Lady Ursula's mother, that is, the countess) just the same case as your poor dear Ma, and though I say it as shouldn't, one of them, at least, only sixpence in the shilling – and who's to wonder, bred up in a damp dungeon like Underwood Priors.'

Aunt Polly had been for a number of years governess, mentor and much-loved guide to the daughters of the Duke of Dungeness, after the early death of their mother. She had, of course, while carrying out her duties in this family, been privy to many matters regarding their cousins, the family of Lord Elstow, and it was owing to her connection with the two groups that Mr Philip Ward had met, wooed and won her when visiting Bythorn Chase on ducal business.

Now Hatty stared at her aunt in deep dismay, only half comprehending this torrent of information. It would take hours, days, weeks to assimilate it fully.

'Ay, ay, my dearie, as I say, I think it an excellent thing for my dear boys that you have come among us. Your uncle would have it that one or other of the lads would fall in love with you, there would be sweethearting, if not rivalry and fisticuffs. But, lord, no! my love, said I, there's not the least risk of that in the world, she will be just the same as a sister to the dear fellows, and she will be daily improving their manners by her example and leading them into milder, more gentlemanlike ways. And so I am sure it will be. Ah, now, here *is* your uncle, come home from business.'

Mr Philip Ward was a thin, waspish man with a leaden complexion, from being generally within doors. The pressure of his business was now so great that he daily brought home large bundles of documents from his office in the town, and also made use of a room on the first floor of his house, which held a desk, and shelves of law books and many cupboards where he kept the more important of his titled clients' papers and archives. He was sharp and curt in his demeanour, in that respect not so different from his red-faced, fox-hunting brother, and

Hatty, never quite easy in his company, was hastily rising to withdraw, feeling that he did not welcome her presence, when he halted her by an inquiry.

'Well, miss! Has any word come yet from your sister – from the new Lady Bertram? Humph! She did a great deal better for herself there than might have been expected – a very great deal! Ten thousand a year! I did not reckon her above two. It is a fortunate thing for her sisters – they may well have cause to be grateful to her. Well, child?'

'No, sir,' said Hatty, faltering. 'At least, my sister Maria has not written to me. But then she would not be very likely to do so. I – I suppose she may have written to Mama and Papa. I have not heard.'

'Very well, very well. Run along, child.'

Her aunt's kinder glance seconding this dismissal, Hatty hastily left the room. Avoiding the schoolroom, noisy haunt of her boy cousins when lessons were over, she repaired to her own little attic bedroom, but found it in process of cleansing by an irritable housemaid, who declared that the new arrival had set her all behind in her tasks. Deprived of this sanctuary, at a loss, Hatty made irresolutely for the haven known as the book room, her uncle's study, knowing that he was still talking over the day's affairs with his wife in the parlour. To Hatty's dismay, she found her cousin Ned, the youngest of the three boys, walking up and down in front of the window-seat, mumbling to himself:

> 'A, ab, absque, coram, de,
> Palam, clam, cum, ex, and e
> Tenus, sine . . .'

'Pro, in, prae,' Hatty prompted him.

He gave her a glance of pure astonishment.

The ages of Hatty's cousins at this time were respectively: Sydney, sixteen, Tom, fifteen, Ned, eleven, and the twin girls, Sophy and Eliza, four years. Hatty's father had frequently sneered at his brother's parsimony in not sending away the elder boys to Eton or Westminster, conveniently forgetting that, from first to last, he had expended remarkably little money on his own daughters' education. But Mr Philip Ward had declared that the only thing the boys would pick up at public schools would be expensive habits and a taste for fashionable frippery associates; they could just as well get themselves a good plain education in Portsmouth and in due course, if need be, acquire a bit of polish at some university. Sydney was destined to follow his father into the attorney's office; Tom and Ned, respectively, were intended for the army and navy.

Tom and Ned had grumbled a great deal at being required to master Latin.

'It is all very well for Syd, who will need lawyers' Latin – but what is the need for a dead-and-gone language in the services?' Tom, a fat, slow-witted boy, had great difficulty in learning anything, and Ned, though naturally brighter, tended to follow his next brother's lead and echo his sentiments.

Hatty had formed no very favourable impression of her boy cousins. The elder pair were rough, loud-voiced, unaccustomed to the company of girls, and wholly lacking in curiosity about any of the things that interested her; but Ned, the youngest, was at least unlike his elders in appearance. Ned was smallish, compact, with dark-brown hair, bright brown eyes and a nut-shaped head. Though younger than Hatty, he overtopped her in height, but not by a great deal. She had already guessed that, left to himself, his natural talents would soon cause him to overtake his brother Tom in schooling.

'You know *Latin*, Cousin Hatty? How is that?' he demanded wonderingly.

'My mother has been teaching it to me. I have been learning it these great many years.'

'But why? What need for a girl to learn Latin? And how did my Aunt Isabel come to learn Latin?'

'Her father, my grandfather, was a bishop. He thought girls should be able to read the bible in Latin.'

Ned stared at such a notion. 'Glory! I am glad he was not my grandfather! What else did your Mama teach you?'

'Oh – Greek delectus and the irregular verbs, and Euclid and Wood's algebra. But I did not get on with the algebra at all.'

'No more don't I,' said Ned with feeling. 'But a sailor has to have algebra, for calculating positions, you know, and that sort of stuff. But what I detest most of all is the history. All those kings and queens and popes. What use are *they*, I'd like to know?'

'Oh, but history is so exciting!' cried Hatty. 'There are so many heroes! Richard Coeur de Lion, and Roland, and Charlemagne, and Hereward – and – and Bonnie Prince Charlie – '

Ned's mouth opened wider and wider. He stared at his cousin Hatty as if she were a conjuror making birds fly out of her ears.

He said: 'You know about all of *those*?'

'Oh dear, yes! And the Greeks – the Spartans, you know, at Thermopylae, and Ulysses – and Marathon – and the battle of Lake Regillus and – and Robin Hood – I used to play at being Robin Hood—'

She came to a sudden stop, blushing. And then added, lamely, 'But I could never make myself a proper bow and arrow. You need yew wood, of course, for a bow, and there are no yew trees in the garden at Bythorn Lodge.'

Ned said, his eyes sparkling, '*I* know where there are some yew trees, Cousin Hatty!'

Hatty's position in the house of her uncle Philip Ward would always, in some degree, resemble a trading-post in hostile, savage territory. She had a few friends – her aunt, her cousin Ned – and she had goods to exchange, valuable goods to those who valued them. But her status was at all times precarious, sometimes perilous.

The boys' tutor, Mr Haxworth, a dour man, and a severe disciplinarian, at first regarded Hatty with considerable distrust, which deepened to outrage when he learned that the instruction of this small, insignificant, uncomely female was to be added on to his duties with the Ward boys.

However, in the course of a few weeks, Mr Haxworth was bound to acknowledge that the presence of their girl-cousin at lesson-times had no adverse effect on the Ward boys, quite the reverse; her questioning mind, her serious attention to instruction, her industry in preparing her lessons, exercised a decidedly beneficial effect on her cousins who, whether out of emulation, shame or simply increased interest, showed a general improvement in their studies that he found quite startling. Tom, the middle boy, it was true, was heard to grumble about the higher standards, the increased amount of work, the more diligent application that was now expected of him.

'In the old days,' he complained, 'I could sleep through half old Hacky's lessons, or whittle a top; now it is talk, talk, and questions. You have to be alert and on the go all the time or he loads you down with tasks and impositions and a lot of deucid extra stuff you have to learn by rote.'

Hatty, the boys considered, possessed a wholly unfair aptitude for learning by heart, doubtless from all the poems she had put to memory to recite to her mother.

So, by degrees, as the weeks and then the months went by, Mr Haxworth was brought to accept Mr Ward's niece with a qualified approval.

Hatty found, however, an inveterate enemy and ill-wisher in Burnaby, the attendant and nurse to the twins Eliza and Sophy. The little girls, as their mother told Hatty, had from their earliest years been of a sickly and lethargic disposition. Their natures were querulous and selfish, and this temperament in them was aggravated by the constant care of a nurse – a close, quiet, hard-featured woman – who saw that, in her oppressive bond with her charges, lay a considerable degree of power for herself in the household. After the difficult birth of the twins, Mrs Ward had at first been obliged to relinquish the larger part of their care to this woman, and later became relieved to have done so, for, as she herself admitted, she greatly preferred her three high-spirited sons to the doleful and demanding infants.

When Hatty first came to Portsmouth, Mrs Ward said to the nurse:

'Now, Burnaby, I know how hard-pressed you are with the care of those sad, ailing children, but I intend that Miss Hatty shall share some of your burden in keeping them company and tending them. She has, you know, been much occupied about her mother, my poor invalid sister-in-law, so she is well accustomed to the fretful ways of sick persons and, if you instruct her, she can be of real use to you in sharing the task and giving you some hours of freedom.'

Burnaby's apparent agreement masked an internal resolve that she would never, while she drew breath, relinquish her two peevish dependants to the care of a little upstart newcomer of no more than thirteen years.

'I thank ye, miss, but I've no need of ye at present,' was her invariable response whenever Hatty tapped at the nursery door and looked in at the two melancholy little creatures captive in their high chairs, either sucking on their coral comforters or wailing dismally for succour. By the age of four they had probably swallowed more physic than any grown person in the British Isles.

Hatty had no wish to make trouble between her aunt Polly and the person who had been selected, presumably with careful thought, by her uncle Philip, to look after her afflicted cousins; but she did feel that Burnaby's regime was not calculated to help or develop the unfortunate twins.

Very likely, if no one takes notice of them soon, they will just *die* of discouragement, she thought in pity.

Hatty wrote copious letters to her mother from Portsmouth. She received very few in return, but she understood sadly that this must be so, because of Mrs Ward's weakness. One of the few she did receive, indited in a very shaky hand, and enclosed in a cover addressed in an unfamiliar hand – perhaps that of Lady Ursula – said:

My dearest H. It is a joy to hear from you. I believe you can help those children. Only by aiding others can we ourselves go forward. Try S.P.S! . . . I miss you with every breath I draw. Not many now perhaps. We shall meet after – Yr loving M.

Hatty wept and puzzled over this letter for weeks. True, she could have written back to Mrs Ward and asked what S.P.S. meant – but her mother was so ill, so frail, that it seemed almost heartlessly slow-witted not to be able to grasp what the letters stood for, to trouble her over such a trifle.

Instead, she consulted her cousin Ned.

Ned, in gratitude for some covert, tactful assistance with his Latin grammar, had, once the boys had grown accustomed to her presence in the family, made his cousin privy to a secret which had never been revealed to his elder brothers. In the grounds of the house were a stable-yard, outbuildings, a flower garden, and, beyond that, a vegetable plot and walled orchard. To the elder boys, the flower garden was unsatisfactory for any games of bilbo-catch or bat-and-ball; in their free time they generally betook themselves to the shore, or the ramparts, or the Dockyard. But Ned was something of a gardener; he had his own small patch where he grew cresses and radishes and marigolds; and, now and then, when his brothers sallied forth to Dockyard or beach, he would announce that he preferred to stay at home in the garden.

'My little oddity,' Mrs Ward called him. 'My little quiddity. But, lord bless me! the radishes he grows are twice the size of any that Martha brings home from the market.' He was her favourite among the boys.

But Ned had another recourse of which his family were wholly unaware.

'Come and I'll show you something, Hatty,' he said one Saturday afternoon when she had been residing in Lombard Street for some months, and his brothers were safely out of the house.

He led his cousin across the walled flower garden behind the house, and through the door in the wall to the kitchen garden and orchard. Beyond the fruit trees rose a further wall, this one covered with espaliered plum and peach trees. These had been somewhat neglected, for the garden required more work than Mr Philip Ward was prepared to finance, and vegetables for the table were his prime requirement. Deakin the gardener could manage no more. Untrimmed currant and gooseberry bushes had grown into a jungle at the end of the plot, surrounding a large leaden water-tank supported on wooden beams, under the drooping branches of a mighty pear tree.

'Look here,' said Ned and led the way along a narrow track among the currant bushes to the back of the water-tank where, half hidden among creepers, a door in the wall could just be seen. 'This is my secret door,' said Ned; and, with some trouble, for the hinges were rusty and the ground piled deep with dead leaves and twigs, he pushed the door open a very little way. 'There is just room to creep through. It is luck that you are not a chubby one, Cousin Hatty,' said Ned. 'My brother Tom could never get by.'

On the far side of this wall lay a small, derelict graveyard. It was triangular in shape. Six large yew trees and a great lime overshadowed the toppled, crooked, untended, lichened gravestones, and the grass and nettles grew waist-high, save where Ned had beaten out narrow runways.

'What a strange, strange hidden place!' breathed Hatty, looking all around her. For a moment she forgot her sorrow and home-sickness. 'Why, Ned, it is like a secret kingdom, all of your own.'

'Is it not!' said Ned, pleased with her. 'Now, look here!' And he showed her his tree-house, a platform constructed of half-rotten logs and planks that he had piled up in the crotch of the great lime-tree. It was reached by a rope-ladder.

Hatty was deeply impressed by all his arrangements, and even more so by the fact that he had kept the hiding-place a complete secret from his brothers.

'How long have you been coming here, Ned?'

'Oh, I don't know. A long time,' he said vaguely.

Even the traffic of Portsmouth seemed a great way off.

Perched in the tree-house, sniffing at the sharp fragrance of a pale green lime-flower, Hatty said hesitantly, after long thought, 'Cousin Ned, do you think that it hurts to die?'

His answer was positive. 'No. Not a bit. It is like falling asleep. I had an old spaniel, Rust, who died last year. I was by him at the time, he had been ill for weeks. He was asleep when it happened. He just stopped breathing . . .'

After that another long peaceful silence fell between the two. Then Hatty said, 'Ned, I have been puzzled by something in the last letter I had from Mama.'

And she told him of her question about the twins, and her mother's answer: 'Try S.P.S'. 'What do you think she can have meant?'

'Why,' he said at once, 'she must have meant Scissors Paper Stone.'

'Of course she did!' cried Hatty, suddenly illuminated. 'How very slow-witted of me not to have thought of that for myself. Thank you, thank you, Ned! I will try it on the twins the next time that old dragon of a Burnaby lets me in to the nursery.'

'I wonder that you should think the twins worth troubling yourself over,' said Ned. 'They are a dismal little pair.'

'But so would you have been, I daresay,' Hatty pointed out, 'if nobody had ever taken any pains with you.'

'Oh well – perhaps. Hatty, you will never, *ever* tell any other person about my secret place, will you?'

'Oh, *no*, Cousin Ned, you can trust me *absolutely* ... If it were not a graveyard,' said Hatty, 'we could some day build a little house here, when we are grown, and have it just for our own. I should dearly, dearly like that – a little house of my very own.'

'We had best go back now,' said Ned. 'I never stay in here for very long, in case people begin to wonder where I am gone.'

After that, Hatty was an accepted visitor in the lime-tree sanctuary.

Next week, having ascertained which was Burnaby's afternoon off, Hatty determinedly made her way into the nursery. Sue, the under-housemaid was there, mending a torn curtain, indifferent to the twins who sat, immobilized as usual, in their high chairs, whining for they knew not what.

'I'll play with them for a while, Sue.'

'Bless ye, miss, no play will cheer that pair,' said Sue, but she departed, willingly enough, to the kitchen.

Hatty planted herself on a stool between the two high chairs. The twins eyed her in a lachrymose, lacklustre manner. They were a plain pair, sallow, like their father, with scanty, straw-coloured hair, bulging foreheads and washed-out blue eyes. Their freckled faces were usually smeared with tears or snuffle. They had identical birth-marks.

'Look,' said Hatty, addressing them both, 'this is a stone.' She clenched her fist. 'And this is a pair of scissors.' She snapped her forefingers open and shut. 'And this is a sheet of paper.' She spread her hand flat. 'So: do you understand? Make a stone, like mine.' She clenched her hand again.

One small grimy fist, that of Sophy, was slowly clenched. After a moment Eliza's followed.

'Good. Very good. Now make scissors – like this, snap-snap.'

The small fingers snapped. Creases of concentration appeared on the bulging foreheads. For once, the twins had lost their look of apathetic woe.

'Good. Now make the paper. Flat, like this.'

Their hands were spread flat, short fingers curling upwards like grubby petals.

'Now, attend: scissors can beat paper, because they can cut.'

The creases on their brows deepened, as they followed this chain of reasoning.

'Right? Scissors can cut paper. Snap, snap. Do you see?'

They did not nod, but their eyes were fixed attentively on her face.

'But paper can beat stone, because paper wraps round stone.'

Hatty demonstrated, wrapping one hand round the other fist.

The four staring eyes were now trained on Hatty's hands.

'You see? And now – stone can beat scissors, because stone can smash scissors. Like this – smash!' Hatty drove her fist between two open fingers.

'Smash!' breathed both twins ecstatically. 'Smash!'

'So, now I play a game. First with Sophy. You shake your fist three times – like this: shake, shake, shake – then you do scissors. Or paper. Or stone. Which ever one you choose. And I do it too. And we see who beats. Are you ready? Shake, shake, shake – *now*!'

Sophy did scissors. Hatty did paper.

'You win, Sophy. Scissors beats paper, because scissors can cut paper.'

Sophy let out a crow of total triumph. Eliza's mouth was wide open with participation.

'Right. Now Eliza's turn.'

Eliza did scissors. Hatty did stone.

'I win that time. Now you do it with each other.'

They played – scissors and stone – and Eliza won. She laughed with pure joy. Hatty wondered whether she had ever laughed in her life before. They played again, and this time Sophy won.

'Now you can play with each other whenever you want,' said Hatty. The twins ignored her. They were utterly concentrated on each other. Hatty sat watcing them for half an hour. When Sue presently returned, with bowls of broth and biscuits, Hatty calculated that they must have played over a hundred and sixty games, and had each won about an equal number. Sometimes they would have long spells of both presenting the same object – two stones, two scissors – but this did not frustrate them, it made them chuckle.

'Bless us, Miss Hatty!' said Sue. 'I've ne'er seen 'em so quiet and biddable. Miss Burnaby should be pleased.'

Predictably, Burnaby was not.

The moment they had finished their meal, the twins recommenced playing and Hatty slipped away and wrote a letter to her mother.

But whether her vivid account of the proposal's triumphant success was ever read by its intended recipient, Hatty did not discover. She received no answer to her letter.

And some months later, word came to Portsmouth of Mrs Ward's death.

'May I not go home for the funeral?' Hatty asked her aunt Polly, who had considerately broken the sorrowful news to her niece in private, summoning her from lessons with Mr Haxworth.

'My dear, your sister Agnes (who writes this letter) recommends that you do not make the journey. And your cousin Ursula Fowldes, who has returned temporarily to Bythorn Lodge (where, Agnes says, she has been a great help during the sad and trying months of your Mama's decline), is strongly of the same opinion. And furthermore – I fear – your father expressly forbids it.'

'But – but – then – may I not go home now? Altogether? Not just for the funeral – to live? I – I was s-sent away so as not to be a trouble to – to M-Mama – now she is gone, may I not return there?' Hatty faltered.

Mrs Ward's gaze was not unsympathetic. She said, 'My child, I know how forlorn you must feel. But consider. Your Mama is what you chiefly miss, and she will not be there. Ever again. Of what avail are empty rooms, if the person you wish to see does not dwell in them any more? Your father does not wish for you and would be no comfort to you. In my opinion a block of granite would be a great deal more use,' she added as a corollary to this, but she spoke under her breath. 'Your sister Agnes and cousin Ursula seem quite bent on preventing your return, so you would certainly receive no welcome from *them*.'

'Will my sisters Fanny and Maria be at the funeral?'

'Agnes does not say so in her letter. Doubtless it depends on Sir Thomas Bertram's parliamentary duties as to whether he can escort them, if Fanny still remains at Mansfield. But, depend upon it, my dear, you do far better to stay with us here, where you have friends. (What you are achieving with those twins passes the bounds of belief.) No, my love, you and I will sit together on Wednesday and read the burial service, and then you may have the afternoon free from lessons and perhaps, if it is fine, walk round the ramparts with your crony Ned. Will not that be more consoling than travelling a day's journey to a home where nobody wishes for you? I grieve to put it so harshly – but so it is.'

'Yes, ma'am. Th-thank you, Aunt Polly,' faltered Hatty, and crept away to weep her heart out in seclusion. One phrase of Mrs Ward's rang in her ears. 'Of what avail are empty rooms if the person you wish to see does not dwell in them?'

Shall I ever, she wondered, shall I *ever* possess a house of my own? A roof and rooms where I shall lead my own life with the person I love?

*

Embarrassed and nonplussed by their cousin's bereavement the boys, in their different ways, did their best to show sympathy. Sydney, now aged sixteen and admitted to a junior post in his father's legal office before commencing law studies in London, bought her a jet mourning brooch. Tom whittled her a top. 'It will soothe you by its spinning,' he said. Hatty was touched. Tom, fat, good-natured and slow-witted, was sometimes capable of giving one a surprise of this kind. Ned said: 'Cousin Hatty, let us teach the twins to play chess. That will take your mind off your sadness.'

Ned's receipt for consolation turned out to be the best of the three. Teaching chess to the twins proved an arduous but rewarding task.

'It is like climbing among brambles,' gasped Hatty, after a particularly fractious half-hour.

'Queen on her own colour,' mumbled Sophy, planting a grimy, sticky white queen on the appropriate square.

'Thank *you*, Miss Hatt, Master Ned, I'll be obliged for the use of my nursery,' snapped Burnaby, coming in, grim-faced, with a can of hot water and a jug of senna-pods. The twins set up wails of protest.

'Pawn to King's four!' shouted Eliza and received from Burnaby a look which made her cower.

Ned and Hatty, knowing there was nothing to be done, left the scene.

'Next I am going to try to teach them to read,' said Hatty, 'with gingerbread letters.'

'I think you will find it a mighty slow business.'

'But at least they will have something to think about in bed. When I think what my poems have been to me ... It is like a river running through one's mind.'

Ned stared at his cousin with affectionate incomprehension.

III

Two years after the death of Mrs Ward, the Portsmouth household received news of another, not of such immediate interest and concern to Hatty, but resulting in a family assembly at Portsmouth which was to have far-reaching consequences for her.

The death was that of cousin Letty, Lady Pentecost, widow of Sir Solomon, Admiral Pentecost.

Cousin Letty had been a connection of Lord Elstow. Her husband, the Admiral, had recently died on board his ship, the *Linnet*, not in battle, but from the smallpox, an epidemic of which had decimated his crew. The widow had brought her husband's body back to Portsmouth for interment, and had then succumbed, not long after, to the same complaint.

'Very inconvenient,' grumbled Mr Ward. 'Now I suppose we shall be expected to put up half the family in this house. And I doubt very much if Cousin Lettice has left us a farthing.'

Hatty's chief interest in this event, since she had never met Lady Pentecost, lay in the fact that her sister Frances would be coming to Portsmouth for the funeral.

'Why only Frances, though? Why not Agnes, or Papa?'

'Agnes, we are to understand, remains at home to take care of your father who recently sustained a broken collar-bone in the hunting field.' (Humph! Mighty convenient for him! was his sister-in-law's internal comment.) 'Frances, it seems, travels here in the company of Lady Ursula, in one of the Fowldes carriages and escorted by two of their men-servants. But it means that we are obliged to invite Lady Ursula ... Lord, though!' Aunt Polly broke off her reading of Agnes's letter to exclaim, 'Here's a fine how-d'ye-do! For Lord Camber is to attend the funeral as well – so your Uncle Philip tells me – and I daresay the pair have never met since the rupture. It is a mercy, at least, that Lord Camber puts up at the Crown – only imagine if we had him in this house, along with Lady Ursula! Though I have the highest regard for him, dear fellow, that would never do!'

'Rupture, Aunt Polly? What rupture?'

'Oh, bless me, my dear, did you not know about it? Well, no, for sure, why should you – 'twas all over long before you might be expected to take an interest in such matters. Though to be sure your dear Mama was a close and loving friend of Lady Ursula, both before she married your Papa and for some time after – so, of course, *she* heard all about the affair – and so did I, for though by then I had ceased to be governess to Lady Susan and Lady Louisa, they still kept in touch with me and they, of course, knew all their elder brother's affairs. And, may I say, they were decidedly critical of Lady Ursula's part in the business!'

'What happened, Aunt Polly?'

'Oh, it all befell some eight or nine years ago when Lady Ursula, I suppose, would be twenty or thereabouts, and Harry – Lord Camber – a couple of years younger. He is the eldest son of the Duke of Dungeness (you have heard your uncle speak of him many times, he handles a deal of business both for Lord Camber and the Duke). Lord Camber is cousin to Lady Ursula and the two families grew up in each other's pockets, as you might say, the children were all friends together, my two dear young ladies with all the Fowldes girls. But then this friendship on the part of Lord Camber and Lady Ursula suddenly blossomed out into as fine a young romance as you could conceive, with promises and posies and vows and valentines ... The parents had no particular objections, especially on the Fowldes side; it would be a great match for Lady Ursula, she'd become a duchess in the course of time, and the Fowldes had all those daughters and were never very well-breeched. Lady Ursula is the eldest, and it would be a fine thing for her younger sisters—'

'And so, what happened, Aunt Polly?' Hatty found it almost impossible to imagine Lady Ursula, that austere, superior, grey-granite pillar, ever being involved in a romance, with posies and sighs and promises. She wondered very much what kind of a man Lord Camber might be to conceive a regard, let alone a romantic devotion, for such a being.

'Why then, Lord Camber brought his best friend home from Cambridge on a visit – he was always bringing his friends, Wandesleigh, and Kittridge the poet, and this Lord Francis Fordingbridge, and, bless me, if *he* did not fall flat in love with Lady Ursula too, so much that she was quite swept off her feet (as the circulating-library novels put it) and forgot all her vows of constancy to poor Harry, and was off with the new love. Gave Harry back his ring.'

'Gracious, aunt! And what happened then?'

'Oh, my dear, such sobbings and heart-searchings. Lady Louisa told me all about it. She is a most faithful correspondent. But everybody behaved *very well*. No duel, no meeting on Wimbledon Common at dawn, nothing at all of that nature, though gossip ran high, as you may well imagine. But Harry Camber, who has the best heart in the world – your dear Mama was used to say he is a veritable saint – and he was always a devoted elder brother to my dear girls – as near a perfect character as you are like to meet in this vale of tears. He made no complaint. He said if his friend and his sweetheart were happy together, then he was happy also; he was not about to stand in their way. And so, and so, off he went to the wars, or at least to the American Colonies, as then they were, and he came back from there only after those Colonists broke away from our king. But in the meantime, not to be outdone, Lord Francis had gone off too, enlisted and left for India, so that, as he said, Lady Ursula should have time and peace of mind to consider what she most wanted. And in India, what do you think, he was killed in the Mahratta Wars, and left a Will, bequeathing all he had in the world to Lady Ursula. (But that proved to be no great matter, only a thousand pounds or so, your uncle heard.) So there the lady was, high and dry, without either suitor.'

'Why, had Lord Camber married somebody else?'

'No, my dear, no, he had not. But somehow, when he came back from the Americas, he and Lady Ursula never took up from where they had left off before. Tastes alter, I daresay. A young man of six-and-twenty perhaps has a different notion as to what he wants in a wife, from what he fancied at eighteen; and he certainly don't want a starched old maid of eight-and-twenty who has been at her last prayers for years and had her own way in the running of the Earl's household for much of that time, since Lady Elstow never troubles her head about such matters. Or so it is said.'

'Poor Lady Ursula.' (Though she still could not avoid a shiver when she recalled that grim figure.)

Hatty's sister Frances — now twenty-three and the only member of the family who ever troubled to correspond with her — wrote to her of life at Bythorn and Lady Ursula's active part in it.

I am come home from Mansfield Park to Bythorn, for there was nothing *doing* at Mansfield. Life there had grown sadly dull, now my sister Maria has one child and is increasing again; for Sir Thos will not permit her to go out into company or up to town; nor, in truth, does she at all wish to. She seems quite content with this interdict — as you know, she was never one to bestir herself unduly — she is happy to recline all day upon a sopha, making fringe. And the house lies shockingly remote, I can tell you, in the middle of its park, and there are no Beaux to be found in the village of Mansfield. The only company we saw, from one week's end to the next, were the Parson and his wife, Mr and Mrs Chauncey, and he is a gouty old Dodderer in his eighties, so you can picture to yourself how diverting *that* was. (If he should die, which seems not improbable, the living would pass to a friend of Sir Thos, a widower, a Mr Norris, and Maria and Sir T have it planned that our sister Agnes should marry Mr Norris and come to Mansfield, but I truly pity her if this should come about, for I have met Mr N & he is most disagreeable, besides which I have it from Katy Sharp, one of the teachers at the Bythorn school, that our sister Agnes is sweet on a Bailiff named Daggett!! Imagine! I am sure Papa would never permit such a match. — But who else is there? She will *have* to take Mr Norris.) Mrs Chauncey, the Mansfield parson's wife, much younger than her husband is, I am bound to say, a pleasant friendly creature, and she has some kinsfolk in Portsmouth called Price, she told me; so, if I can ever persuade Papa to allow it, I may come to visit you and Aunt Polly and Uncle Philip one of these months &

hope to make the acquaintance of Mrs Chauncey's friends the Prices. Life here at Bythorn is no better than at Mansfield – by far too quiet for my liking. After those happy weeks at Bath with my sister and Sir Thos on their wedding journey I have acquired a decided taste for Town Ways. And I have no wish at all to dwindle into an old maid as our sister Agnes bids fair to do, if she will not have Mr Norris; only imagine, she is twenty-eight! Lady Ursula, who comes over from Underwood Priors two or three times a week, is on at her for ever to accept Mr N. (Between you and I, it is Papa that Lady U has her eye on & I do not doubt but that she will fix him in the end if he will stay at home from hunting long enough to pop the question.) I do not think that Agnes will at all enjoy playing second fiddle to Lady U once the lady is mistress of Bythorn Lodge. And I myself detest the notion of such a Stepmother. You are by far best off where you are in Portsmouth, Hatty, I may tell you.

    Yr affc. sister,
    Frances.

Hitherto, Mr Ward had refused permission for Frances to travel to Portsmouth, though Aunt Polly, when shown her letter, had cried, 'Lord! yes, poor thing! She may come to us and welcome. I daresay life at Bythorn Lodge *is* mopish enough, with your poor dear Mama no more, and Lady Ursula hanging over them like a thunder-cloud! I only wonder why in the world the knot has not yet been tied. Does she still have hopes of Camber, can that be what is in her mind? But it is useless to conjecture. When you next write to Fanny, Hatty my love, tell her she may come here as soon as she pleases. I know that Price family a little – they are respectable enough people.'

Such a visit, however, was not achieved by Fanny until the decease of Lady Pentecost and the opportunity of accompanying Lady Ursula in one of the Fowldes coaches provided sufficient excuse for making the journey and the means of doing so without any expense to Mr Henry Ward.

'Though I pity her, poor thing, riding all that way in the company of Lady Ursula,' said Aunt Polly, 'I would not wish it for myself. And, according to Louisa, *that one* only comes for one particular reason – because she hopes that Lord Camber will be at the ceremony. She does still have a hope of him, so Louisa believes.'

Oh, how I pray that I may never love any body so painfully, thought Hatty, that I would travel over a hundred miles for the possible chance of seeing him at a funeral. Does she, *can* she, still hope that he may change his mind and have her after all? I greatly wish that he would! For it is true that he has remained single. And if Lady Ursula does marry Papa – as everybody seems to think is probable – I do not see how I shall ever be able to go home again.

Hatty grew quite curious to see Lord Camber, the object, it seemed, of Lady Ursula's hopeless passion. He had grown up, she knew, at Bythorn Chase, the principal seat of the Duke of Dungeness, who also had various other properties scattered over England, and large estates in the county of Hampshire. Lord Camber, she understood from information let fall by her uncle, had also inherited an estate in Hampshire, from a recently deceased great-aunt, but, apparently, he planned to sell some part of it and give the money to the poor.

'Camber is a strange, unconformable fellow!' remarked Mr Philip Ward with measured disapproval. 'Mind! I can participate in some of his views. His father the Duke has certainly laid out a preposterous, I may say a *ruinous*, sum of money on completely rebuilding Bythorn Chase and improving the park with lakes and grottoes and follies and plantations and I know not what. He has had to sell some of the Hampshire properties to pay for that, and if he is not deep in debt by now I shall be very much surprised. When he does go off, it is likely that Camber will inherit nothing but a fine mare's-nest of encumbrances. I do not wonder that father and son are hardly on speaking terms. If Lady Ursula has any sense at all she will think no more of Camber.'

'Lord! though, my dear, only consider her alternatives!' cried his wife. 'Lady Louisa has told me in a letter that she believes the Lady still dotes on Camber as much as ever, though they have not met for seven years. Mind – if you ask me – she would find marriage to him an uncomfortable business. Why, Louisa tells me that he has founded a Society, the New Stoics, or the Sophocrats, or some such thing, with his friends Wandesleigh and Kittridge, the two poets he grew so friendly with at Cambridge. They are to own no money individually, and will have all their goods in common. Preserve me from such an existence!'

'Do they have their wives in common?' asked Tom wonderingly. The family were sitting round the breakfast table, rather later than usual, as it was Saturday.

'Be quiet, sir!' snapped Mr Ward. 'That is a most improper remark. Another word out of you, and you may leave the table.'

Sydney favoured his younger brother with a superior smile. 'Stupid little boy!' Sydney, now eighteen, attending college in London, took great pains – not without opposition from his father – to appear a smart young-man-about-town. He wore a striped waistcoat, elaborately tied stock, and his reddish hair was heavily pomaded.

'Wretched young puppy!' growled his father. 'I only wish he had taken half as much pains over his studies.' But here he hardly did justice to his son, who found the law an absorbing and diverting subject, and knew a great deal more about the affairs of his father's clients than the latter supposed.

'If Lord Camber should die, sir,' Sydney now said to Mr Ward, 'who would succeed to the title?'

'His brother, Colonel the Honourable Frederick Wisbech – but we have no reason to suppose that Camber is likely to die, not the least in the world. He is a healthy, active man in the prime of life.'

'Just the same, sir, if, as I read in the paper, Lord Camber intends to go abroad to America with his friends and found a co-operative society in Pennsylvania, on the banks of the Susquehanna river – such a life might be full of hazard, might it not, sir – serpents, bears, wild Indians . . .?'

'Pish!' said Mr Ward, impatiently cutting himself a final corner of pork pie. 'For a start, that is a most ill-considered plan, and, in my estimation, it will never get off the ground.'

His two younger sons looked at him sadly. They longed to ask more about the co-operative colony on the banks of the Susquehanna river, but knew they would only be snubbed.

Hatty remained silent, as she mostly did during family meals. Her mind was full of pictures – wild forests, rushing cataracts.

'In any case,' concluded Mr Ward, folding his napkin, 'if Camber *should* be removed from this life, his brother Colonel Wisbech is a sensible, down-to-earth man, without any of his elder brother's whims or fancies, and, in my own view, would make a far better successor to the title. Not that I have anything against Camber *in himself*, mind you; he is a good-hearted, clever fellow, and, I know, was once a great favourite of your mother.'

'Yes, indeed, bless him!' cordially agreed Aunt Polly. 'He was always so obliging, and gave the prettiest presents to his sisters.'

'At what time, my love, is Lady Ursula expected to arrive with my niece?'

'At about four this afternoon.'

Hatty could not help thinking, It is like asking, At what hour will Mont Blanc be with us? Involuntarily she gave a slight shiver. But, she thought, Lady Ursula should not frighten me any more. I am older now. And I shall be truly glad to see my sister Frances.

'I wish you boys to be in the hall at that time, also,' said their mother, 'with washed hands and hair combed, to greet your relations. And you of course, Hatty; you had best put on your white muslin. That India spotted has faded sadly (as I told you it would) and I think it has shrunk also.'

If there was one area in which Hatty's views diverged from those of her aunt Polly, it was in the matter of dress. Despite having passed so many years residing in a ducal household, Aunt Polly's taste in fashion was somewhat gaudy; for her own attire she favoured such colours as salmon-pink, puce, vermilion, and royal purple – perhaps to distract attention from her very high colouring; Hatty, who preferred quiet, sober hues, was sometimes a little dismayed at the brilliantly coloured wardrobe of garments purchased for her by her enthusiastic aunt. But on this occasion she was relieved to find that Aunt Polly was anxious enough about the advent, and possible disapproval, of Lady Ursula, to subdue her spontaneous taste.

'The white still fits me well,' she told her aunt, 'but I do think I have grown a little.'

'Very like, child. No question, you've a far better colour than you had when you first came to us – bless me, you were a poor little ghost of a thing at that time! But you've more countenance now, and your hair is thicker – I fancy your sister will see quite a change in you. Poor Fanny! And so she found no beaux at Bath nor in Mansfield – well, 'tis a thousand pities she is come to Portsmouth on such a mournful errand. But perhaps, even so, she may turn her time here to good account. I am sure she is very welcome to stop on with us after Lady Ursula is gone back to Huntingdon; I daresay your uncle Philip may furnish her with the stage fare later if she will only be a little cajoling to him. Frances used to be a very handsome girl as I recall.'

All the family were duly assembled in the hall to greet the guests at the appointed hour, Mr Ward having returned from his place of business expressly for the purpose of welcoming the titled visitor; and they were not obliged to wait very long before a carriage drew up outside. From it emerged two ladies, one tall, one exceedingly so. Hatty, who had been prepared to mock herself for her former childish dread of Lady Ursula, nevertheless felt a chill reminder of it touch her again, as the forbiddingly gaunt, pale-cheeked figure moved forward, swathed in grey wraps and veils, crowned by a close grey-velvet hat, which made her head more than ever resemble a skull.

Behind her Frances, tall, full-formed and golden-haired, seemed like a creature from a different species.

Mr Ward welcomed his aristocratic guest with formal civility, then speedily handed her on to the easier, kinder, more unpretentious greetings of his wife, who condoled with the visitors over their long journey and offered immediate rest and refreshment. Mr Ward, meanwhile, his manner sensibly softened by appreciation of his niece's handsome looks, was bidding Frances welcome, when Lady Ursula's grating, acerbic tones made themselves heard above the general conversation and chorus of greetings.

'Good heavens, Harriet! How can you hold yourself so very ill? Why, it gives me a megrim to see you slouch so. Stand up, stand up properly! And pull your elbows in, and your chin back!'

Dismayed, speechless, Hatty drew herself up as bidden and did her best to meet Lady Ursula's freezingly disapproving eye.

'Harriet's deportment at Bythorn was *always* deplorable,' Lady Ursula told Aunt Polly, 'due, I daresay, to sitting for hours together huddled up at her mother's bedside. But I had hoped by this time to discover some improvement. I can see, however – ' her eye swept over the gaping Tom and Ned, coming to rest upon Sydney, whose look of smug self-confidence changed ludicrously under her disparaging stare – 'that manners, mien and deportment are not given the consideration in this household that should rightly be theirs. My dear woman, do they attend dancing classes?'

Hatty could almost have laughed at the looks of horror that passed over her cousins' faces. Aunt Polly was obliged to confess that in this area the family's education had so far been neglected.

'In my opinion they should commence at once,' said Lady Ursula. 'That fellow – ' she pointed with her chin at Sydney – 'a great hobble-de-hoy, how can he hope to advance himself in the world with the posture of a rag-and-bone man, holding his elbows out so awkwardly as he does, feet turned in, and his whole aspect so gawky and graceless—'

'Alas, dear madam, will you not come in and take a glass of wine?' cried Aunt Polly. 'All these defects must and shall be put right in time, but at the present moment *your* comfort is our chief concern.' And, taking Lady Ursula's arm, she conducted this critical guest into the house, while Mr Ward followed with Fanny.

'My word, what a Tartar,' he muttered, as Lady Ursula, declining immediate refreshment, asked to be led directly to her chamber, and was taken upstairs by Aunt Polly.

'Sir, sir, you won't really send us to a caper-merchant, will you?' demanded Sydney, as the pair turned the corner of the stairway.

'Certainly I shall, if Lady Ursula thinks it so essential,' snapped his father. 'Now, Frances, my dear – will you take a glass of wine, or do you too wish to retire to your chamber?'

On Frances declaring that she too would prefer to rest and change her dress for dinner, she was given into the care of Hatty, who guided her to the second-best bedroom.

'I have brought you something I thought you would like to have,' said Frances, withdrawing a small silver-paper packet from her muff. 'It is a needle-pouch that Mama embroidered herself – with squirrels.'

'Oh, dear Fanny, *yes*! Thank you, thank you! I shall treasure it!'

'You look well, child,' sighed Fanny, studying her. 'Are you happy in this family?'

'Oh – well – yes – Aunt Polly is as kind as can be. And I have grown accustomed to the boys. I think that my uncle still wishes that I were not here.'

'Well,' said Frances, 'just the same, I believe you are better off here than at home. Bythorn Lodge, with Agnes in command, is grown quite insupportable! And Agnes takes all her ideas from Lady Ursula.'

'But will Lady Ursula really marry Papa? Do you think it probable?'

'I do not think she loves him, not for one single moment. Nor does he have any of that kind of regard for her. But I believe that in the end she will have him, if if nobody else makes her an offer. I think it is plain enough that Papa intends, sooner or later, to propose – hoping that by another marriage he may get himself a son, and so withold the inheritance from my uncle. But, manlike, he is in no hurry, he loves his present liberty too well to buckle himself up before he need, and so he dallies and procrastinates.'

'You would expect,' said Hatty, pondering, 'that my uncle Philip would do his utmost to prevent such a marriage. Since the family here stand to inherit if Papa dies without a male heir.'

'But what could Mr Ward do? I see no way in which my uncle could act in such a matter.' Fanny looked bewildered.

'No, he can do nothing,' agreed Hatty sadly; and seeing Ned beckon from below in the garden, she left Frances to her unpacking and ran down to join him.

'Lord, Hatt, what a she-dragon!' exclaimed Ned when they met. 'I don't wonder she frightened you out of your wits at Bythorn when you was smaller. I just hope she don't stay here beyond the funeral on Monday.'

'I do not imagine she will. I hope not. Poor Aunt Polly looks fatigued to death. And Frances says that the Lady prefers to keep a close watch over Papa. Unless, of course, she and Lord Camber ... Ned, is there time to go to the Kingdom? I have a poem that fidgets me.'

'There's not really time,' said Ned. 'Dinner will be at five, Mama told me, and anyway we are wearing our Sunday things – we had better not. But come into the conservatory.'

This was a large, somewhat dilapidated dome-shaped glass structure, built against the high garden wall, which had suffered considerable neglect under the aegis of Mr Ward, who had a puritanical scorn for hot-house fruit and forced flowers and would not spend a penny on fuel to produce such luxuries. But some pots of bamboo left by previous owners of the place had grown to giant size in its shelter, and various evergreens and citrus bushes, untended but undaunted, flourished, so that its interior was a green jungle.

Apart from the gardener's occasional visits, few set foot in the place, but Ned and Hatty made use of it as a tolerably warm retreat when bad weather prevented their visits to the graveyard.

'I've a thing to show you, Hatt – stay here a moment while I fetch it' and Ned left the greenhouse and ran off across the kitchen garden.

Hatty sat herself down on a comfortable pile of sacking, and pulled out the small notebook which lived at all times in a special pocket sewn into her petticoat. The day had been long and distracted, with many extra tasks relating to the entertainment of the two guests, and the menu for tonight's dinner; Hatty had been called into service for picking over currants, peeling apples, sticking cloves into oranges, whipping cream, and making up posies for bedside tables. But all the while some lines, some words, had been buzzing and scuffling in her mind, noisy and insistent as a bumble-bee caught inside a closed window; now, at last, she had a moment in peace and silence to commit them to paper.

She wrote, thought, wrote again; and then, hearing a step on the brick-paved floor, said: 'I have started my new poem, Ned. Listen, and tell me what you think.' And she read aloud:

> 'Clouds are God's toy —
> Having the first task done
> Having completed earth, moon, sun
> Landscapes and constellations, every one
> And seen the universe well begun
> He wove the clouds for joy, pure joy.'

There was a silence after she had finished reading, and, in expectation of Ned's comments, which were often highly critical, she waited a moment or two. No comments forthcoming, she looked up in surprise, and saw, gazing down at her, a wholly unfamiliar person, much bigger than Ned; indeed, this man was probably as tall as the towering Lady Ursula.

'*Oh* . . .' faltered Hatty, taking in the stranger, as it were, foot by foot. He had on a shooting jacket and breeches, both well-worn; his cravat was loose and untidily knotted; his hair, of a faded foxcolour, must once have been bright red; it grew in an untended bush, thickly all over his head, and descended in side-whiskers, but his angular face was clean-shaven; his eyes were a bright, piercing blue, and his face was amazingly weather-beaten. '*Crazed*, like earthenware,' thought Hatty, trying to find exactly the right words to describe his seamed, wind-tanned complexion. She wondered if he might be a gamekeeper. He had a wide, curving mouth, and many wrinkles, deep grooves pushing up his cheekbones and running out from the corners of his eyes.

He looks, thought Hatty, as if he smiled more often than not.

But he was not smiling now.

'Read those lines again,' he directed. 'I should like to hear them a second time.'

So Hatty read them again.

'Did you compose them?' said the stranger. 'They are remarkable. At least I think so.'

'I am not sure about the last line,' said Hatty. 'Should it be "made" the clouds, do you think, instead of "wove"?'

He considered. 'No, "wove" is better. That long "o" dignifies and strengthens the last line. Have you others?'

'One that I made up this morning which I haven't written down yet,' said Hatty. She recited:

> 'Morning brings labour
> Evening brings rest
> Morning's my neighbour
> Evening my guest.'

She added, 'I believe there might be a second verse. But I can't think of it. Perhaps it will come later.'

'Do they just come like that? Out of nowhere?'

'Oh, yes! And sometimes it is dreadful. If there is no chance to write them down – they just *go* again. Just vanish. Like leaves falling off trees. There is no finding them again, once they are gone.'

'Yes. But perhaps,' said her companion, 'like fallen leaves, they fertilize the ground, so that other plants may prosper.'

'Perhaps. I hadn't thought of that,' said Hatty, pondering.

Ned came running in, flushed and cross.

'I can't find it anywhere. It was a squashed toad, quite dry and flattened out by the garden roller. Most remarkable! I had put it in a flower pot to show you, Hatty, but Deakin must have taken the pot and thrown out the toad – and now it grows late, I think we had better go back to the house—'

He pulled up short in astonishment, for the first time observing the stranger.

'I beg your pardon, sir!'

'No, no,' said the newcomer, 'mine is the fault. I had left my horse in the stable yard and walked round this way in search of Deakin, who used to be an old ally of mine when I was a boy visiting cousins at Gosport. You, I think, must be one of Mr Ward's three sons.'

'Edward,' said Ned, nodding.

'And you are . . .?'

'His niece, Harriet.'

'Your father, then, will be the Mr Henry Ward who lives at Bythorn Lodge?'

In her turn she nodded.

'Oh, so then we are neighbours in some sort.'

He smiled, and the wrinkles rayed out from the corners of his eyes.

'I live in Wanmaulden Wood, near there, in the house that is called the Thatched Grotto. My name is Harry Camber.'

IV

DINNER THAT EVENING was not at all an easy meal.

Mr Ward, later, received a rare trimming from his wife for having invited Lord Camber without giving notice to the household.

He stoutly defended himself. 'What else could I do, my dear? Meeting him – in the street, he staying at the Crown with no previous engagements – it was the barest civility to ask him to come and take his pot luck with us. No harm done that I can discern. He is such an easy, well-bred, conversible fellow – he had so much of interest to tell us about his scheme for the banks of the Susquehanna river – and the indenture system – and redemptionist agreements – and freedom dues – and the triangle trade – that the boys and even little Hatty were quite engrossed. Even Tom – I have never heard them ask so many questions, converse with such good sense and liveliness—'

'But meanwhile poor Frances was quite paralysed with boredom. All I ever heard *her* say was, "Oh, la! I should not have liked that at all!" While as for Lady Ursula – I do not believe that she will ever forgive us. She looked as if she had swallowed an icicle. His appearance! She was so shocked! While you were still at your wine she said to me, "A common *labourer* would be better clad."'

'Well, he is the son of a Duke, he may dress as he pleases.'

'I do not wonder that she retired to bed with a headache.'

'Oh, pho, pho!' said Mr Ward, annoyed. 'What a piece of work about the man's appearance. He has the manners of an aristocrat, of a gentleman, he behaved most civilly to you and to Frances – even to little Hatty – I heard him ask her what books she read. Is it my fault if Lady Ursula chose to behave like a frozen martyr? If she cast him looks like javelins? After all, who invited her to my house? She invited herself. I should have thought she might be glad to see her old playmate again.'

'Playmate!'

'They grew up together as children, did they not? Continually in and out of each other's households.'

'For over a year – you may recall – they were as good as engaged to be married.'

'Well,' pronounced Mr Ward, 'he is probably congratulating himself at this very moment that the engagement came to naught and is never likely to be resumed. Mind – I am sorry for it; her marriage to Camber would preserve my brother Henry from her clutches, and this family from the possible loss of the Bythorn estate.'

'If *that* was why you brought him back to dinner, Mr Ward, it was a most ill-judged scheme!'

Mr Ward said irritably, 'Such a notion never came into my head. That was not my plan at all. In any case, she was bound to meet Camber at the funeral ceremony, was she not? I merely advanced the meeting by a day and a half. How long, pray, does the lady propose to remain in my house?'

'Not above a few days, I believe. I hope!' said Mrs Ward, who seemed unwontedly weary. 'I understand that the lady has many and pressing engagements both at Bythorn Lodge and at Underwood Priors. And, in any case,' she added irrefutably, 'if your brother Henry does not marry Lady Ursula, what is to prevent his taking up with some other lady – now that matrimony is in his mind?'

Mr Ward had no answer to that, but strode away, irritably, while his wife, sighing, pressed her fingers to her forehead.

The day succeeding the arrival of Lady Ursula and Frances Ward was a Sunday, so, pursuing their usual habit, the family of Mr Philip Ward attended morning service at the Garrison Chapel and then, as the morning was a fine one, made their way up on to the ramparts for their regular weekly promenade, during which excursion Mrs Ward greeted her neighbours and exchanged local gossip, while her husband improved his relations with clients and hoped-for clients. Lady Ursula, who had accompanied the household to the service, at this moment made it known that she had yet another headache and proposed returning home directly.

Mrs Ward, all solicitude, would have accompanied her guest, but with brusque lack of ceremony the lady declined the offer, acidly demanding to know if they thought she was in her dotage that she could not walk a quarter of a mile unescorted, and adding that the last thing in the world she desired was to be plagued by a series of unnecessary inquiries as to how she did. Mr Ward, however, insisted that it was out of the question for any guest of his, well or indisposed, to walk through the streets alone, and so told his son Sydney to escort the lady to Lombard Street.

'I promise you, ma'am, Sydney shall not utter a single word, if that is your wish; but accompany you to my house he must and shall.'

Lady Ursula shrugged and nodded, with an ill grace; Sydney silently bowed and took her arm, concealing whatever reluctance he may have felt for the mission under an impassive manner.

Mr Ward chuckled as they walked away.

'Ay, ay, Sydney has not forgotten that yesterday she called him a gawky hobble-de-hoy; he is bent on doing the pretty and showing her that when he chooses he can command all the air and address of a man-about-town. No matter for which, I plan that you shall all go off to Monsieur Lamartine's class next week and learn to frisk and bow and foot it with the best; I'll not have it said that my boys can't comport themselves like gentlemen.'

Ned and Tom pulled terribly long faces at this edict, but they knew there was no purpose in trying to dispute their father's orders. Hatty, on the contrary, was quite pleased at the prospect. She had been used, when younger, to jump about and pirouette with her sister Fanny, to amuse their mother. She greatly enjoyed dancing, and had missed the exercise.

'Never mind it, Ned, I will soon show you how,' she whispered.

'Dancing lessons will do the boys no harm at all,' calmly agreed their mother. 'Oh, see, Frances, there are the Price family – did you not say that the Parson's wife at Mansfield Rectory is related to them?'

'Yes, Aunt Polly, Mrs Chauncey is the sister of Mrs Price.'

'I am a little acquainted with Mrs Price – your uncle transacted some matter of a loan with her husband, who is in a very respectable line of business – I forget what – it will be proper for us to bid them good-day.'

The eye of Frances brightened wonderfully. She had dressed herself with much care for this first public appearance in Portsmouth, and had suffered no small disappointment at the meagre supply of admiring strangers which had hitherto been the reward of all her trouble.

But the Price family – a plain but friendly-looking mother, respectable father, a young daughter somewhat below the age of competition, and, above all, two fine young men, both in uniform, instantly rekindled her hopes and her interest.

Introductions were effected and the two families turned to walk together. The husbands had business matters to discuss, the wives compared notes on the ever-recurrent servant problem in Portsmouth – maids so flighty and always liable to have their heads turned by some handsome sailor – Frances walked happily between the two fine young men.

Hatty and her boy cousins found themselves talking to the Prices' daughter, whose name, she at once informed them, was Nancy, and her age fourteen years. She was a high-coloured girl, well-grown, lively, with black ringlets and an air of great self-possession. Indeed she

chattered so incessantly to the two boys, and took so little notice of
Hatty, that the latter, not at all put out by this neglect, for she was not
especially taken with Miss Nancy, sauntered in the rear of the party,
enjoying a peaceful reverie, happy to feel the spring sunshine, to watch
the continual criss-cross of the ships' masts bobbing at anchor, the blue
sea beyond, and the pearly outline of the Isle of Wight in the distance.
Gulls flashed and shrieked, the air was keen and salty. Words began to
push their way into Hatty's mind, as they so frequently did, when she
had a few uninterrupted moments to herself.

> 'Down the broad flood of light
> Birds scatter loose their songs, pent-up from night . . .'

A man who had been leaning on the parapet turned round and
caught her eye. He smiled. It was Lord Camber. But today he was
dressed with perfect propriety in dark clothes; Hatty concluded that he
too must have been attending divine service.

'Good morning, Miss Hatty! Do I interrupt your train of thought?
You look like a person in the throes of a composition.'

'Well – yes, I was!'

She smiled candidly back at him.

'Would you prefer that I walked away and left you in peace? Or
may I be allowed to hear?'

She told him her two lines and added two more:

> 'Daunted by solitude and hush, they cry
> All their small store of knowledge to the sky.'

'I like that,' he said thoughtfully. 'You have a touch of Milton there,
but Milton is no bad influence. Do you read him?'

'I read *Lycidas*,' said Hatty. 'I liked it.'

'Which lines especially?'

'"But oh, the heavy change now thou art gone, Now thou art gone
and never must return."'

'Ah, yes,' he said in a kind tone. 'Milton teaches us how to turn our troubles to good account. But then there are the "sweet Societies, That sing, and singing in their glory move, And wipe the tears for ever from his eyes." And have you read Andrew Marvell? "Where the remote Bermudas ride ..."?'

'Oh, *yes*! Golden lamps in a green night! Beautiful!'

They exchanged eager smiles. Then his slowly faded and he asked in a hesitating manner. 'Can you perhaps tell me – does Lady Ursula still remain at Mr Ward's house?'

'Yes, she was here with us at church this morning,' Hatty told him. 'But she wished to return home, she did not feel well. My cousin Sydney walked back to the house with her, while we came up on the ramparts.'

'Ah, I am sorry. I had hoped to see her again. Last night she seemed – ill-at-ease.'

'Perhaps my uncle—' began Hatty, but at that moment Mr Ward, looking back, caught sight of his noble client.

'Why, bless my soul! Is that you, my Lord! Good morning, good morning!'

He then, despite some admonitory glances from his wife, went on to invite his Lordship to come and eat his mutton in Lombard Street again, but Lord Camber, perhaps fortunately, had a prior engagement with some acquaintance at the Crown Inn. It was arranged, though, that they should all meet together to take tea after the funeral ceremonies on the following day.

Mrs Ward scolded her husband on the way home. 'How *could* you? Lady Ursula would never have forgiven us.'

'But, confound it, my dear, there was nothing amiss with his appearance today. Perfectly unexceptionable. Except for his red hair, and the man can't help that.'

Frances said: 'Aunt Polly, Mrs Price has invited me to go and stay with the family for a few weeks after the funeral. Is not that kind of her? May I go? Oh, *may* I?'

'We will talk about it when we are at home, my dear.'

The two families bade each other friendly adieux, Nancy pirouetting in front of the two boys, and calling, as they went their separate ways: 'Until we meet at the dancing class! I shall soon teach you all the steps!'

Back at home, in Lombard Street: 'I do not see any objection to Frances passing a month or so with the Price family,' pronounced Mr Ward after some thought, when the matter was referred to him. 'They are entirely respectable. But perhaps we had best find out what Lady Ursula thinks of the scheme. When she has finished having her headache,' he added drily.

That lady, having perhaps ascertained that Lord Camber was not to be present with the family at Sunday dinner, had recovered quite speedily and made her appearance downstairs among the household. Mrs Ward at once began to consult her as to the propriety of Frances accepting the Prices' invitation.

'She is excessively desirous of going, ma'am.'

Lady Ursula, having thought the matter over, gave her qualified approval to the scheme. 'I do not think that Mr Henry Ward would object. The Price family, I understand, are worthy people enough – the two sons both naval lieutenants ... humph ... by no means such a superior connection as that of our dear Maria – but one cannot expect every sister to be equally fortunate. I must avow, I certainly should have hoped that Frances could do better for herself than a mere naval lieutenant – considering her looks ... But it cannot be denied that she is a very dull-witted girl – Not that even Maria could be called intelligent. Agnes is the only member of the family with any brains – '

'Hatty?' suggested Mrs Ward, who looked flushed and tired, as if she heartily wished the next few days were over.

'*Hatty?*'

If a lady with Lady Ursula's elegance of manner could be thought to sniff, and shrug her shoulders, Lady Ursula did so. 'Hatty is a feather-pate. I see remarkably little future for *her*. But I daresay Mr Henry Ward will be reasonably satisfied if one of those Price lads is promoted captain and Frances secures him. Mr Ward is most anxious to get those girls off his hands. I may tell you there is now a tolerably advantageous connection talked of for Agnes: the new incumbent at Mansfield, Mr Norris; a most respectable man (or so I am informed); Agnes herself is not over-eager in the matter, regrettably; the foolish creature had conceived a wholly ineligible fancy for a bailiff – a young man with nothing to recommend him except a smooth face and a plausible manner; Mr Ward soon had *him* removed from his post and sent about his business. I have informed Agnes I do not know how many times, that Mr Norris's offer is the best – if not the only acceptable one she is likely to receive. She had better make the most of her chances, bestir herself (as I am continually telling her) and agree to receive his addresses. "Come, now, Agnes my dear," say I, every time that we are together, "Come now, Agnes, put that ridiculous partiality out of your head, once and for all." "But I love him," she declaims, with a countenance like a tragedy queen. "And he loved me, I am sure of it." "Stuff and nonsense," say I, "a young man, five years younger than yourself? He was only after your portion. Come now: forget him; in your position, my dear, with your lack of looks, and countenance, and so unfortunately circumstanced as you are, an elderly husband is all that you are entitled to expect. And Mr Norris, I am sure, is no more disagreeable than many another. You may be sure, with him, at least, of a comfortable living, since he is a friend of your sister Maria's husband. Come now!" I have told her, innumerable times, "I shall think you a fool, and worse than a fool, if you do not make haste to fix him. He is a widower, he is looking for a sensible person to manage his household, he cannot be expected to wait for ever." But Agnes, for whatever reason, is most tiresomely reluctant to alter her situation. I believe she still, in secret, pines for young Daggett. (Daggett! I ask you! What a name!) And, to make matters worse, she is falling into all the crotchetty, opinionated, self-consequent ways of an old maid, which plagues Mr Ward beyond bearing, and so I have told her, I do not know *how* many times . . .'

'Dear, dear – poor thing – yes, I daresay she had much better follow your counsel at once and have done with it,' sighed Aunt Polly, nodding politely to signify agreement, feeling a great deal of sympathy for Agnes, and deciding within herself that, if ever there was an example of a crotchetty, opinionated, self-consequent old maid, Lady

Ursula was that example. No wonder that poor Agnes was in no hurry to take her advice.

Aunt Polly went on, 'How very fortunate it is that we do not need, yet awhile, to be in a worry about launching little Hatty in the world. *Her* time to look around for an establishment will not be for another two years or so. And I am glad of that, for she has entered with true goodwill upon the task of putting my poor twins in ways of occupying their minds and hands. She has taught them such skills as I would not have thought possible.'

Lady Ursula, however, could never endure to hear Hatty praised.

Sourly, she remarked, 'Well, I am mighty surprised to hear that, Mrs Ward – though, of course, very glad – for, if ever there was a conceited, whimsical, affected, vain fanciful little madam who needed to be *kept down*, Hatty is the one; my poor cousin Isabel was quite worn out, I truly believe, fatigued to death by all Hatty's quirks and nonsense; unfortunately by the time I had become apprised of the situation, and was able to take a hand in the household, and to seek a remedy, it was by far too late for Isabel; but let me warn you, my dear Mrs Ward, you cannot be too strict, or too watchful, in your treatment of Hatty; she is one who likes to go her own way, think her own thoughts, she has a strong spirit of secrecy and wilfulness, believes herself by far superior to all about her, has no notion whatsoever of conforming to the opinions of her friends and governors. No, no, Hatty is one to be supervised and coerced at all times.'

'Gracious me, Lady Ursula!' was all Mrs Ward had to say.

'Where *are* your nieces at this time?' inquired her guest.

At this time Frances and Hatty were still upstairs, somewhat hilariously engaged in dressing each other's hair. Their sister Maria, now become Lady Bertram, had, Frances informed Hatty, acquired a very smart lady's maid, Chapman, who, when working for a previous employer in Paris, had learned a vast number of new and remarkable modes of hair-dressing; and by attentively studying her methods, Frances, during her prolonged visit to Mansfield Park, had picked up a number of useful tips; with much laughter she was attempting to pass on these tricks of the coiffeur's trade to her youngest sister.

Fanny's hair, long, smooth and golden, was easy and rewarding to dress, and could be piled, swept, ringletted and plaited into countless different impressive creations; but Hatty's shorter, dark, vigorously curling locks were by no means so easily disciplined. Frances was still in the middle of attempting to coerce them into a Grecian cluster at the back when the dinner-bell rang.

'Never mind it, Fanny! We had better go down directly. My uncle greatly dislikes it if we are late, especially when there are guests in the house – '

'I will just fasten your hair with these.'

The two sisters hastily ran down the stair to the dining-parlour.

Mr Ward had taken the arm of his titled guest, and his wife followed them from the parlour. The two girls demurely passed into the dining-room, walking behind their elders, ahead of the three boys, who had been at the back of the house preparing lessons for the following day. At the sight of Hatty's hair, twisted into a small black knob with two ivory pins protruding from it, the brothers burst into subdued giggles, causing their father to direct a cold, inquiring eye at them.

'It is Hatty, sir,' explained Tom. 'Her hair. She looks just like a Hottentot.'

Lady Ursula's lorgnette was at once trained on Hatty and her face assumed an expression of extreme severity. 'Girl! How dare you presume to come to the table in such a ludicrous fashion? I am wholly amazed!' she declared in her coldest, deepest tones, and added, 'It is fortunate indeed that your poor dear Mama is not living at this time to see you make such a disgraceful exhibition of yourself – I do not know what she would say.'

The last sentence was too much for Hatty, who blushed miserably and felt hot tears prick at the back of her eyes. Frances, slow-witted and never very agile at responding to a situation, sat mute and open-mouthed, unable to explain her own part in the affair. But Aunt Polly remarked mildly, 'The two girls, I conjecture, have been amusing themselves with hair-dressing. Fanny's coiffure is most becoming. And Hatty does not usually appear in such a trim. Was not that it, Frances?'

'Yes, Aunt Polly. I am very sorry.'

'Well, it is by no means the day, or the occasion, for such foolish pastimes,' pronounced Mr Ward, frowning at Frances. 'And I think, Hatty, that you had best retire from the room and take your meal in the nursery. That may teach you, another time, to come to the table in a proper manner, especially when we have guests. Make your apologies to your aunt and cousin.'

'I beg your pardon, Aunt Polly, Cousin Ursula,' muttered Hatty, half-strangled with tears, and she swiftly made her escape from the room. As she left, she heard Lady Ursula remark to Mrs Ward, 'You see, ma'am, what I mean?' in a grim, self-justificatory tone.

'My dear, why in the world does your cousin Ursula dislike you so much?' inquired Mrs Ward the next day, before the funeral, when Hatty came into her room to be equipped with black gloves.

'Does she, Aunt Polly?' asked Hatty in surprise. 'I thought that was just her manner with everybody.'

'It seems to me that she is especially severe with you.' As if she were your enemy, Mrs Ward thought, but did not say aloud.

'Well, I do not know the reason for it,' remarked Hatty after some thought. 'Unless it is because I broke my sister Agnes's toilet things.'

'That, surely, would not be sufficient cause? Here, this pair fits very well. You may have some drops of my lavender water for your handkerchief, my love. Now run down to your uncle and tell him that I will be with him directly.'

Pondering, while she adjusted her black veil, as to the underlying reason for Ursula's very apparent strong dislike of her young cousin, Mrs Ward wondered if it could have sprung from jealousy. Despite an age gap of sixteen years between Isabel Wisbech and Ursula Fowldes, the two had grown to be very devoted friends when the former was a young married woman and the latter a girl in her teens; could it be that Ursula had felt displaced by her friend's last, best-loved child, who had come by degrees to occupy almost the whole of her affection and attention?

No, no, that is by far too fanciful a notion, thought Aunt Polly, fixing her funeral veil with a jet brooch; a grown woman would not pursue a vendetta against a child for such a flimsy, trifling reason. At all events, it is fortunate for Hatty that she resides here with us; she might have a hard time of it at home, should Ursula Fowldes really marry her father . . .

The funeral of Lady Pentecost was conducted at St Thomas's church in Portsmouth because of the large congregation expected. This consisted mostly of naval persons who had had connections with the Admiral. The Ward family made their way quietly to the rear of the large church as befitted such humble connections, but Lady Ursula was escorted with due ceremony to a front pew to sit with Miss Pentecost, the Admiral's daughter, who had come with the Dean of Romsey. Hatty's quick eye soon detected Lord Camber, again unexceptionable in black garb, by the church gate exchanging remarks with various unimportant-looking persons, preferring, apparently, to remain outside on the pathway, despite drizzling rain, until the last minute before the ceremony should begin. Where he sat during the service Hatty did not see, but she noticed him later at the graveside.

The large church of St Thomas, in Lombard Street, was not very far removed from Mr Ward's residence. Waiting outside, for the last part of the obsequies, Hatty was moved to wonder whether the little neglected graveyard that adjoined her uncle's property had once formed the earliest part of this larger burial-place. Trying to frame in her mind's eye a map of the whole district, with the streets enclosing it, she had given scant heed to what was taking place around her, until she suddenly began to realize that something had gone very much amiss with the proceedings at the grave.

'Oh my gracious – the poor thing!' Aunt Polly was exclaiming softly. 'Somebody should go to her aid – Philip my dear, do you not think—?'

'Not our place!' hissed Mr Ward disapprovingly. 'Let one of the clergy – or Lady Ursula – she who is always so ready to lead the way when it comes to behaviour—'

For – Hatty now saw – the daughter of the deceased, Miss Pentecost, a thin, unimpressive figure in trailing black draperies, had apparently succumbed to a severe fit of hiccups when required to scatter a handful of earth on the coffin – hiccups which quickly graduated to hysterical laughter and then to violent sobs; she appeared to be on the point of casting herself bodily into the grave, on top of the coffin.

'*Stop her!* Oh, why won't somebody stop her?' whispered Hatty in dismay, her eyes and total sympathy trained on the weeping, distracted figure. But all those nearest to Miss Pentecost seemed quite paralysed by horror or embarrassment.

'Mama! *Mama!*' called Miss Pentecost to the black box in the grave. 'Wait – wait for me – I am coming too – I will follow you—'

But before the disastrous act which seemed imminent, another black-clad figure stepped forward, kindly but firmly clasped the distraught lady's arm with both hands, guiding her away from the grave, and from the group of horrified bystanders.

'Come, my poor dear, come with me,' Hatty heard, in Lord Camber's cordial, calm, reassuring tones. 'What you need is a cup of hot negus, and to step indoors out of this wretchedly cold rain.' And, without more ado, he led her away.

A soft, collective sigh of relief arose from the graveside, and the ceremonies were reverently, but without loss of time, concluded.

Back at Mr Ward's house, Lady Ursula was stringent in her condemnation of the hysterical Miss Pentecost.

'Making such an exhibition of herself! Shameful! Before the whole company! And she an Admiral's daughter! I was never so shocked.'

'Lord Camber acted very promptly and considerately,' suggested Aunt Polly. 'It was just as one would expect of him – he is so good-natured and quick-witted. I wonder where he took her?'

Lady Ursula looked as if she hoped it was to the bottom of Portsmouth harbour ...

'I am rather surprised that the Duke did not attend the funeral,' remarked Mr Ward, hoping to lead the talk away to a more innocuous topic. 'He was a great friend of the Admiral's, I understand.'

'My uncle? He is by far too pickled in sherry these days,' snapped Lady Ursula. 'He—'

The door opened and Lord Camber was announced. He came in just as usual, smiling and at ease.

'Forgive me, my dear sir, for not being with you sooner,' he said to Mr Ward, 'but you saw how it was – I had to escort that poor lady back to her lodging – fortunately she has an old nurse, a Mrs Griffin, who always accompanies her.'

'I hope she felt some proper shame at having made such a show of herself,' coldly remarked Lady Ursula to Mrs Ward, but in a tone intended to carry as far as Lord Camber.

He looked across the room at her and said mildly, 'Perhaps you did not know, Ursula my dear, that Miss Pentecost is suffering from a malady which, it is known, will terminate her own life in a few months' time?'

Lady Ursula was silenced. She turned her head away with a sharp movement, and Mr Ward made haste to engage her in a dialogue with Canon Ramsgate, a cousin of the Fowldes family who had helped to conduct the funeral service.

Hatty thought: Lady Ursula has such a great notion of manners and deportment, yet Lord Camber, it appears to me, is much more *truly* courteous and thoughtful of other people's feelings. He is my idea of the perfect knight – like King Arthur, or Sir Galahad, or Richard Coeur de Lion . . . I should wish, when I am grown, to marry somebody like Lord Camber. Only handsomer, of course . . .

On this occasion, Lord Camber did not remain long in Mr Ward's house. Something seemed to have depressed his spirits. He talked little, and soon made his adieux. To Hatty he addressed only one short, friendly sentence before taking his leave: 'I hope, Miss Hatty, that your Muse continues hard at work?' She nodded shyly and he left, explaining that he had an engagement in Winchester. To Lady Ursula he offered a civil bow, raising his brows and proffering his hand; but her only response was, pointedly, to turn her head away and fix her eyes on the person standing nearest to her.

V

Mr Ward had lost no time in enrolling the younger members of his household as members of Monsieur Lamartine's weekly classes in the Terpsichorean art. These classes took place in the draughty Assembly Hall of the Crown Inn, and were very well patronized by the more prosperous families of the town, whose offspring were expected to benefit by an application of Gallic elegance and polish. M. Lamartine (or so he asserted and there was none to contradict him) was descended from an impoverished but blue-blooded French titled family tracing its origins back to the Emperor Charlemagne and beyond. Anticipating calamitous social upheaval in the near future, he had left France and come abroad to earn a living in the British Isles, where life seemed to promise greater security at least. And the scheme had answered remarkably well: attendance at his classes increased, week by week, and they were spoken of as far afield as Salisbury and Winchester.

Escorted by Aunt Polly, Hatty and her cousins lingered in shyness and diffidence by the door of the large bare room with its highly waxed floor, gazing at the animated spectacle that presented itself to their nervous vision.

M. Lamartine, a short square-built man with a whole series of blue-stubbled chins and a wide, smiling mouth shaped like the blade of a sickle, was bounding about the floor with a rapidity astounding for a man of his girth, amending the posture of some thirty pupils of all ages who were marshalled down the room in a long double set. He flew from side to side, demonstrating, commending, reproving and instruct-ing. His wife, meanwhile, a lady built on the same stocky and serviceable plan, her girth further augmented by layers upon layers of draped muslin and cambric and Flanders lace, performed alternately upon the piano and on a miniature violin, and frequently herself stepped in among the dancers to correct the position of an arm, a spine, or a shoulder. Observing the new arrivals she swam towards them, like a tugboat crossing a harbour full of tossing dinghies, and gave them a most affable welcome.

While she was doing so, a curly-black-haired girl bounded forward out of the crowd, all smiles, and ran up to Ned.

'Ned Ward! Capital that you have come! Take my hand, and I will soon show you the way!'

In a moment Ned and Sydney were swept off to the set, Tom was taken in hand by a robust girl with a yellow topknot who appeared to perform the role of assistant teacher. All of a sudden Hatty found herself alone, deserted at the edge of the floor, with everybody else in the room dancing. She felt unexpectedly conspicuous, forlorn and foolish, as if she had been obliged to take part in a game whose rules were familiar to all the players except herself. Yet, on the way to the Crown, she had been comfortably certain of her power to help her cousins, especially Ned. And now he was twirling round, quite happily, in the middle of the set, with the black-haired Nancy Price, while Sydney, frowning in concentration, followed the directions of Madame Lamartine. Hatty who, till one moment past, had felt secure, hopeful, and at ease, now underwent all the pain of an odd-man-out, finding, or believing herself the target of scornful or pitying glances. To make matters worse, she was wearing one of the most unbecoming gowns of Aunt Polly's choice: an orange-tawny muslin with bright yellow trimmings which, she privately considered, made her look like a jelly dessert.

Aunt Polly who, were she close at hand, would have been consoling and supportive, had moved off to the far end of the room where chaperons were seated. Here – to Hatty's even greater dismay – she saw Lady Ursula suddenly appear, doubtless to discover whether her counsel had been followed. She and Aunt Polly were in conference together, observing the dancers; they smiled as Ned and Nancy Price pranced past, followed by Tom, doing his best with the yellow-haired girl ... Lady Ursula glanced across the room, saw Hatty, and her face tightened.

Hatty longed for the floor to open up and swallow her. She felt very wretched. And then, from behind, to her utter astonishment, she heard a familiar friendly voice. 'Good God, what an unbridled scene of dissipation! I come back to the Crown, hoping for a quiet dinner after a long day's business in the country, and what do I find? Wild caperings, as if the whole city had been afflicted by St Vitus' Dance! And only my friend Miss Hatty not participating. But why is this? Have you taken a vow against dancing?'

With a sense of inexpressible warmth and comfort, Hatty turned to Lord Camber. He stood behind her, arms akimbo, surveying the scene with a broad characteristic smile on his face. As on their first meeting, he wore old, untidy clothes. He carried his hat in his hand, as well as a large bundle of papers.

'But why are you not dancing, my friend?' he inquired again.

'Oh, it was just – just that there was no partner,' she stammered.

'We can soon remedy that. Here, my good Barker—' he turned to a waiter who had followed him with a glass of wine on a tray. 'Take these to the parlour – with this.' He thrust the papers and the hat into the man's free hand. 'Now then, my dear – I beg you will do me the honour of a quick turn up and down the set,' and without further ado, he led her out on to the floor. It soon became apparent to Hatty that, whatever fault Lady Ursula might have to find with his appearance, Lord Camber was an adept on the ballroom floor, lively, nimble and confident.

When Monsieur Lamartine claimed the next dance with Hatty, and they waited for the music to recommence, Hatty, facing her partner, noticed out of the corner of her eye that Lord Camber had quietly moved along the wall until he stood close to Lady Ursula. Mrs Ward had stepped away to greet acquaintances, and Lady Ursula was at present standing alone, conspicuous because of her unusual height, morosely surveying the animated scene. She was dressed, as was her invariable custom, in close-fitting grey cambric, with a small severe grey velvet bonnet like a helmet on her head; Hatty fancifully thought that she resembled some female warrior, Joan of Arc perhaps; and, to her own surprise, felt a sudden, a most unexpected prick of sympathy – *could* it be sympathy? – for the older woman who looked so solitary and in some indefinable way unresolved; rather, Hatty thought, like a piece of jetsam that has been washed up by the tide on a reef and now lies waiting for the next wave to float it back into the swell again. Then Hatty caught some words of Lord Camber's as he spoke to the lady – his manner was low and confidential, but all the remarks he had addressed to Hatty herself in the last few days had impressed her so very deeply that she had become extra sensitive to the tones of his voice and felt that she would have been able to pick out his speech cadences amid the uproar of a great crowd or even the howl of a hurricane.

'Ursie!' he addressed her softly. 'Ursie, my dear – can we not remember that we were used to be such friends? I would be grieved indeed – deeply, deeply grieved – to be obliged to forego even that memory?'

She turned sharply and gave him a cold angry stare.

'*Some* of us,' she snapped, '*some* of us in this world, Camber, are not so stupid as to believe that a few cajoling words can re-make a whole time that is lost and gone. What you seem to suggest is laughable. Only look at you! How can you be so outrageous as to stand there – presenting *such* an appearance – how dare you be making any kind of overture – to me! What value, in any case, can there be in any thing you say when I know – when I know now full well – what your intentions are – when I know that your overtures have no more value than – than that feather!' And she fiercely poked with her toe at a plume from some girl's fan that came drifting their way across the polished boards of the floor.

Lord Camber stooped and picked it up and turned it thoughtfully between his fingers.

'There was a time,' he suggested, 'when such considerations did not trouble you. When you would have ventured—'

'Ventured! Hah! Perhaps! If so that time is vanished. Now I would not venture across a duck-pond under your escort. I wonder at your effrontery, Camber, I do indeed! Do you expect me to embark on a career as a lady's maid, as a sewing-woman?'

Madame Lamartine began playing a spirited gig on the piano and the dancing recommenced. Hatty heard no more of the words that passed between the two – if any did; soon she saw Lord Camber walk slowly towards the entrance with bent head, still absently twirling the feather between his finger and thumb. Lady Ursula took a few hasty steps in the opposite direction, then was lost to view behind the line of dancers bounding back and forth.

At the end of the dance Ned made his way through the crowd to Hatty's side. He was pink, panting and smiling.

'Lord, what fun! I say, it is not so bad here, after all, is it, Cousin Hatty?' he said. 'And that Miss Nancy Price is a capital dancer. Is she not? And she tells me she has a white parrot at home! And I may come to the house and see it, if Papa gives me leave. And she says she will ask her brother James to show me over the *Thessaly*!'

As they walked homewards after the dancing lesson, the emotions felt by different members of the Ward family varied greatly, from excited anticipation, through moderate satisfaction, to a kind of sorrowful wonder.

Aunt Polly seemed unusually fatigued, and walked slowly, with her hand pressed to her side. But her sons paid no heed to this.

And, that night, Hatty tossed and turned on her pillow, teased out of sleep by two unanswered questions: what is amiss between those two? What happened once that cannot now be mended?

Lines came into her head:

> The moon is upside down. What power uncanny
> Can toss it, like a pancake, like a penny
> Down into dark?

Next day Lady Ursula took her departure, returning to Huntingdon-shire; and Frances was allowed to remove herself to the domicile of the Price family.

'Poor Lady Ursula!' sighed Aunt Polly. 'She is a queer, harsh, unaccountable creature! Was she really hoping, I wonder, that Camber might renew his addresses? After all this time? Can that have been why she came all this way to Letty Pentecost's funeral?'

'But she seemed so hostile and displeased when she did see Lord Camber,' Hatty said.

'Ay well – there's no denying that he is an oddity too, a wayward fellow enough. And – I suppose – if she *had* been harbouring any schemes of a matrimonial kind – she may have decided to abandon them when she found out that he plans to sail to the Americas as an indentured servant. Such a footing would hardly suit her notions of consequence.'

'*What*, Aunt?' exclaimed Hatty, her mouth wide, her face pale with shock.

'Why yes, he is going quite soon, did you not know? Lord Camber has told your uncle all his plans. He has, it seems, this Quixotic scheme for travelling across the ocean as a common labourer. You know how they do it – the cost of his trip is borne by an employer on condition that he engages himself (he is going as a carpenter, I believe) for a term of years equivalent to the passage money. He must serve any master who will have him on the other side. He says he wishes to ascertain the usage and plight of such poor emigrants. They take children, too, from Houses of Correction. He intends to observe the character of the sea-captains – some of them, it is said, exceedingly venal – and then proposes to write a book describing his experiences after he has established himself in this community that he and his friends are setting up, on the banks of the Susquehanna river.'

'I did not think it was so very definite,' said Hatty forlornly. 'Or would take place so soon.'

'Indeed yes, my dear, within the next few months, I understand. He is selling off some of his estates in this part of the country to raise money for the Society of Sophocrats – your uncle handles the business for him. Of course his family are vastly angry with him about the matter and have all but cast him off, I believe; for he is the eldest son of the Duke, you know, Lady Ursula's uncle, that is; Camber inherits the Dungeness title when the Duke dies, so it is a great scandal for them that he goes gadding abroad in this untoward manner. But Lord Camber himself has said that he is entirely ready to renounce the title in favour of his younger brother, Colonel Wisbech – only it seems that cannot be done, so easily. It would require an Act of Parliament, or some such thing.'

For several nights after this conversation Hatty had agitating dreams, in which Lord Camber was engulfed by waves pouring over his capsized ship, or attacked by wild redskin savages, or pursued by lions and bears through impenetrable forests. The distress and anxiety brought on by these dreams was somewhat allayed by the untroubled appearance of Lord Camber himself, who had occasion at various times during the ensuing months – the date of his departure needed, it seemed, to be continually deferred – to visit Mr Ward on business, and chose, for his own reasons, to wait on the lawyer at his residence rather than in his office. More often than not he might be encountered about the house, and would pause, if he met Hatty, for a friendly word.

'He is so affable and informal,' sighed Aunt Polly. 'I was almost startled to death when I came face to face with him on the stairs – and I in my calico apron and cotton gloves about to polish the lustres of the chandelier because I cannot trust Rebecca not to drop them on the brick floor of the pantry – but his manners are always so engaging and friendly. If *I* were Lady Ursula I'd have had him – red hair, gamekeeper's gaiters, and all!'

'But if it meant sailing across the Atlantic as a servant, aunt!'

'Oh, I dare swear he'd soon enough give up any undertaking of *that* kind if she were to re-engage herself to him,' Aunt Polly said with cheerful confidence.

Hatty did not feel so certain.

'I believe he has a great deal of resolution, Aunt Polly. And perhaps he did not go so far as to mention marriage, when they met this time.' She thought of the words she had heard in the ballroom. 'Can we not remember that we used to be friends?' was all he had said. 'But what puzzles me most of all, Aunt Polly, is, what can he see in her? Or ever have seen? She is so fierce! And – and grim! Was she always thus?'

'Oh, *no*, my dear! You can hardly conceive the change that has come over her in the last seven or eight years. You would not recognize her for the same person! No, she was used to be – in her good moods – quite amazingly lively and light-hearted – flashing and handsome and overflowing with brilliance and wit—'

'*Truly*, aunt?'

Hatty found a brilliant, flashing, witty Lady Ursula very hard to picture.

'I think Lady Ursula is one, Hatty, who needs the encouragement of another person's unstinted love to bring out the best in her – and her best could be something remarkable, I promise you!'

'Another person's unstinted love!' sighed Hatty. 'Do we not all need that, Aunt Polly?'

'Yes, child, and the only way to make your path easy through life is to learn to manage without it,' said Aunt Polly, whose comments now and then had a bedrock of common sense which Hatty found very sustaining. But as Mrs Ward said the words, she sighed, and wiped her forehead with a handkerchief as if, at times, she found her own philosophy hard to practise.

'Well, I do not believe that Lady Ursula will ever learn *that* lesson,' said Hatty.

A month or so after this conversation Hatty met Lord Camber on the stairway as she carefully carried a tray, loaded with gingerbread letters and apples, up to the nursery.

'Good day to you, Miss Hatty!'

'Good day, sir. I cannot shake hands, or I would spill these letters.'

His frowning, smiling gaze rested on the things she carried.

'Now, let me guess! You are going to feed a learned parrot?'

'No, sir. Not a parrot.' Hatty sighed a little, thinking of Ned's ever-increasing devotion and numerous visits to the Price household. 'Not a parrot. My cousins, the twins. It is Burnaby's afternoon off.'

'The twins? I was not even aware that there *were* twin children in Mr Ward's family? And who, pray, is Burnaby?'

'She is – she is – the person who has charge of the twins.'

'They are infants? Why have I never made their acquaintance, I wonder?'

'No, sir, they are not infants – but they very, very seldom go out of doors.'

'And you teach them their letters on Burnaby's free afternoon?'

'Yes. Well – I try.'

'May I be introduced to these unknown cousins? Would there be any objection? What are their names?'

'They are Sophy and Eliza – and, no, I do not believe that my aunt would have any objection. She is lying down at present – I do not like to disturb her. She has been very fatigued and out of sorts lately.'

Hatty did not say in so many words that, since the exertions and unusual social stresses and demands attendant on Lady Pentecost's funeral, Aunt Polly had seemed progressively lower in spirits, anxious and depressed. Or perhaps she worried about Ned?

Hatty repeated, 'I do not believe that my aunt would object to your visiting the twins, if you wish it, sir,' and led the way upstairs to the nursery where the twins spent the greater part of their life. It was a reasonably large apartment but, since it faced north and never received any sun, always remained somewhat lightless and gloomy.

The twins were now eight. Emancipated, at last, from their high chairs, they were permitted to sit side by side at a table, under the supervisory eye of Rebecca the maid. But they appeared forlorn and listless, with no occupation, staring at nothing, waiting for nothing in particular. When they beheld Hatty, however, their dull eyes brightened; they did not smile, but breathed a word in unison: '*Hatt.*'

'Well, my dears,' she said cheerfully, 'I have brought you some things for your reading lesson. (Thank you, Becky, you may run along.) But I have also brought you a gentleman visitor. Here is Lord Camber. Can you say good day to him?'

'Goo' day,' they murmured, rather indistinctly, scanning Lord Camber with their pale, unfocussed eyes.

Lord Camber beamed at them, as if greeting old friends after a long absence.

'Miss Sophie! And Miss Eliza!' he said. 'I am very happy to make your acquaintance. And now I am going to watch your reading lesson – which looks to me also like a very fine picnic – and then I hope I may be allowed to teach you a splendid game of cat's cradle. I always carry a length of twine in my pocket for just such a need.'

He perched himself easily on the window-seat and watched while Hatty peeled the apple, cut it into quarters, and made an A from the discarded rind.

'A is for Apple.'

'Apple,' they murmured acquiescently, munching pieces of fruit.

'And B is for Bread.' Hatty laid a gingerbread letter in front of each twin. These vanished even faster than the slices of apple. 'And C is for Cake. And now I hope you are going to make me some A's and B's and C's with your pencils and paper.'

Slowly, earnestly and laboriously, they did so.

'Good, clever girls. And a few more ...'

'They will never be able to learn even the basic rudiments of education,' their father had said once, furiously, in Hatty's hearing. 'In my opinion it is useless, a waste of time, to attempt to teach them *anything*.'

When the twins had endured as much of the lesson as their energy and capacities would admit, Hatty said, 'And now Lord Camber is going to show you his game.'

Their eyes brightened at the sight of the string. Lord Camber's game of cat's-cradle was an unqualified success. He knew many elaborate variations, and it was remarkable how quickly the twins were able to pick these up, one observing while the other played, and then reversing roles. After that they showed him Scissors-Paper-Stone, which still and always remained their favourite pastime, and then there was time only for half a game of chess before Burnaby returned. Both twins played in partnership against Lord Camber, discussing their moves, it seemed to Hatty, not so much by speech as by some mental process that passed between them without the need for language. Studying them across the board, Camber nodded appreciatively as each move was made, until Burnaby marched into the room with her invariable: 'Now I'd like my nursery to myself, *if* you please, Miss Hatty!'

Lord Camber bowed to the twins.

'Thank you, Miss Eliza, Miss Sophy! That was a very excellent and interesting game. I trust that I may be permitted to come back and resume it some time.'

'Thank the gentleman!' said Burnaby sharply.

'Ang – kew,' uttered Eliza.

'Ooobye,' breathed Sophy.

Lord Camber turned his engaging smile on to Burnaby.

'I know your family, do I not? Burnaby? Did I catch your name correctly? Was not your uncle Jasper transported for poaching?'

To Hatty's utter amazement, Burnaby, with nothing worse than her usual bleak, dour manner replied, 'It was a base, shabby lie. Evidence was planted on him by them as wanted his place.'

'Ah, I always thought that,' agreed Camber. 'I was a boy at the time, my uncle Gilbert was Justice of the Peace in that case. How does Mr Burnaby go on in Australia? Do you hear from him?'

'Now and again. He does well enough,' Burnaby answered laconically. 'Excuse me, sir, it's time for the girls' bath. Come along now, you two.'

The twins uttered faint moans of protest but obeyed. Hatty touched each of them lightly on the head, ignoring Burnaby's malignant stare, and said, 'Goodbye, my dears. Until my next visit!'

Lord Camber remained silent until they had reached the downstairs hall, then said, in a low tone, 'What a very remarkable pair! I am so delighted that you allowed me to visit them. But should they not have been playing out of doors on a fine autumn day such as this?'

'They never do wish to go out of doors,' Hatty told him. 'And my uncle prefers them not to go out into the street. He – he thinks they are frail, and may too easily pick up some infection.'

'And perhaps he is ashamed of their appearance?'

'I – I suppose so. That too. Yes.'

The large blueish-black naevus on the side of each twin's face had not diminished as they grew; on the contrary the marks had expanded and now covered three-quarters of the cheek and forehead, forming a strange contrast to the rest of their pallid and freckled complexions. They themselves were unperturbed by their appearance, but new young nursery-maids were often upset at first and required time to grow accustomed.

'But it cannot be good for them to remain indoors always,' observed Lord Camber.

'I know,' agreed Hatty sadly. 'They do not complain, however. They are very lethargic. The cause of that, I am very much afraid, is that Burnaby pacifies them continually with doses of medicine—'

'Laudanum?' Camber threw her a keen glance. 'You fear it dulls their wits?'

'I am not sure of that – it is only a guess – I believe they are naturally clever – but whatever it is she gives them makes them apathetic and not at all wishful to take pains – as you saw – except when they are really engaged, as they were over your cat's-cradle game.'

'They do lessons?'

'No, sir. Only when I am allowed to go in.'

'And you are their only visitor?'

'Oh well, of course my uncle sees them for a moment each morning.' Hatty did not dare attempt to describe the irritable and perfunctory nature of her uncle's morning duty-visits. But Lord Camber nodded, as if some nuance had nevertheless been communicated.

'And your aunt?'

Hatty looked even more troubled. 'She – Aunt Polly – finds their company deeply distressing.'

By now the pair of them had left the house through the drawing-room french windows and were slowly pacing across the leaf-strewn lawn at the rear of the house. 'I think, after my three boy-cousins were born, Aunt Polly very much longed for a daughter – a girl, you know, who would be company for her.'

'Ha,' said Lord Camber. He gave Hatty a shrewd, understanding glance. 'Poor lady – we can compassionate her. For what arrived instead was *two* daughters who are company only for each other and not at all for her – am I right in my guess?'

'Yes, that is it exactly. And then, they are so plain, poor dears. I think she had hoped for a handsome daughter, in whom she could take pride.'

'Their brothers do not play with them – visit them?'

'Only Ned. He sometimes plays chess with them. The older two – Tom and Sydney – I think they find the twins embarrassing.'

'Yes, boys of their age would do so, of course.'

Lord Camber did not appear to pass any judgement on this state of affairs. He said, musingly, 'One wonders how many other families contain such secrets behind their well-polished brass door-knockers. In my own experience – but no matter for that. Why does Burnaby dislike you so? Because you are a challenge to her authority?'

'I suppose so. There can be no—'

At this moment their talk was interrupted by Mr Ward, who threw open the casement window of his office upstairs and exclaimed, 'My Lord! There you are! I had no notion that you had arrived. Pray step up! I have the papers all ready for your signature.'

'Business, business,' sighed Lord Camber. Again he gave Hatty his broad, all-comprehending smile, and briefly raised her hand to his lips. 'I always learn something of a new and highly nutritious nature from you, Miss Hatty. And your silences, I believe, are as instructive as your speech. I shall miss our salutary encounters. But I have not had time to inquire about your Muse? Has she been active lately? Or is it *he*? Your daemon, perhaps?'

She nodded. 'Yes. But I must not keep you – my uncle is waiting for you,' she murmured, and quickly made her escape into the shrubbery. She wondered very much whether Lord Camber would discuss the plight of the twins with their father, and if Mr Ward would be angry with her for disclosing the fact of their existence. But I do not see what else I could have done, she told herself, walking on in the direction of the kitchen garden. And Aunt Polly? Will she be distressed that Lord Camber – for whom I know she has a high regard – should be privy to the twins' subterranean existence in this family?

Hatty herself could not feel that Lord Camber's admission into the twins' life was in any way undesirable; there was something so open-minded, so good-humoured, so unprejudiced about his way of thinking upon almost any subject that, it seemed to her, his mere knowledge of a situation would have the power of disinfecting guilt, and making anger harmless. How queer, how very queer, though, that he and Lady Ursula—

But here Hatty came to a sudden stop.

Without thinking, she had made her way towards the place always

79

referred to by herself and Ned as the Kingdom – the secret, derelict graveyard with its moss-covered tombstones and giant lime-tree. She hardly ever came here unless accompanied by Ned, for she had felt strongly from her very first days in the household that it was *his* discovery, his domain, that she set foot there by invitation only, and ought not to presume upon his early, sympathetic hospitality when she had been no more than a homesick, unhappy stranger. But today there was so much pressing on her mind, matters about which she needed to reflect without interruption, that, unaware, wrapped in thought, she picked her way among the overgrown currant bushes and slipped through the narrow gap between creeper-hung wall and ancient dusty door.

Afternoon light had begun to dull and thicken already, the autumn dusk was closing in. Soon wintry conditions would prohibit access to the secret place.

And in any case, reflected Hatty sadly, Ned and I are becoming too old for such childish retreats. Soon we shall have outgrown this sanctuary.

During the last few months, Ned had grown very much in height, had become tall and gangling, seemed hardly to know what to do with his long, bony limbs. It was just as well, Hatty thought, that he enjoyed the dancing classes at the Crown and found pleasure in capering up and down the ballroom floor with Nancy Price ... Soon he would be gone into the Navy, it was only repeated pleas from Aunt Polly that had kept him at home until now—

With a sharp intake of breath, Hatty stood still in the doorway. For, across the tops of a couple of tombs, barely visible in the dim light above the tangled grass of autumn, were to be seen two figures: what appeared to be a female sitting on a table-top gravestone, and a male standing very close to her, almost indistinguishable from her.

Nancy and Ned.

Precisely how close the pair were to each other Hatty had only a second's time to estimate, for she must have made some sound, and the two figures sprang self-consciously apart.

Hatty had an immediate, violent impulse to retreat, to try and pretend that the confrontation had not taken place, but it was too late; she heard Ned's voice murmur, 'Thank goodness! it is only Hatty,' and a soft, impatient exclamation from the girl, who stood up, shaking her shawl and dress into order, before beginning to move towards Hatty.

Ned muttered something in an undertone, at which Nancy vigorously shook her head. She continued walking towards Hatty with a languid, gliding gait, recognizably imitated from Mme Lamartine's assistant.

Hatty remained unable to move from where she stood.

'*Lord! Miss Hatty! Is not this fun?*' exclaimed Nancy in a conspiratorial whisper when the pair were only a few feet apart. 'Lassy me! Are you not a lucky pair, you and Ned, to have this charming retreat, all to yourselves? I vow you are the luckiest pair in Portsmouth town! I can tell you, I am quite eaten up with envy, and so I say to Neddy! As soon as ever he told me about this fine hidey-hole I began to tease and tease him to let me have a glimpse of it! An't that so, Neddy?'

Hatty was perplexed. 'But how in the world could you ever make your way here, without being seen? You could not have come through my uncle's house?'

'Oh, *no*, my dear! The simplest thing in the world! I walked out, you see, on an errand, with our maid Sukey and your sister Frances, to buy ribbons, and then I told them I had a blister on my heel, so turned back. After that, instead of going home, I ran down Widdershins Lane, where, you see, there was an old rusty gate, long out of use, fastened by a chain and padlock, which must, I knew, lead to this place; and clever Neddy was there already with a file, and soon filed through the chain that fastened the gate, and hacked a way for me through the holly bushes that grow inside the wall. I vow, though, I am stung and scratched all to pieces – my muslin will never be the same again – look at this monstrous rent! I shall have to bribe Sukey to mend it. (Lucky for me that Uncle Jonathan is so ready with his cash.) The state of my shawl, too, is all your fault, naughty sir, for luring me into your den. You are a sad tempter!'

She gave Ned's cheek a possessive pinch.

To Hatty there seemed several points very unsatisfactory and odd about this explanation. Firstly, how did it chance that Nancy was aware of the existence of the disused gate in Widdershins Lane, a seldom-used alleyway along which, normally, few people ever had any occasion to pass? And when had she managed to communicate the knowledge to Ned? Today, or on some previous occasion? And how in the world had Ned, who was neither quick nor dextrous with his hands, managed to procure a file – from where? – and cut, or break through an old, thick rusty iron chain? An operation which must have taken several hours, surely?

'It grows late,' interrupted Ned nervously. 'Nancy, I think you had best return home. I will see you back to the gate.'

He did not meet Hatty's eye. He was wretchedly discomposed, she could tell, aghast that she should have happened upon this rendezvous of his with Nancy Price; he looked as if beset by a strong inclination simply to bolt off and leave the two young ladies to make the best of their way home. But Nancy thrust her arm briskly and confidently through his, and said, in her chuckling, cooing voice: 'You will have to lead me back to the gate, Neddy, or, to be sure, I shall lose myself entirely in this wilderness of yours, and be taken up in the morning, witless and raving! Goodnight, Miss Hatty; we shall meet, prim and proper, at the dancing class and not betray one another! I fear I cannot give your love to your sister Frances, for she must not know that we have met here!'

She and Ned moved quietly away to a thicket of hollies on the far side of the graveyard, behind which the Widdershins Lane gate must lie concealed.

Sore at heart, and deeply perturbed, Hatty made her way slowly to the conservatory. It was time to change her dress for dinner, but she needed a moment's thinking-time.

In this refuge, not long after, Ned found her.

'Hatty! I had hoped you might be here!' There was a nervous hesitancy about his voice, almost a stammer. Hatty gazed at him in silence, greatly troubled, really not knowing what to say. By now dusk had wholly fallen and she could see little of his face but a pale oval with two black sockets for eyes.

'Hatty! You won't tell about Nancy being there – will you? You won't tell anybody in the house? My father would be so very – I don't know *what* he would say.'

'No,' she said slowly, 'no, Ned, of course I won't tell anybody. But Ned – have you met Nancy there *before* today – has she been there at any time before now?'

'Well – yes! Yes; she has. You see – after I told her about the Kingdom – *she* has so much; I wanted to show that I had something too – she was so interested – and *she* told *me* one day about the gate in the lane – her brothers knew of it – and she said, if I could cut through the chain and open the gate, she could slip away from home and meet me there. She was so wild to see my secret place! And so – and so she helped me file through the chain. In fact,' he added simply, 'she did most of the work. I do not think I could have done it by myself. And various times she has brought cake and wine in a little bottle for a – for a picnic. You see – she is quite used to such secret outings; she has been on many such, she told me, with her brothers when they were younger. Imagine it! They even used to go swimming down by the shore! Nancy as well!'

'Good heavens.'

Hatty had not the heart to ask for how long Nancy had been coming to the secret Kingdom.

'Cousin Hatty!' Ned's voice shook. 'Nancy and I – we have not done anything *wrong* – don't think it – '

Hatty could not help recalling her first glimpse of the pair, indistinctly seen through the mild grey dusk – the girl sitting, the boy standing so close against her – the startled speed with which they had plucked themselves apart.

'Ned,' she said slowly, 'what you and Nancy do is no business of mine. None! But – you do realize – there would be dreadful, dreadful trouble if you were found out – suppose some person were to see Nancy walk down Widdershins Lane? Or go through the gate? Think what my uncle would say if he found out. Or Aunt Polly. She is so – so very fond of you – you are her favourite of the whole family.'

Indeed, Hatty could not help wondering whether her aunt did have some doubt, some unvoiced suspicion – if that might account for her unwonted fatigue, her headaches, her troubled silences.

Ned said, 'Don't, Hatty, *don't!*'

'Or if Nancy's family found out that she has been going out by herself – she must have had to tell a great many lies.'

'Her uncle often gives her presents of money, she tells me, so she pays the maid Sukey to say they have been sewing together, or gone on some errand.'

Curiously, what Hatty minded most was not that another person had been introduced into their hidden place – though she disliked Nancy Price and deeply mistrusted her influence over simple, childlike, guileless Ned – but the fact that another entrance had been opened, leading to a public road. For her, the secret Kingdom was now ruined, violated, laid bare; it would never again, she knew, possess the feeling of utter security, of sanctuary, that it had had before.

At dinner that evening Hatty thought that her uncle appeared graver and more curt-spoken than usual. Aunt Polly had a high colour and seemed uneasy and short of breath. She ate little, as had been her habit of late, and that very slowly, and was by no means her normal, cheerful self.

Was it because of Lord Camber's visit to the twins? Hatty wondered anxiously. Were they angry about his access to this knowledge? Or could they – terrifying thought – have discovered about Ned and Nancy? Nothing was said; the meal was eaten almost in silence. Tom was the only one who seemed at ease. Hatty resolved that, during the brief interval after dinner, when her uncle was left alone with his wine and nuts, before tea was brought in, she would broach the matter of Lord Camber with Aunt Polly and ask for forgiveness.

But Hatty was not given the chance to do this.

At the end of the meal, Mr Ward laid down his knife and fork, wiped his mouth with his napkin, and said in a cold, disapproving tone: 'I suppose the news may as well be disclosed now as later. Though I am sure there is small matter for rejoicing. Today I have had an express from Huntingdonshire informing me, Harriet, that your father is about to celebrate his marriage with Lady Ursula Fowldes.'

Mrs Ward's high colour became even more pronounced; her cheeks darkened to a purplish hue, and, with a sharp choking sigh, she rolled off her chair on to the dining-room floor.

VI

AUNT POLLY'S ILLNESS threw the whole household into disarray. She had contrived to keep all the affairs of the establishment in good order, yet had never been too busy to attend to her husband and the boys, always kind and sympathetic to Hatty. Without her calming influence tempers went awry, tasks were neglected and good habits tended to lapse.

Mr Filingay, the apothecary and surgeon, gave it as his opinion that she was suffering from an acute affection of the heart, that she had been over-exerting herself, probably for years past, and now must submit to a regime of complete rest, careful diet and regular remedial doses. It was a measure of Mrs Ward's lowered state, Hatty thought, that she submitted to this edict with no more than an acquiescent sigh, and the acknowledgement that she did feel rather poorly, could do with a bit of a respite. Hatty, she dared say, would for a while be able to manage the house very well.

Hatty, with all the affairs of the household thus suddenly thrown on her shoulders, found herself stretched, taxed and strained in many hitherto undreamed-of ways. Fortunately for her, she had, unawares, absorbed a great quantity of Aunt Polly's calm good sense and philosophical attitudes during many friendly, peaceful, talkative sessions while hemming household linen or darning the boys' stockings. This involuntary intake of practice and principles now stood her in good stead. Another advantage was the loyalty and devotion of Mrs Ward's household. The cook, the housekeeper, the maids, the coachman and Deakin the gardener were all deeply attached to their mistress and as many of them had followed her from the former house in London, they were anxious to act for her comfort and well-being in every possible way. Any instruction from Hatty beginning with the words 'My aunt wishes' was sure to be obeyed with eager rapidity.

The exception to this was Burnaby, who had been hired in the first place by Mr Ward, and had never taken any particular pains to conceal her scorn for Aunt Polly's undecided, unhappy, unfixed feelings regarding the twins, or her disapproval of the amiable, easy-going system by which the rest of the household was conducted. Hatty, these days, had little time to spare for visits to the nursery and though, in theory, her authority over Burnaby was now greater, she did not attempt to try out such increased powers, wishing, at all costs, to avoid trouble or hostility in the house, which would be certain to have its impact on the invalid. Burnaby's sway in the nursery therefore continued unchallenged, and though Hatty worried a great deal about the twins – who seemed even paler, lower in vitality, and more dejected, when she did have time to pay them a hasty visit – she could only console herself by resolving to give them a great deal more attention as soon as Aunt Polly recovered, which everybody in the family felt sure she must somehow do within a few weeks. Or months, at least.

In the meantime Hatty besought Ned to devote more of his time to his small sisters.

'If you would but play a game of chess with them every day.'

Ned, quenched and melancholy, agreed without protest. Since Hatty's inadvertent intrusion on his secret assignation with Nancy Price, followed so swiftly by his mother's seizure and indisposition, he had appeared exceedingly low-spirited and subdued. Of the boys he had always been his mother's favourite – 'My little quiddity, my little nonesuch,' she used to call him. Now that she had time and strength for no more than a loving smile and faint pressure of the hand during his daily visit to her bedside, he hardly knew what to do with himself, and Hatty, though she felt very sorry for him, was herself so harassed with her additional household responsibilities that she had little time to help or comfort him.

Once or twice he nervously reminded her of her promise, as they passed on the stairs or in the herb garden.

'You won't tell – will you – ever, Hatty?'

'*Of course* I won't, Ned – you may trust me. But do, please, please, be sensible!'

He nodded, but she had no means of knowing whether he followed her anxious admonition, or whether the secret meetings in the graveyard continued. Nancy Price, Hatty believed, was a headstrong, heedless creature, to whom the serious illness of Ned's mother would be of little consequence except insofar as it kept his cousin Hatty conveniently indoors, and occupied with household responsibilities. But winter weather, icy rain, and gales, besides the early dark of December, must make the graveyard, Hatty hoped, an uninviting, cheerless trysting-place; it seemed hardly probable that Nancy would wish to subject herself to much cold and discomfort for the chance of a clandestine encounter with Ned.

A fortnight after Aunt Polly's collapse, Hatty was called to the parlour to greet 'a young lady, asking for you, miss' who proved to be her sister Frances, very stylishly dressed in salmon-pink velvet and brown fur.

Frances was in a great hurry.

'Lord, child! I was so sorry, sorry as can be, to hear the news of my aunt's illness. May I perhaps see her, just for a moment or two?'

With regret, Hatty was obliged to report that at this time her aunt was sleeping, and the poor lady was so weak that it was thought important not to rouse her when she fell into a natural slumber.

'Well, perhaps it is no great matter after all – but, pray, *do* give her my love and say all that is proper. The fact of it is, Hatty, that I am *eloping* – well, you know how things are at home, now, Papa married to Lady Ursula, nothing on this earth would drag me back *there* to be subject to all her sour-grape whims and dictates; and Agnes just as bad, probably worse by this time – unless Lady U has pushed her off on to that Norris—'

87

'But, Fanny, what *can* you mean? *Eloping?* With whom?'

Fanny's face broke into a happy, confiding smile.

'Oh, he is the dearest fellow! My Sam!'

'Is he – is he one of Mrs Price's sons?'

Hatty began to have a slightly nightmarish feeling, that the whole Price family were rising up to tangle round her, like some active, encroaching weed.

'No, a nephew – the son of Mr Price's brother, Mr James Price.'

'What is his profession – Mr James Price?'

'Oh, he is no more than a corn-chandler – but very *rich*, Hatty! I know Papa will not approve – my Sam is only a lieutenant of marines, though so handsome, lively and active – but all that will soon change, I am sure. Mr Price will soon arrange for his promotion – or his father will soon find him a position in his business – or *my* father will come around and endow us with something, once the knot is safely tied. So we only have a comfortable house over our heads there can be no occasion for any trouble, we shall be happy as the day is long.'

Hatty was aghast. She could see, only too plainly, Fanny's very sufficient reasons for not wishing to return to Bythorn, but her hopes of a secure future with Sam Price seemed built on frighteningly insecure foundations.

'Oh Fanny! Do not you think you should wait a while – consider a little longer? Continue staying with the Prices – or, or, you could perhaps come back to this house?'

But Hatty's voice faltered. In the present state of the Ward family she hardly felt entitled to make such an offer; she felt sure that her uncle Philip would not endorse it.

In any case, Fanny threw these suggestions aside.

'No, child, no; the Price household is in uproar at this moment; *two* of the maids have just come down with the measles; one of them went home for a day's holiday to her family in Gosport and picked up the contagion there, and the other one, Sukey, shares a bed with her and has but today thrown out a rash; so Mrs Price is clean distracted. I am off to Bristol with my Sam directly, for we are to be married there by special licence (I sold the diamond brooch that Aunt Winchilsea left me) and Sam has procured a transfer, so we shall live in Bristol until the commotion has died down. I daresay it will not be so very bad. Papa is probably too taken up in his new marriage to kick up a dust or bear a grudge against Sam – and very likely my sister Maria Bertram will come across with a handsome present – she is so wealthy now after all! So soon as we are settled and my Aunt Ward is better you must come and visit us, Hatty, I am wild for you to see my handsome Sam! He is unpolished in his manners, but so sweet and comical and gamesome!'

One of the maids here came in and said, 'Could you come and talk to Cook about the grocery orders, Miss Hatty?'

'Yes, Prue, I will come directly.'

Hatty looked in despair at her sister, who was already gathering up gloves and muff.

'I must be off, Sam is waiting at the end of the road. It is too bad, child, that you are now so occupied with all this housekeeping. I can see they are making a sad drudge of you. But wait, just wait a little time, until Sam and I are settled, and then you shall come to us – and we shall all be so merry.'

Frances kissed Hatty warmly and whisked out of the room, calling back: 'Oh, and do give my love to the boys—'

Hatty had fallen into the habit, after dinner, of playing the piano for half an hour while the boys prepared their next day's lessons and her uncle drank his tea. Some day, she supposed, she must become a governess, and it behoved her to keep up her accomplishments. Whether he listened to it or not, the music appeared to soothe Mr Ward, and she felt that it made for a more comfortable relation between them. He never thanked her for her activities about the house, but his manner to her these days, though not precisely cordial, was calm and matter-of-fact, considerably less chilly than it had been when she first arrived.

'When does my cousin Sydney return home for the Christmas holiday, uncle?' she asked that evening, after having played a couple of sonatas. While Ned was his mother's special son, Sydney was by far his father's favourite among the boys, since he worked hard at his law studies, had become ambitious, and was keenly interested in making a name for himself in his profession. ('Which is just as well,' grumbled Mr Ward, 'now that my brother has married again and Sydney is likely to lose the Bythorn property.')

Sydney had of course been informed of his mother's grave illness, but it had not been thought necessary to summon him to her bedside until the regular Christmas holiday brought him home to Portsmouth for a few days.

'Sydney? He will return on the twentieth. He can bring some papers for Lord Camber, who by that time will probably be making his final arrangements for departure. A sad, hare-brained business, that – sad, hare-brained business,' Mr Ward muttered.

Hatty thought Sydney a very poor exchange for Lord Camber, whose intermittent, unexpected appearances in the house over the past few weeks had sensibly brightened her life. The news of his imminent departure filled her with such deep dismay that she thought: I could hardly entertain a greater regard for him if he were my own brother. And then, taking a survey of the three proxy brothers she already possessed: rather less, indeed – for Sydney is spiteful and conceited, Tom good-natured but very slow-witted, and as for Ned – oh, if Ned is really bewitched by the charms of Nancy Price – then Ned is lost indeed.

Only that afternoon, stepping into the conservatory for some lemon leaves to garnish a flower-piece for Aunt Polly's sickroom, she had been surprised to come upon Ned carrying a very choice little posy, which he had evidently put together himself with considerable taste and care, combining purple michaelmas daisies with a late marigold or two, brilliant rose-hips and a sprig of yew covered with coral berries.

'Why, Ned!'

'It – it is for my mother!' he stammered, but he had turned a deep red, almost as scarlet as the rose-hips, and though she later saw the posy by Mrs Ward's bedside, Hatty could not help wondering if it had originally been destined for another recipient; and then scolded herself for her ungenerous suspicions.

'Uncle Philip,' she said, seizing a moment when both the boys were safely out of the room engaged upon their own concerns, 'I fear I have a dreadfully disagreeable piece of news to communicate to you.'

He looked up, frowning over his newspaper.

'My sister Frances has run off with the Prices' nephew.'

Mr Ward required a full minute to assimilate this information. Then his wrath was cataclysmic.

Scurvy, ill-conditioned, low-class behaviour! The hussy! Taking advantage of a time when her poor aunt was so very unwell – when he himself was constrained to remain at home due to his wife's ill-health – playing such a disagreeable trick on her unfortunate hosts the Prices, who must feel in some sort responsible. How *could* she be so lost to all sense of propriety? The Prices' nephew? Yes, for sure, he knew the fellow – a curst, stupid, cocksure, popinjay – a lieutenant of marines who would never, in his whole life, rise higher than captain. Well, Frances had done for herself now, with a vengeance, a most shocking waste, considering her handsome looks. There would soon enough be an end to *them*, after she had endured a few years trying to bring up a family on a lieutenant's pay – she certainly need expect no help from *him* – and he doubted very much indeed whether his brother Henry would advance a guinea to the miserable pair. Bristol, they had gone to, had they? Ha! Well, let them remain in Bristol, he washed his hands of them, and so would all their respectable connections.

'I wonder, very much,' he concluded, 'that we have not heard from the Prices on this matter.'

A note received on the following morning at breakfast explained this omission. The Price household was in a shocking state of disarray (poor Mrs Price wrote) for not only the two maids and Nancy, but now Mr Price himself, were laid low with the measles, and a very severe form of that troublesome complaint, furthermore, involving a high fever and much pain as to eyes and ears. Mrs Price – though fortunately not stricken by measles – was clean distracted with worry. She blamed herself acutely for not being a more attentive chaperon to Miss Frances, but who could possibly have expected such an eventuality? Naturally she was deeply shocked and distressed over the disgraceful affair, but hoped that the young couple might in due course be forgiven, and the best be made of a bad business, and some reasonably steady, moderately paid position found for her nephew, Samuel Price, who, she could at least say, was the most good-natured young fellow to be met with anywhere and would soon, she doubted not, by the influence of a sensible, well-bred young woman, be cured of a few rough, unmannerly ways and turns of speech and a slight tendency to tippling. Now she begged to conclude, for the doctor was in the house waiting to attend his four patients – Mr Price would indubitably have sent regards but was delirious at present, and she was his very sincerely, etc, etc.

'Measles! Measles!' muttered Mr Ward. 'I wish the whole Price family were carried off by the measles.'

Ned choked on the slice of bread-and-butter he was eating, and found himself obliged to quit the breakfast parlour. He looked unwontedly pale and had black circles under his eyes; Hatty wondered if some of his state derived from worry over Nancy's illness. If they had been continuing to meet in secret, as she half-suspected, and as the sight of the posy suggested, this infection of Nancy's must prevent any further intercourse for many weeks, months even, now that a hard winter had begun to assert its grip over the country. Nancy would not be well enough to go out of doors.

Later that day Sydney arrived off the London stage. His father could still deplore Sydney's stylish mode of dress, from his beaver hat and elaborately tied cravat to the brilliantly polished boots, more suited to a member of the haut ton than a hard-working young lawyer; but Sydney himself was very completely satisfied with his appearance, and combined this satisfaction with a tendency to hold the rest of his family in slight contempt, writing off his younger brothers as scruffy whipper-snappers, his parents as old fogies, and the twins as something too unmentionable to be even called to mind.

By the appearance of Hatty, however, after a six months' absence, he was quite taken aback.

He came upon her when she was discussing Mrs Ward's rate of

progress with the surgeon, and making a list of medicines to be purchased.

Mr Filingay had taken his departure.

'Is my mother *very* ill, then, Hatty?' Sydney asked in a subdued tone, impressed by the gravity of the surgeon's demeanour.

Hatty sighed, tucking the memorandum she had made into a notebook which travelled at all times in her reticule.

'Yes, cousin; it seems that she has been over-tasking herself for years past.' She did not go on to tell Sydney Mr Filingay's explanation for her aunt's disability, that the birth of the twins had put too severe a strain upon her heart, which, at the time, had passed unregarded. She did not think Sydney would find this information of particular interest. Indeed he sighed and said, with more than a touch of irritability: 'Does that mean that she will be laid up in bed over Christmas? And we all have to tiptoe about the house? I had hoped to invite some of my friends in.'

'You had better speak to my uncle about that,' Hatty said, feeling quite certain that Mr Ward would veto any such proposal.

'Shall I go up and see her? Perhaps I can cheer her – make her feel more the thing with a few London tales.'

'Better wait for half an hour – the nurse is with her now.'

'The nurse? Good heavens,' said Sydney discontentedly. He glanced again at Hatty, taking in her appearance more carefully. 'So *you* rule the rookery now, hey, Cousin Hatty? You have properly got the reins in your hands, I can see! And I won't deny it suits you – you must have grown a couple of inches since I saw you last – filled out, too and looking as smart as ninepence. That is a deuced smart way you have found of doing your hair – upon my soul it is! I recall when I was here last what a sight you had made of yourself with Cousin Frances – how we did laugh at you! By the bye, is that right, what Tom tells me, that she has thrown her bonnet over the windmill with that oaf, Sam Price? If that is really so, she has properly done for herself – might as well go upon the town at once.'

Hatty stared at him in silent, astonished disgust, but was spared the need for making any reproof, as Mr Ward came in at the front door, returning from his place of business, and said, 'Ha! Sydney! I am glad to see you. Have you brought those papers for Lord Camber?'

The law office in London where Sydney was now employed also handled business for Camber and his father the Duke; indeed it was through Camber's influence that Sydney had obtained the position.

'Yes, sir, I have them here.' Sydney smartly pulled from his portmanteau a bundle of documents, tied with blue tape.

Hatty slipped away towards the pantry to confer with the housekeeper. As she crossed the hall she heard Sydney say, 'Cousin Hatty is turning into a deuced fine girl, is she not, sir? I suppose she will soon have a prodigious deal of beaux coming around?'

And his father replied in a tone of deep disapproval, 'Beaux? Why, no, sir. I should hope not, indeed!'

At dinner-time Mr Ward remarked to Hatty, with something of a return to his old style of chilly censure: 'Hatty. Among the documents Lord Camber dispatched to me by Sydney, I find there is a note addressed to *you*. I am somewhat surprised, and not best pleased, I must aver, to discover that there exists a correspondence between you and his Lordship.'

Hatty blushed a hot vivid scarlet and sat speechless for a moment, while the boys gazed at her with interest. Then she said, 'I am sure, sir, whatever is in the note is not – is not at all – there has not been – this is the first—'

'I believe you must allow me to open it and see for myself,' said Mr Ward.

'Of course, sir. Pray feel free to do so.'

With another frowning glance at Hatty, her uncle prised up the seal, and read the contents of the communication inside – only a few lines.

'My dear Miss Hatty: here is the address I promised you. I regret that press of business will keep me in Huntingdonshire from now on, and that I shall not have the pleasure of visiting your uncle's house again and bidding you goodbye in person. I hope that your Muse continues active. Your sincere friend H. Camber.'

'*Muse?*' demanded Mr Ward. 'What is this about a *muse?*'

'Oh, it is nothing – only a kind of joke. I had shown Lord Camber some of my verses – which he was so good as to – as to admire – and he promised to give me the address of an acquaintance of his who edits a journal which – which sometimes publishes such pieces—'

'*You*? Write *verses*? This is something quite new,' pronounced Mr Ward, in a tone suggesting that the production of verse came rather lower in his estimation than cleaning the gutters.

'No, sir; it is not new; I have done it all my life. Ned knows about it,' said Hatty faintly, wishing that her uncle would hand her Lord Camber's note; she would have liked to see it, to handle it for herself. But he put it down by his plate and turned his censorious gaze on to Ned.

Ned, however, was in no state to take up the cudgels on behalf of his cousin. From deathly white, his complexion had changed to a uniform brick-coloured flush, and as his father addressed him – 'Ned?' – he gasped, 'I am s-s-s-sorry, sir – I feel uncommonly s-sick—' and incontinently bolted from the dining-room.

Two hours later Ned had thrown out a rash which covered his entire body with small red papules set so close together that a pin-head could hardly pass between them. His eyes and nose ran continually, he was slightly delirious.

'Nancy?' he mumbled. 'Nancy, I am so sorry – I could not come to the glass-house. Chess with the twins. Pawn to king's four – pawn to king's five—'

'I am afraid, sir, that Ned has the measles,' said Hatty, at the bedside, to his father, hoping that Mr Ward had not made any sense of Ned's disjointed mutterings.

'Oh, good heavens. Good *heavens*! As if we had not troubles enough in this house!'

Mr Ward looked down without a great deal of sympathy at his restless, feverish son, who rolled miserably among the bedclothes, crying out at one time that he was so thirsty! then that his ears pained him so much that he could not bear it another minute.

'How are we ever going to manage?' demanded Mr Ward. 'Have *you* had measles, Hatty?'

'Yes, sir – fortunately. Frances and I had it at the same time, when I was eight.'

Hatty's voice quivered as she remembered, with a pang, how their mother, though not well herself, had tended them, how they had shared jokes, and grapes, and games, during their convalescence. Another life, gone for ever.

'Let us hope that, as it has come out on Ned so fast, it will be quickly over for him. But I am afraid there is a quarantine period of two weeks for those who have not had it.'

Mr Filingay confirmed this, when summoned to the house. He prescribed Fellow's Syrup of Hypophosphites and ordered the curtains of the room, which Ned shared with Tom, to be kept drawn at all times.

Hatty was in dread that some mention of the Price household should provide the clue as to where Ned had picked up the contagion, but that danger seemed by-passed; Mr Filingay said there were numerous cases of measles in the town. Fortunately both Tom and Sydney had had the disease already. And, even more mercifully, Aunt Polly (who had also contracted measles in childhood) at this time took a slight turn for the better and was able to lie on a sopha in her bedroom and receive visits from her family, two at a time.

Hatty had managed to take possession of the note from Lord Camber, at a moment when her uncle and cousins were cast into confusion by Ned's collapse. (Let her not be blamed unduly if, during this hectic period in the history of the Ward household, the piece of paper containing Lord Camber's few kind lines was never parted from her during the twenty-four hours, tucked under her pillow at night, hidden in her reticule during the hours of daylight.)

Perhaps he has already embarked now, she thought sorrowfully, as she went about her household duties or lay wakeful and worried in the dark. My uncle said he would probably embark from Bristol – that is where most of the emigrant vessels take on their human cargo. Bristol! I suppose Fanny is there. How strange if she were to encounter Lord Camber. He said he might write to me from Pennsylvania. It takes at least two months to sail across the ocean. And another two months for a letter to come back. Sometimes the people on board may have been taken by force, he told me; if the captains have not enough passengers to make their trip profitable they snatch a few more. Suppose some disease breaks out? Sometimes the vessels arrive with smallpox aboard and are turned away from the ports. Oh, how can I bear his being so far away? I may very likely never hear from him again.

Sometimes, at night, she would re-light her candle, sit up, and write a few lines.

> Perhaps, perhaps,
> This strange word slips through gaps
> escapes from traps
> is never found
> on signs or maps.
> Perhaps we shall get a letter
> perhaps we shan't.
> Perhaps we can meet again
> perhaps we can't.
>
> Perhaps is just
> a word we cannot trust

She could not solace herself in this way too often, however, for Burnaby, whose attic bedroom was opposite hers, would remark, with her dour sidelong glance: 'Wakeful in the night again, were you, Miss Hatty? I saw your candle-glim shine under the door. No wonder the bills for tallow and wax is so high!'

Burnaby, for some mysterious reason, perhaps because of her sour disposition, had Mr Ward's confidence, and if there were disputes among the servants, it was Burnaby's version of the controversy that he would be inclined to favour. Hatty was sure that her policy of keeping the twins in monotonous, unstimulated subjection stemmed directly from Mr Ward; he saw no future for them, so was prepared to lay out as little as possible, in time and human effort, on their welfare or instruction.

Sydney, for some obscure reason, was Burnaby's favourite among the boys; they had been allies from a time when he was much younger. Perhaps it was, Hatty thought, because they both preferred to conduct their lives in a devious, diversionary, undercover manner. Sydney, Ned once told Hatty, had several times procured the dismissal of servants he did not like, or who had attempted to discipline him, or been severe with him, by spying on them until he found out something discreditable, or which could be made to sound discreditable, and then informing Burnaby, who would carry the story to Mr Ward.

'It is too bad that Burnaby and you ain't better friends, Cousin Hatty,' observed Sydney one day. 'She's a close, quiet one, but she's as shrewd as she can hold together; with her on your side, I can tell you, you'd have an easier time of it, running the house.'

'Thank you, cousin, but I fear I will have to manage as best I can without Burnaby's goodwill. She has always chosen to resent my attempts to instruct or develop the twins in any way. So long as she is in charge of them I fear they will make but little progress.'

'Oh, hang the twins! Who cares a straw what becomes of *them*?' said Sydney impatiently. 'I am sure my father has written them off long ago. It is too bad that creatures of that sort cannot be drowned at birth, like unwanted kittens. What a useless drain on my father's resources!'

And Sydney commenced a long discourse, to which Hatty, hemming sheets, paid little heed, about Economy, and Management, Thrift, Good Housekeeping, and How to Make Every Penny Work. One's life should be planned with extreme care from the very beginning, he informed Hatty, that was the only way to get on; as an example of the horrendous foolishness and misjudgement, one had only to look at the example of Hatty's sister Fanny!

'How can Frances have been so cow-witted, when your elder sister Maria did so well for herself – far better, indeed, than Maria had any right to expect? And I hear that your eldest sister Agnes has left off her foolish repinings and agrees to marry the new incumbent at Mansfield, Mr Reginald Norris. So she does not do so badly and will at least never want for a comfortable establishment, as Norris is an old friend of Sir Thomas.'

'From whom did you hear that, cousin?' asked Hatty, surprised, breaking off a thread.

'Lady Ursula, when she is staying at the Fowldes town house, sometimes visits the Chancery Lane office on behalf of her father the Earl, who is sadly gouty; and she has been so affable and condescending as to stop sometimes and chat a little when she passes by my desk. She was so good as to recall the time when I was privileged to escort her back to Lombard Street after the Sunday service.'

How unexpected, thought Hatty, re-threading her needle, that Lady Ursula, proud and stand-offish with almost everybody, should bestow her favour on Sydney, of all people! How very odd.

Sydney, smirking, took a turn about the room. He was bored and restless in Portsmouth, Hatty thought, for all his suggestions as to inviting friends in for Christmas festivities had been instantly negatived by Mr Ward, and he was probably as eager to get back to his London ways and acquaintances as Hatty was to see the end of his visit. He made a great deal of extra work for the servants, for he was decidedly fussy about his food, demanded clean linen every day, and required his boots to be polished at inconveniently frequent intervals.

He was like a tiresome bluebottle about the house.

'Lady Ursula won't stop in London long now, though,' he divulged. 'For Lord Elstow has commenced another of his *friendships*.' Sydney sniggered. 'He won't want his daughter in Grosvenor Place when anything of that sort is afoot – no, by Jason, he won't! She will be despatched back to Underwood, with her bride-linen, you may be sure. And she probably will not be sorry to leave London now that *her* particular friend, Miss Kittridge, has set sail for America with her brother.'

'Kittridge?' Hatty's attention was caught by the name. 'Is her brother Jonathan Kittridge? The poet? Lord Camber's friend?'

'Ay, Camber and Kittridge and Wandesleigh are all cronies together. Founders of that fanciful, holier-than-thou Society of Sophocrats. *That* precious scheme will soon founder, you may be sure; it is very certain to collapse.'

To avoid fruitless argument, Hatty left the room. She wondered whether Lady Ursula minded the departure of her friend Miss Kittridge on a venture that she herself had spoken of with such scorn. Was her friend's departure the event that had decided her in favour of marriage with Mr Henry Ward? Had Miss Kittridge paid her own fare, or did she travel as a servant? Was she also a friend of Lord Camber?

There are so many things I do not know, Hatty thought.

By Christmas Eve the weather was worsening. Rain and gales swept the country. Hatty shivered, thinking of Lord Camber, perhaps by now a passenger on some ill-found ship, laden with poverty-stricken people, desperate to start a new life in unknown surroundings, mortgaging their future in order to get away from their past. What kind of travelling companions would they make? Hatty wondered about the conditions on the ships. Did they have separate bunks? Or hammocks? Or cabins? What kind of food was available and who served it? Who cooked it? Hatty glanced at her watch. In a moment she must go upstairs and superintend the swallowing of a posset by her Aunt Polly, who was still permitted only the lightest of nourishment; then she must visit the bedside of poor Ned, who, fractious and miserable, a bad patient suffering an exceptionally severe case of measles, could not be soothed, cried out continually that he was going mad with pain and irritation, took very little food, and was the despair of his attendants. He might not even read, usually a solace for Ned, since his eyes were so inflamed.

Hatty, much occupied with hemming sheets to augment the household's depleted supply, had suggested that Sydney read aloud to his brother, a proposal which met with a very curt rejoinder: 'What? Waste my time droning out *Orphans of the Forest* or some such rubbish? I thank you, no! I did not come back to Portsmouth to wet-nurse that pitiful fool!'

Hatty could scarcely conjecture why he had come back; it could hardly be filial devotion to his mother, for his visits to her bedside were brief and perfunctory. Tom he seldom, if ever, addressed, and he never went near the twins.

He did, it was true, spend time with Mr Ward discussing legal matters, and showed considerable interest in the family's business affairs and relationships.

'Even though my uncle Henry has done his possible to chisel me out of the entail by marrying Lady Ursula this week,' he remarked, 'I reckon 'tis all Lombard Street to a china orange that he don't succeed. After all, he is getting on in years. And she's no spring chicken either. My guess is that nothing will follow. There won't be any issue. I'll come into Bythorn Lodge in the end, no matter for all his plots and his ploys. And then shan't I laugh! And a devilish good base Bythorn Lodge will afford me – handy for town, and close in among all the nobs.'

Hatty sighed, thinking of her home. She had no wish to go back there and see it under the governance of Lady Ursula, but she still pined for the green fields and woodland walks of childhood.

She stood up, shaking out heavy crumpled folds of bed-linen.

'I say, Cousin Hatty!' said Sydney, with a sudden change from easy self-occupied satisfaction to what he evidently hoped was a languishing, flirtatious manner. Unexpectedly he crossed the room, stepping over Hatty's mound of piled-up draperies, and sat himself down plump on the window-seat, where Hatty had been sitting. He looked up at her, as she struggled to fold the sheet, and went on: 'I can tell you, Cousin Hatty, I didn't come back to Portsmouth with matrimony in my intentions – no, curse me, I didn't! But marrying, you know, is no bad thing for a young fellow at the start of his career. It settles him. It keeps him out of mischief. And then – and then – well, the truth of the matter is, I had never thought of *you* in that regard, Cousin Hatty, such a little quiz, such an ugly scrawny little thing as you were when you first came here; 'tis quite wonderful how your looks have improved in the past year. Quite a woman you've grown! And now I spend most of my time in London, you know, I am well qualified to judge! But that ain't the whole of it, Cousin Hatty: I never expected, truth to tell, that you'd turn into such a deuced clever housekeeper! Why, the place seems to go on just as well, with you in charge, as when my mother held the reins.' He gave her an encouraging smirk. ''Tis a monstrous fine thing to set up house with a clever manager! That's what *I* think. And I daresay you'd not object to be back in your old home – hey? – and be queen of the nest in Bythorn again? Hey?'

Hatty, now, for the first time, began to pay attention and see whither this overture was tending.

She clapped her needlebook together decisively, and said, 'Cousin, I think you had better say no more. The subject is not at all pleasing to me, nor suitable for our present circumstances, and I—'

'Hey, hey!' he cried. 'Not so hasty, miss! *Not pleasing?* You have not heard yet what I have to say!'

'I must go to my aunt. It grows late. And Ned is waiting for his soup.'

'Let them wait!' decreed Sydney. 'Cousin Hatty – my little charmer – I haven't even told you about my feelings yet! Haven't said what a devilish regard for you I have! Let me inform you – there's not a girl from Whitehall to Ludgate Circus that's fit to hold a candle to you – and I've looked at them all – with your dark eyes and glossy hair and your clever ways and neat ankles – *and* a trim waist, too, I'll be bound, under that apron—'

Unexpectedly he slid his arm round her waist. Hatty, springing back, dealt him a box on the ear. And he, lurching forward in pursuit of her, tripped over the entangling sheet and fell headlong.

Hatty, whisking herself out of the way, snatched up the folds of sheet, flung them untidily on to the window-seat, and started across the room. Tears of wrath and mortification were pouring down her cheeks.

Oh, if my uncle comes to hear of this, she thought, how angry he will be!

Behind her she could hear Sydney picking himself up, muttering maledictions. As Hatty sprang to the doorway a figure appeared there, blocking the way. It was Burnaby, with a doom-laden countenance.

'I beg pardon for *interrupting*, Miss Hatty – ' Burnaby's sneering tone made Hatty wonder precisely how long she had been standing just outside the door and how much she had heard. 'I beg your pardon but I thought it my duty to come at once and tell you that both twins have thrown out a rash. They'll have caught the measles from Master Ned, I don't doubt. Didn't I say that no good would come of all those chess games?'

VII

AUNT POLLY HAD become very thin during the weeks of her illness. Her round pink face, with lively twinkling eyes, once so responsive, had grown hollow-cheeked and pale; her former animated interest in all the doings of the family had wholly abated; she lay, most of the time, in a quiet lethargy as if husbanding her strength for some possible forthcoming emergency. Mr Filingay had been most emphatic that she be spared any worry, problems, or bad tidings, lest such news bring on another seizure, which might easily be enough to terminate her existence. She lived, therefore, in a kind of bubble, thought Hatty, sitting at her aunt's bedside and administering the posset, sip by careful sip. She knew nothing of all the agitation and trouble in the house. And, at all costs, she must remain in this condition of peaceful unawareness.

'Thank you, my love,' whispered Aunt Polly from time to time. 'You make me so comfortable!'

Then she would fall asleep for a moment or two. Sometimes, on waking, she seemed to imagine that Hatty was one of the twins, Sophy or Eliza.

'How you have grown, my dearie,' she would whisper. 'But where is your sister? I like to see both of you together.'

This aberration of her aunt's for some reason gave Hatty a most complicated pain.

'I am *Hatty*, dear aunt! Your niece! Don't you remember? You shall see the twins, I promise, as soon as you are a little better.'

Nobody dared tell Mrs Ward that the twins were dangerously ill. Mr Filingay shook his head over them, visited them half a dozen times a day.

'They have so little strength for resistance,' he said. 'I fear their frail constitutions simply cannot fight against this infection. It is terribly unfortunate that they should have been exposed to the germ.'

The most grievously sad thing, Hatty thought, was that no other member of the family but herself seemed to have any interest in whether the twins lived or died. Mr Ward made perfunctory, brief inquiries each morning, but otherwise paid no heed to their state; Tom and Sydney never made any inquiry at all; Ned seemed troubled about them, but, still seriously ill himself, appeared to feel more guilt at having passed the germ to them than real concern about their prospects. 'Poor little things,' he sighed, 'but what future had they, after all? Life could never be any benefit to them. They have a strange gift for chess, certainly, but what use is that? No man is going to marry them for their chess. And they could hardly be separated. No, to me it seems the kindest fate for them to die and be together. But supposing only one should be taken? What in the world would happen to the other?'

'Oh, Ned, *don't*!' Hatty would cry out, as he rambled on in this way, his own enfeebled state lending a bleak sadness to his speculations.

The only person in the household beside herself who took an active, positive interest in the survival of the twins was Burnaby, grimly battling for their imperilled lives, cooling their fevered heads with lavender spirits, nourishing them with drops of broth and brandy, changing their soaked bed-linen ten times a day.

Can she have discovered at last that she loves them? wondered Hatty at first, helping as much as she was permitted, which help was now dourly and ungratefully accepted because there was too much work for one person. But it was not love that drove Burnaby's labours, Hatty soon realized; it was the knowledge that, without the survival of the twins, her own position in the household would be in danger. The care of the twins was her sole responsibility, her only function; if they were gone, nobody would need her, nobody would want her. Few in the house liked her; only Mr Ward had a kind of taciturn respect for her. Sydney, it was true, sometimes gossiped with her, but Hatty had not noticed him doing so since her own rejection of his advances had left him in a state of humiliated, resentful rage. Hatty still did not know how much of the scene Burnaby had witnessed. At present, perhaps, she was too much preoccupied with the state of the twins to allude to it; but Hatty felt certain that, sooner or later, she would turn it to account in some malicious and trouble-making way; most probably by telling Mr Ward about it. Hatty thought that she ought to forestall this by informing him herself, but, just at present, she did not feel equal to the ensuing scene. She was sure that her uncle would deeply disapprove of any such alliance, that he did not expect Sydney to marry for years to come, and, when he did, it must be an advantageous, profitable match, preferably to the daughter of the senior partner in his law firm, or some young lady with a comfortable fortune of her own, certainly not his penniless cousin.

But Mr Ward, just then, was in no mood to be burdened with any additional anxieties. He was beginning, most reluctantly, to realize that his wife's state was much more severe and problematical than he had, at first, been willing to acknowledge; that she might, indeed, never return to full health. He was still excessively angry about the infamous behaviour of his niece Frances who, he felt, had disgraced him and the whole family in the most open, bare-faced way possible, in view of all his neighbours, colleagues, and trade and professional connections. If the hussy had to run off with some good-for-nothing, why could she not have done so in Bath or Huntingdon or Northamptonshire, where Mr Ward did not live and was not known? But to elope within throwing distance of her own uncle was the outside of enough!

Another worry, not the least, was the condition of his son Ned, who was still extremely weak and debilitated. Ned ought, at this time, to have been commencing his naval service, in fact he should by now already have done so, but this step had already been postponed a couple of times due to the intervention of Ned's mother who, steady-minded and sensible in most ways, had a quite unreasonable attachment to her youngest boy; he was her darling, the apple of her eye, and she had up to now managed to defer his departure from home; she had been used to fall into a most exaggerated anxiety when she envisaged his rough and dangerous life at sea. And now, reflected Mr Ward, the parting, when it came, would be a thousand times worse, with the boy still thin and pale and pulled-looking, and his mother so frail that a breeze might knock her over, and full to the brim of sick fancies!

Then there was a worry about Hatty – the girl, though she looked tired and drawn, seemed to be tackling her household duties well enough; in fact, Mr Ward was obliged to acknowledge, it was hard to see how they could have managed without her during the present embarrassment; though that, to be sure, was no more than ought to be expected of her, considering the comfortable home she had been granted all these years. But what was all this about *poetry*? And Muses? And corresponding with Lord Camber – that was a thoroughly undesirable development.

Living on the fringes of the aristocracy had its problems, Mr Ward admitted to himself; upper-class gentry felt themselves so much less bound by social restrictions than persons in his own hum-drum middle-class walk of life that dealing with these high people (though profitable) presented one with not a few difficulties. Now and then I even wish I'd never asked the fellow to step in and take his mutton with us, mused Mr Ward; well, it is a thoroughly fortunate thing that he has gone off to the banks of the Susquehanna river, and I trust that he will remain fixed there for some years. Though what will happen to the Duke in the meantime I hate to think.

Hatty, for the remaining week of her cousin's sojourn in Portsmouth, tried her best to avoid being left alone with him. She did not anticipate a renewal of his addresses, for he eyed her with such hostility when they were together in a room that she felt she had made him into an enemy for life. So she was greatly surprised to be intercepted by him, one afternoon when she had hurried out into the garden in hopes that some of the twins' night-wear, hung out earlier in the day, might have been sufficiently dried by the wintry gale to be ready for use. Sydney came walking from the direction of the conservatory, stood directly in her path, and said, 'Cousin Hatty: have you given any more thought to the offer I made you last week?'

She stared at him in astonishment. He went on rather stiffly, 'I took you by surprise on that occasion, I fear I should have been more deliberate in my approaches and given you time to reflect.'

'My dear cousin,' she told him with a certain degree of impatience, 'if you had given me five years to reflect – if you had given me ten – the answer would still be the same. We should not suit one another at all. I should put you out of patience all day long and I cannot imagine *ever* being happy as your wife. We know one another far too well to allow of any doubt on the matter. Now – pray – excuse me, I am in a hurry to supply your poor little sisters with clean bed-linen.'

He still barred her way.

'I have not finished yet, Cousin Hatty. Listen. You cannot remain in this house for ever. Suppose my mother should die? That is not improbable. What are your prospects? I am probably better informed about them than you. It is very unlikely that my uncle Henry will be able to provide you with any portion at all. His recent marriage to Lady Ursula has been a decided drain on his resources. I know this for a fact. And your sister Agnes's simultaneous wedding to Mr Norris has also embarrassed him to a considerable degree. With no portion, I can assure you, my poor cousin, your chances of receiving any other offer than mine are quite negligible. Who would want you? You have no expectations, you have no fortune. You will have to earn your living as a nurse-maid or as a governess. Do you realize that?'

'Of course I do! The prospect does not terrify me in the least. I might even enjoy it. Teaching – attempting to teach – your sisters has been no penance, I assure you. On the contrary. If – if I had been permitted more freedom with them – but excuse me. I really cannot stand talking now, Cousin Sydney. And my feelings about your offer are perfectly firm. I am greatly obliged to you but I am sure, too, that when you are returned to London, you will be relieved that I said no.'

He looked at her with a lowering brow. Then he said, 'Cousin

Hatty, you will be sorry, very sorry for this. I warn you! I can make your position in this house exceedingly uncomfortable. I can even – very likely – put a period to your residence here. My father—'

'Have you ever considered, Sydney,' she interrupted, 'how very, *very* much your father would dislike it if you were to go to him with news of your engagement to me? He has quite other intentions for you, you may be sure. I heard him once tell your mother what a fine thing it would be for you if you were to marry Miss Brabham.'

'*Miss Brabham?*' Sydney looked thunderstruck. Miss Brabham was the daughter of the senior partner in his law firm, had ten thousand pounds of her own, and was aged thirty-two. Hatty had never laid eyes on the lad, who lived in London, but had heard Sydney describe her as very evil-tempered and a regular antidote.

This distraction gave Hatty the chance to slip past Sydney with her bundle of laundry and run indoors. He was to travel up to London that evening by the mail, so she was in hopes of not encountering him again, or at least only briefly. And indeed her last view of him was when the diminished family party – Mr Ward, Tom, and herself – stood on the doorstep to wave Sydney goodbye. He shook hands with the two males, threw Hatty a cold glare, shouldered his portmanteau, and walked away in the direction of the mail-coach stop.

Hatty drew a large breath of relief. She had not taken his last threat very seriously and soon forgot it in the pressure of other cares and the comfort of having him out of the house.

She had, however, intended, that evening, to inform her uncle of Sydney's proposal – she felt it her duty to do so, though a most disagreeable one, in furtherance of the better, more communicative relations now obtaining between her uncle and herself – but was prevented from this by the presence of Ned, allowed downstairs for the first time in his bed-gown to join the family for tea. He hardly seemed to relish the privilege – sipped his tea half-heartedly and nibbled without appetite at a morsel of cake.

'Ha! Ned,' said his father. 'Now you are back on your pins we must begin to set about getting you on to a ship. The *Bulfinch* had to sail without you, but I have made overtures to Captain Hardwick on the

Endeavour; she is in dock re-fitting but he tells me that he hopes to sail within four or five weeks, and if you have your strength back by then he will be happy to take you on board. Sea air will complete your recovery, I dare say.'

'Thank you, father,' said Ned faintly.

'There will be a deal of work, I daresay,' said Mr Ward, 'getting you outfitted and ready with all your gear. It is too bad your poor mother is not in health enough to take a hand in the business. She has such a head on her shoulders for such matters. But your cousin Hatty will do her best, I am sure.'

'Do you think Ned will be well enough to leave home in four or five weeks?' inquired Hatty doubtfully.

'In course he will!' Her uncle returned with a frown to the newspaper he was reading.

'I – I think I will go back to bed, Hatty,' said Ned unhappily. 'Will it – will it be in order for me to visit my mother to say goodnight?'

'Yes of course, Ned, but pray do not stay with her too long so as to fatigue her.'

He nodded and crept away.

Now I ought to summon up the courage to tell my uncle about Sydney's offer, Hatty thought. Tom was in the schoolroom whittling a top, to add to his already large collection. No interruption was likely. But she found she simply did not have the heart to break up the quiet interlude, and fracture her uncle's peace. He may think I *wish* to marry Sydney and this is my roundabout manner of approaching the subject. That would be dreadful. And he is fond of Sydney, has such a high opinion of his good sense and ability; this would certainly lower Sydney in his estimation and annoy him very much; but is the truth simply that I am too much of a coward to tell Uncle Philip what happened?

Suddenly it occurred to Hatty to wonder what Lord Camber would advise, supposing him to be present in the room and a party to the situation?

Oh, how I wish he was! thought Hatty with a deep sigh. She imagined Lord Camber's comforting presence, his time-scoured, weather-beaten countenance, nearly always with a broad understanding smile on it, his friendly comprehension and slow, thoughtful manner of commenting on what he had been told.

'We-e-ell, do you know, Miss Hatty, I believe I would not trouble your poor uncle with such a confidence at this time. He has so much else on his mind! And it would be rather telling tales out of school, would it not?'

With a huge sigh of relief, Hatty thought: no, I will not mention the episode to my uncle. Ten to one, as soon as he is back in London, Sydney will forget all about it. He too has plenty of other things to occupy his mind, I am sure.

In her turn she bade her uncle good night, and went upstairs to visit Aunt Polly, impelled, in part, by a wish to ensure that Ned had not stayed too long with his mother and distressed her with too much talk about his forthcoming departure to sea.

Arrived at her aunt's room she thought, indeed, that she had come none too soon. Ned was half-kneeling, half-crouching by his mother's bedside, clasping her hand, addressing her in a low, urgent murmur; Mrs Ward looked distressed and confused; she was stroking his head, but her eyes were sad and unfocussed, staring over the bowed head as if she did not quite hear him and her attentions were half elsewhere, on something that lay beyond him.

'Poor Neddikins; dear Neddikins,' she murmured. 'It will get better. Things often do get better. Or else they seem less important. Or they go away.'

'And I am afraid *you* must go away now, Ned,' Hatty said gently. 'We have to get your mother ready for the night.'

Ned gave her an apprehensive, shame-faced look, and took himself off; Hatty, approaching the bedside, saw at a glance that her aunt's pulse and temperature were both higher than they should be, that her breath came much too fast, that she was in a dangerous state of disturbance.

'Oh, the children!' she said sadly. 'They are always asking for treats and sweetmeats. Mr Ward will never agree – very likely he is in the right of it; how can one decide what is for the best?'

'Never mind it, Aunt Polly,' Hatty soothed her. 'Very likely in the morning it will seem much simpler. Here is Nurse coming, look, with your night-time dose, which will make you feel like going to sleep. Just forget about the children. They will come to no harm.'

But outside Mrs Ward's door Hatty met Burnaby, arriving to summon her with a baleful countenance.

'Miss Hatty, the twins is mortal bad, both of 'em. I wish ye'd send the boy for Mr Filingay, though I misdoubt there's little he can do.'

Mr Filingay, when summoned, agreed. All that could be done he did, but his efforts were unavailing, and, towards dawn, Sophy, the smaller of the pair, murmured, 'Pawn to king's four' for the last time, turned to her sister, and died. Ten minutes later Eliza followed her example.

Tired out, wrung, and utterly defeated, Hatty burst into tears.

'Oh, poor little things! What did they ever have? What use were their lives?'

Mr Filingay was soothing.

'Now, Miss Hatty! Now, my dear young lady! They did not have bad lives. They had far better care, a better home, than hundreds of others with such problems. Many in like case would not have lived for half as long. Don't I speak the truth, Miss Burnaby? *You* have taken famous good care of them, I know!'

Burnaby deflected her malignant stare from Hatty long enough to give him a nod.

'Now I am going to give you a calming dose for yourself, Miss Hatty, and you must go to your room and lie down.'

Hatty drank the potion Mr Filingay gave her and went off to her own room, feeling that she left the household in a dangerously explosive and undefended condition.

She slept for a short time, but heavily.

When she woke, it was to a strange silence. The usual sounds of the house were completely stilled.

She lay for a few moments in a state of great confusion. Was it Sunday? Christmas come again? Or had all the maids caught the measles?

Then she remembered about the twins. She was able to feel more calmly about them now, thankful, at least, that their deaths had been easy and without pain, that they had been together; and it was true, as Filingay had said, that, in poorer or more uncaring households their lives might have been a great deal worse; at least they were fed, clothed, washed, and attended to, if the latter only to a minimal degree. But oh, poor Aunt Polly, Hatty thought; their death is going to strike her a mortal blow. With a deep, premonitory pang she knew that this was so. I wonder if she has been told yet? Or will they keep the news from her? It would be best to do so. But she will be sure to find out. How can she not?

Hatty sprang from her bed and made a hasty toilet. As she did so she saw one reason for the household's unwonted silence: snow was falling heavily, and must have done so for some time; a layer of white, two or three inches thick, lay on branches and twigs, the posts and chains in front of the house, the doorsteps, and the street beyond. Few tracks marked the snow. Very little traffic was moving. Yet it was late, Hatty discovered, far past the usual breakfast hour.

She hurried downstairs.

The hush outside, she found, was echoed by a hush indoors. Meade, the cook, met her in the hall, laid a finger on her lips, and whispered, 'We've saved your bit breakfast for ye, miss, in the kitchen. Will I bring it to the breakfast parlour?'

Hatty shook her head.

'Thank you, I am not at all hungry.'

She felt as if she could never eat again.

'Not even a cup of tea? In that case, Miss Hatty, Master wants ye in his book room.'

'Oh, is he not gone to his office? But no,' said Hatty recollecting, 'I suppose that today he feels that he must stay at home.'

She went upstairs to the first floor. There, outside the door of Mr Ward's work room, she found her cousin Tom, seated, rather dejectedly, on the window-seat. He had a row of his own tops in front of him and was endeavouring to keep them all spinning at once.

'Hilloo, Cousin Hatty,' he said in a dismal tone. 'The devil's to pay, in there.' He nodded towards the book room door.

'What can you mean, Tom?' she asked, her heart falling. 'Is it – is it about my aunt? Is she worse?'

'My mother? No, not that I know on. No: it's Ned. Burnaby had some tale to tell. *I* don't know what. Poor Ned was in a rare quake, I can tell you. And I heard Burnaby say, should she fetch you, and my father said no, let her have her sleep out.'

Hatty knocked on the book room door and went in.

Of the three people in the room, Mr Ward sat at his desk, Burnaby and Ned stood at equal distances from him and from each other. Burnaby was as usual, hard-featured and impassive; only, there was a pale gleam in her eye which Hatty had not seen before. Ned had been crying, Hatty saw; his cheeks were smeared with tears. But he was not crying now. He looked at Hatty, cleared an obstruction from his throat, and said, 'Sir, it is unfair to bring my cousin into this. She is not – she has nothing to do with it.'

'That's not true,' said Burnaby sharply. 'You'll pardon my speaking out, sir, but that's a lie. She knew *all along* what was going on. The note proves it. And, as well, before that, in times gone by, it was *her* and Master Ned what used to go off and get up to their nonsense in the old graveyard. Oh, I heard about that! I had it from Deakin. He knew it was as much as his place was worth not to answer my questions.'

Hatty looked dumbly at her uncle. He was pale and grave. He held a piece of paper which, from its creases, had once been folded into the form of a cocked hat. He said, 'Your cousin Sydney found this in the conservatory and – I suppose not wishing to distress me – gave it to Burnaby.'

Ned's eyes met those of Hatty.

'What is it, sir?'

Hatty, like Ned, found that her throat wanted clearing.

'It is a letter. To my son Ned.' Mr Ward handed it to her with a gesture of disgust, and Hatty, casting her eyes over the lines, read aloud:

'My darling Neddy: I am lade up at Home with a bad sore Throat
& so not alloud out of Doors, so cannot come to Meet you at our
Usul tristing place. What a sad Shame! I'll pay Sukey 6d to give this
to Deakin with another 6d to put it in our flourpot in the hot-house.
So hope youll find it their. And hope to be better by the dance-class
next week. How can I wait til then for your Sweet Kiss & caresses?
But perhaps at least your Cross Cousin will bring me a note from
you? I will hope – hope – hope –
    Your Sweet-heart Nancy.'

There was a silence after Hatty had finished reading the note. Poor
Ned had flushed a deep burning red. Burnaby pressed her lips together
and looked at the floor, as if to veil the satisfaction in her eyes. Mr
Ward snatched back the note and tore it to pieces and cast the bits into
the fire. Then he said, 'It seems that all the Price family are birds of a
feather. But that *my own son* – my own niece whom I have treated as
if she were my daughter – ' (*That* you have not, thought Hatty
rebelliously. But then she recollected the twins, who really had been
Uncle Philip's daughters. How had he treated them?) He went on:
'That such a system of regulated deceit, lies, and subterfuge should
have been going on under my own roof – clandestine meetings in the
conservatory – and in the *graveyard*, of all unsuitable places. How long,
may I ask, sir, have you been sneaking off to the graveyard?' he asked
Ned.
    'I suppose – six or seven years. Ever since I found the door,'
mumbled Ned.
    'And you took your cousin in there too?'
    Ned looked at Hatty, who said firmly and clearly, 'Yes, sir. Ned and
I used to play at house in the big lime-tree. We pretended that it was
our palace.'
    '*Played house!*' Mr Ward's tone of disgust turned the words into
something else. 'And then you brought that Price hussy in there.'
    'Sir, Nancy is not—'
    'Be quiet, sir! I say she *is*! In any case – thank goodness – you will

see no more of *her*. She is being sent off to stay with cousins in Holborn
– so her wretched mother informs me.'

Hatty had not thought that Ned could look more miserable, but this
information really seemed to demolish him. He let out a sound like a
puppy's whimper, and pressed his knuckles to his eyes. Mr Ward
surveyed him without the slightest sympathy. Hatty thought in pity of
poor Mrs Price, at the best of times a rather untidy, distracted-looking
lady; now, as well as all that sickness in the house, she had a disgraced
daughter to be sent away.

'And now *you*.' Mr Ward turned his attention to his niece. 'I had
thought that you were a decent, honest, straightforward girl, but it
seems I was mistaken. Not only did you abet my son Ned in these
clandestine goings-on – in this tawdry hole-and-corner trafficking with
that pitiful little hoyden – but it seems that you yourself have been
encouraging the addresses of my son *Sydney* – enticing him with I do
not know what arts and wiles—'

'No, *that* I have not, sir!' interrupted Hatty indignantly.

'Sydney, whom I did think to be a lad of sense and decorum,
resolved on climbing high in his profession—'

'I never enticed him! I would never wish to! I cannot abide Sydney!
He made an offer of marriage to *me*, and I refused him.'

'That is not what I hear from Burnaby. She tells me that you were
encouraging him, leading him on, with the intention of accepting him
in the end.'

'It was no such thing! She is completely mistaken. I said no. I boxed
his ears!'

Mr Ward drew himself up and pursed his lips, as if the mere thought
of such a scene were repugnant to him.

'Well, I am truly thankful that you, Ned, will be off to sea in a few
weeks; a life in the navy will soon cleanse your mind and rid you, I
trust, of such vulgar propensities. As for *you*, miss – ' he turned back
to Hatty, 'it is an excellent thing that your father is recently married to
Lady Ursula. In regard to you, at least, my course is clear. I am going
to send you straight back to Bythorn.'

'Oh, no!' Hatty's gasp of protest came out as a whisper. She cleared her throat again, and said in a louder tone, 'But what about my aunt? What about Aunt Polly? Who will take care of her? And the house?'

'You need not concern yourself about your aunt,' said her uncle. 'Burnaby can do that very well, now that she will no longer have the twins to look after.' Burnaby looked coldly triumphant. 'You do realize, both of you, do you not,' continued Mr Ward, impartially addressing his son and niece, 'that if it had not been for this disgraceful entanglement with that pernicious girl, the measles infection would not have been carried into this house, and the twins would not have caught it from Ned? You do realize that you are responsible for your sisters' deaths?'

'No, sir! That is not so!' Hatty was hoarse and trembling at the horror of her own prospects, but she still had enough tenacity to argue. 'That is not fair. Ned could have caught measles at the dancing class – from Nancy or – or from anybody else. Mr Filingay says that it is all about.'

'We will not discuss that,' Mr Ward said shortly. 'Harriet, you may as well go directly and start to pack up your things. I am arranging for you to travel to Bythorn under the care of Lord Camber's steward, a very respectable person named Godwit who is taking some papers for me to be deposited at the Duke's bank in Bythorn. He travels tomorrow. So you will have the day in which to make your arrangements.'

Almost stunned, Hatty said, 'But what about Ned's clothes – his outfit for going to sea – who will take care of that? All the linen requires to be marked – and half the shirts are not yet made up—'

'One of the maids – some person – will take care of it. That is of no consequence. You are not indispensable, you know – don't think it. Now, Harriet, I do not wish your aunt to be hearing about *any* of these matters. It would only distress her and serve no useful purpose. You will oblige me by remaining out of her room today. She can be told that you are indisposed. You may see her in the morning to say goodbye before you leave – if I think fit – that will be sufficient.'

'Yes, sir.' Now Hatty did not wish to meet Ned's eye. She had no comfort to offer him, and was sure that he had none for her. They must each struggle out of this nightmare as best they could.

She went up to her room and began packing her clothes.

VIII

THE COACH JOURNEY from Portsmouth was unredeemedly wretched. Godwit, Lord Camber's steward, travelled outside during the first half of the trip, so Hatty saw little of him. He was a spare, middle-aged man with a pear-shaped head, narrow above, wider below. That was the only impression that Hatty formed of him. He was attentive to her comfort, however, procured her a room when they stopped for the night at an inn outside Oxford and had a meal uniting dinner and supper sent up to her there on a tray. The next day's travel proved even slower, for snow continued to fall, making the roads treacherous, and towards the end of the journey there was nobody inside the coach but Hatty herself. Godwit therefore moved in, observing that it was cold enough outside to give chilblains to a brass monkey, and with the snow that was coming down now, he feared they'd be late reaching their destination.

'You'll be met at Wanhurst, miss?' he asked, naming the nearest large town to Bythorn.

'No, my uncle sent an express, requiring my father to have me met at Wanmaulden Cross. That will save them full seven miles – fourteen, going and coming.'

'Eh,' said Godwit thoughtfully, 'that's true enough. But Wanmaulden Cross is a no-account sort of place to meet in bad weather. There is but one inn, The Woodpecker, and that's naught but a paltry hedge-alehouse; not a proper place for a young lady to be kept waiting, should some mishap chance to delay one of the parties; not a proper place at all; at least, not to my way of thinking.'

'You know that country well?' asked Hatty.

'Why yes, miss – 'tis not far from Wanmaulden Cross that Master Harry has his cottage – Lord Camber I should say, miss – right in the thick of the wood, he lives, and has these five years; the road past Wanmaulden Cross is his nearest coach-road.'

'Oh, do tell about his cottage!' cried Hatty, greatly interested, and glad of any distraction that would prise her miserable thoughts away from the trouble she left behind her – Aunt Polly abandoned to the untender care of Burnaby, Ned bereft, not yet fully recovered from the measles, about to face a strenuous, unfamiliar new existence in the Navy; Tom, poor Tom, soon to be left all alone; and the twins – but Hatty could not bring herself to think of the twins. And to contemplate the prospect ahead of her was even more distressing and fearsome: the wrath of her father, the scorn of Lady Ursula, the dislike of Agnes; Hatty was not certain if Agnes and Mr Norris were already gone off to Mansfield parsonage, but if Agnes were still at home she would be in no easy humour ... What would the family do with her, Hatty wondered. Uncle Philip's anger seemed mild in comparison with what she might have to face at Bythorn.

So it was with interest and relief that she asked about the cottage. Anything concerning Lord Camber would be worth hearing.

She had thought Godwit a rather stolid-looking man, with his odd, humorous, pear-shaped face; when invited to describe his master's way of life, he became cheerful and discursive. His small, grey-blue eyes darted from side to side with wicked humour as he enumerated all the terribly expensive and needless 'improvements' made by the Duke at Bythorn Chase – the follies, the grottoes, the fountains, shell-houses, orangeries, lakes, water-gardens, temples, obelisks and monuments the Duke had erected, the avenues he had chopped down; meanwhile his unfortunate tenants lived in discomfort and squalor, with rotting thatch and crumbling walls.

'My grandma was one of 'em,' said Godwit. 'Storm two winters ago blew half her roof off, and his Grace's man of affairs said it could not be repaired until they'd finished the pavilion. Living in a puddle, my gran was. The pavilion! Who wants a pavilion half a mile from his house, that's what I'd like to know?'

'What happened to your grandma?'

'Lord Camber took her in to live with him. She's a prime knitter and needlewoman, is my old gran; takes care of all his Lordship's mending. And she's company for Mrs Daizley, that's his housekeeper, and they both keep an eye on the boy, Dickon. Ay, they'll all be missing his Lordship sore, now he's gone off to the Americas,' Godwit ended thoughtfully.

'But what have the Duke's pavilions to do with Lord Camber's cottage?'

'Why, miss, my master's what you'd call a Democrat. He believes that the things of this earth were given to mankind to share out freely.'

'I wonder if that is so?' said Hatty, half to herself.

'I've often asked myself the same question, miss,' said Godwit unexpectedly. 'Why did the Almighty create dukes and earls and marquises if he did not mean them to have more worldly goods than the rest of us? He must have had *some* purpose in mind.'

Hatty's internal question had gone off in a different direction. She had been wondering if the human race had not quite unjustifiably snatched control of the animal, vegetable and mineral resources of the globe; what right had they to do so? We write verses, she thought, we make up tunes and invent clever machines; is it reasonable to expect the whole world to be given to us as a reward? Just for a bit of cleverness?

As often, when a poem was incubating in her mind, ideas and the words to frame them seemed to float towards her simultaneously from some dark nowhere.

'So,' continued Godwit, 'even when my master was a lad in his teens, he began to worrit at his father to look after his tenants and his estates a bit better, and not spend all his cash on furbishing and altering and improving. He said the tenants had as much right to comfort as his Grace. But the old Duke's neither to hold nor to bind, miss – except by the Duchess, and after she died and my master went up to Oxford, and from then on, it was nought but argification and fritsomeness. So when Master Harry came into a bit of property at twenty-one – that's Wanmaulden Wood, miss, and the cottage on it – he moved out of Bythorn Chase altogether, and he and the Duke don't see each other, not if they can avoid it.'

'When did the Duchess die?' asked Hatty.

'Oh, a long time ago, miss; when his Lordship was but a boy. And Lady Suzanne and Lady Louisa were just little things. So, since then, there's been no one to, as you might say, keep an eye on his Grace.'

'What about Lord Camber's brother?'

'The Colonel? He's mostly off with his regiment, miss. And the young ladies is married now, living up north.'

'Oh, yes.'

Hatty had a sudden flashing recollection of the Assembly Rooms at the Crown, the girls dancing and laughing in their pale muslins, Lord Camber holding her by the hand, Monsieur Lamartine inquiring after the ladies Suzanne and Louisa. What a long time ago that seemed! And that was because Lady Ursula had decreed that we must all have dancing lessons.

That is twice that Lady Ursula has come into collision with my life and sent it shooting off in a different direction, Hatty thought. What a powerful influence the woman has. She is like a hurricane or a volcano.

'What about Lady Ursula Fowldes?' she asked. 'Does she ever visit the Duke? She is his niece, is she not?'

'Yes, miss. But since she and Master Harry broke it off – and that's a decent few years ago now – she don't go next or nigh the Chase. Now, here we are,' said Godwit, peering through the snow-dappled window glass. 'Here we are, if I'm not mistaken, drawing nigh to Wanmaulden Cross but I don't see any sign of another carriage a-waiting for you, miss.'

Hatty's heart sank. Their journey, across white-blanketed, fog-wrapped countryside, had been long and excessively cold, for the last five or six miles through uninhabited woodland; she was filled with dread at the prospect ahead of her, the return to a strange, changed home, the unwelcoming people she would encounter there, most particularly the thought of Lady Ursula ensconced in her mother's place; but she had braced herself to face this bleak arrival, and the thought of its postponement froze her with dismay. Especially since, if there had been some accident or misunderstanding, she felt very sure that she would be the one to incur the blame for it.

The coach drew to a standstill.

'You bide in there a moment, missie,' advised Godwit. 'I'll tell the driver to wait, while I ask at the inn whether anybody's come for ye.'

The snow was falling again, softly and steadily; Hatty watched his figure dim and disappear through the pelting flakes. The inn was no more than a grey shape seen against a background of darker trees; a pale light shone in one window; the curve of the thatched roof was like an inverted cup covered with snow. There was no other dwelling.

The coach-driver called something impatiently as Godwit reappeared, shaking his head, and the two men held a brief colloquy. Then Godwit returned to Hatty.

'It's bad news, I'm afeered, miss. No one's been for ye.'

'Oh dear,' said Hatty. 'Do you think this driver would take me back to Wanhurst?'

'No, miss. I asked him that, but it's not on his road. He has to be on his way to Peterborough.'

'Then I shall have to stay at the inn, or try to hire a chaise to take me to Bythorn.'

'No, miss. I asked that, but there's none to be had, not in this weather. And the Woodpecker Inn is no fit place for ye to be staying. The landlord's a swinker, miss.'

'A *swinker*?'

'A tippler. He's half-seas-over already, for in this weather there's no customers, and he's got no housekeeper nor chambermaid; indeed 'tis doubtful if he has so much as a decent bed in the place.'

'Good heavens!' said Hatty rather faintly. 'I appear to be in quite a predicament. Can you give me any advice, Mr Godwit?'

'Why yes, miss. We'll leave your boxes at the inn – the driver's a-fetching them down now – they'll take no harm there, I'll see them stowed away in a loose-box – and you can come home for the night with me to his Lordship's cottage. There'll be my old gran and Mrs Daizley to see after ye, so ye'll be as safe and snug as an egg in a hencoop. And tomorrow we'll see about hiring a chaise to take ye to Bythorn. Which of your boxes would you be wanting for the night, miss?'

Startled, but immensely relieved at having her affairs so sensibly and expeditiously put in train, Hatty jumped down from the coach into what felt like about five inches of snow, and pointed out the small bandbox which contained immediate necessities for the night. Then, without further ado, the driver clambered back on to his seat and whipped up his horses, who trotted off into the snowy dusk with no great eagerness. Poor beasts, thought Hatty; I suppose they still have about twenty miles to go.

Godwit carried her other two bandboxes away to some outhouse behind the inn.

'Now, miss,' he said, returning and shouldering the small one, 'if you would not object to taking this satchel for me – 'tis full of papers to be delivered later to his Grace's bank – then you can hold on to my other arm, for I'm afeered we've a half-mile walk before us, and we had best step out smartly. *I* know these woods like the palm of my hand, but the path is on the rough side for a young lady, and dark will be on us in the flick of a lamb's tail.'

They took none of the four roads which met at the Woodpecker Inn, but struck away obliquely along a cart track which bisected one of the right-angles. Hatty was thankful that the boots she had on were a stout pair purchased not long ago under the guidance of Aunt Polly: 'For, say what you like, my love, having your feet dry and warm is the first step to good health; never mind all your fine bonnets and pelisses and shawls, a girl's feet are her fortune and money spent on them is never wasted.'

Oh, Aunt Polly, mourned Hatty silently, as she struggled to keep in step with Godwit who, despite his years, was setting a vigorous pace through the untrodden snow. Dear, dear Aunt Polly, shall I ever see you again? You gave me such good advice about taking care of my health, why did you not follow your own precepts? 'A diet consisting mainly of bread and tea has thoroughly depleted her constitution,' had said Mr Filingay furiously. 'And she seldom troubled to step out-of-doors for a breath of fresh air; indeed it is a wonder that she did not collapse long ago. Whether her system will now have the resilience to withstand, to bear up under the death of the twins, I do not dare predict—'

Has the awful news been broken to her yet? Hatty wondered. The funeral of the twins was due to take place on the following day – no, today, she remembered; there was not the least possibility that Aunt Polly would be well enough to attend, or would even be told about it. Hatty was suddenly overwhelmed by such strong feelings of grief and fury at the fact that she herself would not be at the ceremony, was not permitted to be there, to comfort Aunt Polly through the impending dreadful revelation, that she would have liked to stop, stamp her feet in the snow, and scream aloud; but she was constrained to keep moving by her companion's unflagging pace, and his firm guiding hand on her arm.

'All these are Wanmaulden Woods, what we're walking through now, miss,' Godwit informed her in a comfortingly matter-of-fact voice, so that her impulse of hysteria abated and died down. 'Been here since before Saxon times these woods have, so 'tis said. And Master Harry likes to keep them so; there's not so many tracts of ancient British woodland now, he says. I daresay there was bears and savage things a-plenty, running wild here in those old historical days; but these days the woods are safe enow.'

'Yes,' said Hatty, 'when I was little, living at Bythorn Lodge, my sister Frances and I would sometimes go into the woods. We always hoped to see bears. But we never did.'

'I daresay there may be bears where Master Harry's gone now – grizzly bears they say there is in those American forests, do they not?'

'I hope he will not meet with one.'

Godwit chuckled, his rather gnome-like, eldritch chuckle.

'I'd like to see the bear that could down Master Harry. Five minutes, and he'd have it marching up and down the bridleway with a placard that said, "Votes for bears".'

'Do you think he will stay in America for the rest of his life?' Hatty inquired, in a voice which she hoped sounded suitably detached and disinterested.

'As to that, I can't rightly say, miss. It's Master Harry's whim to go as an indentured servant – ye know that? – so, properly speaking, he'd have to work out his time for his master over there, five years or whatever it might be, first. And then he wants to help with the formation of this new community that he and his friends are setting up. They have already bought thirty-five thousand acres of land. They plan to have mills and factories, they will weave silks and broadcloths, they will farm the land, plant orchards and vineyards, raise cattle, mill timber, print books and weave woollen goods from their own sheep. That is what they reckon to do. There will be no money used within the community, and each family will be given all that they need in goods or clothes.'

'It sounds – it sounds like the kingdom of heaven upon earth, Mr Godwit! Are *you* not curious, yourself – would you not wish to go there and take part in it?'

'Me, miss? Well, I'm plenty curious – that I won't deny – but I'm too old for such a new venture, I reckon. And I've duties this side of the water. His Lordship has asked me to take care of the cottage – and there's my old gran and Mrs Daizley and the boy, who's a bit simple.'

'The boy?'

'Mrs Daizley's boy Dickon – and then, also, his Lordship have asked me to keep an eye – to the best of my compass, miss – on his Grace. Or at least, keep his Lordship informed about his Grace's state of health.'

'Why,' said Hatty, 'this is a most serious responsibility Lord Camber has laid on you, Mr Godwit. Shall you be able to carry it out?'

She wondered how, from a cottage in the middle of the forest, Godwit could keep an eye on the Duke of Dungeness. But he seemed unperturbed.

'I've a-many friends at the Chase, ye see, for that's where I was reared, working my way up from a pantry-boy to the steward's position – we all know one another. And 'tis the same at Underwood Priors.

There's little that's not known in the servants' halls of great houses. Somebody is sure to keep me posted.'

'But how you will miss his Lordship himself, now he has gone overseas,' exclaimed Hatty involuntarily.

'That I shall, miss. It will be like losing the sunshine. But now, look, you can see the light of the cottage, far ahead through the trees. My gran and Mrs Daizley will be expecting me. And they'll be right astonished to see a pretty young lady along of me.'

By now it was full dark, so the glint of candlelight over the snow made a useful aid to their progress, which had slowed down insensibly as they proceeded; Hatty could not help thinking that Godwit's half-mile was rather a long one. Her feet were icy and her skirt and petticoats soaked six inches deep and heavily clogged with snow, impeded her motion; her shawl weighed heavy on her head, cold, stiff, and crisped with the layers of snow that had fallen on it.

Nevertheless, and despite her discomfort and anxiety, she could not avoid a lift of the heart as they approached the tiny light, glimpsed intermittently through flying snowflakes and black branches. This is like a fairytale, she thought, and remembered stories told by her mother long ago: Red Riding Hood, the Three Bears, witches in gingerbread cottages among the trees. Perhaps it will be a magic little house, perhaps it will transform my life in some wholly undreamed-of way. Nothing like this, at all events, has ever happened to me before.

They reached the house, which was lapped around with trees, almost up to its doorstep, and Hatty saw that the window was curtained by muslin, behind which the candle glowed in a pale aura.

Godwit tapped on the door and called, 'Grandma? Jenny? Open up, it's me, Eli, I'm back!'

Immediately there were high, delighted female cries inside, footsteps, fumblings, rattlings, the excited bark of a dog. Then the door was flung open.

The space inside seemed full of figures. More than three, surely? Females in caps and aprons, a leaping, capering hound, somebody holding a candle, somebody restraining the dog, a chorus of joyful welcome.

'We thought ye'd never be here – that ye were lost for sure – such weather as we've had – come in, come in. Never mind shaking yourself – do that indoors – come in, come in, do. Good sakes, Eli, ye look like a snowman!'

'I've brought a young lady with me who's in trouble,' Godwit said, and gently urged Hatty ahead of him through the narrow doorway. A wonderful warmth came out to meet her, and the scent of woodsmoke. Her eyes began at once to water in the smoky heat – she could hardly see. The group inside the door gave way in wonder and concern.

'A young *lady*? Eh, dear, whatever next! Come this way, my poor love, ye must be clemmed. Come by the fire directly.'

Urgent, friendly hands propelled her along a short passage-way and into a room, dimly lit, but kept deliciously warm by a red fire which burned behind bars and was contained in a stove, itself set into a chimney-piece in the wall; Hatty found herself gently but firmly thrust down on a wooden settle by this stove, while voices and fingers fluttered about her like birds: 'Lift her shawl off, her fingers are friz. Dickon, set a pan of milk to hot up – now the bonnet-strings – eh, me, they are as stiff as wire. Fetch a towel to rub her hair dry – and Jenny, run up to the attic for a spare mutch and a shawl and my best flannel petticoat. His lordship will have to go in the back kitchen for a minute – and you too, Eli – while we set her to rights.'

His Lordship? thought Hatty confusedly. His Lordship? How many Lordships can there be?

Now the room was cleared of all but two female figures in white aprons over stuff dresses – a plump, rosy-faced woman with brown-grey curls escaping from under her calico cap, and a much older, tiny gnome-like creature with a spikey pointed face and bright little black eyes – she is like a wood-mouse, Hatty thought, as the old lady attacked her petticoat strings, with minute, bony fingers, and skilfully undid them.

'Are you – are you Mr Godwit's grandmother?' she asked.

'Ay, that I am dearie, and right pleased to see my Eli safe back in such a storm as it has been! And this is Mrs Daizley,' as the rosy-faced woman enveloped her in a capacious brown wool gown, evidently one of her own, and wrapped a brilliant knitted shawl round her shoulders.

'Mrs Daizley – *thank* you – I am so grateful to you both.'

'Never name it, my dearie – 'twas Eli fetched ye in out of the snow – and now I know who ye are – aren't ye Mrs Ward's youngest gal, her as used to be Miss Isabel Wisbech? I thought as much – you are as like her as two peas in a pod. Leave the lady's hair to hang on her shoulders a while, Jenny, it will dry better that way. Now you may tell his Lordship and Dickon they can step back in.'

With complete bewilderment Hatty saw Lord Camber's tall figure come into the room, followed by a skinny boy dressed in leather and sheepskin. Lord Camber was smiling and at ease, just as she had seen him, so many times, in her uncle's house.

'Miss Hatty! What a wholly delightful surprise! The last person I expected to see! And the most welcome! I can see that you have had many adventures, but I will ask no questions until you have drunk this posset that Jenny is preparing for you.'

'But you—' she stammered – 'you *here* – I thought – by this time – you would be halfway to Pennsylvania?'

'Ah, and so I should have been. But Fate decreed otherwise. And I must confess, since this gale has been blowing for the last two days, I am not sorry to have escaped encountering it in the Irish Sea or the Atlantic Ocean. But drink your posset.'

The posset was heavily flavoured with nutmeg and some powerful spirit – rum? – Hatty sipped it with caution and felt a wonderful thrill of warmth travel with lightning speed to the extremities of her fingers and toes.

'Why did you not set sail as planned, my Lord?' she asked.

He grinned, somewhat wryly.

'Ah, well, you see, my old father – by some mischance – came to hear of my embarkation plans. Now – I do not know if you are aware – he and I are not on good terms.'

Hatty nodded.

'We seldom meet – and, when we do, dissension is sure to follow.

But – well – I suppose blood is thicker than water and when the old fellow heard on some grapevine that I was due to set sail – he fell into a fret, decided he was dying and had a message sent me to that effect. I, of course, took said message with a bushel of salt – but – but—'

'You had to go,' said Hatty.

'Of course. You, I am sure, would have done so on such a call.'

'Oh yes,' agreed Hatty. 'Yes, I would.'

'So,' he said smiling, 'when I got to his bedside I was greeted with a storm of reproaches and recriminations – all very familiar – but as I could see that the old fellow was no worse than usual, in fact rather better than I have sometimes known him, had taken to his bed in a pet rather than from any real infirmity – I left as fast as I had come. But my ship, by then, of course, had sailed, so now I must wait for another.'

'Master Harry, come and get your soup,' interrupted Mrs Daizley briskly.

While he had been talking she and old Mrs Godwit had been setting bowls on a table in one corner of the room. 'And before you sit at table, pass the young lady this bowl of soup to eat by the fire. Dickon, give Eli a call – he should have changed into dry things by now.'

Indeed at this moment Godwit came back, having changed his snow-covered outerwear for a plain manservant's suit of black.

Hatty was served an earthenware bowl of soup by the fire, while the others sat round the table and listened to Godwit, who told the tale of how nobody had been there to meet her at the Woodpecker Inn. This was received with nods and clucks of sympathy.

'But what else could you expect in such weather? A dozen accidents might ha' befell the other coach – and no way to send word – '

'It was just so lucky for me that I was with Mr Godwit and that he could bring me here,' said Hatty faintly. She was beginning to be overwhelmed with drowsiness.

'The young lady's for bed,' decreed old Mrs Godwit. 'She's as dozy as a cockle-pig. Come along o' me, my dearie, a good night's rest will set ye all to rights.'

Hatty, heavy-eyed and stumbling, had no wish but to obey. She followed the old lady up a steep narrow stair, which turned several corners, and into a sloping-roofed room with two beds, both covered by patchwork quilts. 'That's Jenny's bed,' said the old lady, nodding at one of them, 'but she won't disturb ye, a quiet sleeper she be. Now, here's a night-robe for ye.' She pulled it out from the bed, where it had kept warm, wrapped round a stone bottle filled with boiling water. 'There's a goose-quilt under the patchwork, so ye'll be plenty warm enow.'

Nimbly and with great cordiality the old lady assisted Hatty's speedy disrobement. No time was wasted for the room was icy cold. Helping Hatty into the sagging, capacious bed – 'That's it, then, bless ye, my dearie – I mind your mother when she was just your age' – the old lady stooped and kissed Hatty's brow. 'Sleep sound now – I doubt there will be little need for stirring in the morning.'

And she took her candle downstairs again.

In two minutes Hatty was deeply unconscious.

IX

NEXT DAY THE snow still fell; and the sky was thick and brown with it, like lentil soup, until long past noon.

Hatty slept very late, and nobody roused her.

'What use?' said old Mrs Godwit. 'Ne'er a soul will be stirring between Bythorn and Wanmaulden Cross this day.'

'Her poor father!' said Mrs Daizley, who had a soft heart. 'Worried to a ravelling he'll be, wondering where she's to.'

'They should have sent to meet her at Wanhurst,' said Godwit. 'Penny-pinching, that was. Then, if aught went amiss, at least she'd be in a town, with inns, and coaches for hire, and a post-office.'

'Well,' pronounced old Mrs Godwit, who had once been chief nursemaid at Bythorn Chase before she married the head gardener, and whose sister Jess had held the like post at Underwood Priors with the Fowldes family, 'that Lady Ursula, who's took and married Mr Ward at Bythorn, she was never one to spend sixpence on a pint of shrimps if she could get them farther down the road for fourpence.'

Her grandson's eyes slid from side to side with amusement though his face remained sober. 'Ay, they make a pair, she and Mr Ward, no question,' he said. 'And I reckon t'other Ward in Portsmouth is the same. It's my belief they won't keep Miss Hatty at Bythorn Lodge longer than it takes them to find another roof to lodge her under.'

'But where?'

'Oh, likely they'll send her off to Mansfield Parsonage with Mrs Norris, Miss Agnes Ward that was.'

'Miss Agnes won't want her, for certain sure. My grand-niece Jenny, that was named for me, she went as housemaid to Bythorn Lodge, and she used to say as how Miss Agnes was always tormenting of Miss Hatty, putting upon her and laying into her, over one thing or another.'

Hatty came down the steep stair, heavy-eyed and apologetic.

'I have slept so long! It must be dreadfully late.'

'Never fret your head for that, miss, dear! See how it snows still. There will be no wheeled traffic along the roads this day. You must just bide with us, and we're happy to have you. Eli, make the young lady a bowl of toast-and-milk. There's nigh a foot of snow outside, dearie; we must all take the weather that's sent us and make the best of it.'

'Well,' said Hatty, 'I hope in that case you will allow me to be of some use. I'll do anything you ask me.'

She looked with pleasure round the plain square room, which last night she had been too weary to observe with close attention in dim firelight and candlelight. Today, although there was no sun, a white-reflected light shone up from the snow-covered ground outside the windows and threw a pale radiance on to the cedar-wood-panelled walls, the dresser holding blue plates and cups, the simple solid table, chairs and settle, the white ceiling and row of thriving plants on the windowsill. A large grey dog was peacefully asleep stretched over the hearthstone, and a tabby cat lay crossways, using the dog as a pillow.

The room seemed to combine the function of kitchen and living-room. Hatty wondered where Lord Camber might be.

'His Lordship's up in his study,' said Godwit, accurately reading her thoughts. 'He mostly spends the mornings in there writing. But he said to give him a call when you roused up. He'll likely want to show you over the place.'

'Is it very old?'

'Nay, nobbut a hundred years. It used to be the old laundry. Then his Grace's father, he took a fancy to have a *hermit* living on his estate; so he had this place turned into a hermitage, called it The Grotto. But never a hermit could he find – ' Godwit's eyes slipped to and fro in amusement – 'so the place was not used, and was nigh to falling down when Master Harry came into the property. He added some more rooms and made it snug and weatherproof.'

Everybody in the room had some occupation, Hatty noticed, except for the dog and cat. Mrs Daizley was plucking a pheasant, Godwit was polishing spoons with hartshorn powder and spirits of wine; old Mrs Godwit was making another rag rug like the brilliant red-and-blue ones that lay on the stone floor. From outside came a sound of wood-chopping.

'May I learn to do that, Mrs Godwit?' Hatty asked. 'I should dearly like to know how to make a rug.'

'For sure you may, dearie; I'll be glad to teach you. And it's not hard. But here's his lordship coming now – we'll wait to start till he's showed you round the place.'

Lord Camber appeared, in a sheepskin shooting jacket and corduroy breeches. His benevolent smile fitted so comfortably into this scene that Hatty wondered how he could ever have the heart to leave it and sail across the ocean to work as a carpenter for some unknown master. What an extraordinary man he was . . .

'Good morning, Miss Hatty. I hope that you slept well?'

'Like a dormouse, thank you, sir. I was just asking Mrs Godwit if she would show me how to make a rag rug. Since they tell me there will be no chance of reaching Bythorn today.'

'No travel today, nor tomorrow, by the look of it,' said Lord Camber cheerfully. 'Neither you to Bythorn, nor I to America. We must just make the best of our circumstances. Let me conduct you over my mansion.'

'Thank you, sir, I should like that.'

He took her up another narrow twisting stair, which had been concealed behind what looked like a cupboard door, and along a dark hallway with sloping ceilings, carpeted by more of Mrs Godwit's brilliant rugs.

'Bedrooms on each side – ' he gestured – 'and here is my workroom which lies at the end of the house above the stable and cart-shed.' He threw open a latched door and revealed a lofty attic room, its roof sloping down to the floor on each side, lit by three large dormer windows, two facing each other, one at the end, all of which let in clear snow light. The roof was of thatch, very thick; that, and the massive cedar boards which formed the floor gave the place a pleasant, spicy farmyard odour. A row of well-filled bookcases, waist-high, back to back, ran down the centre of the room; and each of the side windows had a large desk in it. A brazier beside one of the desks kept the room only moderately warm. By the far window it was bitingly cold. But Lord Camber did not seem affected by the temperature. Opened books and piles of paper lay everywhere.

'Oh!' breathed Hatty. 'What a beautiful room! How can you ever bear to leave it?'

'Well, in winter weather it does become a trifle chilly. But the horses and cattle down below help ameliorate the worst of the cold. And now, my dear Miss Hatty, do you want to tell me what unexpected upheaval in the Portsmouth household sent you flying north in this sudden and precipitate way, up into the wilds of Huntingdonshire – or is it a private matter which you would prefer not to divulge to me?'

Hatty hesitated.

'Will you not be seated for a moment or two?' suggested Lord Camber, and drew out a wooden armchair by the desk that was nearest to the brazier. 'We must not remain here very long; it is not warm enough for you.' Hatty sat down in the chair, and her host, having first wrapped his sheepskin jacket round her, pushed aside a pile of papers covered with handwriting, and perched himself on the desk.

'I am writing a book,' he explained, 'but it will probably take me till my dying day and not be finished even then.'

'What is it about?'

'Too many things. Clothes – and how they affect character; climate – and how climate affects clothes. How can you tell a king from a savage? By his crown. But the savage would not necessarily recognize the crown as a symbol of royalty.'

'Nor he would,' said Hatty. 'That is true.' She reflected. 'I should *like* to tell you, Lord Camber, what happened at my uncle's house – but some of it is not my story to tell, so I must leave that part out.'

'I am at your disposal, and my ear is as private as when I listen to your poetry.'

She told him about Aunt Polly's illness and how, with the cares of the household on her shoulders, she had persuaded Ned to play chess with the twins, and how they had caught measles and died. His face puckered with sympathy.

'Poor, poor little creatures. Theirs would have been such an interesting and difficult, such a *remarkable* existence. It is sad, sad indeed, that it has been cut off. You must feel it deeply.'

'I do. I do. I cannot think of them without misery.'

Tears had been running down her cheeks as she told the story, and she now stopped and dried them.

'Was that – was their death – why your uncle sent you away?'

'Only in part. He was very angry with me about that – that I had persuaded Ned to play chess with them and that they had taken the infection from him. But my uncle's anger had another cause as well, and on that head you must excuse me – I cannot go into the other part. It concerns my cousin Ned; and my cousin Sydney.'

'I see,' said Lord Camber.

He looked at Hatty very kindly.

'But what troubles me *very much*, sir,' she went on, staring down at her tightly joined hands, unaware of his sympathetic, frowning scrutiny, 'what makes me very anxious is that, in part, I believe my being sent away was engineered by the twins' nurse, Burnaby. She, you see, would have had no duties in the house now the twins are – are gone. But – but now, as matters are, she will be occupied in caring for my aunt, so she will be secure of her place; she is needed. But oh, I am afraid – I am so afraid that she will not take sufficient *care* of my aunt – that she will not be kind, or solicitous enough, but will simply use her as she did the twins.'

Hatty came to a stop, her voice shrivelling in her throat.

Lord Camber studied her in friendly silence for a few minutes. Then he said, 'I do not think that – perhaps – you need worry unduly about Burnaby's care of your aunt. After all, Mrs Ward is a grown person, not like the twins, who were small and helpless and without sufficient wit to defend themselves. Mrs Ward is a lady of excellent good sense. And she has a solicitous, affectionate husband, who will be frequently at her bedside. And now Burnaby, who does not lack for shrewdness, will see that her position depends on that very thought and care which you fear is in doubt . . .'

'Yes, of course,' said Hatty. 'You are perfectly right. It was selfish of me to feel that I was indispensable to my aunt's comfort.'

'Not altogether! I have no doubt that she will miss you a great deal. But are you not happy to be returning to your childhood home?'

'You see—' began Hatty.

But here she came to a complete stop, due to the impossibility of telling Lord Camber how much she dreaded the prospect of Lady Ursula as a stepmother. For was not Lady Ursula his long-time friend – his childhood playmate? His lost love?

And what did Lord Camber think of Lady Ursula's marriage to Mr Ward?

'You see, I was never my father's favourite,' Hatty went on slowly. 'He had hoped for a boy – he was not pleased when I was born – it was because of the entail. It was he who arranged for me to be sent away to my uncle's and he may not be at all happy to have me back.'

'Oh, come,' said Lord Camber. 'When you left home you were, how old? – ten? eleven? – just the most difficult age. Now he receives back a complete young lady, accomplished, skilled in all the household arts, pleasing in every way. You will be a friend and companion for my cousin Ursula. Which I do not doubt she will be glad of, since I believe your father still goes out hunting as often as he is able? Nearly every day?'

'Yes, I think so,' said Hatty. 'But whether—'

She had been about to voice her doubts as to Lady Ursula's acceptance of her as a companion, but at that moment the boy Dickon passed below the window, waving something that looked like a large, flat basket, while, simultaneously, from the foot of the stair, Godwit could be heard calling: 'My Lord! My grandmother says it is too cold for the young lady to be any longer above-stairs!'

'She is quite right! Let us go down. Besides, I believe the sun is on the point of breaking through the cloud. And I see that Dickon has made you a pair of snow-shoes, so that we can walk in the wood.'

Back in the kitchen Dickon proudly demonstrated the products of his labour: flat, pear-shaped frames of willow-saplings woven with a tight criss-cross, and leather straps to fasten over Hatty's boots.

'They seem clumsy at first, but you will soon grow accustomed,' Lord Camber promised.

'Now, Master Harry, don't you keep the young lady out too long!' cautioned old Mrs Godwit. 'Mortal cold out there it be!'

'Half an hour, no longer,' promised Lord Camber. 'I will just take her as far as the Viewpoint.'

They went out into a suddenly dazzling world, shutting the door on old Mrs Godwit's protestations that the Viewpoint was by far too far for the young lady, not used to snow-shoes. She'd be worn to a bone, if she didn't break her ankle coming down the sheep-track . . .

'Nonsense, nonsense, Lena!' Lord Camber called back, laughing, and he said to Hatty, 'You can manage to go as far as half a mile, I am sure, can you not? There is a little hill from which one is able to see twenty miles in every direction; it is a favourite spot of mine. I am certain you will be able to walk as far as that without the least difficulty.'

Hatty was not so sanguine about her ability, and felt some scepticism as to whether Lord Camber's half-mile would be any shorter than Godwit's. The snow-shoes felt amazingly cumbrous at first, on her unaccustomed feet; soon her ankles began to ache. But, by following his directions and example – 'No, no, don't try to pick your feet *up*. Slide, just keep sliding as you see me do, that's right, now you have it!' – she began to acquire the necessary competence.

'It is mighty hard work, though!' she gasped.

'That is because we are, all the time, going slightly uphill. This path winds very slowly round and round until it reaches the summit. There you will be able to sit and rest.'

The track was indeed slowly, steadily ascending through different layers of woodland: first a beech grove, with a little frozen brook in a deep gully far below them; then oak forest, then birch, then pine; at last they came out on a treeless slope with clumps of snow-covered heather and furze; and the last circuit of the hill brought them to the bare crest, where there was a simple seat, made from two posts sunk into the ground with a plank nailed across them.

'From this we can measure how much snow has fallen,' said Lord Camber, wiping the snow from the plank with a bunch of heather, and spreading his thick-knitted scarf for Hatty to sit down. 'I would say there has been six inches at least. I very much doubt if there can be any travel tomorrow. But now, look about you at all the kingdoms of the earth!'

It was indeed a dazzling prospect. Below them the woods wrapped the hillside like black fur; in the distance, beyond the woods, a rolling, snow-covered landscape shimmered and gleamed.

'That brick-chimneyed house,' said Lord Camber, pointing, 'in the shade at the foot of the wooded hill over there, that is my Uncle Gilbert's place, Underwood Priors, where my cousin Ursula grew up. Poor things, they get no sun from December to February. And the house in the opposite direction, on the hilltop, that is Bythorn Chase, my father's principal residence. As you probably know. And beyond it lies Bythorn village – there is smoke rising from the chimneys, but you cannot see your father's house, it is hidden behind a fold of land. And over there eastwards is Mansfield Park (can you detect the church steeple?), home of your sisters Maria and Agnes. On a clear day from here you may see as far as Peterborough to the north and Bedford to the south – but now the air grows hazy – I believe we shall have more snow. Come, I had better take you home, or I shall receive a terrible trimming from Nanny Godwit. You will find that the return journey is a great deal faster.'

So it proved, for the homeward path was a breakneck descent straight down the side of the hill; Lord Camber held tightly on to Hatty's arm as they slid, panting and laughing, down the snowy slope. At one point she fell over completely into a heathery tussock, but he picked her up and dusted her off.

'Never let them know that happened, or I shall be made to eat my dinner in the stable! There! Now we are back on our original path. And here comes Godwit, who has been to the Cross to find out the state of the roads.'

Godwit's report, when they met him, was negative. The roads were still blocked, there was drifting to the south and east, even the way to Bythorn was impassable with drifts. There were no horses or carriages to be hired.

'And more snow coming,' Godwit predicted. 'Old Chicksand, from Copse Gate, was in the Tap, he's a wonderful wise head for weather, he reckons another two–three inches will fall by tomorrow's morn. I doubt you'll get to Bristol afore Saturday, my Lord, or the young lady to her folks ...'

'Then there is nothing we can do but resign ourselves,' said Camber happily. 'Now Miss Hatty has learned to walk on snow-shoes, I can show her all my favourite paths. The person we should be feeling sorry for is Miss Hatty's father, deprived of his hunting.'

'Nay, my Lord, old Chicksand said the Underwood pack would meet on Friday, as usual, that's unless there should come a hard frost, but he don't think there will be.'

They were now back within view of Lord Camber's dwelling, and he asked Hatty what she thought of it.

Struggling to combine truthfulness with honesty, she said, 'Well, it is not just in the common way—'

He gave a shout of laughter, and Godwit allowed himself a small dry smile.

'We call it the Thatched Grotto,' Lord Camber told Hatty. 'The front porch, you see, is supposed to represent a cave mouth. It was constructed during the period when my grandfather hoped that a hermit might be found to come and inhabit it. He had the Greek words inscribed on the lintel. They mean "A place for leisure is the best property".'

'From Plato,' said Hatty.

'Just so. Then the pillars were added as a kind of afterthought by a different architect. The original roof was of slate, but it was in very poor repair when I inherited the building, so, as Godwit has a cousin who is an excellent thatcher, he re-covered it for me, and taught me the trade at the same time, which I hope will stand me in good stead during my sojourn in Pennsylvania. I believe they use wooden shingles there, rather than thatch, but doubtless there is straw to be had.'

Godwit sighed. 'They say *maize* is grown there, my Lord, rather than wheat or barley,' he observed. 'Maize straw would not be suitable for thatching, perhaps.'

There was a shade, Hatty thought, of reserve or disapproval in his tone; she wondered if Godwit privately considered his master's project a hare-brained scheme, but was too loyal to voice his doubts.

But Lord Camber, perhaps catching the tone also, clapped him on the shoulder. 'Set your mind at rest, old fellow! If shingle roofs are the mode, I will soon find somebody to teach me how it is done.'

The boy Dickon came out of the house, capered round Hatty, evidently admiring her proficiency on the snow-shoes, then knelt in the snow to help unlace them. When he had taken them off to the stable, Hatty asked in a low voice, 'Does he never say anything? I have never heard him speak.'

'No,' Lord Camber answered in the same tone (Godwit had followed Dickon to the stable), 'he has been dumb since his father was transported for poaching when he was a little lad of two or three. But his wits are bright enough.'

'Poor child! Is it known what became of his father?'

'Word came back that he had died on the transport ship. Many do,' Lord Camber added briefly. 'But come in, and warm your cold hands. From the fragrance indoors I conclude that Nanny Godwit has been making some of her pheasant soup.'

During the next couple of days Hatty learned that housekeeping for a family of eight or nine in a large house with an ample staff of servants in kitchen and garden is a very different matter from undertaking all the work of the house oneself, making soups and stews, kneading bread-dough, fetching vegetables and coal from icy outhouses, plucking birds and washing soiled linen. Mrs Daizley and Mrs Godwit took her at her word and allowed her to help with everything they did.

'I have learned more from you two,' she said, panting over the heavy iron mangle, 'than in six years at my aunt's house – and yet Aunt Polly is an excellent housekeeper.'

'Ah, 'tis the doing it yourself that learns ye, dearie,' agreed Mrs Godwit. 'And the things that me and Jenny teach ye will stand ye in good stead for the rest of your life, I'll lay.'

'I shall always remember these days,' Hatty said with certainty. 'Now I know what real happiness is like.'

When the essential household tasks were finished, Nanny Godwit taught her the craft of rug-making, which was done with rags of cloth ('We gets their worn-out gowns from the ladies at Underwood Priors – there is always a-plenty') threaded and knotted on to a coarse canvas foundation. Or, from Dickon, she learned to whittle clothes-pegs. Or how to lay mortar, from Godwit and Lord Camber, who were building an internal wall to partition off one end of the stable. Or how to make patchwork from Mrs Daizley. Or how to make corn-dolls from Dickon. When the sun shone, briefly, between snow-showers, Lord Camber took her out along his favourite rides through the woods, which covered a hilly rugged area including a small lake and a winding stream.

In the evenings, when early winter dark had fallen, they sang. Lord Camber had a modest tenor voice, Mrs Daizley a firm contralto, and Mrs Godwit an aged, faint, true soprano. Godwit had no voice at all, he croaked like a raven and could not tell one note from another, but, to counterbalance that, he had in his memory a vast store of folk songs, ballads, rounds, glees, and catches, and beat time vigorously while he gave out the words. Hatty was able to add a few to this repertory from those she had sung with her mother. And, noticing Dickon's interested eyes following the rhythm of their opening and shutting mouths and Godwit's gestures, she had the notion of contriving him an instrument, halfway between a drum and a tambourine, made from canvas stretched over the mouth of a round basket. On this, while they sang, he happily thumped with a wooden mallet.

'He keeps very precise time, too,' said Lord Camber, watching attentively. 'I believe you have discovered something, Miss Hatty.'

'I am going to try to teach him to read,' said Hatty, and cut a set of letters from a thin sheet of paste-board. With these she produced DISH, BREAD, PLATE, TABLE and could have no doubt of Dickon's instant comprehension, as she matched the words and pointed out the appropriate objects.

'I wish I could come over here from my father's house and go on working with him,' she said to Mrs Daizley. 'But I'm afraid they will never allow me.'

'We'll keep on with him, never fear,' said Mrs Godwit. 'Next time you come this way I believe the lad will be reading all Master Harry's books.'

'I wish I need never leave here,' sighed Hatty. 'This is the sort of house I have always wanted to live in, all my life.'

She drew a picture of a house among trees for Dickon and laid the letters H O U S E beside it. He nodded gravely and fitted in lines up and down the roof to represent thatch, so she added the letters T H A T C H.

Lord Camber, descending the study stair, said, 'I am sorry to interrupt your lesson – but the sun is out, had you noticed? And I believe it grows a little warmer.'

'Maybe tomorrow the young lady will be able to leave us,' said Mrs Godwit.

'I shall be very sorry to,' said Hatty.

Today, when they climbed Lord Camber's Viewpoint hill, their snow-shoes slipped and sank in soft, moist snow, and a mild wind blew gently in their faces.

'Yes, a thaw is coming,' said Lord Camber, 'you can feel it. Perhaps it will rain tonight and clear the roads.'

Hatty did not confess how heavy-hearted this prospect made her. But her companion went on: 'I shall miss our conversations when I am gone abroad, shall not you? What a great deal of ground we have covered, from our arguments as to whether sunlight or lamplight is more beautiful, and the best way to fry an egg, to discussions about poetry and moral questions. I do not believe there is a single question on which we agree!'

'Except about the egg!' said Hatty, laughing. But there is one thing we have never discussed, she thought.

'I'll write to you – shall I? – from Pennsylvania? To tell you about the ocean voyage, and what kind of employment I am fixed in?'

'Oh, yes! Do, please! I should like that of all things. But will you have time? It seems so strange to think of you employed as a servant . . .'

Privately she thought that, unless his employers were exceedingly autocratic and difficult, they would soon be on the easy comfortable terms with him that obtained in the Thatched Grotto, with no distinctions between different members of the household.

'And you will answer my letters – from time to time – will you? And send me specimens of your newest verses?'

'As soon as you let me have your address!'

'Oh, you can always write to me in care of the Sophocratic Community at Amity Valley, and my friends Wandesleigh and Kittridge; they will make sure that letters are sent on to me. But where shall I direct my letters to you?'

'Well – I suppose – at my father's house, at Bythorn Lodge,' Hatty said slowly. She wondered if her father would disapprove of her receiving letters from Lord Camber. Almost certainly he would, very strongly, remembering Uncle Philip. But then, she probably would not remain at Bythorn Lodge any longer than it took Mr Ward to find her some eligible situation as a governess; she felt certain that would be her immediate destiny.

A faint hallooing and the sound of a horn came from below them to the east.

'Oh, see! There are the hounds! Just as Godwit predicted!'

Below them on the hillside a ribbon of black and white and tan poured out of the pines, circled around the hill, then vanished back into the trees again. Men in scarlet coats galloped after them on horseback and likewise disappeared into the trees.

'A queer pursuit,' said Camber. 'When you think about it in a detached spirit.'

'Did you never go a-hunting, sir?'

'Oh, certainly, when I was a boy. And *then*, I found it very exciting. But it was the rush across country that I enjoyed, not the pitiful business of tearing the fox to pieces— Talk of the devil, there he goes!'

A small brown creature, mouth lolling open as if he laughed, slipped between the heather tussocks, going in a contrary direction to the pursuers.

'He has doubled back on them, clever little beast.'

'Oh, let us hope that he has given them the slip. No, see, they are following the scent back again,' Hatty said regretfully. She was always surprised at the *smallness* of a fox; it seemed a puny prey for a whole troop of large men on horseback with half a hundred dogs.

The hounds once more poured over the hillside below, a good deal closer now to Lord Camber and Hatty, who stood on the summit by the snow-covered bench.

'View halloo-oo, there he goes!' shouted somebody, and a clump of riders tore by them, splashing up great clots of the caked snow, which, in the sunshine, was beginning to thaw quite rapidly.

'Did you see him? Where is he?' one rider called back to Camber, who shook his head.

In the distance the hounds yelled and pealed, sounding mad with excitement; a voice close beside Hatty and Camber suddenly said: '*Good gad* – it's m'daughter!' A red face under a black top hat turned to give them a disapproving glare, and then its owner, a tall, solidly built man on a massive bay horse went thundering off down the hill, kicking up a spray of melting snow with his rear hoofs. A moment later there came a terrible outburst of shouts, the triumphant cry of hounds, and more notes on the horn.

'Come,' said Camber, 'let us not stay for the kill – ' and he caught Hatty's arm, urging her away down the steep track on the opposite side of the hill.

Well, thought Hatty, at least now Papa knows that I am alive; not that the knowledge seemed to give him any pleasure.

She felt a vague surprise that he had been able to recognize her, after a six-year absence, forgetting how much she was said to resemble her mother.

'Would you wish to try to catch up with your father?' Camber asked, loosing her hand at the foot of the hill. 'It sounds to me as if they have gone into the wood looking for another fox. I daresay they are all regretting that they caught up with that one so early in the day.'

'No, I am sure that would be a great mistake,' said Hatty. 'We might trudge over half the country and still never come up with him again. And he would hate to be interrupted in the middle of a run. Perhaps at the end of the day's sport he may come round by your house – he recognized you, did he not?'

'Oh yes, we have met each other on various occasions.'

Camber did not pursue this. They made their way back to the cottage in silence. There Godwit met them with the information that the road from the Cross to Bythorn would be passable by the following morning, and he had succeeded in hiring a chaise to transport Hatty at that time from the Woodpecker Inn to Bythorn Lodge.

Mrs Daizley and Mrs Godwit were touchingly grieved at the prospect of Hatty's departure. 'Like a ray of sunshine you've been,' said Mrs Daizley, and wanted to load her with pots of blackberry jelly and strings of dried mushrooms. But these Hatty thought it best to decline in case Lady Ursula or her sister Agnes considered them a slur on the housekeeping at Bythorn Lodge. Lord Camber offered to accompany her on horseback, but this offer, too, she put by, though with considerable regret. She could not feel, though, that another meeting between Camber and Lady Ursula would be in any way desirable, or would be likely to ameliorate her homecoming.

Camber himself, therefore, was to set off for Bristol at the same time. Godwit had heard, from a packman who had called at the Woodpecker, that the roads westward beyond Oxford were not so badly affected by snow.

At this announcement Mrs Daizley broke down entirely.

'Oh, Master Harry! When shall we see you again?' she wept into her apron, and he laid an arm round her shoulders.

'Should not you and Nanny like to come and join me at Amity Valley? When I am free of my indentures? I am sure the life there would suit you both very well.'

'No, no, Master Harry dear, we are too old to shift as far as that and leave all our friends.'

'Well then,' he said, 'we must just think of each other kindly. We shall be sure to do that, shall we not?'

'But you'll be back *some* day – won't ye? – For you will be obliged to when his Grace is no more?'

'Well,' he said laughing, 'we shall see. Perhaps that task may be offloaded on to my brother's shoulders.'

'Colonel Wisbech? Never! All he thinks about are his guns and his waistcoats!'

'We shall see,' Lord Camber repeated.

His farewell to Hatty, on the following morning, was brief. Characteristically, he was to set off on foot, with no luggage but a knapsack, to pick up the Oxford mailcoach at a west-lying crossroads.

'Well, Miss Hatty – ' he grasped her hands, looking down at her with the smile that dispersed a hundred tiny creases from his eyes – 'I shall not be likely to forget all the things we have said to one another. And I shall not lose your poems. I have them in my notebook.' He patted a poacher's pocket. 'Some in my head, too. I shall expect to see them in reviews and periodicals before very long. And I shall hope that the sun shines on your path.'

'Goodbye, Lord Camber,' was all Hatty could find voice for.

She turned away hastily to where Godwit and Dickon were waiting to escort her to the Woodpecker Inn.

X

HATTY'S UNCLE PHILIP had supplied her with a modest sum of money for travelling expenses; she feared that it would not extend to the cost of a private chaise from Wanmaulden Cross to Bythorn. In order to distract herself from this worry, and from the effect of parting from Lord Camber and the informal but congenial existence at the Thatched Grotto, she stared resolutely out of the chaise window at the snow-patched meadows bobbing past, and engaged her mind with a poem:

> Useless to put the question to the grass
> As to: he loves me or he loves me not;
> The nodding field's indifferent, divided
> Exactly on the matter, which is what
> The law of averages made one fear.
> Daisies the same,
> One can't believe a word
> Since each negates the last ...

I wonder what Lord Camber would think of that. I wonder if it is rather vulgar to have a rhyme at all? I wonder how far Lord Camber has travelled by now? Is he on the Oxford coach yet? I wonder how soon I can possibly expect a letter from him? Not for at least four months, I suppose. And then he may be too busy, too involved in new experiences, to find time for writing to such a chance acquaintance as myself. Or he may not have access to writing materials. Or he may have forgotten me entirely. Oh, parting is such pain ...

Very fortunately, when the chaise pulled up at Bythorn Lodge, the door was opened by Firle the footman, an old ally of Hatty's.

'Oh, Firle, I am so glad it is you. Can you please see that the driver is paid off?'

He gaped at her in astonishment.

'My word, miss, ye've come fast! Yes, I'll get the money from Mrs Ayling – we're all in a pucker here, as ye can imagine.'

Indeed the house did show signs of unusual disorder: mud on the mat, Mr Ward's hunting-hat and whip lying on the hall table amid a scatter of unopened letters. Jenny the housemaid, arriving as Firle returned with the chaise fare, cried out, 'Oh, Miss Hatty! What a to-do! The poor master!'

'Why, Jenny? What has happened?'

'Didn't ye know, then? He got throwed yesterday, a-hunting – fetched home on a hurdle. Mr Jones says it will be only a matter of hours now, if as long—'

'Oh, good God!' whispered Hatty. 'Yesterday – when Papa was out hunting – then—'

It must have happened not long after we saw him, she thought. How strange – how terribly strange. How awful.

''Twas on account of the melting snow,' Jenny went on. 'Very slushy it was, and Master's horse, Fiddler, slipped as he was about to jump a gate at Hickley Wood, and threw the Master, and the poor gentleman fell on his head – the horse fell on him too – there was a-many falls yesterday, Mr Gridley said, the slush was that treacherous. Missus had begged the Master not to go out in the morning, but he would not listen, he said he'd been confined to the house three days, and that was quite long enough—'

'And that is quite enough from *you*, Jenny,' snapped a familiar voice from the stair; Hatty, looking up, saw her sister Agnes. The sight of Agnes – her sharp face, pursed-up mouth and disapproving, gimlet eyes, instantly recalled that former occasion, the calamitous fall, the ivory hairbrush, broken mirror, the shattered Venetian flask. I bring bad luck wherever I go, thought Hatty in despair.

'So, Harriet! You are come at last!' pronounced Agnes sourly. 'Too late for any farewell to our father, I fear. It is a pity that you delayed your return for so long.'

'I came as soon as I could,' Hatty protested. 'Yesterday there was no chaise to be had.'

'Well! I may say that Mr Norris and I made our way on *horseback*. Sir Thomas was so kind as to let us have two safe old hacks from the Park stable. *We* spare neither time nor trouble to do our duty in such a case. As soon as the news came to Mansfield about poor Papa – we must be off, my dear, directly, said I to Mr Norris; and he was quite of my mind and asked Sir Thomas for the horses directly; he is upstairs now, sitting with poor Papa, and with dear Lady Ursula, offering what solace and comfort he can; it is a most grievous mishap, and, what shocked me more than *all*, was that, while Papa was still able to speak last night, he told us that he had seen *you* walking with Lord Camber, carefree as you please on Coppice Hill. I have no doubt whatsoever that this encounter with you, in such disgracefully untoward circumstances rendered Papa somewhat careless in the control of his horse; for, all these years he has followed the hounds and such an accident never befell him before – or not very often—'

Lady Ursula now came stalking down the stair, thin and pale as a spectre.

'It is over,' she reported briefly. 'Mr Ward is no more.'

'There, miss, you see!' said Agnes. 'You arrived too late to be at his bedside.'

'I do not suppose that he would have been at all pleased to see me,' pointed out Hatty forlornly.

'That is hardly relevant – or respectful to the departed,' snapped Lady Ursula. 'And where, pray, have you been these past three days? Certainly it was unfortunate that the vehicle Mr Ward had ordered to meet you was unable to proceed – but could you not have despatched some message as to your whereabouts? Your father was quite concerned about you – so were we all – or would have been if we had known. Why did you not contrive to send word from the inn?'

'Because the landlord is a swinker,' said Hatty.

'I *beg* your pardon?'

'He drinks. He was under the influence of liquor. And there was nobody else about the place to send with a message.'

Agnes and Lady Ursula exchanged disgusted glances. That a member of this family should have such a tale to tell was the burden of their looks.

'So what did you do?'

'I could not stay at the inn. Godwit – Lord Camber's manservant who had escorted me from Portsmouth – took me to Lord Camber's cottage in the wood. It was too late and dark and stormy to go anywhere else. So that was where I stayed.'

'You stayed in *Lord Camber's cottage*? That was a most unseemly thing to do!'

'How could I help myself? It was not possible to go farther – it was snowing hard.'

'How thankful I am that our dear father had not lingered on to hear *this* tale!' declared Agnes with upraised eyes.

'*I* had understood that Lord Camber was already departed for America,' observed Lady Ursula with a contemptuously curling lip. 'What caused him to delay his departure?'

'His father was ill and sent for him.'

'Humph! So *he*, at least, has some filial feelings.'

'But then,' said Lady Ursula, 'he returned to his cottage. Pray, who else was there in this – this abode?'

'His housekeeper, Mrs Daizley – a very excellent woman,' said Hatty defensively. 'And old Mrs Godwit. And Godwit himself. And a deaf-and-dumb boy, Dickon.'

'A thoroughly respectable household, upon my word!'

During the whole of this interrogation the three females had stood in the front hall, at the foot of the stair. But now a gentleman came slowly down the stairway. He was a heavy-looking, elderly clergyman, who wore on his reddish countenance an expression of fixed gravity and disapprobation. Hatty guessed him to be Mr Norris.

'And whom have we here?' he inquired.

'This is my youngest sister Hatty – Harriet,' Agnes informed him.

'Ah – so. It is a regrettable circumstance that she has arrived too late for her father's last moments.'

How was I supposed to know that he was dying? Nobody told me, thought Hatty. But she had the sense not to utter this question aloud.

'And why, pray, do we stand here thus in the cold hall?' Mr Norris inquired.

Hatty wondered if she might retire to her bedroom to remove her bonnet and pelisse. But did she still *have* a bedroom in this house?

Lady Ursula decided the matter. 'Well – you had best remove your outer garments. You may go up to your old bedchamber, then return to us in the breakfast parlour. By then we shall have decided what is best to be done about you.'

Hatty found that the servants had already anticipated Lady Ursula's instructions. Jenny was in her old room, had lit a fire, and was unpacking her boxes.

'Oh, dear Miss Hatty! I'm *that* pleased you're back – though, sure, 'tis a sad home-coming for ye. And will Miss Fanny be coming too?'

'Gracious me, Jenny, I don't know. She is in Bristol. I am not certain whether anybody has her address. I suppose my uncle Philip may let her know. I suppose he may come himself—'

At this moment a sudden and shocking thought overtook Hatty. Upon her father's death the ownership of the house reverted to her uncle Philip. Would he arrive forthwith and take possession?

No wonder Lady Ursula had appeared so grey and grim. She was now a widow.

Not that she doesn't always look like that, thought Hatty. I once saw a picture of the stones in a circle at Stonehenge. She is like one of those great monoliths:

> Grey as a boulder, harder than granite
> more distant, colder than a dying planet . . .

But wait! Wait a minute! Suppose that by any chance Lady Ursula is with child? Suppose she is increasing? Aunt Polly said that was not very likely – but still, I suppose that no one can be sure yet, not at least for some period of time – how long? If she were to have a boy child, I suppose he would be the heir. My half-brother. How strange! And then he would inherit the house. But suppose she had a girl child? I would be sorry for that girl . . .

Hatty's knowledge of the probabilities and time intervals involved here was minimal; she longed for Aunt Polly's useful and sensible company and experience. Oh, dear Aunt Polly, how are you? Are they taking good care of you? Who is looking after the house?

The atmosphere of *this* house, for Hatty, seemed to offer nothing but grief, anger and calamity.

Again, Jenny anticipated her. 'Your uncle, Mr Philip Ward – he'll have this house now, won't he, miss? Since the new Missis isn't in the family way—'

'Oh, Jenny! But how do you know that? How can you be certain?'

'Lord love ye, Miss Hatty, us in the servants' hall knows all that kind of business. Fanshaw, that's Lady Ursula's maid, *she* knows. And so do the rest of us. There ain't naught in the wind of *that* sort. No, no, Lady Ursula will just have to pick up sticks and be on her way out of this house. And nary a soul here will be sorry for that, I can tell ye! She's not at all like your poor sweet lady mother, Miss Hatty.'

'But they cannot make her leave at once, surely? There must be a – a period of – of grace?'

'Oh, ay – 'tis around a month or two, summat like that; Mr Firle, he've a cousin in the law line, a lawyer's clerk, he told us it'd be a while before she had to walk her chalks. Then – word has gone round – 'twill be your cousin, Master Sydney Ward, as comes here – what do you think? Is that like to be so, miss?'

Hatty remembered Sydney saying, 'I'll come in for Bythorn Lodge in the end. And then shan't I laugh! A devilish good base – handy for town, close in among the nobs.' And he had gone on to say, 'I daresay you'd not object, one day, to be back in your old home, Queen of the nest in Bythorn?'

Good gracious! she thought. Suppose I were now, after all, to take Sydney at his word!

For a moment, her fancy toyed with the notion. She tried to imagine Lady Ursula's look of amazement, of horror, at the revelation that she was to be displaced by her disgraced step-daughter.

But no; it would not do. Nothing, no fleeting moment of triumph, could make up for the misery, the tedium, of being obliged to spend the rest of life with Sydney Ward; the prospect was unthinkable.

Hatty braced herself, and went down to the breakfast parlour. There, she found that the conclave of Lady Ursula, Agnes and Mr Norris had already resolved on her future.

'It is, on the whole, a timely and expedient circumstance,' announced Lady Ursula, 'that the Governess, Miss Stornoway, who, for the past five years, has undertaken the guidance and education of my two youngest sisters, Barbara and Drusilla, at the Priors, has, it appears, of late, been almost entirely incapacitated by a tiresome rheumatic disorder, which renders her wholly unfit for her duties. The girls are become quite disgracefully idle and unruly, since Miss Stornoway cannot discipline them as she ought. "Mama!" I have said to the Countess, on I do not know how many occasions, "Mama, you *must* get rid of that woman! The girls are entirely out of hand." "I know, my love, I know," she replies, "but where am I to find a person with the necessary authority to rule them, a person, moreover, who will not object to our remote, secluded situation? Nearly all the applicants are deterred by that aspect of the house." But undoubtedly, for this post, my unfortunate step-daughter will do well enough. She is sufficiently well-connected so that the girls must use her with at least minimal respect. She is young enough so that she may hold the position for as many years as may be needful; and the seclusion of the situation is, in her case, an added benefit, since her scandalous history will not be exposed to public notice. Harriet may therefore take up her duties at once. The life at Underwood is wholly retired, my sisters never go out, they see nobody; visitors do not come to the house; and so this disreputable incident may be forgotten. Among ourselves, of course, word will spread no further – especially since *one* of the protagonists will by now, I trust, have departed abroad.'

Agnes and Mr Norris wagged their heads approvingly. 'But will your lady mother – will the Countess have no objection to the young person?' gravely inquired the latter.

'Not if I myself propound to her the merits of the case. I shall write her a letter. Mama, I shall say, your problems are now at an end. You may feel no further anxiety. Miss Stornoway may be sent packing without more ado. And that will relieve poor Mama of a great deal of inconvenience, for the wretched woman has been eating and drinking at her expense for the last two months, at least, to my knowledge, without doing a hand's turn of work – so there will really be no more to be said. All will be well at Underwood Priors.'

'Underwood Priors?' repeated Hatty doubtfully.

She remembered Lord Camber pointing out the low-lying, irregular old mansion, huddled down half out of sight in its elbow of wooded downland; at the time, happy with her companion in the brilliant sunshine on the hilltop, she had thought: yes, it appears a picturesque and interesting old place, to be sure, but I should certainly not care to live there; it looks so very dark, damp, and secluded.

Perhaps it was her childhood, growing up in that gloomy place, that imbued Lady Ursula with such a sour and carping disposition?

Oh, Lord Camber! What a long time ago – a whole lifetime! – that first carefree walk in the snow seems to me now! And yet it is only three days. And I have the rest of life to live without seeing you again.

'Must I go there? To Underwood Priors?' she said with reluctance.

'Obstinate, ungrateful girl! Certainly you must! And the sooner the better.'

'Ought she not to remain here until after Papa's funeral?' suggested Agnes.

'No. I believe she had better set out as soon as possible. Other people, as well as Mr Ward, may have seen her wandering the hills in the company of Lord Camber. It is best that she do not appear with us in public, especially at the interment. I will despatch a note to my mother asking that a conveyance may be sent for her as soon as possible.'

'Yes, you are right,' agreed Agnes, eyeing her younger sister with disfavour. 'Moreover if she remained here she would require a complete mourning outfit for the funeral. At Underwood a black gown will be sufficient, for, as you say, she will not be going out, she will not require a new pelisse. She appears to have grown a great deal at Portsmouth, much faster than might have been expected.'

By now – in any case – the day was found to be too far advanced for Hatty's immediate transfer; her removal was accordingly fixed for the following morning.

(In fact, with poor Mr Ward lying dead upstairs, there were a great many duties to be discharged, orders to be given, news to be sent out; also, in the mysterious underground fashion of the countryside, tidings of the sudden fatality had percolated from one household to another, so that neighbours now began to come calling to pay their respects to the bereaved family, and must be appropriately entertained.)

In these circumstances Hatty's presence proved quite useful; she was sequestered in her father's business room upstairs (which he had used very little himself) and employed in answering notes of condolence and writing letters to distant relatives who had to be informed of her father's decease. An express was sent off to the family in Portsmouth. Hatty wished she could think that Aunt Polly would be well enough to come to the funeral, but felt sure that she would not. In any case, she herself would be gone to the Priors before the Portsmouth family arrived.

So the day passed, drearily enough.

Jenny brought up a tray of cold meat at about an hour after noon, and Hatty seized the opportunity to ask about her cat Simcox. 'Is he still in the house?'

'Oh, no, miss, he died a while back; he got hurt by a fox and never mended. But miss – Lady Ursula – she has a cat of her own, so it's as well Simcox is not alive; they say two cats in a house never agree.'

'Lady Ursula has a cat?' repeated Hatty, rather surprised.

'Indeed yes, miss, and a nasty disagreeable brute it be; not that it was helped by Master kicking and laming it one time when he'd taken a drop too many. He've been tippling a fair bit, miss, since your lady Mama died.'

'He used to, before, when he was out of humour,' Hatty remembered.

'It got worse, miss. Most nights he'd be fair foxed and Firle would have to put him to bed. And he'd take a flask along when he went out after the hounds. We thought it might ease off when he wed the lady – but it did not at all. She used to go to London, for a night or two, at times, to stay with her Papa – to get away from him, we thought. And that riled the Master.'

Harriet felt a twinge of pity for Lady Ursula. Mr Ward's temper, surly at best, could become violently irritable when clouded by liquor; marriage to him must have been bleak enough, unless he were put in a better humour by the possibility of an heir. And to somebody like Lady Ursula – accustomed, all her life, to her own way, to her own consequence ... Hatty wondered if the unexpectedly sudden death of her husband might not have come to the lady as something of a relief.

But where would Lady Ursula go now? What would she do? Would she return to Underwood Priors? (Heaven forbid!) Had Mr Ward left her a sufficient competence so that she might form an independent establishment somewhere? Hatty suspected that this was unlikely. From various remarks that her uncle Philip had let fall now and then she believed that her father might have been in straits, that his income had diminished even from what it was when the first Mrs Ward was alive.

No doubt all the particulars of Mr Ward's bequests and reversions were well known in the servants' hall, but Hatty felt that it would be undignified to apply for particulars to such a source.

Information she was soon to receive, however, and from an unexpected quarter. The next day she rose early, after a restless night in her own bed, the bed she had once longed for so acutely. Now the bed, the room, the whole house seemed foreign, hostile territory and it was no hardship to re-pack her belongings. Entering the breakfast room she was not particularly surprised to be eyed malevolently and hissed at by a limping, moth-eaten ginger cat who squatted by the meagre fire and stared with pale green eyes.

'That's Lady Ursula's Copper,' said Firle. 'Nasty bad-tempered brute he be. Don't go next or nigh him, Miss Hatty.'

Nobody else was down. Not wishing to be the first at breakfast,

Hatty found an old cloak of her sister Fanny's in the pantry and went out to stroll on the gravel sweep, which was now mostly free from snow. Here she was soon surprised by the arrival of a carriage, which approached at a spanking pace, drew up smartly, and disgorged her cousin Sydney.

'Well I'll be blest! Cousin Hatty! I hardly thought to see you here so soon!'

Sydney appeared in high spirits, and not unfriendly. Hatty supposed there might not have been time for him, in London, to receive news of her expulsion from Lombard Street; he might think she had simply come to Bythorn because of her father's death.

He was even more smartly dressed than when last seen in Portsmouth, with a black band round his arm, and bore, altogether, a very triumphant, satisfied expression. He carried a portfolio of papers.

'So! Cousin Hatty! All has turned out as I foretold. Has it not? And even sooner than my expectations. Here I am, you see, ready to take possession. But I'm not one to bear malice, no, curse me, I ain't! How about it, Cousin Hatty? Will you reconsider what you said to me in my father's house and make me a happy man? Will you be Mrs Sydney?'

'No, Cousin Sydney, I thank you, but I cannot. The answer is still no—' Hatty was beginning, when interrupted by the irate appearance of her sister Agnes, black cap-ribbons twitching and almost standing on end with anger.

'What, *pray*, is the meaning of this, what are you doing, Hatty, to be stepping outside the house against our express instructions – in this uncalled-for manner – putting yourself forward – as if you were not in disgrace?'

Agnes's nature had certainly not been ameliorated by marriage to Mr Norris, Hatty decided. Did she still pine for Daggett the bailiff? Mr Norris seemed a dour and taciturn character, though, to be sure, Hatty was not meeting him under the most favourable circumstances.

'This is our cousin Sydney Ward, Agnes,' she explained pacifically, and, to Sydney, 'My sister Agnes, Mrs Norris—' But her introduction, instead of placating, had the reverse effect.

'Indeed! I suppose, young man, you think you can come to this house, take possession of it, and drive me and poor Lady Ursula out into the fields! With your poor uncle not yet cold on his deathbed!'

'Why yes, Cousin Agnes, I do think that,' he replied coolly. 'Though such is not my immediate intention, I assure you.'

'I should like to know how you got wind of your poor uncle's demise so fast,' snapped Agnes. 'I am sure nobody from *this* household has informed you yet.'

'Oh, we lawyers have our means of exchanging information,' Sydney told her with a self-satisfied smile. 'The attorney in Wanhurst owes me a favour – he sent me an express about the unfortunate accident to my uncle. And I have, as well, some business to transact with Lady Ursula so I thought I would just step down this way and cast an eye, while I was at it, over my uncle's affairs. Which, as his heir and executor, I am fully entitled to do. Killing, you see, two birds with one stone.' And, without waiting permission to do so, he instructed his driver to take the carriage round to the stable-yard.

Red with anger and frustration, Agnes said, 'Well, I suppose you may as well come into the house. I do not suppose I can stop you.'

Breakfast was a thoroughly uncomfortable meal. Sydney ate and drank with good appetite, the two Norrises maintained a hostile silence, Lady Ursula spoke only when necessary. Hatty escaped as soon as she could to her father's business room where she had, yesterday, left a letter to Aunt Winchilsea unfinished. She felt she might as well complete it while waiting for the carriage from Underwood Priors.

Sydney soon afterwards joined her there and began inspecting Mr Ward's papers.

'So, Cousin Hatty, I understand that you are in disgrace all round,' he remarked complacently, running his eye down a column of figures in an account book. 'You were expelled, Mr Norris tells me, from Lombard Street for assisting Ned – the silly fellow – to hold secret trysts with Nancy Price. And now you are in more trouble on account of having passed three nights in Lord Camber's cottage. So you are to be shipped off to Underwood Priors. Very convenient for one and all! You will be shut up there for the rest of your life, working like a slave, for next to no salary, until you succumb to illness and old age, like their last schoolma'am.'

'But,' said Hatty protestingly, 'the girls are in their teens, surely? They will very soon be grown, and no longer need a governess?'

'I doubt that very much, Cousin Hatty; I have heard queer rumours about the two youngest girls at the Priors – they are maniacs, or malefactors, or unteachable, or all three. I wish you joy of them. You may soon be sorry, very sorry indeed, that you did not accept my offer. There is still time to change your mind!' Sydney said.

'I thank you, Cousin, but my answer remains the same.'

A shabby carriage soon after drew up outside the house, and Hatty with relief went downstairs. She found Lady Ursula curtly instructing the driver; her luggage had already been loaded.

'You may inform my mother, the Countess, that I shall come over to see her in due course. And pray give her this letter.'

Hatty took the letter, wondering why neither the Countess nor the Earl were to be expected at their son-in-law's funeral. Perhaps they had not approved of the marriage?

Lady Ursula nodded brusquely and retired indoors; neither Agnes nor her husband had appeared to say goodbye.

Just before Hatty stepped into the carriage, a small boy came running along the driveway, clutching a letter in his grubby hand.

''Tis for Miss Hatty Ward,' he panted, and thrust the crumpled missive at her.

'Thank you, my love.' Hatty gave him a threepenny piece.

'Too much for the likes of him,' said the driver, eyeing this transaction with disapproval. 'A ha'penny would have been sufficient. Step in quick, now, miss, for I'm to call at Elstow End on the way back and pick up a load of tallow.'

And he whipped up his horses the moment Hatty was seated, and drove off at such a vigorous pace that the carriage rocked from side to side and there was no possibility of reading her letter; she tucked it into her reticule for later perusal.

The approach-road to Underwood Priors – after the tallow had been taken on board – was long, narrow and melancholy. The ill-kept rutted track made the driver at least abate his pace, but still the carriage was thrown from side to side by the bumps and puddles all along the way. The woods here were very badly maintained also, Hatty noticed; the trees had been allowed to grow tall and spindly, their half-dead boughs weighed down and netted over with trails of ivy, wild clematis, and mistletoe. A grove of acacia trees enclosed the house, crowding in to the very verge of the moss-covered carriage sweep; and these, too, were so heavily clustered over with mistletoe that they appeared to be still green, though it was midwinter. The bricks of the ancient mansion were dark with damp and veined over with moss, and the roof tiles were covered by lichen, so that the house, Hatty thought, resembled nothing man-made, but seemed like some natural growth, a fungus or a toadstool, which had sprung up from the damp ground.

Hatty shivered as she stepped from the carriage, noticing that the house lay in shadow, though the hour approached noon. She remembered Camber saying: 'For three months in the winter they receive no sun, for they are at the foot of a north-facing slope. The monks who first built there set more value on the purity of the spring, and the watercress beds, than they did on winter sunshine.'

An elderly manservant emerged from the main entrance and received Hatty soberly. She handed him Lady Ursula's missive to her mother, and was shown into a waiting-room at one side of the main hall. The hall itself was a damp, shadowy tunnel, with antlers sprouting all over the walls, leading to a shallow stairway. The waiting-room, barely lit by a tiny greenish window, was a dim and fireless little cell. Pulling out the note the boy had handed her, Hatty saw there would be no possibility of reading it here. She sat down on a straight-backed chair and resigned herself to wait. This is an uncommonly silent house, she thought. What a contrast to my arrival at Lord Camber's cottage – or even to my father's house, for that matter! There, all had been bustle and exclamation; here, not a sound could be heard. No voice, no step. But then she recalled the large, rambling nature of the building. The inhabitants may be two hundred yards distant, across a courtyard, in another wing.

Now, however, she thought she did hear cautious whispers outside the door. Another moment's listening convinced her.

'What shall we do?' Hatty thought she heard, 'what shall we do about the other?'

'Throw her to the wolves!'

'Glastonbury says—'

'Hush!'

There was a rustle, and a scuffle, then silence again. Hatty was sorely tempted to step towards the half-closed door and snatch it open, but felt this would be derogatory to the dignity of her new role as governess. She waited for another seven minutes, amid renewed silence, then the manservant reappeared.

'You are to walk this way, if you please, miss,' he said, eyeing her with gloomy curiosity, and he preceded her up the flight of broad, shallow stairs at the rear end of the hall. The stairs curved around and arrived at an upper landing with cedar-panelled walls and a number of doors leading from it, all closed. Light came from a large but small-paned window over the stair, and from a few candle-sconces on the walls. The servant tapped on one of the doors and was admitted.

'You may go, Glastonbury,' said a harsh voice from within. 'Young woman! Come in, walk across the room, and stand *there*, where I may see you.'

The servant bowed and retired. Hatty stepped to the designated spot, where she stood, interestedly observing her new employer, who lay reclined on a *chaise-longue*, wrapped and swathed around in a number of shawls. This room was quite well-lit by a number of wall candles and several lamps placed about on tables.

'I am the Countess of Elstow,' said that lady, 'and you, I understand, are Miss Harriet Ward.'

Hatty curtseyed in silence.

The Countess, under her shawls, appeared to be a tall and massive woman. On her head she wore an imposing lace turban, wound with a dark-green velvet ribbon, fastened beneath the chin by muslin lappets, and topped by a magnificent, but dirty, emerald brooch. The turban was raised on the left-hand side to expose one of the lady's ears. On a small table by the *chaise-longue* lay a silver ear-trumpet and a well-worn pack of cards.

This is Lady Ursula's mother, remembered Hatty, and she studied the lady for signs of family likeness.

There were not many. Lady Elstow's face was larger than her daughter's flat one, and extremely high-coloured, especially over the cheekbones. Her nose was fleshy and prominent, her mouth a thin, straight line, almost lipless.

Her voice – the loud, toneless voice of somebody who has been deaf for many years – bore no trace of feeling in it as she said, 'Your first duty as my daughters' governess will be to get rid of your predecessor. Tell Miss Stornoway that she has to go, as soon as possible. You look like an active, capable young woman. See to that, at once, and then I will instruct you in your further duties.'

'But, ma'am—'

'Speak up, speak up when you address me! One thing you must understand *immediately*, Miss Ward, is that, so long as you are employed by me, you must neither argue, ask questions, nor raise difficulties. Just do as you are told. Ring the bell, now, for Glastonbury.'

Thoroughly startled, Hatty did so. The manservant reappeared with a celerity that suggested he had been only a short distance outside the closed door.

'Take Miss Ward to Miss Stornoway,' ordered the Countess. 'Then bring Lady Barbara and Lady Drusilla here.'

'Yes, my Lady.'

When they were safely out of earshot, and ascending another, narrower stair, Glastonbury said, 'I'll take you to the young ladies' schoolroom first, miss, and then I'll fetch Miss Stornoway.'

'Glastonbury!' Hatty stopped on the top step and turned to face him. 'What did Lady Elstow *mean*, get rid of your predecessor? That was what she told me to do. Am I to dismiss her?'

'I'm afraid, miss, she meant just what she said. You are to tell the young ladies' previous instructress to go. Her Ladyship always gets somebody else to perform that kind of task.'

'I am to tell the poor woman that she is dismissed?'

'Yes, miss.'

'But where will she go?'

'That is not for me to say, miss.' But he looked very troubled.

'But what about – what about her wages?'

'I understand that her Ladyship considers that none are owing – due to Miss Stornoway's incapacity during the last two months.'

'Good God! – Does she have friends – family – somewhere within reach?'

'No, miss. Miss Stornoway comes from Scotland. I understand she has no living connections.'

'You mean – she may have to go to the workhouse?'

'It is to be hoped, miss, that the lady has some savings.' But Glastonbury's anxious look remained. A bell pealed imperiously behind him, and he added in haste, 'Excuse me, miss. I will leave you in here. The fire is not bad. I daresay Miss Stornoway will be along very soon. And I will carry you up a nuncheon, later, and see that your boxes are taken to your sleeping apartment. Excuse me—' he said again, and was gone, leaving Hatty just inside the door of a large, bare, battered chamber which she had no difficulty in recognizing as the schoolroom. A deal table, cut, scarred and ink-stained, bore the signs of many years' misuse; piles of tattered books lay on unpainted shelves; the keys of an unimposing pianoforte were brown with age, and a harp in a corner had several broken strings; some tattered maps and a few bad watercolours were pinned to the walls. It was easy to guess that no studies had been carried on in this room for a number of weeks. A small handful of fire burned in the grate. A large, but small-paned window looked out over a wide stable-yard.

At least, reflected Hatty, stepping nearer to the window, at least it is a little lighter in here; and at last she was able to pull out her note and read it: 'My dear Miss Hatty,' it said, in Lord Camber's black, untidy, distinctive handwriting,

I have been considering your future, not, I must confess, without a good deal of anxiety. I know your wish to become a poet, and I think it is a valid one. But the pursuit of poetry requires, I am sure, a calm and trouble-free environment, and I cannot be satisfied in my own mind that this is what you will find in your father's household – or in any employment as a teacher.

Should you at any time wish for a peaceful and solitary refuge, I therefore invite you to make use of the Thatched Grotto – from today it is yours to command, and I have left instructions with Godwit and the rest of the household to receive you (and of course any friends you may care to invite) whenever you like to find shelter there. Feel free to take advantage of this offer at any time! I shall like to think of you and your Muse under its roof. And my odd little household will be truly happy to welcome you back.

    Yours very sincerely,
    Camber.

Then there was a post-scriptum which, unfortunately, had come just where the paper folded and, on account of the fold, because the ink had run, and because some dirt from the hand of the boy who brought it had rubbed in, was almost wholly illegible. 'To make all square I xxxxx xxxxx xxxx' and some words that might have been 'Turtle Doves' 'Thistledown' 'Tidal Waves' . . .

It was no use. Hatty could not decipher the last lines. But the rest of the message warmed her to such a degree of happiness that she stood clasping the paper against her heart, smiling out at the pigeons who pecked about on the cobbles, even, for a single instant, forgetting the horrible task that lay ahead of her.

A slight sound behind her was enough to break the spell. She turned, and saw a lady in the doorway supported on two sticks.

Miss Stornoway had once been tall, but was now so bowed, so bent over, so crumpled and twisted that she seemed like an aged, wind-contorted tree. Thin hands, knotted and gnarled with arthritis, clasped the handles of the sticks. Wispy grey hair, only half-controlled by a worn velvet ribbon, surmounted a pale face from which two greenish-brown eyes gazed fearfully at Hatty.

'Miss Stornoway? I – I am Hatty Ward – I do not know how to begin – I do not know if anybody has said anything to you?'

Hatty felt desperately awkward and guilty; there was no possible means of sweetening what she was obliged to say. But to her surprised relief the thin, defeated creature before her accepted the situation with great dignity.

'Och, my dear, ye need not be embarrassed. I am fully aware of what ye have been instructed to say. Ye need make no bones about it. I am tae take my marching orders. My only wee bit problem is – *where* shall I march to? *That* is the question! Where shall a poor useless discharged person take her auld body? And that, I may tell you, is a problem indeed!'

'You have no money? No friends?'

'Not a soul, not a shilling in this world, my dear. The wage, ye ket paid by her Ladyship is remarkably small – and every penny of that has been disbursed on warm clothes and a wee supply of extra nourishment, tae keep body and soul together.'

Miss Stornoway was, indeed, wrapped in a mass of thick garments and woollen shawls. Good heavens, thought Hatty, to what sort of a place have I come?

She said with great diffidence: 'Miss Stornoway I I hope you will not be offended at this – but I have just received a kind of invitation – to stay in somebody's cottage; I don't know if – I daresay you may have heard of Lord Camber the Duke's son?'

'Och, yes, Lord Camber's name is not unknown – he will be the first cousin of my charges – my ex-charges, your future pupils, Miss Ward.'

'Yes, that is it – it happens that I – I have become somewhat acquainted with Lord Camber – my uncle, in whose house I have been living, was his attorney – Lord Camber has now gone to America but he was so good as to write me this letter, inviting me to stay, to live in his cottage – perhaps you know where that is, not too far, I think, from here?'

Miss Stornoway nodded.

'Och yes, I have heard tell of Lord Camber and his radical views and how he preferred to live in a simple manner, like the poor and needy. And he has offered you the use of his wee house in Wanmaulden

Wood? That sounds exactly like his Lordship's benevolence! But, my dear, would ye not wish to take advantage of the offer yourself?'

'I am not sure about that,' said Hatty, surprising herself. She clasped Lord Camber's letter between her hands like a talisman. 'I – I think not yet, not immediately. I think it might – it might be rather cowardly to run away from the world at my very first exposure to it.'

'Hech, my lassie, I can see that ye have in ye the spirit of a crusader! (And I am afeared ye will need every morsel of it in dealing with Lady Drusilla and Lady Barbara.) But are ye certain that ye can make such use of Lord Camber's offer, on behalf of a chance-met acquaintance such as maself? It is most remarkably generous.'

'No, *that* I am quite sure of,' said Hatty roundly. 'Lord Camber's generosity extends to anybody in – in trouble. And his household – Mrs Daizley the housekeeper, Mr Godwit and his old grandmother – they are the kindest people imaginable. I am sure they will make you welcome.'

Despite these words, she did feel a slight qualm; *was* she making outrageously free with Lord Camber's kind offer? Was she loading the three adults in the Thatched Grotto with a wholly unjustified responsibility? But then she felt she heard Camber's voice saying, No, no, of course you must do it, my dear Miss Hatty! Indeed what else could you possibly do?

'The only difficulty that I can see,' she went on, 'is how to transport you to the cottage.'

'Och, as tae that – I've a notion – ' a wintry smile overspread Miss Stornoway's harassed countenance – 'I've a notion that Glastonbury may render me some assistance there … he's no' a bad soul, poor fellow; in the past I have written some letters for him relating to a cousin of his who was transported for poaching … I think he will contrive my removal.'

'Oh, well, in that case … Can I help you with your packing, Miss Stornoway?'

'Och, ye are a fine, kind lassie! But Hannah the housemaid will do that – she's no sae dreich as some o' the others. And ye had best get back to her Ladyship and your charges – now ye have performed the first difficult task!' Again the wintry smile. 'But a word of warning in your ear, my dear – these gairls are adversaries that ye will need all yer strength and all yer wits tae contend with! I can see that, fortunately, ye possess both strength and wit. And ye will require them both. I came tae the task too auld and infirm – they defeated me. But you are young – ye may prevail. Do not make the mistake of thinking Drusilla the weaker – of the two she has the more guile—'

A bell had been sounding impatiently while Miss Stornoway said this, and now Glastonbury appeared again.

'Her Ladyship is asking for you, Miss Ward. Will you be so good as to come with me.'

He had scanned Miss Stornoway with a doubtful expression, but what he saw appeared to reassure him.

'I am going to my room now, Glastonbury,' she said. 'I will see you there.'

'Yes, miss. I will be with you as soon as I can, Miss Stornoway.'

'Goodbye, my dear.' To Hatty's surprise, Miss Stornoway planted an awkward, glancing kiss on her cheek. 'I wish ye all the good luck in the world. And I fear ye will need it!'

XI

BACK IN LADY ELSTOW's room, Hatty saw that two girls had arrived and were sitting on a sopha in attitudes of exaggerated indifference at some distance from their mother. Hatty would have liked to study them, but her attention was claimed by the Countess who demanded at once: 'Well? Did you give that dismal woman her marching orders? Have you sent her to the rightabout?'

'Miss Stornoway understands, ma'am, that she is to leave your employment,' Hatty said loudly and coldly.

'You made sure she knew that she is to go today – without loss of time?'

Hatty merely bowed her head. The Countess studied her sharply through a lorgnette.

'Very well. Now, these are my daughters, the Lady Barbara and the Lady Drusilla. Come here, girls.'

With seeming reluctance the girls slowly approached. Lady Elstow eyed them with a total lack of enthusiasm.

'Well, girls, this is your new preceptress, Miss Ward. She is the step-daughter of your sister Ursula. And her mother was a Wisbech. Bear that in mind.'

The girls curtsied stiffly and favoured Hatty with a cool appraisal which she, now that she had licence to do so, returned with considerable interest. Lady Ursula's two youngest sisters were of very different heights and complexions. Barbara, aged perhaps fifteen or sixteen, was tall and massive, resembling her mother in build. She had a shock of untamed frizzy black hair, thick wrists and ankles, a large, not unhandsome face with a rough skin, bright complexion, alert dark eyes, a wide mouth and an expression of sullen ferocity. Drusilla, the younger, was completely different in build: much smaller, with spindly limbs, a pale skin, thin protruding lips and bulging ophthalmic, brilliant, positively glittering blue eyes. Blond hair draggled forward over her forehead in a sparse fringe and was gathered behind her head into a knot. Both girls were untidily dressed in ill-fitting clothes that did not suit them. Drusilla – perhaps about twelve, Hatty thought – eyed her new governess with less absolute hostility than did her sister, but with a look of cool contempt. Barbara's baleful stare was made even more belligerent and sinister, Hatty realized, because the poor girl suffered from a severe cast in her left eye; while one eye was fixed on her new governess, the other one stared off into a distant corner of the room as if it were focussed on some subversive concern of its own.

'You may leave me now,' said Lady Elstow impatiently. 'Be gone! Glastonbury – ' for he had remained by the door – 'bring me my egg-nog.'

'Yes, my Lady.'

'At once.'

'Yes, my Lady.'

The two girls left the room without troubling to look round and see if Hatty followed them. She did so, feeling all the awkwardness of her situation. To her relief they went to the schoolroom, where they stood on either side of the meagre fire, eyeing her in a combative manner.

'Well!' said Barbara. 'What are you going to teach us?'

'Yes!' echoed her younger sister. 'What are you going to teach us?'

Drusilla had, Hatty noticed, a slight impediment in her speech; not exactly a lisp, but a kind of hesitation. Her eyes were really extraordinary: so brilliantly blue, they ought to have been beautiful, but they seemed like the eyes of some bird, lacking in any warmth or recognizable human expression.

'What did Miss Stornoway teach you?' Hatty countered.

'Oh – sad stuff! The principal rivers in Russia and the dates of the kings of England with the principal events of their reigns and the Roman Emperors . . .'

'As low as Severus . . .'

'And the Heathen Mythology . . .'

'And all the metals, semi-metals, planets and distinguished philosophers.'

'A well-educated pair of young ladies,' remarked Hatty calmly.

They stared at her in astonishment.

'Was that intended as a joke?' demanded Barbara. She had a harsh, carrying voice, very like that of her mother.

'Not at all. I merely wondered how such a random assortment of information would be likely to help you through life.'

'My good Miss Ward,' said Barbara coldly, 'we need no help of that kind. We are to have no life. We shall remain in this house until, in our nineties, we die the death of desiccated spinsters.'

Hatty did not ask why this should be so. She could see that marriage, the only escape for either of these girls, was hardly to be considered as an option, secluded as they lived, and that with their disabilities, they had no such hope. Even the prospect of earning their own living was denied them; the daughters of an earl could not seek employment.

Although they were looking at her with a dislike that almost amounted to enmity, she bore no particular ill-feeling towards them, but only considerable pity.

'You could not go and live with your married sisters?' she suggested. 'Lady Mary? Lady Anne?'

'Hah!' A single derisive syllable disposed of that possibility.

Hatty stared about the comfortless room. Had Miss Stornoway already packed up her belongings, had Glastonbury arranged for a conveyance to take her to Lord Camber's house? What, she wondered, would Lord Camber prescribe for *this* doleful pair? She thought longingly of Camber's small establishment with all its resources of literature, philosophy, music and outdoor pursuits.

Walking over to the piano, Hatty ran her hand down its keys. They were disgracefully out of tune. 'First of all this must be put in order,' she said. 'And the harp mended.'

'A man from Bedford has to do that,' said Drusilla, as if that put it out of the question.

'Then he must be sent for. I can tune the piano.'

'*You* can?' Barbara demanded in a tone of flat disbelief.

'I am lucky enough to possess absolute pitch. Then – has this house a library?'

'Yes, there is Papa's library.'

'Is he here now? Does he object to your using it?'

'*Papa?*' The girls bestowed scornful smiles on their new governess. 'Papa is not in the house. He is hardly *ever* here. He is in London, at the house in Grosvenor Place.'

'With his friends,' added Barbara in a sour undertone.

Hatty chose to ignore this.

'Then he will not object if we make use of his books?'

'I – I suppose not,' said Barbara doubtfully. 'Very likely he will never know.'

'Let us go there directly. I can see there is nothing useful in this room.'

The two girls looked at one another, scowling and wary. They were not natural allies, or even particularly fond of each other, Hatty could see at a glance; only force of circumstances obliged them to side together against a common enemy.

Indeed as they took their way downstairs, with Barbara striding ahead, Drusilla, sidling along close to Hatty in the wide hallway at the stairhead, murmured, in her shrill, faulty voice, 'You will have to keep a careful watch on my sister Barbara, Miss Ward! She will do you any harm she can – tell lies, report on your conduct to Mama, put you in a false position—'

'Indeed?' said Hatty, startled out of caution. 'Why should she do that?'

'Why? It is her nature. Like the scorpion that stung the horse. She enjoys making trouble. She likes to make people enemies to one another. Like our sister Ursula.'

Hatty was surprised at the spite with which these words were poured out by the blue-eyed angelic-looking little creature at her side.

When they reached the library, a long, dank, unheated chamber on the ground floor, its windows overlooking a dense untrimmed shrubbery, Drusilla danced off into the gloom, exclaiming, 'Wait there! I will ring for Hathill to bring more candles.' She tugged a bell rope at the far end of the room.

Barbara stood still until Hatty was near her, and then said sharply, 'Do not place too much belief in anything that my sister Drusilla tells you, Miss Ward! She is quite lacking in any moral sense.'

Before Hatty could make any response, Drusilla came skipping back, chirping, 'Hathill will attend to the lights. He was my sister's very first love, Miss Ward! He is quite her ideal of manly beauty. Just wait until you see him!'

'Behave yourself!' Lady Barbara hissed at her younger sister.

A snub-nosed, fair-haired footman came along the room, cast a startled look at Hatty, and began lighting the wall sconces. He was not particularly handsome, and Barbara showed not the least interest in him. Either she was an excellent actress, or her juvenile partiality had long since died away. Or, her younger sister was a troublemaker. Hatty decided to reserve her judgement on these questions. Meanwhile she told the footman to kindle a fire.

'A fire? In here, miss?' he said, astonished.

'Yes! At once, if you please. It is as cold as a barn in this room,' Hatty replied absently, casting a covetous eye over the tooled and gilt leather-bound contents of the shelves which ran all along the rear wall of the room facing the windows, with added bays here and there. Molière, she saw, Racine, Plato, Aristophanes, Sophocles, Shakespeare, Jonson, Dryden, Pope, Virgil, Catullus ... There would be enough here to keep the girls occupied for many a day. And herself as well.

'Mama wishes us to study Italian,' Barbara informed her. 'Miss Stornoway could not teach it for she did not speak it.'

'No more do I,' Hatty remarked. 'Do you think your Mama will send me packing on that account? We shall have to find Dante, or some Italian poetry, and read it with a translation alongside. I can offer Greek, Latin and French, however.'

Barbara seemed a trifle nonplussed.

'Oh,' she said blankly. 'Latin and Greek. What use would they be to us?'

'Some very entertaining stories are written in those languages,' suggested Hatty, wondering what use it was to learn lists of Roman Emperors and Heathen myths while remaining in a state of complete ignorance about their lives and contents. She glanced longingly at the volumes of poetry: Crabbe's *The Village*, Collins, Goldsmith, she saw and promised herself a later visit to the library in her free time, if she was allowed free time in this strange household. Many of the volumes on the shelves showed signs of damp, decay and old age, but new ones had been added here and there, and the books were ranged in an orderly manner.

'Have you a librarian?' she asked.

'There was Cousin Septimus Wisbech, but he died last year. As Papa spends most of his time in town he has not troubled to provide a replacement.'

'So you do not think he will object to our using the books?'

'Oh, la, no! Why should he?' Barbara said disdainfully.

'What books did you read with Miss Stornoway?' Hatty wished

there had been time to consult and compare with that lady. She picked out a volume of *The Idler*. 'Did she ever read you these pieces?'

'I do not recall.' Barbara peered at the volume distastefully.

'Well, you sit here at this table – it is quite warm now that the fire has burned up – and make a list of any familiar titles you find.'

'And if there are none?'

'Then put down any ideas that may occur to you arising from the text.'

'The ink here is all dried up.'

'Then use a pencil.'

Drusilla, during this exchange, was eyeing Hatty with the horrified fascination shown by a wild animal which sees a trainer approaching with whip and club. You cannot do anything like this to me! said her expression. Hatty had found on the shelf handsomely illustrated collections of Aesop's *Fables* and those of La Fontaine. She opened Aesop at the fable of the fox and the grapes.

'Here,' she said to Drusilla. 'Let me hear how well you can read that tale. It is not very long. And then you can copy the picture of the fox looking up at that tempting bunch of grapes.'

Drusilla gaped vacantly at Hatty, then at the page. She remained completely silent and motionless.

'You don't like that one? Well, then, here is another: here it is, also, in French with the fox and the crow. "Maitre Corbeau, sur un arbre perché" Did Miss Stornoway never read it to you?'

Barbara, on the other side of the table, had made no attempt to perform the task set her, but was watching the scene with ironic brows raised. Now she shrugged and said, 'You'll get no good of my sister that way, Miss Ward. She does not read, so she is incapable of learning by rote.'

'*She does not read?* At her age?'

'No, she has never been able to do so. Nobody has managed to teach her. You will be quite wasting your time, I promise you.'

Good heavens, thought Hatty. Why, even the *twins* ... But that path of memory was too painful, so she said instead: 'Well, can you draw me a picture, Drusilla? Draw me the crow with the lump of cheese in his beak.'

Even such a simple task appeared beyond Drusilla's capacity. Furnished with a sheet of paper and a pencil, she scratched a few random lines, some of which met, it seemed accidentally, in a rough triangle.

'Is that the crow? Very well, black it in with your pencil.'

The child began to do so, slowly and reluctantly; then, becoming impatient, crumpled the paper into a ball, and threw it into the fire. The sight of the burning paper pleased her; she would have proceeded to burn all the rest of the sheets had not Hatty removed them out of reach.

'Listen, then, I will read you the story of the crow and the fox.'

But, as she read aloud to the frowning Drusilla, Hatty's heart sank; how was she ever going to find ways of filling this vacancy? Now she remembered her cousin Sydney saying, 'They are maniacs, or malefactors or something; I wish you joy of them.'

'Did Miss Stornoway teach you French?' she asked Barbara.

'Yes, she read us history in French. *La Guerre des Deux Roses*. We had just got as far as the murder of the Princes in the Tower.'

'Oh. Well, I shall see if I cannot find something more entertaining from these shelves while you finish the task I have set you.'

Scowling, Barbara looked down at *The Idler*, and her blank paper.

Hatty strolled away from the sisters, partly to give herself a moment's respite, at a distance, from the miasma they exuded: hostility, resentment and lack of the least intention to cooperate. At the end of the library clusters of sconces dangled on each side of a large picture. As she came closer, Hatty saw that it was a portrait of two people standing under a tree in a garden. She began to think that the pair looked familiar – then, standing below the canvas, attentively studying it, she felt almost certain that she knew them. But so young, so beautiful! Radiant, confident, they laughed out of the summery, flowery landscape into a future that must have seemed as idyllic as the verdure that surrounded them.

Returning to the sisters, who sat each doing nothing, gazing at vacancy, one at the table, one on a stool by the hearth, Hatty asked, 'Of whom is that portrait at the far end of the room – the two people under the tree?'

'Why,' said Barbara, yawning, 'it is our sister Ursula and our cousin Harry Camber. It was done years ago by a painter that Papa thought well of at the time. Ursula and Harry were great friends then. He would often ride over here from Bythorn Chase. They were going to marry. But then they had a quarrel, so Harry stopped coming.'

'*I* remember the quarrel,' said Drusilla, lifting her intense blue eyes from the paper she was mechanically tearing to shreds. 'It was about us.'

'*You?* You could not possibly remember. You were only an infant.'

'I remember,' Drusilla said with a fey chuckle. 'Harry made Ursula promise to stay and look after us. She did not wish to, but he made her, and in the end she promised.'

'Oh, what nonsense! The quarrel was about something quite different.'

'Whatever it was,' Hatty pronounced, 'it was their own affair and no possible business of ours. I think we should now return to the schoolroom. I have picked out some books to read with you, and I have found some of Dante's poetry with an English translation, so that should satisfy your Mama's wish for you to study Italian.'

Barbara made a grimace. 'Must we move? Just when it was growing quite warm and pleasant here? *I* think we should ask Mama if we may study in the library.'

'By all means, if you wish to. But for now, since we don't have permission, let us return upstairs and I will tune the piano.'

Privately, she was anxious to remove Drusilla, who had now helped herself to a whole quire of paper, from close proximity to the fire. But at the magic word *piano* the latter jumped up, scattering paper like confetti.

'Oh, yes! You will play us a tune and we shall dance and sing. Come, Barbara!'

Hatty followed the sisters, thinking with something like anguish of that pair of lovers, so young, so hopeful, so radiant, so lost.

173

How could he ever pay any heed to *me* when he has a memory like that in his heart?

Following the girls along the damp dim passages and up the creaking stair, she wondered about the child Drusilla. Plainly there was something radically amiss with the girl's learning capacity and yet in conversation she seemed normal and quick-witted enough – indeed rather unusually so for her age. And though several of her remarks were of a spiteful nature, there was something undeniably taking about her pale-skinned, little, lively pointed face with the prominent lips and those remarkable eyes.

Barbara too, though she was very evidently bent on resistance and antagonism to her new teacher at every turn, seemed not wholly dislikeable; and although almost entirely deficient in a sense of humour, Hatty imagined that she could be genial enough if she so chose; the lack of humour no doubt was inherited from her mother who appeared utterly devoid of any such attribute.

What kind of person could the girls' father be?

After forty minutes spent wrestling with the schoolroom piano, Hatty pronounced it tolerably fit for service. Meanwhile she had taken unobtrusive note of the sisters' occupations during this period of time: Barbara hunched herself in silence over a little notebook in which she occasionally jotted down a word or two; perhaps she kept a journal? Drusilla, to Hatty's great surprise, squatted on the floor close to the piano stool, following and listening to Hatty's scales and shifts and modulations with what seemed the keenest, most breathless attention. When Hatty finally said, 'There! That is the best that can be done with it. One note is dumb entirely, but by good luck it is a high register and will not be required a great deal,' Drusilla jumped to her feet and said, 'Now let *me* play!'

'Certainly, if you wish.'

To Hatty's great astonishment Drusilla sat down on the piano stool and plunged into a medley of airs and harmonics: Hatty recognized melodies from Gluck, Arne, and Purcell, besides ballad themes, Christmas carols and hymn tunes. The child seemed to have an inexhaustible memory for musical themes and a natural gift for harmonizing them. Hatty heard passages from Haydn piano sonatas, all jumbled up with chants from religious services and popular songs from street and meadow.

'Who taught you this?' she asked when Drusilla came to a stop and looked up at her, for once with a smile of pure delight. 'Did Miss Stornoway?'

'Oh, *no*! Miss Stornoway could not play at all. My sisters Mary and Anne had a teacher, when they lived at home. I used to listen to them. They learned the harp too.'

'Well, we must have that mended. Perhaps you should play the fiddle as well.'

Drusilla nodded, as if this was only her right.

'Can you read music?' Hatty pulled down a set of simple exercises from the tattered heap of manuscripts on top of the piano. But Drusilla looked at the staves, minims, and crotchets with blank incomprehension.

'Music in my head,' she said.

Then she flung herself down on the worn rug and went instantly to sleep.

'Should we not lift her up and put her to bed?' Hatty said, disconcerted.

Barbara shrugged.

'She will be well enough there. Very often she goes off like that, quite suddenly, after she has tired herself out with music.'

'Her music is remarkable.'

Another shrug from Barbara.

'It is of no *use*, however. She will never be able to learn to read music, or remember a piece right through correctly. As she said – it is all in her head.'

'Has no one ever really taken pains to teach her reading and writing?'

'I tell you, it is a waste of effort. She cannot learn. She is incapable.'

We'll see about *that*, Hatty thought militantly, but from Barbara's look of derision she could see the girl guessed what was in her mind.

'You will only be throwing away your time, Miss Ward. As you will in teaching me to speak Italian or read French plays.' Impatiently Barbara pushed aside the *Purgatorio* and plays of Molière which Hatty had brought from the library. 'We do not *want* to be done good to. We do not want to be improved. Who in the world will care one jot if we speak with superior French accents or can translate Italian arias? Where did any of her education take my sister Ursula? She had to marry your father! Now she will very likely have to come back here again.'

Barbara gave Hatty a shrewd, penetrating look out of her dark eyes, and said, 'You have sisters, have you not, Miss Ward?'

'Why yes – three,' said Hatty, rather surprised. 'Agnes, Maria and Fanny.'

'And which of them do you love best?'

Caught off her guard, Hatty hesitated before replying. Barbara laughed – a sardonic chuckle.

'I see how it is. You do not really love any of them.'

'We were all so different. And they were a great deal older than I,' Hatty defended herself. 'The person I really loved was my mother. But she died.'

'You were lucky,' Barbara said flatly. 'You were lucky to have that one person at least. *Nobody* could love Mama – as I daresay you have discovered. That is why my father interests himself elsewhere. While there might still be some faint hope of a male heir he made a pretence of devotion but once that was past, enough! And he will not take Mama to London any more – he says she is too deaf. And too disagreeable.'

'Barbara, you really should not be telling me these things! They are not at all a proper subject of conversation for Lord Elstow's daughter – or from a young lady to her governess.'

'Oh, stuff! What difference can it make? And you are hardly a proper governess. Why, I do not suppose you are much older than I.'

'No,' said Hatty firmly, 'but I am far better educated. And I have a greater knowledge of the world and society.'

'Fine words! Just because you have lived in an attorney's house in

Portsmouth and attended dancing classes, you need not assume grand airs.'

'Your cousin Lord Camber was not too proud to pay frequent visits to my uncle's house in Portsmouth,' Hatty could not help retorting. 'And his conversation was always very delightful and instructive.'

Barbara eyed her even more narrowly.

'Ah. I see how it is. You have fallen in love with Harry Camber. Many do. Even when he was betrothed to my sister Ursula there were a dozen young ladies in London all dying for love of him. And so it has been ever since. Very queer, when you consider how plain he is. My sister Mary was off her head in love with him before she married Finster; and Ursula, of course, never recovered from the blow of losing him. Look at her now!'

'Barbara you really *must* not speak so.'

'Why? Because Harry Camber is thought to be a saint? If you ask *me*,' said Barbara forthrightly, 'saints do far more harm in the world than ordinary wicked people. Their expectations are too high, nobody can come up to them, everybody feels guilty who has anything to do with them, and they waste themselves in preposterous schemes like this one of my cousin Camber – going off to found some idealistic society on the banks of some swampy river in America. What use is *that*, I ask you? It will last three years, a lot of money will have been spent, some people will probably die – and for what? It is all balderdash!'

Hatty said: 'This scheme in itself may fail. But all such efforts add to the sum of human progress. In a hundred years' time, perhaps, some future society may profit by learning from the experiences of your cousin's design. His name may be remembered, along with that of Sir Thomas More and Francis Bacon.'

'Who, pray, are *they*?'

'Both wrote fables about imaginary societies. Thomas More about a place called Utopia, Bacon about an island called Bensalem. Both men were imprisoned in the Tower of London,' Hatty added.

'Oh. Why?'

'Bacon, I think, for bribery. Thomas More because he would not approve Henry the Eighth's divorce from Queen Catherine. He had his head cut off, though Bacon was let off with a caution. Your cousin may think himself lucky that he lives in quieter times. People's heads are not cut off so often nowadays.'

'Henry the Eighth? Was he the one with six wives?'

'Yes, and the Field of the Cloth of Gold. Sir Thomas More was present on that occasion.'

'I never heard of it,' said Barbara dismissively. 'We did not get as far as Henry the Eighth – we stopped at Henry the Seventh.' After a moment she added, as if in spite of herself, 'Was it really a whole field covered with a cloth of gold?'

'I'll tell you about it some time,' said Hatty. 'What does that bell ring for?'

'Oh, that is to let us know that our cold meat is served downstairs.'

'Should we not wake Drusilla?'

'No. She seldom eats anything but fruit. And not much of that. She may as well go on sleeping.'

Hatty was decidedly relieved to discover that the light repast of cold meat, very welcome after her chilly drive and long, difficult morning, was not consumed in the company of the Countess. She, it seemed, kept to her own apartments for the greater part of the day.

'Mama is very lame,' Barbara explained, 'and finds coming downstairs too fatiguing, when there is no company but us. I suppose she may do so again if Ursula returns home. But I hope not. They do nothing but fight. Mama has always detested Ursula, and, after the business of Harry Camber and Francis Fordingbridge – losing two husbands at a stroke – of course it grew much worse.' She stuffed her mouth inelegantly full of cold mutton.

'Tell me,' said Hatty, in a determined effort to lead the talk away from Harry Camber, 'is that a portrait of your parents over the mantel?'

'Yes; but executed long before I was born.'

Like Lord Camber and Lady Ursula in the library, this couple were young and elegantly dressed, though in clothes long since out of fashion, the lady with hoop skirts and a high wig, the gentleman in a long-skirted embroidered coat and buckled shoes. She was recognizably

Lady Elstow, he had a long face, protruding teeth, a prominent nose, and slightly receding chin. He was taller than his lady, so must be very tall indeed, thought Hatty, and, like her, stared off into the distance with a look of extreme boredom and distaste for his surroundings.

'I always go riding on horseback at this time of day,' announced Barbara, abruptly leaving the table and starting towards the door of the small dining-parlour where they had eaten. 'You, I presume, will wish to renew your labours with my sister. I wish you joy of her.'

And she vanished round the door.

But Hatty asked the footman who waited at the meal to direct her to her sleeping chamber. She felt that she required some time to herself, and wished to discover if her boxes had been brought upstairs.

It is going to take me weeks to learn my way about this house, she thought, as she followed the servant up yet another stair and along a different series of narrow, ill-carpeted passages.

From the view of overgrown shrubbery glimpsed outside its small-paned window, she judged that her room must be located above the library. It was a large enough chamber, scantily furnished with somewhat antique pieces, but, she thought, might be made pleasant enough. It was, however, bitterly cold; no fire burned in the grate.

'I shall need a fire,' said Hatty.

'No orders were given about that, miss.'

'Well I am giving you one now. Please see that a fire is kindled directly,' Hatty told the man with more authority in her tone than she privately felt. But he said, 'Yes, miss,' in a docile manner, and not long after a maid appeared who proceeded to kindle and light a fire.

'Do you know if Miss Stornoway was driven to Lord Camber's house?' Hatty asked.

The girl gave a sudden quick smile. 'Yes, miss, she was! Frott, the under-coachman, he drove her in the gig. And when they got there the old ladies took her in – Mrs Godwit and Mrs Daizley. Mrs Daizley's my dad's second cousin, miss. At first they was mighty surprised to see her; but Frott he gave them your note and told us he left her there all right and tight; he reckoned they'd be glad to have her.'

'I am very glad to hear that,' said Hatty, much relieved. 'Thank you for telling me. What is your name?'

'Bone, if you please, miss. Would you like me to help unpack your things?'

'Thank you, no, I can manage,' said Hatty, nodding at the small boxes.

'Well, just you ring if you want anything stitched or pressed out, miss,' Bone said, and departed, leaving Hatty with the feeling that the servants here were friendlier than their employers.

As she unpacked, and piled her belongings in the one small chest provided (resolving at the same time to investigate the rooms on either side of hers, which appeared to be unoccupied, and see if she could not equip herself with a writing-desk and a cupboard with shelves), Hatty pondered about her pupils. Drusilla certainly presented a formidable challenge, perhaps insuperable; her problem seemed a medical one, not to be overcome by tuition, however lively or affectionate. And precious little help would be forthcoming from their mother, it was plain. Lady Elstow was bored by her children, bored by her household, bored by her whole life. And, if the Earl came home so seldom, and took so little interest in his property, an appeal to him seemed likely to be equally unprofitable. Neglect and despair suffused the atmosphere of Underwood Priors. It is as if there were a curse on the place, thought Hatty; and put the thought on one side for a possible poem.

What about Barbara? She at least was imbued with active emotion, even if that emotion was anger, mistrust and dislike. Her need for a companion was very evident; something might be built on that, thought Hatty. She resents me, but at least she converses.

Wrapping a shawl round her shoulders, for the air in the passageways was glacial, Hatty carefully built up her fire, hoping that it would last, then left her bedroom and began the troublesome process of finding her way, by trial and error, back to the schoolroom. As she neared her goal she was guided by the sound of music; evidently Drusilla had woken from her nap of exhaustion and was once again utterly absorbed in her delirious game of tunes and variations.

A footman who had been mending the fire came out as Hatty

entered the room; he cast up his eyes to heaven and murmured, 'She'll go on like that all day, miss!'

Drusilla was too engrossed in what she was doing to take notice of Hatty's entry, until the latter tapped her on the shoulder. Then she turned, rather impatiently, as if a fly had bitten her. Her expression was rapt, lost, infinitely distant. But as the lustrous blue eyes slowly focussed on Hatty, their look became less ethereal, and she smiled again.

'Come now,' said Hatty. 'We shall try and see if we can play a duet.'

PART TWO

XII

Letter from Midshipman Ned Ward to Miss Harriet Ward
Dear Cousin Hatty:
Here I am at sea & it is none so bad. The first three days I was sick
as a Cat & Oblig'd to keep to my hammock in the Midshipmen's
Mess for the wind blew a gale & I felt like to die. But on the 4th day
a Marine help'd me dress in my midshipman's rig & I was fain to
totter up on deck & much amus'd to see how all the men's
garments, wet from spray & rain, were hung up to dry; the whole of
the rigging being loaded with shirts, trowsers & jackets. All the wet
sails were spread on the booms or tric'd up in the rigging, the decks
were white & clean & the sweepers hard at work with their brooms.
At first I knew not where to go or what to do, but the other
midshipmen are a decent set of fellows & soon sho'd me how to go
on. We have been in several engagements with privateers & I was
sore Frit at first but now am becoming tolerably accustom'd to the
gunfire & shocks of battle. The lads I pity are the powder-monkeys.
They must bring up the powder from the magazine in small tubs &
then sit on these tubs in a row on deck so no sparks shall get into
the powder from the men working the guns. I do not envy them
this task!

 The Captain is kind & after 4 months at sea tells me I am in line
for promotion to 2nd Lt but shall have to go before a Board on the
Admiral's Flagship where they ask terrible questions about
quadrants & sextants & what to do if you are in charge of a ship that
is embayed on a lee shore with a hurricane blowing. If I manage to
pass this & gain my promotion it will all be thanks to you, dear

Hatty, who help'd me so many times with my multiplication and division!

At night in my hammock I often while myself to sleep with remembering those pleasant Hours we us'd to spend in the old Tree House & the Poems you us'd to tell me. I hope that you still make up poems, Cousin Hatty, for yours were some of the best I ever listen'd to and I am very sure they deserve to be publish'd in a book. Well no more now from your devoted cousin Ned. By the bye, do you know how the family go on at home? I have heard no news for months. This may be because mail is slow to catch up with us. I send this to Bythorn hoping it may find you.

Midshipman Edward Ward.

Letter from Mrs Frances Price to Mrs Agnes Norris
My dear Aggie:
I have been meaning these months past to write & wish you Joy upon your Marriage. If you are half as happy as I with my dear Mr Sam Price, you will do uncommonly well. It is a great comfort to know that you are so Respectably settl'd in life & when you think of it, I wish you may be able to send me and my dear Sam a trifle . . . perhaps £10, for his present wage is hardly enough to keep a Bird alive & I am in a promising way. You might mention me also to our sister Bertram – she is grown so grand now that I am nervous of approaching her but do, pray, send her my dear love & Remembrances.

Yours etc.
Yr affct Sister Fanny

Letter from Mrs Norris to Mrs Price
My dear Frances:
I was somewhat surpris'd, I must confess, at your application to me for aid, since you must know that it is quite out of my power to find any such sum as that you mention out of the very modest allowance that Mr Norris provides me with for maintaining his Establishment. Not that he is a parsimonious man, no indeed, but he must keep a respectable Establishment, suitable to his Cloth, and

is of course ever mindful of the Poor and observant of his duty to them. Therefore I regret that I cannot assist you but fear that your misfortunes have been brought on by yourself through your own foolish indiscretion & you must endure them accordingly. I did not inform our sister Bertram of your application, as I know she feels as I do that you brought Disgrace on our family by your most ill-judg'd Escapade & must therefore brook the consequences. When ever she speaks of you she refers to you as 'Poor Sister Fanny' with such a sigh as would break your heart to hear. We do, of course, very constantly remember you in our prayers.

    Yours etc.

    A. Norris

Letter to Lady Ursula Ward from Sydney Ward

Dear Madam:

I write to remind you that four months have now elapsed since the unfortunate demise of my uncle, your late husband Mr Henry Ward & the period of grace allow'd you to find another domicile has long since passed by. I must ask if you will be so good as to vacate the premises as soon as possible, since I propose to take up residence there myself & am much inconvenienc'd by this delay.

    Yr Obdnt Srvt

    Sydney Ward

Letter from Lady Ursula Ward to Mrs Norris

My dear Agnes:

You will, of course, have heard of the unfortunate Situation I am plac'd in, due to the very regrettable Entail on this property and the disgraceful and heartless behaviour of Mr Philip Ward's family. I am oblig'd to remove from this house at the end of the month and since your father, Mr Ward, left me sadly ill provided for (I was grossly misled as to the size of his Estate and, I may say, had I known more of his tendency to squander his resources on horseflesh would never have been persuaded into such an injudicious Matrimonial venture) – but enough of that – unless kind friends offer to receive me, I have no recourse but to return home to Underwood Priors. You know, I feel sure, my dear Agnes, how repugnant such a step would be for me and what dismal recollections it would unfailingly evoke. You – after your dear Mother – have always been one of my most cherish'd friends, especially since my other friend Miss Kittridge has sailed the Atlantic on this foolish venture to Pennsylvania – I have therefore not the least hesitation in applying to you first as the one likeliest to offer me a Refuge in my present predicament. I should be so happy to reside with you in Mansfield Parsonage and to enjoy the company of yourself, your esteem'd Husband and of course your dear sister Lady Bertram, not to mention her greatly admir'd Lord, Sir Thos. And, I venture to suggest, I should be able to add my own touch of Distinction and Harmony to your small but select Neighbourhood. How do Lady Bertram's charming infants go on? They must, by now, be reaching a most Interesting Age. I look forward, dear Agnes, therefore with the liveliest expectations of mutual satisfaction to your sisterly (and step-daughterly) response to my suggestion. Pray give my very kindest regards to Mr Norris and to your dear sister Maria.

    Your affectionate friend (and step-Mama),
    Ursula Ward
    P.S. I can of course bring my own bed-linen.

Letter from Mrs Norris to Lady Ursula Ward
My dear Lady Ursula:
I was of course highly gratified that you should have turned to myself and Mr Norris as a first possible refuge in your most unfortunate situation. Had we been able to come to your Assistance we would naturally have done so without the least hesitation, as you may well imagine, but, alas, it is quite out of the question. My dear Mr Norris is, as you know, of a delicate and gouty constitution, and requires, at all times, the most complete quiet in his household. The presence of another, a third person under the same roof, even such a dear and valu'd friend as yourself, would be more than his frail

constitution could tolerate. I feel sure that you will understand this, and will find many, many other good friends who will be only too happy to offer you a home. But if you, in the end, decide to return to Underwood Priors, may that not be all for the best? Then you will have the satisfaction of being with your dear Mama and your charming sisters Barbara and Drusilla. I recall your telling me that your cousin Lord Camber had in past times recommended the girls especially to your care and attention and I daresay you will find happiness in the knowledge that you are acting in accordance with his wishes. The mention of Lord Camber reminds me that, through your kind recommendation, my young sister Harriet is still, so far as I know, attending, or so at least I hope, to the educational needs of your sisters. It may be an excellent thing for all concerned if you return to oversee her activities in this sphere. Hatty, as we all know, is of an obstinate, headstrong, perverse nature; she has about her a spirit of wilfulness and waywardness, of nonsense and whimsicality; she likes to go her own way and will not brook interference; your dear and greatly admir'd Mama may find her hard to govern. But I am positive that you, dear Lady Ursula, will soon, if you return, have matters going along as they should. We shall, of course, always rejoice to see you at Mansfield Parsonage – Mr Norris as you know has the most hospitable nature in the world when his health permits him to be sociable. And if, in a few months' time, the weather is more open, and if Sir Thos permits the use of his landau, we may, perhaps, be permitted to come, likewise and wait on you at the Priors some afternoon. I always enjoy an opportunity to revisit that grand old mansion and benefit from the conversation of your esteem'd Mother the Countess.

Your affectionate friend
A. Norris

Letter from Lord Camber to Miss Harriet Ward:
My dear little Miss Hatty:
You will note that I give as my direction the address of Amity Valley & not some factory in Philadelphia or farm in Pennsylvania.

The history of this is as follows: when I parted from you last January the coach took me straight to Bristol. The Customs House there keeps a register of outgoing passengers who wish to enter into what are known as Redemptionist agreements. They were not a little surprised that I, apparently a person of some standing in the world, should wish to hire myself out in this manner, but such cases are not unknown when men have lost all their fortune at Play, so I allowed them to assume that I had suffered some such Reversal and did not submit myself under the principal family name Wisbech but chose the minor one of Harry Liss. I had to go before a magistrate and sign a form binding me for two years to an unknown master. Such other applicants as had no clothes of their own were issued canvas suits, woollen drawers, shoes, a boat cape, and blankets; about £5 worth of stuff, which would later on be subtracted from their wages. We were inspected for the French disease. Then we were despatched to a respectable boarding-house, where we were to wait our turn until the next vessel was ready to set sail for Baltimore. By good luck, one was due to sail in five days' time. During that period I was able to fit myself out with a set of carpenters' tools. Other trades of men in my ship: weavers, fullers, button makers, tile makers, and farmers.

We accordingly set sail on the sloop *Sea Flower*. The accommodation for the Redemptionist passengers was a 'Bed place' some six feet square for each four adults. We were therefore oblig'd to sleep in turn, two at a time. Then, for eating, we were divided into 'messes' and so much flour, meat &c allotted to each mess, to be cooked by whoever was capable. There was great over-crowding – our sloop had 106 passengers, not counting the seamen. We were at sea for 16 weeks, many of which were stormy. During a storm, hatches were battened down and passengers must remain below. There was terrible misery, stench, vomiting and many kinds of sickness, dysentery, pox, and lice. Many died. I counted at least thirty who did so. It is shocking that such conditions still prevail. I shall write a report to Parliament about it. Most of the provisions were spoiled by the end of the journey, the meat went mouldy, the butter rancid.

You may well imagine with what cheers of jubilation the first sight of land was acknowledged.

As we sailed up the Delaware River in late April the servant-passengers all spruc'd themselves, hair was cut by those who possessed scissors, faces washed, wigs donned, lists made of names & accomplishments of those who had survived. On the dock side the masters and hirers stood eagerly waiting and scanning the emigrants for the strongest and likeliest looking servants. I can tell you, dear Miss Hatty, we were not a promising looking group. Many thin, pale, scarred or spotted by disease. I counted myself fortunate that, since the ship's carpenter had early succumb'd to the smallpox, I had been able to take his place & so escaped the worst conditions under hatches. I was also lucky to be chosen almost at once by a very decent 'master', a Mr Claiborne, who, when he discovered my various abilities, insisted on using me in a most distinguishing manner. He had a large estate to the north of Baltimore, named Piccadilly, so there was no great distance to travel on land. The method and style of building houses here was of great interest to me as you may imagine, dear Miss Hatty. There are many half-timbered houses with thatched roofs, as in England, so my skills will not be wasted. There is little lime for mortar in the countryside, so few brick houses. A ploughman here may earn £5 a year. It is no wonder that many still emigrate. My master, James Claiborne is a liberal-minded and intelligent man and we have many friendly discussions and arguments as I go about my duties. He has promis'd that, if another skilled carpenter should come this way, he will release me from my Indentures before my 2-year term is completed. Meanwhile I have been in communication with my friends at Amity Valley and hope to join them as soon as fortune permits. If you should be so good as to write a letter to me, it may safely be sent there. I wonder so much, dear Miss Hatty, how you go on, and where you are? Did you receive my scribbled note, sent from the cross-roads, and are you installed at the Thatched Grotto, I ask myself? Or have you chosen some other domicile? Are you writing poetry? Indeed I hope so! I have a little time in the evenings after the completion of my duties in which to make notes for my work on language, clothes, and climate, and my narrative of the sea-voyage. I have been reflecting a great deal on the importance of *light* and how it affects men's dispositions. There are many brilliant, sunny days here, more than in our own country. I think the people are proportionately more cheerful and conversible. England is a land of fogs and rain and inturn'd, gloomy dispositions. When I think of my cousins at Underwood I can see how natures may be permanently affected by an unfortunate geographical location. But some natures can triumph over adverse conditions better than others. – Pray, Miss Hatty, do let me hear from you and, if you are able, send me a new poem.

     Your affectionate Friend,

     Harry Camber. (Do not forget that my name here is plain Harry Liss.)

Letter from Miss Harriet Ward to Mrs Pauline Ward
Dearest Aunt Polly:
It is now seven months since I have been living at Underwood Priors and *still* I have no word from you in answer to my several previous letters & do not know how you are going on. I am so very anxious about you, dear Aunt Polly & wonder so very often how you are, if you are well, if you have left your bed, and what is happening in the family? I am so very fond of you all, it seems so queer & strange & sad not to know about you. Is my uncle well? And did Tom go to boarding school or does he still live at home? Does Burnaby still take care of you? Did Sydney go to reside at Bythorn Lodge? What became of Lady Ursula, where did she decide to settle? I wrote to my sister Agnes at Mansfield asking these questions, but receiv'd no Answer. Doubtless she is very busy looking after her husband's parishioners. I had a letter from Ned & am so happy to know that he enjoys the life at sea & no doubt has quite forgot Nancy Price! – As I wrote to you in my last, I am living here at Underwood & endeavouring to instil a little education into Lady Barbara & Lady Drusilla. I have been paid nothing yet,

but perhaps that is only fair, for I do not progress very fast. I am sorry for the girls, they lead lonely lives & I do not think the little one, Drusilla, will ever be able to learn reading, writing or arithmetic. She will always require some person to look after her. Barbara, the elder, hated me at first and set her face against receiving instruction from me at all & for some weeks the situation seem'd hopeless. But she is so bored here that, in the end, I suppose she felt that any diversion was better than none, so now we read French, Latin & Italian together & I am in hopes of Greek. A lucky circumstance proved to be my ability to ride horseback & I was thankful for that more genial period in my father's fortunes when he kept a pair of ponies for me and Fanny, so that I am now able to accompany Lady Barbara, who likes to ride out into the woods every fine day. Now that the weather is benign and there are leaves on the trees, the woodland paths are become very pleasant. And it is always a Joy to get away from the house which is, as I told you, cold, dark, and unbelievably damp. A fine bloom of mould is to be seen on the dancing shoes you bought me, which are never worn . . . However there is to be one alteration in our mode of living: the Earl is to return home for a short period in August, in order to look into some affair relating the Estate; not before time, I imagine, for all about here appears ruinously neglected. The Earl, I learn, is a great friend of Mr George Fox & H.M. the Prince of Wales, so I assume he must be very grand and will pay less than no attention to his daughters' governess. We see little of the Countess; suffering greatly as she does from her rheumatic Disorder she keeps her room all day and takes Opiates to relieve the pain. She dislikes conversation for, being so deaf, she can hear only shouted remarks so any simple conversation or exchange of views is almost out of the question. The girls, I am sorry to say, have fallen into the habit of exchanging highly disrespectful comments about their mother even in her presence, secure in the knowledge that she cannot hear. I have endeavoured in vain to check this habit. Barbara is a strange girl; she has considerable Parts and, when she takes a fancy to use her mind, can be excellent company & do good work, but this is

193

sadly rare. The greater part of the time she spends in a lethargy or kind of angry Sulk. The two married sisters, Anne and Mary, do not ever come back here; both of them reside so far away in the north as to make visiting out of the question. I wonder where Lady Ursula has set up her establishment after she was oblig'd to leave Bythorn Lodge? I feel most cut off here, for no news travels to this house, 'tis like dwelling in the Sleeping Beauty's castle . . .

    Your loving Niece

    P.S. Do, *do, pray* Aunt P write to me if you are able –

Letter from Miss Harriet Ward to Lord Camber

Dear Lord Camber:

I address you, as requir'd on the outer cover as Mr Liss but cannot think of you in any other way than as Lord Camber so hope you will excuse this. I was so very glad to receive your letter & to know that you had safely survived the Perils of the sea-voyage. Indeed I could hardly believe it was true & must carry your letter about with me for many hours & keep re-reading it, to assure myself of its truth & reality. I wonder if, by now, you have left your 'master' Mr Claiborne & been able to join your friends in Amity Valley? As you see, I write to you from Underwood Priors where I am establish'd as a governess to your two cousins Barbara and Drusilla. Lady Ursula arranged this as soon as I returned home to Bythorn Lodge. This return coincided with the sad death of my Father from a hunting accident, so Lady Ursula herself will soon be oblig'd to leave the house, which becomes the property of my cousin Sydney Ward. Indeed she may have done so already. I am not sure where she may be residing; perhaps with my sister Agnes (now Mrs Norris) at Mansfield Vicarage. I did receive your kind little note offering me the hospitality of the Thatched Grotto. The thought of that offer infinitely warms my heart but I do not like to retreat there until I am able to earn enough money from my poetry to keep myself – I would not wish to be a charge on you. Instead I took the very great liberty of installing there your cousins' former governess, a poor lady who was thrown on the world and had nowhere to go. I felt certain that your Benevolence would approve this action. – I have sent various pieces of work to the *Gentleman's Magazine, Bentley's Miscellany* & *The Analytical Review* (by good fortune I was able to find some Numbers of these journals in the Library here) and have had encouraging letters from the Editors but so far no poems have been sold. Naturally I am eager to earn some money as soon as may be to recompense your kind Hospitality. I have been writing a Threnody on the death of the twins but it is not ready to be shown yet.

There is a colony of Rooks not far from my window:

> Rooks flaunt high nests in open view
> And mock their foes in raucous sound
> But oh! the risks their fledglings rue
> So high above the heartless ground . . .

Dear Lord Camber, I am so grateful to you for that happy, happy visit to the Thatched Grotto. I think I shall remember snatches of those lively and easy talks that we had, walking about Wanmaulden Woods, until the very conclusion of my life. The things we said to one another continually recur to me: your saying how important it is that the things we *do* should be done to the very best of our ability, no matter how trifling they seem, since we have a duty to future generations. How very true that is. I bear it constantly in mind. I am sure that in your Sophocracy all the common tasks of every day are performed very carefully and beautifully. I love to think of the life that is carried on there. When I first came to Underwood Priors I thought it an unutterably dismal dwelling for that time was in the Depth of winter & the surrounding woodlands appeared shaggy & decay'd & sodden with snow; but now they are green with summer verdure & amazingly more cheerful. The house, however, is still in a very wretched condition with plaster falling from ceilings & damp running down the walls; it is sad to see a fine old place so neglected, but I understand from Lady Barbara, who sometimes now has fits of communicativeness, that the Earl has lost huge sums at Play & thinks it a waste to spend money on the upkeep of his property as there is no Male heir to inherit. This seems to me a shocking pity. A female would surely be likely to take better care of the estate. Females are natural housekeepers. Perhaps it is this thought that makes Lady Ursula so indignant with the world. I should tell you that I gain great pleasure from musical exercises with little Drusilla. At first I thought her unteachable; & in many ways she is so, but I have had the Harp re-strung & she will play that whilst I accompany her on the piano so that what seems to us both very beautiful music is produced. These 'duets' leave Drusilla wonderfully calm and smiling, but alas they do not please Barbara who has no interest in music & often goes off into the woods for a Sulk when we play. Try as one will, one cannot satisfy everybody. I find this letter grows too long, you will never find time to read it.

    Yr Affte friend,
    H. Ward

Letter from Miss Nancy Price to Midshipman Ned Ward
Dearest Neddikins,
You will laugh when you see the name at the foot of this letter & indeed I can hardly help laughing myself when I think how different my life is now from those days in Portsmouth when our only Diversion was to meet together for Frisks and Gambols in the damp freezing graveyard. I am sure it is a Wonder we did not catch our Mortal end from the chill and 'tis not to be admir'd that we both came down with so bad a Go of the Measles. But no matter for that, dear Neddikins, those sweet Kisses & Caresses we exchang'd are still amongst my fondest Memories & will remain so I am sure for Many a Long Time. As you may not know when I recover'd from the sickness I was sent up to London in disgrace to reside with my aunt and uncle Chauncey in High Holborn. This was intended as a punishment, but, lord! 'tis no such thing at all, for, apart from being separated from you, dearest Neddikins, life here is by far more pleasant & entertaining than ever it was in P'mouth for my

Cousins, Grace and Clara, are a merry-hearted pair of girls and my aunt Chauncey no bad sort. She makes no objection to the girls & myself sitting downstairs in my Uncle's Shop which, as you may imagine, is by far more agreeable than remaining mew'd up in the parlour Upstairs, so we are well entertain'd & see plenty of Life and Miss Clara and Miss Grace have no lack of Beaux as you may believe. But I remane always faithful to the memory of my dearest Neddikins. My brother Robert who you may remember is a 2nd Lt on board the *Adonis* writ me from Gibraltar that he had seen you & knew you to be aboard the *Harpy,* so I take the chance of addressing you there & hope this letter finds you happy & doing Well. If your ship should ever dock in the Port of London, do not forget your loving Sweetheart Nancy.

Letter from Lord Camber to Miss Harriet Ward
My dear little Miss Hatty:
Your letter directed to me from Underwood Priors gave me infinite joy and satisfaction. This made a resolution of several difficulties which it would not have occurred to me to suggest, but now that it has come about I rejoice from the bottom of my heart. Your presence at Underwood I am certain will do my poor little Cousins all the good in the world; you with your active joyful nature will both enliven and instruct them and Open out their lives in a manner which might hitherto have been thought impossible. You may even perhaps have some beneficial effect upon my Aunt, who is always in sad case from lack of cheerful Company. It would be no bad thing either, if my cousin Ursula were also to return to the Priors but I know this is not very likely to happen if she can find herself a home elsewhere, perhaps with your sister Agnes.

I shall like to see your Elegy for the twins when it is ready. I am sure you will be able to do Justice to their sad, short, but poetic and Interesting lives.

Now to my life in Amity Valley. As you may have guessed my kind 'Master' James Claiborne lost no time in freeing me from my indentures as soon as he was able to find another skilled carpenter. I

had performed some paid thatching services for neighbours & so
was able to refund the moneys owing to him for the complete
period of my services. Then I purchased a mule & rode here,
passing through various German and Swiss townships on the way.
Since the commencement of the century this area has been settled
by various Sects such as the Dunkers and the Marienborn Society.
These Fellowships are similar in their observances: their garb is
very simple, the women in clear-starch'd Cap with handkerchief
crossed on the breast, the men in slouch hats & woollen breeches.
They are very abstemious and hard-working. Then I came – with
what happiness – to Amity Valley where my friends observe many
of the same practices. Wooden cabins have been constructed and
more are in process of being built. But all eat together at night in
the main hall of the village where there is a central kitchen. The
hall has lines of benches which may be turned on a pivot to form
the top of a long table. This is covered with a white cloth, and each
day different brothers and sisters take charge of the cooking,
making soup, bread, pies, roast lamb, etc. After dinner comes
Discussion Time when plans for the next day's labour, as well as
Ethical Matters, are debated. Sometimes these discussions may last
all through the night! as the male Sophocrats are by no means all of
one Persuasion – some are Christians, some Freethinkers, some
Dualists, while some have views so individual that no name has yet
been assign'd to them. It has been laid down as one of the prime
tenets of the Group that no action or decision be taken until a
Unanimous Vote be cast, so you can imagine, dear Miss Hatty, how
hard it is, at times, to attain such Unanimity. However there is great
friendship and goodwill among the Brotherhood and so these gulfs
are always somehow bridged in the end. I think the women may at
times find this communal life harder, as they have sometimes come
here from fondness for their menfolk (like the Sister of my friend
Kittridge) & not from Personal Belief in the constitution of the
group. But I may be wrong about this. I have plenty of occupation
myself, building roofs and thatching them for the new houses; and
have a little time also to work at my Book. I share a cabin with my

friend Humphrey Kittridge & we have great Chats together when Discussion Time is ended. Kittridge is an ardent Naturalist & when the agricultural business of the community is in a good train, he intends to travel on a Botanical Excursion to the as yet unexplor'd Regions of this great Continent where there are doubtless all manner of new & wonderful Species to be discovered. No more now from your affectionate friend Harry Camber.

P.S. I too remember *well* those enjoyable, talkative walks we took in Wanmaulden Wood. Since you are at the Priors, which is none so far from my Thatched Grotto, I should be oblig'd if you might find time to ride over there, perhaps with my cousin Barbara, who I recall is an enthusiastic horsewoman, to see how my friends do at the Grotto, for Godwit is very Sparse of his correspondence, writing only when there is some urgent business matter to communicate, while the ladies are not gifted in epistolary matters & never write at all. So news as to their welfare and that of your predecessor would be most gratefully received.

Letter from Miss Harriet Ward to Lord Camber
My dear Sir:
I was most happy to receive your last with engrossing descriptions of your happy Colony at Amity Valley. Long may it thrive and prosper & I shall always be deeply interested to hear more about the life and Activities there.

I shall be glad, so soon as opportunity presents, to pay a visit to your dear little house, if I can persuade Lady Barbara to take her ride in that direction. I shall rejoice to see your kind friends there again. Also I shall like to see how poor Miss Stornoway goes on under their care. And I can offer something towards her Maintenance as I am happy to report that I sold two Poetic Pieces to *The Analytical Review*.

We have news here of a somewhat dismaying nature. Lord Elstow plans to visit his home during the late summer; he is to bring with him an acquaintance, a young Frenchman whom you may remember, as Lady Barbara informs me that he has been living in London for a number of years – the Abbé du Vallon; he has been invited not as a friend but because of his knowledge of books & he is to make a complete catalogue of all the volumes in his Lordship's library with the object of presently disposing of them to some would-be purchaser & thereby relieving some of the Earl's financial Distresses. (The girls speak of this quite freely.) I am, as you may imagine, greatly troubled at this News, since the excellence of the library here is one of the great amenities of the Establishment & without it, I do not know how I would manage to play my part in Improving the mind of Lady Barbara. I do not mention her sister, for nothing written on paper is of the least use to her.

He
throws the ball to *me*
But *I*
throw it to *him*. Why?
I and Me, Him and He
What a fuss
when there are only two of us!

Your affectionate friend,
H. Ward

XIII

WHEN HATTY AND Lady Barbara went out together on horseback, they often rode in silence for extended periods. What engaged Barbara's mental processes at such times, Hatty could not imagine. For herself, she enjoyed the long, untroubled, contemplative interludes, when the horses jogged along at their own choice of pace, and Harris, the elderly groom, followed some way behind, also immersed in his own thoughts, while the rhythm of the horses' trotting, the hush of the woods, the continuous flow of cool air against her face provided Hatty with ideal conditions for the generation of poetry; often, after their afternoon rides she was able to note down themes, lines, sometimes whole verses, or to discover solutions for what had previously loomed as insoluble problems.

The silent company of Barbara on these excursions appeared to hold an element of friendship, which, at other times, her presence signally lacked; they rode together in what seemed like amity, silently acknowledging and appreciating such minor occurrences as a woodpecker's sudden zigzag flight, a wild cherry's white tower of blossom, a fox slipping sidelong and soundless away from the track. And Hatty thought that, after these shared small pleasures, Barbara too returned from the ride in a more softened, approachable humour; but this seldom lasted very long.

Barbara, familiar from childhood with all the lanes and bridle-ways, always chose their route; she seemed disconcerted, and not best pleased, when Hatty, one afternoon, made the suggestion that they should take in Lord Camber's cottage on their ride. 'For I have a message to deliver there. And I have looked at the big map in the Estate Room and I find it is not far from one of our usual bridle-tracks.'

'But why,' demanded Barbara curtly, 'why in the world should you wish to go *there*?'

'Your cousin asked me in a letter last month to pay a short visit there some time and find out if his household go on as they should. For it seems none of them are very good correspondents.'

'You correspond with Lord Camber?' Barbara's voice just then strongly resembled that of her mother.

'Why, yes. As I had mentioned before, he was a frequent visitor at my uncle's house in Portsmouth. He wrote to me about his sea voyage, and somebody forwarded the letter from Bythorn Lodge.'

Hatty saw no reason to speak of her subsequent meeting with Lord Camber. She was a little dismayed by the immediate reappearance of Barbara's sullen, glowering manner. However, no objections were raised, and they turned their horses in the desired direction. Barbara, though, urged her mount on and kept up a hasty, impatient pace all the way, as if to convey that she felt the errand to be supremely tiresome, and wished it over with as soon as possible.

Hatty was amused to find that the Thatched Grotto, though now surrounded and embowered in summer verdure, had not lost its appearance of slight absurdity, as if a pastry-cook's confection, wearing a mob cap of thatch, had been set down in the middle of a budding grove.

Godwit was to be seen, as they approached, digging in a vegetable patch at the side of the house. He straightened up with care and, as soon as he recognized the callers, came hurrying towards them, his plain, pear-shaped face broken up into creases of delight. His shout had brought the boy Dickon from the rear of the house, who capered round them with energetic joyfulness, and, as soon as they dismounted, led their mounts away to the shed.

'Miss Hatty! You are a sight for sore eyes, *that* you are! And you have brought Lady Barbara with you, I see, to honour us this day. Mrs Daizley will want to put out her best table-cloth.'

Barbara looked faintly astonished.

'This person knows me?' she said to Hatty.

'Why, of course, Lady Barbara, I am sure you are known by sight to everyone for twenty miles around. How could it be otherwise? This is Mr Godwit, your cousin Camber's — what are you, Mr Godwit?' Hatty asked, laughing. 'His bailiff? His steward? His butler?'

'All of those three, I reckon, ma'am,' Godwit replied, his eyes doing their sideways dance of amusement. 'And his gentleman's gentleman as well — bar the fact that his Lordship's given up being a gentleman, by all accounts, in those American parts. But come in, come in, my Lady and Miss Hatty — there's three inside as'll be rejoiced to see ye.'

'Oh, I think I will remain out of doors and stroll about,' Barbara said instantly. She had gazed at Godwit while he was speaking with a kind of haughty wonder, as if a badger had suddenly addressed her, not only in human speech, but in *French*. Now she moved away and stared impatiently about her, conveying her dislike of being made to wait. 'You will not be long, surely?' she added.

But at this moment the door opened and two persons emerged from it with great rapidity and cries of astonishment and welcome. One was plump Mrs Daizley; Hatty hardly recognized the other, so rejuvenated and transformed did Miss Stornoway appear. They surged towards Hatty, kissed her, and made much of her, while Barbara Fowldes regarded the scene in silent amazement.

'My *dear* Miss Stornoway! How very well you look! And dear Mrs Daizley. Is Mrs Godwit well?'

'Ay, miss dear, but she grows powerful short-sighted, so she bides mostly indoors. 'Twas a real lucky stroke you sent Miss Stornoway to us, for she's a wonder at reading his Lordship's books out loud – reads by the hour, she do, and Mrs Godwit fair laps it up. But come in, come in, do, and take a dish of lime tea. Ye'll do us that honour, Lady Barbara dear, will ye, now? Ye'll be pleased to see Miss Stornoway, here, and talk over old times, to be sure you will.'

Barbara, it seemed, felt no such pleasure, and would plainly have preferred to decline the invitation, but was so startled at the appearance of Miss Stornoway that she put up no resistance to being shepherded indoors, where she sat in mute discontent, eyeing her surroundings in a series of small glimpses, as if afraid that a prolonged gaze might render her liable to some infection.

Old Mrs Godwit, by the hearth-side, was seen and greeted; Mrs Daizley bustled about, putting a kettle on the hob and bringing out plates of nut cake and bowls of dried cherries.

Hatty could not get over the alteration in Miss Stornoway. 'You look so much better, ma'am, than you did when we last met – it is really a most remarkable transformation.'

'Och, my dear, dear Miss Ward, it is you I have tae thank for the change – and indeed I am aware of it myself with every breath I draw – Mrs Daizley here and Mrs Godwit – they have fairly taken me tae pieces and made a new person of me.'

'But how was it achieved?'

'It was nettle broth and nettle ointment, my dearie,' Mrs Daizley explained, pouring out cups of lime tea. 'Nettles, you know, are *sovereign* for all rheumatic ills – and that was what chiefly plagued the poor lady – so we fair dowsed her in nettles the first two months she was with us – luckily Eli had cut down a great patch of them last summer and I had made twice my usual brew of nettle essence. We rubbed her and we fomented her, she drank nettle beer eight times a day—'

'But as well as that,' Miss Stornoway broke in 'the ladies here have permitted me to make myself *useful* – which was such a great joy to me.'

'Useful, Miss Stornoway?'

'Och, well, I didn't like tae sit idle when every one about the house was occupied from morn tae night.'

Hatty nodded. Nostalgically she recalled the atmosphere of constant peaceful industry in the Thatched Grotto.

'And my fingers,' continued Miss Stornoway, unabated, 'were over-crippled at first tae knit or sew – but then Mr Godwit recalled the shells his uncle had collected in Bermuda when he was a sailor – and brought them doon – and I have been permitted, ye see, tae fashion a variety of wee playthings and ornaments – which Mr Godwit is able tae dispose of for me at a market stall in Bythorn. So I need not be altogether a charge on my kind hosts.'

And Miss Stornoway pointed triumphantly to a tray full of objects which Hatty had been eyeing with a vague sense of puzzlement, wondering what in the world they might be. They were made, it seemed, from large tropical shells, adorned with bits of black velvet ribbon, tinsel and scraps of fabric. Some of them appeared to be grotesque dolls, others were evidently intended for strange little animals, hedgehogs, bears or monkeys.

'They are quite remarkable,' Hatty said truthfully. She thought them hideous, but Godwit said, 'I've a friend at Bythorn market, Miss Hatty – well, he's a bit of a gipsy, but honest with it – he and I have known each other since we were boys. He disposes of them for us on his stall, and they go like hot cakes, he tells me, can't sell enough of them. Folk buy them for lucky charms, like.'

'What a very fortunate thing,' Hatty said warmly. 'I am so happy for you, Miss Stornoway, that you can contribute in this way. Is that not a great piece of good fortune?' she said to Barbara, who had been sitting for the last five minutes with her eyes turned to the window as if trying to detach herself from the scene. She roused herself to say, 'Oh – yes. We must leave now, Miss Ward, or we shall be late back for dinner.'

Hatty was sorry to part from her friends but, after a few moments' more conversation, saw that it would not be prudent to detain Barbara here any longer. Accordingly she pulled from her reticule a sheet of paper and handed it to Godwit. 'I had this letter from Lord Camber describing his life in Amity Valley – I copied it out, thinking you would like to have it to read over among yourselves.'

'Oh, that was kind of you, Miss Hatty dear – it is grand news indeed that he is safely there and with his friends at last. Maybe he will have time now to honour us with a line himself.'

'Well – he says that *you* are very poor correspondents,' Hatty said laughing. She stood up and followed Barbara, who had made for the door and was waiting, in haughty silence, for Godwit to open it, which he did with leisurely dignity.

'The boy will bring your nags round in a moment, my Lady,' he said to Barbara, who nodded distantly, moving away; then Godwit addressed Hatty in a low tone. ''Twas a real work of rescue ye did there, Miss Hatty, sending us yon poor lady. Another month in the misty murk at Underwood and she'd have been dead and buried. 'Twas not only the damp, but the *unkindness* of the place.'

'It is an unhealthy spot,' Hatty agreed, shivering.

'You mind for yourself, now, miss! I've heard tales of *them* – ' he threw a glance at Barbara, who was mounting her mare. 'Don't let them put upon ye, or put ye down, Miss Hatty; but come back to us here any time – we'd be proud and glad to have ye.'

'Oh, thank you, *dear* Mr Godwit. I will remember that. I promise. But Lord Camber said in his letter that he was very glad I was teaching his cousins and hoped I would stay with them.'

'Lord Camber lays out notions of conduct that's sometimes too high for ordinary flesh and blood,' Godwit surprised her by saying.

'I'm sure, Godwit, he'd never ask anyone to do something he would not undertake himself.'

'Nay, that is true, for certain, but his Lordship is nearer to being a holy angel than most of the rest of us sinners. 'Tis easy enough for him. But it may not be so for us. The proof of the pudding,' said Godwit thoughtfully, 'the proof of the pudding 'ull be how those folk all get on together in Amity Valley. For I reckon the rules of that place is all laid down according to his Lordship's notions.'

'I thought it had been decided between him and his friends.'

'Most o' the deciding was done by his Lordship, I reckon.'

Godwit did not smile; but his tone conveyed his view of the matter.

Hatty said thoughtfully, 'Yes, I see what you mean.'

Barbara had mounted by now. 'Do make haste, Miss Ward,' she called impatiently.

Dickon threw Hatty up on to her horse and she hurried after Barbara, who was already making off at a fast trot.

'Why in the world, Miss Ward,' demanded Barbara as Hatty drew alongside, 'why in the *world* did you take it upon yourself to send that wretched woman to lodge with those people? I had no idea that you had done such a thing.'

'Well,' said Hatty mildly, 'she had to lodge somewhere. And she had nowhere else to go. And no resources.'

'But who gave you leave to make such use of Harry Camber's house?'

'Why, he did himself.'

'*He* did? *Very* strange, indeed.'

'Living there seems to have had a wholly beneficial effect upon Miss Stornoway,' Hatty pointed out.

Barbara made no reply to this, but pressed her lips together and spurred on at an even faster pace. The mare, displeased at such cavalier treatment, tossed her head and swerved sideways along by some thickset low-growing hazel bushes, which slightly grazed Barbara's cheek and forehead. She cried out angrily and slashed at the mare with her whip. Fortunately Harris, the old groom, had seen what occurred and came hurrying up level with her in order to grasp the bridle and bring the mare to a halt.

'Nay, never use Firebird like that, my Lady, she 'on't stand for it,' he admonished. 'Leave her go her own pace, she'll be mild as the moon, but chivvy her, she'll act umbrageous! Lucky it is ye bain't much hurt – 'tis only a scratch.'

'It is bleeding,' said Barbara angrily. 'It is very painful! I shall not ride this bad-tempered beast any more. She had better be sold.'

Harris shook his head.

'There bain't many mounts left in the stable now, my Lady. Better ye think again about that. Maybe ye'd better change mounts, now, with Miss Ward.'

Hatty declared that she was very willing to make the exchange, and inquired with solicitude after Barbara's graze, which she could see was in fact of a very trifling nature; but Barbara exclaimed that she did not wish to ride on that slow old pig, matters had better rest as they were. She rode the rest of the way home frowning with discontent.

'I have some tincture of witch-hazel, Lady Barbara,' Hatty said as they dismounted. 'It is very efficacious for scratches and small wounds. I will bring it to your bedroom directly.' She did not mention that the witch-hazel had been given to her by Mrs Daizley.

Barbara acknowledged the offer by no more than a nod, and strode off to her chamber, where Hatty followed soon after with the little flask and some pieces of old clean cloth.

'You will find this very soothing,' she said after she had knocked and been invited brusquely to enter. 'Here – let me apply it for you.'

Barbara, sitting on her bed, submitted in silence and without thanks to this ministration. As Hatty completed the small operation and looked about her for somewhere to dispose of the soiled scraps of cloth, she saw, to her shocked astonishment, lying upon Barbara's bureau, her own mother's little linen bag holding needles and pins and embroidered with tiny squirrels.

'Oh!' she cried out irrepressibly. '*There* it is! My mother's bag! I wondered where it could possibly have got to – I looked for it everywhere and asked Bone—'

In fact she had wondered if the maid had taken it, and mourned it as stolen, for she knew very well that she had never taken it out of her room. Not wishing to accuse the maids, she had grieved for its loss in silence.

Now Barbara stared at her in what seemed haughty incomprehension. 'I *beg* your pardon, Miss Ward! That bag is mine. It is mine and always has been. My grandmother gave it to me.'

Hatty refrained from pointing out that her own initials, H.W., were embroidered among the squirrels. For all she knew, Lady Barbara's grandmother might have been named Helen Wisbech.

She made some monosyllabic, non-committal noise in reply. She could not even bring herself to add, 'Perhaps there is some mistake,' since she knew the bag was hers. But there would be no profit, none, in bringing matters to an issue. Better let the bag go.

'You should lie down for a while, Lady Barbara,' she said quietly.

'The bag is mine!' asserted Barbara, swinging her booted feet up on to the counterpane.

'No doubt,' answered Hatty.

She turned to leave the room.

As Barbara flung herself on to the bed a small object had rolled from her pocket and fell to the floor with a thump. Hatty picked it up without comment and placed it on the bureau beside the embroidered needle bag. It was one of Miss Stornoway's sea-shell monsters, adorned with black velvet ribbon and spangles.

XIV

HATTY GREATLY REGRETTED that, during the visit to the Thatched Grotto, there had been no opportunity for herself and Miss Stornoway to hold a brief private conversation about the Fowldes sisters. She felt that lady, now, it seemed restored to health and good spirits, might have some valuable advice and comments to offer on the temperaments of her two difficult ex-charges. At first Hatty had been inclined to think Drusilla the more peculiar and unteachable of the pair, but she was now coming to revise that judgement. She could comprehend that there was no way in which the younger child might ever receive a normal education, but she had the capacity to be docile and tractable, and, in her own way, lovable. The bond of music with Hatty was a very strong one and, under its influence small doses of information might be administered and good habits inculcated. But Barbara, taller and more physically robust, almost old enough to be considered grown up – and certainly adjudging herself sufficiently mature to be accorded adult status – Barbara was a much more difficult proposition. By now Hatty had discovered that there lay a deep substratum of jealousy in her nature: so long as she was accorded first preference, and given as much as she required and expected in the way of praise, acclaim, respect, friendship and consideration, all went well enough; but let her receive ever so little less than what she felt to be her due, and a balefully sullen black temper was aroused which took days, sometimes weeks, to abate. Friendly relationships between other parties she could not tolerate; with every person she must always come first. Hatty wondered very much what the terms had been between Barbara and the elder sisters who were now married: had she been fond of them? had she missed them when they left home? did she envy their escape into the great world? Hatty often wished that it were possible to discuss Barbara's character with her mother. Did Lady Elstow, for instance, know of her daughter's propensity for stealing other people's belongings? Was that why it was so firmly accepted that this daughter, like her younger sister, stood no possible chance of matrimony, but must always remain at home, at Underwood Priors? Was this awkward characteristic talked about, discussed, among the elders of the family? Was that – perhaps – why Lord Camber had urged his cousin Ursula to remain at home always to look after her younger sisters? (Supposing that to have been a true story; it did seem to contradict Aunt Polly's alternative version of the engagement to Lord Francis Fordingbridge and the fatal voyage to India.)

Oh, Aunt Polly, how I wish that you were here and that I could have a comfortable coze with you!

But all letters to Aunt Polly went unanswered. And any such discussion with Lady Elstow was quite out of the question. Lady

Elstow kept her bed all morning, and her chamber until the dinner hour; she discouraged visits to her room and if her opinion was sought on any problem relating to her daughters, merely said, 'You must wait until his Lordship comes to Underwood and ask him about that.'

Drusilla's teeth protruded, a defect which, in part, led to her speech difficulty; Hatty thought that a dentist might be able to advise on this matter but when it was suggested to the Countess she shrugged and said, 'Her father must decide. Pray do not trouble me about such trifling affairs.'

But the Earl's visit had now been postponed again until September.

'May I write to him about it, ma'am?'

'Good heavens, no! Wait until he is here. Now leave me. I am excessively fatigued today. Ring the bell for Glastonbury.'

Encountering Glastonbury in the hall on the day following her visit to the Thatched Grotto, Hatty had paused to felicitate them both on Miss Stornoway's unexampled improvement in health and spirits. 'If you had not arranged her removal, Glastonbury, I do not know how she could have survived. You would not recognize her now for the same person.'

Glastonbury, as she had rather expected, was no stranger to the news of Miss Stornoway's recovery. 'It was a good piece of work, that, miss, for sure. Maybe the lady will be able to find another post now.'

'You think she will wish to leave Lord Camber's house?'

'Well, miss, there's talk about Lady Ursula.'

'*Lady Ursula?*'

'Yes, miss. There's talk she might remove herself and go to the Grotto. There's talk that Lord Camber gave her leave to do so.'

'Good heavens! Where is Lady Ursula now? Not still at Bythorn?'

As might have been predicted, the gossip of the countryside was well up to date regarding the movements of the gentry.

'Lady Ursula went up to London, Miss Hatty, when your cousin Mr Sydney Ward took over occupation of Bythorn Lodge. Lady Ursula went to stay with her sister Lady Mary Finster, who had hired a house in Berkeley Square. But the house was only hired until July and now Lady Mary is gone down to Kirkudbright again and Lady Ursula did not wish to travel all that way – or 'tis possible that Lady Mary did not wish to have her any longer,' Glastonbury added in an expressionless tone. 'Anyhow, Lady Ursula is now residing with Lady Bertram and Sir Thomas at Mansfield Park.'

'Is she indeed? Well, I hope that she remains there a long time. My sister Maria Bertram is very good-natured.'

'No doubt, miss.' Glastonbury's face suggested that he felt even Lady Bertram's good nature might not be unlimited. And Hatty added thoughtfully, 'It is true, my sister Agnes is now at the Mansfield parsonage. She and Lady Ursula were used to be great friends. But they are two of a kind,' she added, half to herself. 'They might not always agree.'

Her thoughts moved anxiously to the happy household at the Thatched Grotto. Had Lord Camber bestowed on Lady Ursula the same carte blanche as he had to Hatty, to go and stay there whenever she wished? Hatty felt a moment's indignation. As Godwit had said, 'Lord Camber lays out notions of conduct that are sometimes too holy for the rest of us.' Did he really think that his household would be happy to accommodate Lady Ursula? Besides – supposing Hatty herself had already been there? What then? Or was that – Hatty thought next – was that what he had intended? To oblige his cousin and Hatty to make friends? This idea needed some careful thought.

'Glastonbury,' she said, 'do you have any definite intelligence as to Lord Elstow's return home?'

'No, miss.' And Glastonbury added cautiously, 'I believe it depends mostly on His Majesty's state of health.'

'*His Majesty?*'

'Yes, miss. Apparently His Majesty has run mad, and was recently seen conversing with a tree in Windsor Great Park, addressing it as the King of Prussia. There is talk of confining him to a special establishment, and the Prince of Wales would then become Regent.'

'Good heavens, Glastonbury.'

'In that case, you see, miss, his Grace being a great friend of Mr Fox – and Mr Fox being a great friend of His Royal Highness – and Mr Fox being asked to form a government—'

Such an eventuality would be very favourable towards restoring the Earl's fallen fortunes, Hatty perceived at once.

She asked impulsively, 'Has it ever been suggested that Lady Barbara should go and stay with Lady Mary or Lady Anne?'

Glastonbury's flat, impassive face became even more mask-like. He said, 'No, miss. It has not.'

Feeling that she had been guilty of backstairs gossip, Hatty went off to the schoolroom, where Barbara greeted her with a glare. But how, Hatty wondered, other than by backstairs gossip, is one to acquire information in this house?

May gave way to June. Hatty's rides with Barbara were discontinued. On the day following the visit to Lord Camber's cottage, arriving as usual at the stable, Hatty was told by Harris that Lady Barbara had given orders for the mare to be sold; Lady Barbara would ride alone with the groom in future and Miss Ward's company would not be required.

Discomposed but not greatly surprised, Hatty replaced the rides with Barbara by walks with Drusilla. The child was delicate and liable to catch cold very easily; during the winter and early spring months it had not been thought advisable by Winship, the elderly nurse who had had charge of all the Fowldes girls, that she should set foot out of doors, at all. But now the weather was mild, croquet in the garden or gentle walking exercise might be permitted. Drusilla indeed throve visibly under this regime. Her cheeks had a better colour, she slept longer at night, her tiny appetite increased and, Hatty thought, so did her intelligence and memory span. She could now learn short passages by heart, especially if these were accompanied by music; and so their strolls were enlivened, as they walked along, by singing games: multiplication tables, rules of grammar and historical dates all chanted to the tunes of nursery rhymes, or ballads, or the airs that Drusilla made up herself as they walked. Of these she seemed to have an inexhaustible supply, and Hatty often thought that they were not just a child's jingles but real melodies with shape and structure such as would have done credit to an adult composer. These the child could always recall when required, and Hatty wondered, over and over, at the strange anomaly that her memory for facts and words and pictures should be so faulty and inexact, her memory for music so precise and absolute.

Unfortunately Hatty's growing rapport with Drusilla had a maleficent effect upon the temper of the latter's elder sister. Barbara's solitary rides, also, seemed to feed her gloom and jealousy, as if she spent them entirely in angry, repetitive rumination; she would return from them sunk into a black mood, speaking to nobody and replying in snappish monosyllables if addressed. Even Lady Elstow, who was generally wrapped in a cloud of her own abstraction, noticed her elder daughter's silence and surliness.

'Hey-day, Miss Ward! What have you done to Lady Barbara, to throw her into the sullens? You are supposed to be *enlivening* her, not casting her into a permanent huff. To be faced with black scowls at dinner is what I have no patience with, and not what I pay you a salary for, let me tell you.'

'Perhaps this might be a suitable occasion to remind your Ladyship that you have not paid me *any* salary as yet,' Hatty pointed out in the mild but clear and carrying voice which, by a process of trial and error, she had discovered was best calculated to penetrate the Countess's deafness.

This remark surprised a reluctant snort of laughter from Barbara as she sat morosely chopping her roast mutton into small portions and pushing them around her plate.

Lady Elstow chose not to hear, which was her invariable tactic for dealing with domestic difficulties. She said: 'Well, you girls will need to improve your manners next week – I want no sour looks and ill-natured silences when du Vallon joins us. In himself he is of small account, but I do not wish him returning to London and telling all your father's acquaintance that Elstow has a pair of ill-conditioned lumpish daughters who are unfit for polite company.'

Drusilla's face lit up. 'Is he coming? Mr Abbey? Oh, I like him, I like him!'

And even across Barbara's lowering, down-turned visage, a gleam of interest could be observed.

'Though I daresay *we* shan't get much of his company,' she muttered.

213

'Mama will occupy all his attention as she did before.' These words were uttered in a tone too low to be caught by the Countess. Hatty frowned at the girl, who made a grimace of disdain, pushing up her lips. To distract the Countess's attention from this ill-bred behaviour, Hatty asked, 'Who is M du Vallon, ma'am?'

'Oh, he is a penniless young scapegrace who is nevertheless perfectly well-connected – his family disowned him some seven or eight years ago. He is a relative of our cousin the Duc de Pierrefonds de Bracieux; he came to England to make his way and Mr Fox has befriended him.' Lady Elstow was incapable of telling a connected narrative.

'Why does he come here, your Ladyship? To this house? Does he accompany Lord Elstow?'

'No, no, my husband has no intention of returning to Underwood at present – not while political affairs are in such an uncertain state. He sends du Vallon to make a complete catalogue of the books in the library. He has the intention of selling them, it seems – since they are of no use to anybody here – if they will fetch a sufficient sum to make it worth while—'

Hatty let out a gasp of dismay and protest. 'Oh, no! But then, what will the girls and I read?'

'*You*, Miss Ward? You and the girls? You can have no possible occasion to read the books in Lord Elstow's library.'

Hatty did not remind the Countess that most of the girls' lesson hours were now passed in the library. She said mildly, 'I did ask your Ladyship – if you recall – whether I might supplement the lesson books in the schoolroom, which are extremely old—'

'What was good enough for my grandfather, the late Lord Aberfoyle, is good enough for these girls.'

'Certainly, ma'am, but they have outgrown them. *A Lytel Pretie Picture Boke* is not adequate reading for Lady Barbara. We have found it needful to augment the schoolroom reading-matter with some of his Lordship's volumes.'

'You did? And which books have you selected as suitable reading-matter from the library, may I inquire?'

'Aristotle. *The Nicomachean Ethics.*'

'*Indeed?* What, pray, can be your object in reading the girls such a work?'

'I thought it might be useful for the girls to think about the purpose of life.'

'And they are to learn this from *Aristotle?*'

'Why not? He says that to live temperately is not pleasant to most people, especially when they are young. So they must be taught early, in order to grow used to the discomfort.'

Lady Elstow's large unfocussed grey eyes stared at Hatty in almost vacant astonishment, as if she had suddenly grown wings and a tail.

Barbara, unexpectedly, let out a dry chuckle.

'So you see, Mama,' she declared in a loud, flat, triumphant tone, 'Aristotle is good for us. And so are many of the other books in the library. M du Vallon must not take them away from us.'

'What else do you read?'

'Oh, Milton, Cervantes, Dante – you *said*, Mama, that you wished us to learn Italian.'

'Not *Dante*. I wished you to learn Italian in order to be able to converse in that language.'

But already Lady Elstow's interest in the argument was waning; she yawned and said, 'Well it is all most unfortunate and, I am sure, not at all what your Papa would wish. But it must wait until he comes to Underwood ...' Her eye glazed. She added, 'Tell Glastonbury that I will take tea in my boudoir.'

'And we may go on working in the library, ma'am?'

'Oh ... I daresay you may as well ... unless your father tells du Vallon to have all the books packed up and sold.'

The Countess trailed from the room, yawning again.

Barbara said: 'She will swallow a dram of laudanum with her tea and forget all about the matter, ten to one.'

The glance of complicity that she gave Hatty was almost friendly. What a strange creature she is, thought Hatty. The most trifling occurrences send her spirits shooting up or crashing down.

'Well, we had best read in the library while we may. Tell me about this du Vallon,' taking advantage of Barbara's more approachable humour, 'is he an old friend of your father?'

'Oh, well, nine or ten years back. There was some scandal in France – the du Vallons are cousins of my father's aunt, they have estates near Compiègne – and so Marcel came to England. I was only about six or so then, I never heard what the scandal was about. But Papa quite took to him. He used to come and stay here, he was very amusing and stylish. "*Tiré à quatre épingles*" – he taught us a bit of French too.'

'I wondered how you came to have such a good French accent,' Hatty remarked. 'I did not think it could have come from Miss Stornoway,' and then could have bitten out her tongue.

But Barbara gave her no more than an absent-minded scowl, and went on: 'Yes, he and Papa were quite bosom-bows for three or four years. And he used to come down here for long visits. Mama found him very amusing too, he used to set up charades and impromptu theatricals – this was when my sisters Anne and Mary were still at home.'

'Have you seen him lately?'

'It is above a year since he last came down with Papa. But he is grown more serious. They were talking politics a great deal of the time.'

'Does he never go back to France, to his family?'

'No, it seems they have quite cast him off.'

Hatty wondered what the un-named scandal could have been that exiled the young man from his connections for such a long period. Something relating to a woman, perhaps . . .

A few days later, returning from a walk with Drusilla, she saw a carriage pulled up in front of the house, and a vast deal of luggage unloading from it.

Drusilla, catching a glimpse of the passenger, darted forward.

'Mr Abbey! Mr Abbey!'

He caught her up and embraced her.

'*Ma mignonne! Petit choufleur!*'

Then he saw Hatty and swept her a low bow. 'Mademoiselle! A thousand pardons! But your pupil and I are old acquaintances, as you see.'

His English was faintly accented and very rapid; otherwise it might have been that of a native.

'How do you do, Monsieur,' Hatty said. 'Yes, I am Miss Ward, the girls' governess, as you may have guessed.'

'*Enchanté*, Mademoiselle.' Another bow. 'I hope that we shall be great friends.'

'On the contrary, Monsieur. We are already enemies. For you are to arrange for the sale of Lord Elstow's books. And that is an act of vandalism to which I am most vehemently opposed.'

He gave her a conspiratorial glance. 'Ah, then! We see what ensues! Perhaps, after all, I find the library is not worth selling! But now – excuse me – I go to pay respects to Madame la Comtesse. We meet again later.'

He darted into the house, after his luggage.

What a strange little character, Hatty thought. He reminded her of an engraving she had found in one of Lord Elstow's Natural History textbooks – a praying mantis (found, perhaps, in the Americas?) – an attenuated, wispy creature, with a triangular face, topped by two huge dispassionate eyes like marbles. His small wrinkled brow fell away behind them, his mouth was similarly small. His skin, pale and soft, was like that of a larva emerging from a cocoon. Not quite human, Hatty thought. He is like a talking lizard, or an intelligent cricket.

At dinner he reappeared, very handsomely attired – '*tiré*,' as Barbara had said, '*à quatre épingles*' in satin knee-breeches, a velvet jacket, and silk stockings. He wore a wig, and exuded a strong odour of orris root. The girls, in their usual evening muslins, took in his appearance with admiring eyes.

The Countess chatted to him in a lofty manner, putting questions about her acquaintance in town, all of which he answered with practised ease and vivacity in a high, clear carrying voice. He seems to know everybody in London, thought Hatty, or else he has excellent sources of information and gossip. Some of his tales caused Lady

Elstow to emit a brief, gruff laugh which Hatty had seldom heard before.

'Well, well, du Vallon, I must say that you are more entertaining by far than my two sulky girls and their preceptress,' she remarked.

'Ah, well, Madame,' he smiled, 'nobody is to blame for that. After all, my sources of scandal, rumour, and tittle-tattle are so much better than theirs. But I have taken the liberty, Countess, while I am under your roof, of ordering a London newspaper to be sent to me from town – which I hope you will do me the favour of sharing with me.'

'Oh! Well, I see no harm in that. Much obliged to you, Mossure.'

'It will be a pleasure, my Lady.'

'Now, girls and Miss Ward, we will leave M du Vallon to his wine.'

Wine had appeared at table for the first time since Hatty's arrival at Underwood. Normally, of an evening, the girls and Hatty drank water, or lemonade, while the Countess had a small flask of colourless liquid by her place from which Glastonbury filled her glass every now and then. Often she became extremely drowsy as the evening meal progressed, and would retire to her own chamber directly afterward; but tonight she repaired to the drawing-room which, unusually, was warmed by a small fire – for all the rooms at Underwood were dank and chilly after sunset, even in the middle of summer. All the candles were lit, also.

During the meal Hatty had hardly spoken, except when questioned or directly addressed. The girls had sometimes put questions to the guest, or reminded him of episodes during past visits. It was plain that both of them were eager to reclaim his regard, and jealous of his notice. He divided his conversation equally between them and seemed to take pains not to favour one above the other, for which Hatty mentally commended him; she felt that, while perhaps not naturally kind-hearted, he might be judicious and fair. He has remembered, she thought, what a highly complicated and potentially explosive situation there is between those two girls. Towards Hatty his eye seldom strayed, but just occasionally, if it did, she thought she caught a brief sparkle, what he himself might have described as a '*clignement d'oeil*' and, when, after dessert, Lady Elstow left him alone with the half-bottle of wine, she caught the vestige of a brief rueful grin, an infinitesimal shrug. Indeed he appeared in the drawing-room after a minimal interlude; Hatty imagined him swallowing the wine at one gulp and pulling a face over its sourness.

'Well, sir,' said Lady Elstow, when du Vallon made his entry, 'what is your opinion of matters now in France?'

Barbara and Drusilla threw up their eyes and grimaced with boredom. Du Vallon, perhaps observing this, said, 'Ah, Madame, you ask *me* that? Me, who have been an exile for so many years?'

'But you still have friends there – kinsfolk, who write letters to you?'

'Ah, so seldom! But I read the French press and know there is now a shocking national deficit, which could be remedied most easily by an additional tax of six or seven francs per head, levied on the middle and upper classes – but the nobles, my family among them, cannot be persuaded to pay their share! I hear there is to be an Assembly of Notables – perhaps that will succeed in putting an end to the impasse.'

'The nobles?' said the Countess. 'Why should they pay? I see no need for that.'

'Well, Madame, as you may have read in the works of Jean-Jacques Rousseau – his *Discours sur l'origine de l'inégalité* and *Du Contrat social* – he believes that we were all created equal and should perhaps return to that condition.'

'Disgraceful nonsense,' said the Countess. 'No one but a Frenchman would dream of such a perverted theory, let alone writing it down.' She gave a tremendous yawn and added, 'I beg you won't talk of such works to my girls.'

'No, Madame, I should not dream of it! And I am very sure they would not listen.' He flashed a smile at Barbara and Drusilla, whose expressions of utter boredom faintly lightened.

'I am very fatigued and must leave you now,' said Lady Elstow. 'Miss Ward, pray do not permit the girls to stay up after ten o'clock.'

'No, ma'am.'

Trailing her voluminous satin draperies, the Countess made for the door, and du Vallon was agile in leaping to open it for her.

As soon as the door was closed behind her — 'Monsieur du Vallon!' cried the girls in one breath, 'Do you remember the battle game?'

'*Ma foi*, how could I forget it? But do you young ladies still take an interest in such masculine, warlike pursuits?'

'What else is there to do?' said Barbara with a curling lip, while Drusilla cried, '*Malbrouk s'en va, Malbrouk s'en va!*'

Greatly interested — it was the first time that she had heard the child volunteer any words in French — Hatty inquired, 'Pray enlighten my ignorance, Monsieur du Vallon, what is the battle game?'

'Why, it was one summer when Lord Elstow was so unfortunate as to break his ankle — so, for a month, he was confined to the house here. I had been reading a life of Alexander the Great, with very detailed descriptions of his battles and campaigns, so we invented this game, which we used to play on a great table in the room next to the library — even his Lordship was quite amused, *faute de mieux*. And from Alexander's battles we progressed to other famous contests — Hastings, Lutzen, the Siege of Troy, Malplaquet, on which field both sides claimed the victory—'

'Oh, do let us play it again!' cried Drusilla. 'We can easily find some plaster — and I daresay the pieces we used are still laid away in the game larder or one of the lamp rooms—'

'Or we could create some new pieces — that is if Mademoiselle Ward permits?' Again his strange eyes sought those of Hatty, and this time they flashed a distinct message — *We are of one tribe, you and I.*

'Well,' she said, 'I certainly do not see any objection. It sounds a most educational pastime.'

On another man's face it would have been a grin.

XV

Hatty feared that the educational routines, such as they were, of Barbara and Drusilla were likely to suffer after the arrival of the Abbé du Vallon; both girls were wild to resume the much-discussed battle game. In some degree, she thought, this was just an excuse to be in the Abbé's company, but also, she soon discovered, it was a genuine craving to play the game for its own sake.

'Why did you never mention this pastime before?' she asked Drusilla, who shrugged.

'What use? You would not know how to play it.'

An old laundry table, twenty feet long, was fetched from a disused wing of servants' offices, and set up in an empty pantry near the library. The table had been used for the same purpose on the Abbé's former visit, and was encrusted with old putty or plaster, dried hard, which one of the footmen was set to scrape off. When he rebelled, which he soon did, saying that builders' work was no part of his duties, the girls quite willingly applied themselves to the task, and had it complete long before Hatty would have expected, to the fearful detriment of their hands. Fortunately Lady Elstow, soothed and diverted by the Abbé's company and conversation at meals, took even less than her customary notice of her daughters during this period, and their blisters and broken fingernails escaped comment.

While the table was being prepared, the Abbé set himself to a systematic sorting and re-organization of the books in the library, preparatory to cataloguing them. Hatty, unobtrusively observing him at work, was impressed by his intelligence and method. Misled at first by his eccentric looks, she had wondered if he might be just a parasite, presuming on his friendship with the Earl to supply himself with comfortable board and lodging and a sinecure occupation. (Not that he seemed overjoyed by the accommodation and diet provided at Underwood Priors, but beggars, thought Hatty, cannot be choosers, and she gathered that he had no other means of subsistence.)

'How were you employed before you came here?' she asked him once, and he shrugged and replied, 'Oh, *comme çi, comme ça*. Sometimes I am engaged to teach French to the young sons of nobility, sometimes I do translation work. I live from hand to mouth.'

When the girls came eagerly to announce that the battle table was now ready for use, du Vallon, who seemed to enjoy his conversations with Hatty, said, '*Très bien*. But where are the pieces? We cannot fight battles without armies.'

After further rummaging in an old game larder, boxes of pebbles were unearthed – the infantry, explained Drusilla – as well as a dusty, musty collection of corks, entangled with moth-eaten cocks' feathers. Half the pebbles were white, half brown; but they were all so dirty that the Abbé decreed they must be washed and laid out to dry before use.

'Otherwise Drusilla, who, we know, is colour-blind, will not be able to tell one from the other.'

Hatty was interested to hear the Abbé refer so unconcernedly to Drusilla's disability, since her affliction was never alluded to in the family. A blanket of silence lay over her difference from other people, as over Barbara's habit of helping herself to other people's belongings.

'These feathers are all moth-eaten and must be burned,' pronounced the Abbé.

'Oh yes!' cried Drusilla, and began piling them eagerly on the fire.

'*Not* the corks also, fool-child! The corks are unspoiled and may be used again – *du reste*, I do not imagine corks are now so plentiful in the house as when his Lordship is at home.'

'No, that is true,' said Barbara. 'We used to get big bags full of corks from Glastonbury when Papa was in the house. But Mama does not provide such a supply. Her tipple is laudanum, not wine.'

'So: we require a few more corks, a basket of feathers from the hen-wife, some siege weapons – clothes-pins and twigs will serve – and ink to colour the feathers.'

Hatty was much interested and not a little amused to see how readily even Barbara lent herself to this childish game of creating two toy armies. On their own, or in her company only, this would never have been achieved. It was the interest and participation of the Abbé that engendered their enthusiasm; they were prepared to work all the hours of the day under his guidance.

'Now: what battle shall we re-create? Agincourt? Malplaquet?' And he hummed, '*Malbrouk s'en va, s'en va, s'en va t'en guerre . . .*'

'Oh yes, Malbrouk!' clamoured Drusilla, excited by the singing. But Barbara said, 'No, let us have one further back. Alexander and Darius, or the Romans and Hannibal.'

'The Romans always lacked good cavalry; that is why Hannibal won. It is queer, and interesting, how the Italians have never been very successful on horseback. Who first invented cavalry, can you remember, young ladies?'

'Cyrus the great,' Barbara amazed Hatty by replying.

'*Formidable!* In the year 550 BC. But the Greeks, under Alexander, had excellent cavalry, trained by Xenophon. *Bien*, we have us the battle between Alexander and Darius on the plain of Gaugamela, between Nineveh and Arbela. Alexander led the cavalry himself. Now, we make this plain with sand. Drummond, the second gardener, has promised me a sack of sand.'

'Why not plaster?'

'Too much trouble to scrape off, once it has become hard. Sand we can re-form for each new battle.'

The girls saw the sense in this, but complained that the sand slid about and made their hands dirty. It also stained the fronts of their dresses, until Hatty decreed that for the game they must wear enveloping aprons. The battle of Agincourt required a wet terrain so that the French army might sink in the bog; this rendered both girls so extremely filthy that Hatty demanded they both take baths and change every stitch of clothing before appearing at the dinner table.

She noticed, with interest, that the presence of the Abbé in the house had effected a considerable change for the better in the manners and appearance of both girls. Besides being extremely elegant himself in his choice of attire – which, though plain and sober during the hours of day was always of the very best quality, his linen freshly laundered, and his shoes brilliantly polished – he was critically observant of any niceties in the wardrobe, style and trim of those about him.

'I observe a young lady with very, *very* clean, shining hair,' he congratulated Hatty one evening, when she had washed hers; and she was amused to notice that both girls the very next day followed her example and had their hair washed by Winship, the elderly nurse who looked after them. They voluntarily put on clean dresses without being urged to do so, and submitted to lying on back-boards and having their nails trimmed with a better grace than they had hitherto manifested.

The Abbé also volunteered to ride into Bythorn in his curricle and purchase muslins to make the girls new summer dresses.

'For it is plain to me that you wear outgrown and very faded toilettes.'

'Oh yes,' sighed Barbara. 'They are dresses left behind by our elder sisters when they married and went away.'

'*Pauvres petites!* Well, I am a very excellent judge of materials and shall bring you back some superb bargains, trust me.'

'Oh, Monsieur! But how in the world will you be able to persuade Mama to part with the cash?'

'Oh, I shall promise to buy her some of those bon-bons that she likes.'

'I wish we could go with you!'

'No, *that* I believe she would never permit.'

Du Vallon offered to perform the same service for Hatty. With considerable tact he suggested that it was a pity a young lady with her charming appearance, and, he could judge, very superior personal taste, should be afflicted with a wardrobe of such gaudy and unflattering garments. 'I am perfectly sure they were not chosen by yourself, Mademoiselle.'

Hatty sighed and laughed. 'No, you are entirely correct, Monsieur du Vallon. They were chosen by my aunt, and, dearly though I love her, I cannot agree with her taste in colour.'

'Then – Mademoiselle – it would be the simplest matter—'

'Alas, Monsieur, you are exceedingly kind, and I am vastly obliged to you, but it cannot be. I have no money to expend on my wardrobe.'

She still had received no payment from Lady Elstow and, though she had a few guineas from poems she had sold to *The Analytical Review*, felt it prudent to retain what she had, in case of some sudden emergency. She did not trust Lady Elstow's erratic temper and felt it not improbable that she might be dismissed with the same staggering unexpectedness and irrationality that had despatched her predecessor.

'But this need be no concern,' suggested the Abbé. 'Madame la Comtesse gives me money for her daughters – the sum can most readily be distributed among the three of you.' The Abbé seldom smiled outright, but a kind of wintry twinkle now passed over his strange countenance.

'Oh, thank you, Monsieur, but that would not be honest,' Hatty said very firmly indeed.

'*Dommage!* You would *so* repay clever dressing, Mademoiselle.'

'But what does one's appearance matter, tucked away here in the wood?'

'The eye of God sees you,' said he sententiously.

This was the first time he had referred to religion; Hatty could not feel that he took his calling very seriously. On Sundays when the girls, Hatty and Lady Elstow repaired to the down-at-heel little church which was all that remained of Underwood village, the Abbé remained at home and performed his own, presumably Catholic, devotions.

Now he went on: 'Besides, *I* see you, Mademoiselle, and I have the eye of an artist, let me tell you. It grieves me to contemplate you in a dress like an orange fondant.'

'Well, I am truly sorry for your plight, Monsieur, but I am afraid that you must continue to suffer,' Hatty said laughing.

He bowed, hand on heart, and acquiesced; when, later, he returned from Bythorn with a considerable bundle of charming and intelligently chosen fabrics bought, all, he assured them, at bargain prices, over which the girls exclaimed in ecstasy, his eye caught that of Hatty and he shrugged and raised his brows in exaggerated grief at her obduracy. But Hatty had a curious and powerful conviction that she had passed some kind of test with the strange little visitor, and that it was lucky for her that she had not acceded to his suggestion.

He gave the girls excellent advice as to how the materials that he had bought them should be made up, and personally superintended the process.

'How does it come, Monsieur, that you are such an expert on fashion?'

'Why, Mademoiselle, it is because I was brought up, so to speak, on the knees of the royal family at Versailles. My mother, you see, was a lady-in-waiting to the Queen and had to attend all Court functions. So we lived at Versailles (in a small apartment in great discomfort) and I, as a child, was dandled by all the royal personages. I was a very pretty child, with a mass of golden hair – yes, yes, I know I am very different now – my mother dressed me as a girl until I was five years of age, and in my little cambric frock I perched on many a royal knee. I was a child prodigy, learned to read at two, at the age of three could recite Racine's tragedies by heart, and sat in the royal box when the royal family attended the theatre and amused them all with my comments.'

'Good heavens, Monsieur.'

'Your surprise is natural, Mademoiselle.' He gave her a melancholy nod. 'But I am glad to have had such experiences; good taste, thus acquired, can never be lost. (Take care, Miss Winship, you are cutting too close to the border.) Elegance of appearance and manner is, without question, the first step to a civilized life.'

'I wonder if Lord Camber would agree with that?' Hatty remarked, half to herself.

'Hein? Camber? You are acquainted with him?'

'When I was living in my uncle's house in Portsmouth I saw him frequently,' Hatty explained. 'You know him also?'

'I knew him at Cambridge.' A curious shade passed over the Abbé's face; as with so many of his expressions, Hatty did not know what it meant. Distaste? Wry amusement? Regret?

'A man of much charm,' he pronounced. 'But I fear that his ideas do not – how do you say it? – they do not hold water. They have no validity. But it is some years since I saw him, he may have changed his opinions already.'

'Oh no! He is a man of very strong convictions. He has lately gone as a servant to Pennsylvania.'

'Indeed?' Hatty suspected that this was no news to the Abbé. 'Well, I pity his master, unless he is fond of argument! *Chère Madame*, pardon me, you make the tuck *here*, like this – so. Now, you will see, the gown will fit very well.'

Drusilla was not so interested in the new clothes as Barbara, since colours and patterns meant nothing to her.

'Monsieur, Monsieur, will you not come out and play croquet with us? See, the sun shines!'

'If Mademoiselle Ward permits?'

'Oh yes – provided you promise to talk to us in French all the time we are playing!'

'You are a stern taskmistress, Miss Ward!' But he went with the girls amiably enough. He was ready to fall in with everybody's requirements, Hatty thought. In the evenings he played backgammon or cards interminably with Lady Elstow and entertained her with an inexhaustible (it seemed) supply of political and society gossip.

'And is it true that the King is out of his mind?'

'No, no, Milady, that fear has passed; his Majesty is quite himself again.'

'And is it true that the Prince of Wales has a different pair of shoe buckles for every day of the year?'

'Oh yes, *indeed*, Madame, and more besides.'

Hatty, along with the girls, benefited from the daily newspaper that the Abbé had caused to be despatched to him by post; and he also received a French journal, *Le Moniteur Chrétien*, which came weekly, and which he perused with great attention. 'So that,' he explained, 'if my affairs mend, and I can ever return to France, I shall not feel too much of an ignorant foreigner.'

The Abbé never, at any time, gave any account of what unfortunate or discreditable occurrence had obliged him to leave his native land and take refuge across the Channel; he occasionally had letters from Paris. 'From a friend,' he explained, but he did not divulge or allude to their contents.

Hatty wondered what had obliged him to come abroad; he seemed so very discreet and sedate in his behaviour that it was hard to imagine him involved in any wrongdoing; something political, perhaps? The affairs of France appeared to be in a sorry state, judging by the contents of *Le Moniteur Chrétien*. It might be easy, in France, to make some dire political mistake.

Hatty had persuaded Lady Elstow to have the harp repaired, and lessons on it now formed part of the girls' daily timetable. Barbara had very little talent, but liked the idea of herself giving an elegant performance well enough to make her take some pains in practising; Drusilla, as with the pianoforte, seemed unable to apply herself to a systematic routine of learning and practising, but, by instinct, it appeared, had the ability to improvise and produce melodies for as long as she chose. Music had the power to penetrate Lady Elstow's deafness better than voices, and she seemed quite well pleased, now and then, of an evening, to have the harp carried down to the drawing-room and sit nodding her head while her daughters played and sang.

Du Vallon had a strange, creaky voice like a cricket chirping, Hatty thought, remembering her first impression of him, but he was cheerful and obliging about taking part in their after-dinner music-making, hummed along with them when they sang, and himself sometimes burst into odd little French nursery rhymes and songs:

> *'Qu'on m'apporte ma flute*
> *La tzimm, la tzimm*
> *La tzimm*
> *La la!'*

During the mornings he applied himself diligently to the task of making a library catalogue.

'You know, there are some treasures here,' he confided one day to Hatty. 'I am very sure that Lord Elstow, who is no reader, has no conception at all of what valuable items his library contains.'

'For instance, Monsieur?'

'For instance, a folio Chaucer printed in 1687 – "The Works of our Ancient Learned and Excellent English poet Jeffrey Chaucer" – see, here it is – look at that beautiful page, together with "The Siege of Thebes" by John Lydgate.'

'Would that be one for the girls to do in their battle game?'

'Now you tease me, Mademoiselle Ward, but indeed the book is a treasure. Look at the engraved portrait of the poet Chaucer with his "lyttel sonne".'

'It is charming,' agreed Hatty. 'Would it be worth a great deal of money?'

'Oh, a hundred guineas at least, I should imagine; and, see here, "Seats of the Nobility and Gentry of Great Britain and Wales, illustrated by engravings, bound in morocco and gilded" and "Works of Quintus Horatius Flaccus, 1733 edition with vignettes and floral gilt decorations".'

'Perhaps I could borrow that one for the girls' Latin lesson.'

'*No*, Mademoiselle Ward; I hope you are jesting. And look here, Malory, Sir Thomas, "*Le Morte d'Arthur* Wynken de Worde 1498".'

'That I must certainly borrow. I have always loved King Arthur.'

'I beg you will do no such thing. The volume should be locked up in a chest lined with velvet cloth in a warm dry room.'

'Where is one to be found in this house?'

'I know. It is terrible what the damp has done already. But, seriously, dear Miss Ward – here are treasures enough to supply a *dot* for one, at least, of the young ladies – or—'

'You think they will marry, then?'

He shrugged. 'The little one? *Jamais à la vie*. The elder? Perhaps. Mind, it is unfortunate about *la kleptomanie* . . .'

'I beg your pardon?'

'Her penchant for helping herself to other people's valuables.'

'Oh, goodness!' said Hatty in horror. 'Has she—?'

'No, no. *Soyez tranquille!* She has taken nothing of mine. I am fully on my guard. I lock my door. But I have a memory from former visits. Do not disquiet yourself, dear Miss Ward! And indeed you are doing wonders with her. It is not too impossible, I begin to believe, that, in the end, she should find a *parti*. But you interrupted me, Mademoiselle. I was thinking how simple, how very simple it would be to forget that these books had ever been here in the library, for who knows of their existence except you and I? Not Lord Elstow, for sure!'

'I do not think I understand you,' said Hatty, who had turned quite white.

'Do you not? But you have not yet been paid a single sou for your labours with these young ladies, I believe? Nor have I, for that matter. Just *one* of these volumes would amply cover our wages as preceptress and librarian, for one year, or even for two.'

'You are joking, of course,' said Hatty, after she had taken a careful, silent breath.

'Oh, of course!' He studied her calmly and said, 'Now we will forget this conversation.'

'If you please.'

'*Why* forget the conversation? What was it about?' asked Barbara, who had just walked into the room. She looked black, suspicious, and lowering, as always when she interrupted a conversation between two other people who seemed to be getting on well with each other and without her.

'We discussed whether Quintus Horatius Flaccus should be added to your syllabus of education. You should be glad, Mademoiselle, that we decided against it. And you are wearing one of your new gowns and look charmingly in it! What a pity that Miss Ward has to go on wearing her old orange-coloured jaconet.'

Barbara was only partly mollified.

'Can we fight the Battle of Hastings?' she demanded.

'From where had Harold brought his troops, the night before?'

'Stamford Bridge.'

'And whom had he fought there?'

'The Norsemen.'

'And why did not the English return the Norman archery fire?'

'They had no archers.'

'Very good girl. They had learned better by the time of Agincourt. We shall play. Set up the ridge of Hastings on the table. But where is your sister?'

'Asleep on the schoolroom floor.'

'*Eh bien*, you had better wake her up.'

Barbara went to do so, after giving the Abbé another suspicious glance. But Hatty had already left the library and was running upstairs to her own chamber. As she did so she clasped her reticule which contained a folded paper.

It was a letter from the *European Review*, announcing their acceptance of two of her poems and offering payment of half a guinea apiece.

Another step on the road to freedom, she thought.

XVI

As well as knowing all about London society, the Abbé du Vallon was a mine of information regarding the Wisbech and Fowldes families and their idiosyncracies and ramifications. The Duke of Dungeness, for instance, he said, had a rooted dislike of a half-filled cup or glass, and would never drink but from a full one. His butler had to be constantly at his elbow to keep the beaker topped up . . .

'All that family are somewhat strange,' the Abbé told Hatty. 'The Duke's aunt, Lady Flimborough, tore off all her clothes, once, at a Queen's Drawing Room.'

'Dear me! Did not that make quite a sensation?'

'Well, it was during the first period of the poor King's madness, so the people at Court were quite accustomed to odd behaviour. And then there was her husband, Lord Flimborough, who left a clause in his Will stating that he bequeathed his whole fortune to his beloved daughter Jane upon condition that, within the twelve calendar months after his death, she should marry a man not below the rank of a baron. If she should *not* do so, the money would go to his wife, not otherwise mentioned in the Will.'

'Gracious me! What happened? Did the daughter marry a baron?'

'No, she did not. (Though, as you may well imagine, there was no lack of applicants, for his fortune was an immense one.) She announced that it would be an insult to her father's memory to marry within a year of his decease, and, after the expiry of that period, she entered a religious order, for she was of a serious cast of mind.'

'So the wife inherited after all.'

'No, the poor lady died of a flux five days before the conclusion of the year.'

'So who got the money?' This story would interest my cousin Sydney, thought Hatty.

'Alas! The fortune was all dissipated in lawyers' fees as different members of the family tried to claim it.'

The Duke of Dungeness was a decided eccentric, du Vallon told Hatty; if he had not been a duke his mental state would have been termed madness.

'But so it is with many of these noble families. They are so inbred that such singular aberrations are commonplace among them.'

Hatty thought of Drusilla's visual deficiency and Barbara's pilfering.

'But the Duke's children are normal enough, are they not?' she asked, hoping that the Abbé would say something friendly about Lord Camber.

But, to her dismay, he exclaimed, '*Au contraire,* Mademoiselle Hatty! Of the girls I know little harm – Suzanne and Louisa married well enough and seem to have settled satisfactorily with their spouses. But Camber! Some say that he is no worse than a Holy Fool – though even in that role he has done untold harm – but I find him *insupportable*! He has a habit of telling the truth – or what *he* considers to be the truth – in and out of season, at the most inappropriate moments. At Cambridge he was known as Candide.'

Such a look of venom momentarily distorted the Abbé's countenance that Hatty did not dare make further inquiries in this area, but du Vallon went on: 'See what harm he did his cousin Ursula. As you may know, they were fiancés. She had a passing weakness for his friend Fordingbridge – it was a nothing, no more than an *amitié tendre* – would never have come to anything, but Camber had to make a grand drama out of it with renunciation scenes and heroic relinquishment and resignation. All quite unnecessary, believe me.'

'But,' suggested Hatty cautiously, 'perhaps he had come to the conclusion that he and Lady Ursula were really not – really did not suit? After all they are very, very different from one another. And they never did resume their engagement.'

'*Now* they are different,' snapped the Abbé. 'But if they had remained together, who knows? He might not be such a Holy Fool, she might be less angular and intransigent.'

'But if she loved Fordingbridge?'

'Pfui! That would have come to nothing. I know, I!'

'Why?' Hatty asked obstinately. 'How do you know?'

'Fordingbridge was not of a kind to love any woman for long. At the beginning he had been *Camber*'s friend.'

'Oh,' said Hatty rather blankly.

'Fordingbridge wrote Camber a letter from India, making Camber promise that, if misfortune should come to him, Camber must look after Lady Ursula. Did Camber do so? No, he did not. In fact he worked upon her, almost compelled her to return and look after these tedious girls—'

Hatty longed to ask how in the world du Vallon had known about this letter from Fordingbridge to Camber. It did not sound as if he and Camber had ever been on sufficiently close terms to make such a confidence likely between them. And what, she wondered, had been the incident, presumably at Cambridge, that engendered such a strong dislike for Camber in the Abbé?

But at this moment Barbara entered the library, picking up the Abbé's last phrase.

'*What* tedious girls?' she demanded instantly.

'The girls who read this volume,' promptly replied the Abbé, holding up a book. 'Fordyce's *Sermons for Young Women*. See, it is already the ninth edition, and it was first published only twenty years ago. It must be in great demand. I have been exhorting Miss Ward to read you and your sister one of these edifying homilies each day as you lie on your back-boards – the author requires young ladies to wear at all times an air of bashfulness, to eschew *any* kind of wit or humour or spriteliness, to show sedate manners in company, to be quiet, demure and humble. Love of *shining* is most particularly discouraged.'

'Sad stuff! *Pray* do not read it to us, Miss Ward.'

'Well, I will not,' promised Hatty. 'I don't detect any particular love of shining in you and Drusilla, fortunately – perhaps because there is no company to shine at.'

'Aha!' said Barbara. 'But we are to have company. Papa has written to Mama that he will certainly be here in September and that he may bring a party of friends.'

'Then you must remember not to be spritely. Or to shine,' said Hatty.

Barbara pulled a face at her – the nearest she ever approached to a smile – and demanded, 'Marcel, may we have Thermopylae?'

'Have you completed your devoir for Miss Ward? And you should not call me Marcel in her hearing.'

She put out her tongue at him. 'Yes, yes, we have done it, we have done it.'

'Which kind of men did King Leonidas take with him to the Pass of Thermopylae?'

'Only men with sons to succeed them.'

'Why?'

'Because he knew they would all be killed.'

'And where were the rest of the Greeks?'

'On Salamis Island.'

'Very well, go and set up the battlefield. But before our battle I think we should play a game of battledore and shuttlecock. Drusilla looks a little pale.'

Drusilla, who came in behind her sister, had stood looking wistfully at the fire which, even on this warm August day, was, by the Abbé's command, kept burning in the library.

The two sisters ran off to set up the battlefield.

'You have done those girls much good,' du Vallon pronounced. 'More, I am bound to admit, than their sister Ursula would have achieved.'

'Oh, but so have you, Monsieur!'

A footman came in and said to Hatty, 'Miss, there's a visitor for you. A young – gentleman.' His hesitation on the last word was noticeable. 'I have put him in the lobby to the left of the front door.'

'Thank you, Firkin.' Who in the world can it be? Hatty wondered, her heart leaping up, then falling again.

The visitor proved to be Hatty's cousin Sydney.

'Well, well, Cousin Hatty,' he said, scanning her up and down. 'Have not the Fowldes paid you any wages yet? That gown looks to me like one of my mother's choosing! Did I not see you in it last year?'

'Oh,' cried out Hatty, 'how *is* my Aunt Polly? I long to have news of her. Did she make a good recovery from her illness?'

'No,' said Sydney flatly. 'Did you not know? She had a second seizure in April and died two days after.'

'Oh no!' whispered Hatty. '*Oh no!* She has been dead five months?'

'That is so.'

'And nobody wrote to me! Nobody told me! Here have I been writing letter upon letter – and nobody thought to let me know. Oh, that was *cruel*.'

'Well, what would you expect from my father? He had cast you off – he is not one to make a change, once he has decided upon a course of action. He never speaks of you, never mentions your name.'

'Does he know that you have come to see me?'

'Oh, very likely. For I am here on business. My mother left you fifteen pounds in her Will. It was hers to leave – from her dowry. She had always saved it.'

Sydney handed his cousin a small cloth bag. 'And furthermore she left you her book of kitchen receipts, though I do not suppose that you will have any need of *that* in this establishment. No doubt they look after you hand and foot.'

He gave Hatty a sour smile, glancing superciliously round the shabby little apartment. '*Have* they paid you yet?'

'Well – no,' admitted Hatty. 'But Lord Elstow will be here himself next month. I have not met him yet, he has never been home since I came here. I daresay he will arrange to pay me then. Lady Elstow does

235

not take much part – much interest – but is, I think, quite approving of what I am teaching the girls.'

'Well, you are a stayer, I am bound to admit that, Cousin Hatty! I had not thought it possible that you would settle in here. I knew you had a strong constitution, but still I am surprised. You look well enough, too.'

'I can say the same for you, Cousin,' Hatty retorted, not without a touch of malice, for since she saw him last, Sydney had put on weight to quite a degree, and now looked the image of a plump, self-satisfied young man of business. His clothes, hat, and complexion were all glossy; and the latter decidedly rubicund. 'You have a most prosperous air. I hope that is a true indication of your condition?'

'Thank you, yes. I spend three days a week in London and the other four in Bythorn where, already, I have enough business to keep me well occupied.'

'And my – my stepmother, Cousin Ursula? Where did she go?'

Hatty had hardly, yet, felt the full pain of Aunt Polly's death; she was talking and asking questions mechanically, in an instinctive attempt to postpone the final shock of grief. To have been deprived of the right to mourn all this time, to have been kept in penitential ignorance – or so it seemed to her – increased the sharp sense of unjust punishment. That is the second death, she thought, in which I have not been permitted to participate as I had the right to. Unbidden, a memory flashed into her mind of the rainy graveyard in Portsmouth, the distraught daughter of Lady Pentecost attempting to throw herself into her mother's grave, Lord Camber stepping forward and kindly, with perfect sympathy and understanding, guiding the poor creature away to some comfortable haven.

Oh, he is *not* a Holy Fool!' Hatty thought passionately. He is not, he is not! He is a truly warm-hearted, understanding person. Oh, how I wish he were here. He was so fond of Aunt Polly too...

Half-unconsciously, she compared her mental image of Lord Camber with the two men she had most recently talked to – du Vallon, clever, amusing, but, she felt, untrustworthy, lightweight, swayed by who knew what strange unaccountable objectives or desires, while the motives actuating her cousin Sydney were all too plainly visible in his every look and gesture. Self-interest governed him and always had and always would.

Now he was glancing discontentedly round the bare little room. 'Lady Ursula?' he said carelessly. 'Oh, she went to stay with one of her sisters but that was only for a month or two; I fancy she was hoping after that to quarter herself on your sister Lady Bertram at Mansfield Park ... I hear Lady Bertram is very good-natured. Your stepmama can probably hang up her hat at Mansfield for as long as she cares to; that is, if she don't get across Sir Thomas or rub your sister Agnes up the wrong way. Lord save us, what a harpy *she* is. I should think you were not sorry to leave her behind when you came to reside with us at Portsmouth, hey, Cousin Hatty? But how do they treat visitors in this great damp barrack of a place – is there any chance of a glass of Madeira, or something to warm the cockles of a man's heart? After I have rid all this way to see you?'

'I am rather surprised that you did,' replied Hatty, jerking the bell pull. 'Could you not have sent a messenger? Or have you business with Lady Elstow? And are you not presuming rather far in expecting that visitors to the governess may hope to be entertained in the same style as visitors to the family?'

'Oh, not in the same *style* – but, after all, plague take it, you are related to them, your mother was a Wisbech, and Lady U was your stepmother. And I could give Lady Elstow news of Lord Camber if she were interested.'

'Which she would not be in the very least; she has a decided prejudice against him. But you may as well tell the news to me,' said Hatty, masking intense interest in a casual tone. 'How do you come to hear from him?'

'Oh, he wrote asking for another piece of land to be sold. He and his father, in their different ways, are just as feckless as one another.'

The door opened and a footman came in.

'You rang, miss?'

'Fetch us a glass of wine, will you?' said Sydney. The man bowed and vanished again.

'So has Lord Camber now left his master and settled in Amity Valley?' Hatty inquired, still in a negligent manner.

'No, but he is about to do so. It must be said that they obtained that land on most advantageous terms.' Sydney was evidently put out that somebody had concluded a successful piece of business without his intervention. 'They have acquired another thirty-three square leagues of land with a mineral spring on the banks of the Susquehanna river – the ground rent is only one red rose in the month of June for ever.'

'Good gracious,' said Hatty. 'That is a bargain indeed. I wonder who the rent is paid to?'

'Oh, doubtless some native Indian tribe,' Sydney said irritably. He added in a casual manner which Hatty instinctively felt had a false ring to it – for when was any action of her cousin Sydney ever casual? – 'By the bye, Hatty, I suppose you are not informed as to the present whereabouts of the title-deeds to Lord Camber's little place in the woods – Thorn Grotto, is it called?'

'Title-deeds of the Thatched Grotto?' Hatty was puzzled. 'No, indeed! I have no idea at all. Why should you expect *me* to know such a thing?'

'Well, you spent some days there, did you not? Some member of the household might have chanced to mention the matter.'

'Why, are they lost?'

'Oh, merely mislaid. They are sure to come to light.'

Sydney moved to the window, through which the Abbé du Vallon could be seen with Drusilla and Barbara, playing at battledore and shuttlecock on the carriage sweep, which was about the only level piece of ground in the vicinity of the house.

'That, I suppose, is du Vallon, the Frenchman who comes to catalogue Lord Elstow's library?'

'Yes, that is the Abbé.'

'He takes time off from his labours to play with the daughters of the house? He must be very good-natured.'

'Yes, but he is very diligent also.' Hatty defended the Abbé. 'He works long hours in the library – he informed us that there are some very precious and interesting old volumes there.'

'Ah, indeed?' Sydney's eyes momentarily lit up. Though not at all interested in old books, his mind was naturally alerted at once to anything of pecuniary value. But he continued doggedly with his inquiries about the Abbé. 'And how does Lady Elstow receive the Frenchman? Is he likely to be a suitor for one of the daughters?'

'No, I do not think that is at all probable.' Hatty was quite startled at the suggestion. 'He behaves to them more like an older brother, a relative. Well, he *is* in some way connected to the Fowldes family. But he has no money, none at all, I am sure Lady Elstow would not for a moment entertain any notion of such a match. Besides, he is such a strange, dried-up little creature – the girls enjoy his company, but it is for lack of any other – I do not think they would ever look upon him in the light of a suitor.'

'He is civil to *you*? Uses you with propriety?'

'Oh, perfectly. Indeed, he is very good company. Why, Cousin,' exclaimed Hatty, with an irrepressible chuckle, 'were you afraid that the Abbé might offer me some affront? Nothing, I am quite certain, is farther from his thoughts. Is *that* why you rode all this way to Underwood? To protect my virtue?'

Sydney scowled. 'If I did so, Cousin, it would be no joking matter. Your reputation is already somewhat in question, after those nights spent under Lord Camber's roof.'

'Oh, who in the countryside cares a fig for my reputation? Who, indeed, knows about that visit?' But Sydney's inquiry about the title-deeds had made Hatty anxious. 'Lord Camber is not proposing to *sell* the little house, is he?'

She thought of the happy household established there – Godwit, his grandmother, Mrs Daizley, the boy Dickon, and Miss Stornoway. What refuge could they find, if the house were to be sold? She thought of Lord Camber's offer of the place as a haven for herself, but did not mention this to Sydney, who would almost certainly put some disagreeable construction upon the gesture.

'You must understand, my dear cousin, that I cannot discuss Lord Camber's business transactions with you,' Sydney said chidingly. His repressive air annoyed Hatty, who felt that she was probably more conversant with Lord Camber's plans and wishes than her cousin. But he was still intent on the subject of du Vallon.

'I wonder that Lord Elstow allows him the freedom of the place here, thinks fit to establish him in the same household with his daughters. He has a somewhat unsavoury reputation, I understand.'

'Oh?' Hatty was not wishful to hear demeaning stories about the Abbé from her cousin Sydney, who, even as a schoolboy, always had a predilection for telling malicious tales, generally much exaggerated, about all his acquaintance.

'They say—' Sydney began, but Hatty interrupted him.

'Cousin, if you have no more business to transact, I must return to my charges, and not be loitering here, listening to gossip. Or I should certainly merit a rebuke from Lady Elstow.'

'Oh – very well! But, Cousin, there is one more thing I have to say – I ask – I wonder very much—' Sydney suddenly lost his assured air and looked merely like a fat, plain young man, rather over-dressed, nervous and mistrustful. 'Do you – *can* you like it here?' he brought out at last. 'Do you go on as you should in the household?'

'Why, yes.' Hatty was surprised at this unexpected solicitude. 'Quite to my own surprise, I get on comfortably enough. Lady Elstow does not interfere with my authority over the girls, they mind me tolerably well, and, what is most important to me, I have sufficient peace and lack of disturbance – and a most wonderful supply of books to provide a foothold – a good environment – for my own work.'

'Your *own* work?' Sydney looked wholly puzzled.

'My writing.' He still looked blank. 'My poetry.'

'Oh, good heavens. You still do that scribbling? I had thought you meant *work*.'

To this statement Hatty did not choose to make any reply. She waited in cold silence.

'Cousin Hatty, have you given any more thought to my offer?' Sydney brought out at last. She continued to look at him blankly. 'My offer of marriage? It still stands! Consider how very comfortably circumstanced I now am with my own house, a number of excellent connections, more coming in all the time. It cannot but present a most favourable contrast to your own circumstances and future. What lies ahead of you but more drudgery here, or similar drudgery in some other household? I assure you, Cousin Hatty, that you are *never* likely to receive a more eligible offer than mine – and you know that I have always felt a decided partiality for you,' he added as an afterthought.

Hatty gave an impatient sigh. 'How many times, Sydney, do I have to tell you that my answer is No, and would always be No, were you to stand here till Judgement Day? As for your partiality, I cannot recall any manifestation of it in the past. I think you deceive yourself there. You certainly do not deceive me. We should not suit. Now, let me see you out – I wish to join the girls on the carriage sweep.'

She opened the door and passed through it ahead of him, observing, but without any particular concern, his expression of sullen chagrin.

'How do they all go on at the house in Lombard Street?' she inquired politely, as they passed a couple of footmen in the hall. 'Does Tom still go to day school? The household must be very much diminished now. It makes me sad to think of your father. He must be lonely. Do you go back there often?'

'Hardly ever!' snapped Sydney, as they left the house. He looked round for his horse, which a groom was holding and now led forward. 'I understand,' he went on sourly, approaching the stocky cob – evidently Sydney was not one to waste his cash on ostentation when it came to horseflesh – 'I understand from Tom that my father has every intention of marrying Burnaby when he is out of his blacks for my mother. It will save her wages,' he added.

'*What?*' Hatty stared at Sydney, transfixed, as he rather clumsily mounted and gave the cob a kick. Then she suddenly ran after him.

'Oh, Cousin!'

'Yes, what?' He turned to give her a malevolent look.

'You said that dearest Aunt Polly had left me a book of household receipts – do you have it with you?'

'Oh. Yes. To be sure.' Clumsily, ungraciously, he delved in a saddlebag and handed her down a small volume wrapped in brown paper.

'Much good may it do you – I suppose even the Fowldes do not expect you to help in the kitchen?' he inquired disagreeably, and urged his horse into a trot.

Gazing after him, Hatty realized, with rueful amusement, that part of his bad temper was indubitably caused by the fact that the footman had never returned with the glass of wine he had asked for. Momentarily she felt a touch of pity for her cousin. Poor fat Sydney. However much he prospered in his legal career, he would never acquire that effortless air of command, of inborn, natural authority that Lord Camber, however shabby his appearance, or the Abbé du Vallon, with all his peculiarities, would always excercise.

Tucking the wrapped-up book under her arm, she joined du Vallon and the girls. Watching their cheerful antics as they bounded about, she pondered Sydney's statement that the Abbé had an unsavoury reputation. Unsavoury in what way? she wondered. And remembered, unexpectedly, from long ago, a gardener at Bythorn Lodge, whom her father had had occasion to dismiss, unpaid and even with angry threats of legal penalties, because he had made undesirable overtures to two of her sisters, Fanny and Maria.

Maria would not ever state, precisely, to her sisters, what had happened. She merely said that it had been most disagreeable.

'But what did he *do*, Fanny?'

'Oh, he kissed me – in a very horrid way.'

Hatty herself could remember the man – Fawkes was his name, a thickset, burly man with bristly hair and prominent red lips, and he smelt always of sweat and sacking. He had kissed her too, though she was only six or seven, and had clutched her against him in a way that she strongly disliked, wriggling free as soon as it was polite to do so.

Whatever there might be of an unsavoury nature about the Abbé du Vallon, Hatty felt perfectly certain that it was in no way similar to the delinquencies of Fawkes the under-gardener. They seemed of a different species.

Suddenly grief overcame her. She turned to du Vallon.

'Monsieur, my cousin – that young man – came to me with most unexpected news of the death of a near relative – my aunt, who brought me up. I need to be by myself for a while. Will you ask Lady Elstow to excuse me from dinner? And keep the girls entertained?'

The girls came inquisitively to hear what was being said. She felt three pairs of eyes fixed on her with interest, but without the faintest touch of sympathy.

But du Vallon was always equal to any social requirement.

'Most assuredly I will tell her Ladyship, Mademoiselle,' he said, bowing. 'You must rest and grieve in peace. It is perfectly understood.'

'Thank you, Monsieur. Good night, Barbara. Good night, Drusilla. Enjoy your game. I will see you in the morning.'

Toiling, with a weariness unwonted to her, up the stairs, Hatty wondered why Sydney had given himself the trouble of riding all the way to Underwood Priors. Was it just to inspect the Abbé du Vallon? And if so, why?

PART THREE

XVII

Letter from Mrs Fanny Price to Lady Bertram

Dear Sister Maria:

I write to appeal to you, since I get but Harsh words from Sister Norris and, latterly, not even very many of them. But you was always a kind sister to me and I remember many a Laugh and Comfortable Coze we had together brushing our hair by candlelight. Sister I do not deny that I was villainously misled in my Estimate of Mr Sam Price & should never have taken him if I had known of his Hasty Temper, Gross personal habits, Intemperance, Ignorance, and Nasty Ways in general. But, Sister, I put it to you, how many women, when they go to marry, do know anything more about their future Mates than I did about mine? A young lady meets a gentleman at an Assembly – they dance together a few times, he dines at her family's house, they may take a stroll or two together – in the great majority of cases, that is the entire acquaintance a couple may have before they are united at the altar. I collect that you were fortunate in your alliance with Sir Thos who, my Sister Norris continually assures me, is all that could be desir'd in sobriety, benevolence and sagacity. But consider! It might have been far otherwise! You had met him on no more than 5 occasions (a picnic, a ball, and three dinner parties as I recall) before he offered for you, and I can well remember you crying all night because you had no mind for this heavy, dispiriting person and were in love with Ensign Stephen Tillinghast, who had not three farthings to rub together.

Dearest Sister Maria, pray consider my plight. Meat costs 6½d per pound, coals are 12s a ton and my husband allows me but 4s a week and often I have to look Sharp if I am to get that out of him. How am I to take proper care of my poor girl, my little Fanny, not to mention William and Sam, out of that? As often as not I am oblig'd to wrap Sam in an old Towel for lack of proper swaddling clothes. Do, I beg you, Sister, out of your abundance, send me but £10 – or even £5; or at the very least a parcel of linen. I hear from Sister Norris that you already have a fine family in your nursery. I daresay some of them may by now have outgrown their first clothes. And, Heaven help me, I am increasing *again* . . .

Your affectionate but despondent sister, F. Price.

Letter from Mr Nathaniel Claiborne in Baltimore to his cousin Luke Claiborne in Connecticut.

My dear Luke:

I send you this with a load of Salt Pork in exchange for the Maple Sugar which we are so glad to receive from you. It will be delivered by the hand of my ex-Master Carpenter Harry Liss who will see it to its destination and then go his ways to the Settlement which he is to join on the banks of the Susquehanna river. I shall be sorry to lose his services, for he was an excellent carpenter and many of the articles he made will see my grandchildren out. But in other ways I shall be greatly reliev'd to lose him, for never was there such a talker! My ears became tired at the very thought of his voice! One subject, one idea led on to another without intermission. From the first crack of daylight his voice could be heard, and though (I am bound to admit) much of what he had to say was full of sense, wit, and original thought, I am a peaceable simple fellow, as you know, and like to spend my days in quiet labour and contemplation. It does not suit me to be for ever discussing or arguing, or (what is worse) listening to some other person involved in discussion, however rational and virtuous. So I was glad to compound with Master Liss for the second half of his indenture and (I may say) I am heartily sorry for his colleagues in the Settlement of Amity Valley for unless they are of a like mind with our friend, I fancy that after a few weeks they will be worn out with conversation and disputation. Yet he is a likeable fellow and I wish him well. I do not, though, entertain very high hopes for the future of their community if it is composed of Similar spirits; they will expend all their time and forces in discussion and nothing practical will be achieved.

All good wishes to your esteem'd wife my good sister-in-law Adelaide, and hope that the coming winter will not be too severe on you.

    N.C.

Letter from Lady Ursula Ward to her sister Lady Mary Finster.
My dear Mary:
I hear from our sister Anne that you plan to travel up from Scotland and hire a house in Bath to spend the winter there for the sake of your husband's Rheumatic Disorder. I was greatly interested to learn this, for I have had a few rheumatic twinges myself & should be glad to join you in Bath. As you know, I was oblig'd to leave Bythorn Lodge which, due to a most unfortunate and ill-conceiv'd Entail, passed into the ownership of my late husband's nephew, Sydney, a thoroughly disagreeable and unmannerly young puppy of whom the less said the better. I accepted a very kind invitation from Lady Bertram (Mr Ward's eldest daughter) and have spent some time at Mansfield Park, but the increase in that family (they have two sons and two daughters and all of them exceedingly healthy, well-grown, lively children) makes the Bertram establishment less comfortable than formerly, and Sir Thos, with his usual gentlemanly consideration, has suggested that I might prefer to find accommodation in some other household. I therefore with confidence in your sisterly hospitality, propose myself to you. I shall be glad to support you in your entry in to Bath society. I can of course bring my own bed-linen.

    Yr affectionate Sister,
    Ursula Ward

Letter from Lady Mary Finster to Lady Ursula Ward
Dear Ursula:
I am afraid that Finster will in no circumstances permit of your
joining our household in Bath. He remembers too forcibly the
continual dissension about the oatmeal at breakfast and the bread
sauce. If you wish to visit Bath and take the waters there, I
understand there exist professional ladies who, for a fee, accept
guests and supply them with an introduction into Society there. I
have heard of a Mrs Partridge who does this, and can supply you
with her direction if you wish it. We shall then have the pleasure of
meeting you sometimes at the Pump Room or the Bath.
    Yours affectionately,
    Mary Finster

Letter from Sydney Ward to Lady Ursula Ward
Dear Madam:
With regrets for imposing upon your Ladyship's time, I write to
inquire as to whether, by any singular chance, you are cognisant of
the whereabouts of the Title Deeds of Lord Camber's little property
Thatched Grotto – as his cousin, it occurred to me that his Lordship
might have apprised you of the document's disposition, or, he might
indeed have left it with you for safe keeping. If this is the case, I
shall be most exceedingly oblig'd for the assurance that you have it
in your possession.

    I had occasion recently to call at Underwood Priors on a matter
of family business & am glad to be able to inform you that your
esteem'd Parent, Lady Elstow and your sisters, the Ladies Barbara
and Drusilla Fowldes are all in excellent health. I am glad that my
young cousin Miss Harriet Ward continues to give satisfaction in
her position as Cicerone there and is herself acquiring a touch of
that Elegance which residence in such an Elevated Establishment
must necessarily bestow.

    (I am the more grateful for this as I intend to espouse the young
lady myself at no very distant date and so have her interests and
situation very much at heart.)

Did you by chance see the messenger from Foale's Bank who called at Bythorn Lodge on the day following Mr Ward's decease?

Yr Obdnt Srvt

Jos Sydney Ward

Letter from Lord Camber to Miss Harriet Ward

My dear little Miss Hatty:

I cannot tell you how it rejoices my heart to know that you are still residing at Underwood and superintending the education of my young cousins Barbara and Drusilla. I know the young ladies display some little difficulties and oddities, but these, I feel sure, will soon yield to your friendly and inventive company and amiable handling, and I am happy to know that the peace and seclusion at Underwood proves a suitable nursery or pasture for your Muse to browse in! I remember so well your excellent treatment of those hapless twins. I greatly admired the Verses you so kindly sent and congratulate you with all my heart on your success in selling some poems to the *European Review* and *The Gentleman's Magazine*. I admire your *nom de plume* and shall in future look out for stanzas by Anthony Bailiff. Members of our community receive several of these journals which are eagerly passed round here and discussed, so I shall hope to discover you in print before too long and shall pride myself on my secret acquaintance with the author. – I was a little concerned to learn that the Abbé du Vallon has been retained by Lord Elstow to make an inventory of his library; the Abbé is a clever man, and a man of parts, but I consider his company a trifle unwholesome, especially for the young. But I know that young digestions are able to consume almost any diet and derive nourishment from it – so I will try not to concern myself too greatly. However I hope that the Abbé does not continue for too long at Underwood.

Your sincere friend and well-wisher

H.C.

P.S. By the bye, do not forget that my offer of asylum at T.G. still holds – though I must reiterate that you are of infinite benefit residing where you do at present . . .

Letter from the Abbé du Vallon to his cousin Marcus Dariole
Mon Cher:
I remain here, as you see, a little bored, but lying low in safety;
inquiries were coming rather too close in London, so this sinecure
of an occupation fell at a most providential moment. And it has its
advantages, as you shall learn in due course! I hope that matters go
prosperously on your side of the Channel and shall look for good
news before long.

Yours in fraternity,
Marcel

Letter from Lady Ursula Ward to The Honourable Lucy Kittridge
My dear Lucy:
Doubtless you will be surprised to hear from me after so long, but I
thought that, cut off as I imagine you are in Amity Valley, you
might be glad to have news from your English connections and to
know that your sister Kate has been safely delivered of another son,
making, I believe, her fourth. I have not seen her myself but receive
copious bulletins from Aunt Sarah Chornleigh who keeps all the
family news in circulation.

I wonder how your Society of Sophocrats progresses? Frankly, I
give it five years, no longer; any association with three such diffuse
and harum-scarum figures as Wandesleigh, your brother Humphrey
and my cousin Harry Camber as its originators must soon crumble
under its own weight of dialectics! It is sad, I grieve to predict the
downfall of any well-intentioned enterprise, but so I fear it will
always be. You may tell my Cousin, if you should think of it, that his
father was in good health four weeks ago, by the account of Cousin
Fred Wisbech, though the Duke continues decidedly eccentric and
wayward; also that young Miss Harriet Ward who was, I believe,
something of a little protégée of my cousin's, will soon be married to
her cousin, Sydney Ward, the attorney who handles part of the Duke's
business affairs. I daresay it is considered quite a good match for her.

With all good wishes,
I am Ursula Conway Fowldes.

Letter from Miss Letitia Stornoway to Miss Harriet Ward
My dear Miss Ward:
I hesitate to trouble you when it is entirely due to your good offices
that I am alive and residing in this delightful household and still in
this World at all. But what I have to tell you is, I believe, germane
to your interests; and even if it were not, my sense of Rectitude
would not permit me to remain silent. Can you, dear Miss Ward,
find the time and the means to pay another visit here? I would not
ask if I did not believe the matter to be of Serious Importance . . .
   (unfinished)

XVIII

SEPTEMBER CAME, BUT Lord Elstow did not pay the promised visit to
Underwood Priors. His wife displayed perfect indifference to this non-
arrival, but his daughters were disappointed and resentful.

Barbara wanted a new horse. 'Firebird is long past her best days and
has no more pace than a tinker's donkey. She shuffles along so slowly
that I might as well go out on foot.'

'Then Drusilla and I may accompany you,' said Hatty cheerfully.
Barbara scowled at her. 'But could you not write to your father and
ask him to send money and instruct Harris to look out for a new
mount for you?'

'Useless! He never pays the least heed to my letters. It is most
aggravating that he does not come home for the cub-hunting – then,
he might have seen for himself how hopeless Firebird is becoming –
besides, I love cubbing.'

This was another annoyance. Lord Elstow had allowed the master-
ship of hounds to pass into the hands of Colonel Wisbech so that the
meets, which had formerly taken place at Underwood, were now held
at Bythorn Chase, or even farther away at Market Saltby, almost on the

other side of the county. Lady Elstow would not permit Barbara to attend these with only the escort of Harris. Both girls missed the sociability and excitement of the meets.

'It is most vexatious! And Harris is such a slow old niggler. He wanted to stop this afternoon and go down to the brook in Sparsholt Wood – the silly old man said he thought he heard somebody call out – wanted to go and see what it was, but I soon put a stop to *that*. I told him that if we were not home by four o'clock he could start looking for another situation.' Hatty thought how like her sister Ursula Barbara sometimes sounded. 'But what do you suppose keeps Papa in London?' Barbara went on discontentedly. 'He used to be so fond of hunting.'

'He has been much plagued by the gout this past year,' suggested du Vallon tactfully. 'I have seen him at his club when both feet were so swelled that he was obliged to wear slippers – and, you know, in such case he could not possibly get his feet into hunting boots – let alone stirrups.'

To Hatty, next day, privately, the Abbé said: 'And I understand Lord Elstow had other reasons for remaining in London. It is rumoured that his Majesty has gone mad again, so mad that he called Mr Pitt a rascal and Mr Fox his friend. For a man interested in office, this is not a time to leave the capital.'

'But do you think that Lord Elstow will ever really achieve any high office?' said Hatty, who had, somehow, at long range, acquired a rather low opinion of Lord Elstow's capacities.

'Well, he has good friends – Lord Foley and Charles Grey. But, in fact,' said du Vallon, 'I believe what keeps his Lordship in town is another new friendship, with young Mr Matthew Artingstall.'

'Who is Mr Artingstall?'

'Oh, he is a poet,' said the Abbé, as if poets rated fairly low in his catalogue of respectability. Later, Hatty was to remember this. 'One of these new Romantic poets. But the thing is, he is very beautiful, with flowing black locks and rolling black eyes.' He gave a philosophical shrug and raised his brows to indicate that such a friendship would be enough to keep *anybody* from their home, family and boring country duties. Hatty, not wholly comprehending, felt that he knew what he was talking about.

'You and I, Miss Ward, must resign ourselves to wait for our wages.'

'We are lucky that there is nothing to purchase around here.'

As a matter of fact, Hatty was feeling quite rich, for she had sold two more poems to the *European Review*. 'Dear Mr Bailiff,' said the editor's letter, 'We think so highly of your work that we wonder if you may be contemplating the compilation of a volume? Our rate, as you know, is Half a Guinea per hundred lines, and thirty guineas for a full volume. A Commentary in verse on the present troubled situation in France would be of interest.'

Thirty guineas! A year's wages!

Glastonbury came in with a distressed countenance. 'If you please, Miss Hatty – something dreadful—'

By insensible degrees, the servants had formed the habit of turning to Hatty in the event of household problems and crises. Lady Elstow took so little interest, and was so slow to respond that it often required half a day or longer to extract any reply or decision from her.

'Oh, what is it, Glastonbury? Lady Drusilla has not suffered another convulsion?'

'No, miss, there's been a body found in the Sparsholt Brook and – and – and I'm loath to tell ye this – but it's the other lady—'

'The other lady?'

'The one ye replaced, Miss Hatty. 'Tis Miss Stornoway.'

'*Miss Stornoway?*' repeated Hatty through numb lips. 'You mean – a *body* – you mean – she is dead?'

'Ay, miss. I'm afeared that's so. They're a-fetching her up now. Harris, he thought he heard somebody a-crying out, when he rode past that way yesterday with Lady Barbara – but they never stopped then, Lady Barbara was wishful to get home and said *she* heard nothing. And Harris, he was not certain sure he'd heard a voice – but troubled enough in his mind to go back this morning to take a look – ye see—'

'But – but how terrible – you mean – she *drowned* – in that small brook? She was there all night?'

'There will have to be a Crowner's Quest – won't there, miss? The men are out there now, fetching her in. The Crowner, he'll have to say – won't he? – if the poor lady drowned. But 'tis a nasty unchancy place, on the corner of Tanner's Piece and Yaffle Bank.'

Hatty knew the place Glastonbury meant. A narrow, tree-bordered bridle-track ran across a wooded hillside some twenty feet above the brook, narrow and deep here, and sunk between high banks. The woods and paths were slippery at present with fallen leaves and heavy recent rains. If somebody, walking along the narrow path, had chanced to slide or trip, and had rolled down the steep bank into the stream ... for a young, active person it would be no great task to climb out of the brook, but for an elderly frail lady, handicapped by her clothes – of an arthritic tendency ...

But what in the world was Miss Stornoway doing there, some five miles from the Thatched Grotto?

'They are quite sure who it is? That it is Miss Stornoway?'

'Oh yes, Miss Hatty. No question.'

A gloomy muttering and shuffling presently announced the arrival of the group of men bringing home Miss Stornoway's body on a hurdle. They were directed to a disused still-room in a semi-derelict wing, far from the family's living-quarters. The Coroner was sent for. Hatty, mastering terrible reluctance, went along to view the body, which had been laid out on a work-bench.

It took a moment or two to recognize Miss Stornoway, for the poor bent figure was so soaked, splashed and coated with mire that only the bony nose and the wispy grey hair, now draggled with wet but still bound close to her head by a drenched black velvet ribbon, gave proof that this was indeed the ex-governess. She looked more as Hatty remembered her from their first meeting, much less like the trans-formed figure of the Thatched Grotto.

'There's mud plastered all over her face and in her nose,' said Harris. 'I'm afeared the poor lady smothered in the mud. Don't ye think so, miss? 'Tis deep mud there in the bed of the stream. The water itself is none so deep – a matter of two foot – but she'll have rolled in and couldn't muster up the strength to get herself out again. There's naught

to hold on to. Oh, if only I'd gone when I heard that voice a-calling –
but Lady Barbara she said no, and I was just not certain in my mind –
it could have been a kingfisher's cry, or a heron ... Reckon that'll
haunt me now.'

When the Coroner – who turned out to be Mr Jones, the apothecary
from Bythorn – arrived, he was of the same opinion. The marks below
the sloping, slippery track, when inspected, told the same tale. The
unfortunate lady had slid off the edge of the path – probably in trying
to avoid a very miry stretch of the path itself which had been deeply
cut by horse-tracks – she had then rolled or slipped uncontrollably
down the steep hillside. Broken saplings and crushed leaves of wild
garlic bore witness to this. She had tumbled headfirst into the stream
and there lain helplessly, unable to raise herself out of the water, calling
out faintly for aid, until she had succumbed to weakness and exhaustion. She had drowned in a mixture of mud and water.

'There is no indication of foul play?' asked Hatty nervously.

'Oh, none, my dear miss; none at all. The idea!' said Mr Jones,
scandalized. 'No, the poor lady was merely subject to a shockingly
unfortunate mishap. She should never have been permitted to roam the
woods alone, at her age, and in her state of disability. What could her
friends have been thinking of?'

'They will be dreadfully sad about it,' said Hatty. 'A message has
been sent off to them – they must have been wondering   they will be
so worried—'

Hatty then, to her own subsequent shame and mortification, succumbed to a combination of strain and the sorrow that had been
assailing her since hearing of the death of Aunt Polly; she fainted away,
and only recovered, an hour or so later, to find that she had been
carried to her own chamber, where the maidservant Bone and Winship,
the young ladies' nurse, were ministering to her with burnt feathers
and aromatic vinegar.

'Oh, good gracious,' she said weakly. 'Where am I? What happened?'

'You fainted, miss; and small wonder, for a shocking thing to see, it
was, and not at all the sort of spectacle a poor young lady should be
expected to look at – 'tis the mercy of Providence Lord Camber's

257

people came and fetched the corpus away as quick as they have done. What such a sight would have done to Lady Drusilla I do not dare to think—'

'Poor Miss Stornoway. Her body has been taken away already?'

'Yes, miss. Her Ladyship said she didn't care to have a corpus remaining in the house – and Mr Godwit and two others came with a tumbrel and took the poor lady's remains off to Garrett, he's the undertaker at Wanmaulden village. The funeral's to be Monday, miss. Mr Godwit he left a message for ye, miss, that he was sorry you'd been taken bad and that he had no chance to see you. But he sent his best respects.'

'I hope I may have the opportunity to see him at the funeral.'

Indeed, Hatty much regretted not having seen Godwit who was, next to Lord Camber, the kindest, most reliable man she knew; and no fool, either, she thought, remembering with a small spark of amusement the look that sometimes came into his eyes while he listened to Lord Camber's more high-flown asseverations. And yet Godwit is truly, truly fond of Lord Camber, thought Hatty, rising cautiously from her couch, and I wish I had had the chance of seeing him.

'Take care, miss. You're full weak yet.'

'Where are the young ladies?'

'In the drawing-room, miss, with the French gentleman and her Ladyship.'

Drusilla was playing mournful, mysterious tunes of her own invention on the harp, while Lady Elstow slumbered and the Abbé du Vallon told Barbara about the siege of Tyre. But Barbara was paying him very little heed. In fact, studying her, Hatty's heart sank; she was only too familiar with the sullen, resentful expression which had settled on the girl's face. It meant that Barbara knew she was in fault, would rather go to the stake than admit it, and so was prepared to defy the whole world, be as hostile as she could to whomever she chose, rather than yield a single inch. Her lowering look at Hatty, entering the room, dared the latter to allude in any way to the circumstances of Miss Stornoway's death, to the fact that it might have been prevented if

258

Harris had been allowed to investigate the source of the cry he thought he heard.

'Are you feeling better, Mademoiselle Ward?' asked du Vallon solicitously. 'Viewing the poor cadaver must have been a sad shock.'

Barbara puffed out her lips contemptuously but said nothing.

'Yes, thank you, I am quite better,' Hatty answered.

Lady Elstow roused from her slumber sufficiently to say: 'What *can* the ridiculous woman have been thinking of, to walk about the woods all alone, like that, at this time of year, with the ground so dirty and treacherous underfoot? Such an undignified way to end one's life – too stupid, upon my word! So inconsiderate, too! Making such a stir! She might have thought of *that*, before she started out.'

'I wonder why she did start out?' mused the Abbé. 'It seems she must have been coming here. Perhaps she wished to pay a visit to her old pupils. But how would she ever have returned home before dark fell?'

He gave his nearest approach to a smile, a roll of his large, extraordinary eyes, to Barbara, who jumped to her feet with a clumsy, abrupt movement, exclaiming, 'Oh, who cares what the stupid creature planned to do? I have the headache. I am going to bed.' And she flounced out of the room.

For ten days after that Barbara kept to her chamber, asserting that she was ill. To Mr Jones the apothecary, summoned to her bedside, she complained that her head ached, she had pains in her back, her neck, her legs; she refused to eat, saying that food sickened her. She demanded that Hatty sit and read aloud to her, hour after hour, day after day. So far as Hatty could discover, she never listened to a word that was read, whether it were poetry, Shakespeare, French or Latin. Hatty felt that this insistence on being read to was a hostile act, an assertion of power; in this unspoken battle Hatty's only recourse was to comply calmly, and wait until the aggressive impulse had worn itself out. It meant that Hatty was unable to go to Miss Stornoway's funeral, which may have been the intention. This might not in any case have been possible for Lady Elstow did not attend the service and so the carriage would not have been available. It must, Hatty thought, have been a matter for some gossip in the countryside, that none of the family from the Priors attended the last rites of their old governess; still, doubtless the behaviour of the Fowldes family was nothing new to the neighbourhood.

'Were many people there?' she asked Glastonbury.

'Nay, miss; nobbut the ladies from the Grotto. And Mr Godwit and the lad. Or so I'm told.'

'You don't really believe that I am ill, do you?' Barbara said to Hatty one day. 'You think I am just malingering.'

'Why should I think that? Nobody submits to a boring regimen day after day just for fun; what could possibly be the object?'

'Then,' said Barbara challengingly, 'what do you think is the matter with me?'

Hatty was silent for a moment or two.

'I think something has poisoned you.'

After a startled silence, Barbara said: 'What?'

'How can I tell? The poison may have passed out of your system by now; you may be just suffering from the after-effects.'

Barbara stared at her through narrowed eyes.

'What can *you* possibly know about it?' she said sharply. 'You don't know any more than I do.'

'I have nursed quite a number of sick people, though,' Hatty replied calmly. 'And I know how they behave. Sickness is not only spots or vomiting or belly-ache – not only what you can see or feel. It can be in the mind, too.'

'Oh, so you think I am mad – like Aunt Flimborough?'

'No I do not. I think you are unhappy.'

'Oh, go away! Leave me alone.'

Next day Barbara got up, declared that she was better, and resumed her usual occupations. But she maintained a hostile manner to Hatty, never spoke to her unless it was essential, hardly ever looked at her, and avoided being left alone with her. She hates me, thought Hatty, sighing. But what can I do about it?

There seemed little to be done.

XIX

Lᴏʀᴅ Eʟsᴛᴏᴡ ᴄᴀᴍᴇ down to Underwood Priors for a brief visit in January. He was a tall, pale man with a freckled complexion and an underhung jaw. He had a vague, hesitant, sleepy manner; Hatty thought that he and his wife seemed very well matched. He addressed Lady Elstow in a high, weary voice which was apparently gauged to penetrate her deafness and must have been achieved by years of practice. She, for her part, seemed mildly interested in what he had to tell her of their London acquaintance.

'Parliament and the King have refused to pay the Prince of Wales's debts.'

'Well, why should they indeed?'

'The Duke of Richmond insists on his right to control Sarah Napier's annuity.'

'Well, I daresay he has his reasons.'

Barbara was annoyed that her father had arrived during a prolonged period of black frosts when no hunting would have been possible even if he could have accompanied her. But in any case his gouty affliction would have prevented his going out with the hounds. He did, however, put in hand the purchase of a new mare for Barbara's use.

Drusilla was ecstatic to see her father – she was very fond of him, it seemed, much fonder than Barbara; but unfortunately her excitement at his arrival brought on a series of severe convulsions which so weakened her that she was obliged to remain in bed for days on end. The winter was always a bad time for Drusilla; her narrow little weak chest was prone to bronchial disorders. Regrettably, her father was terribly embarrassed and disconcerted by her seizures and avoided seeing her as much as he could, which gave Hatty a very poor opinion of him.

She was interested to observe the Abbé's behaviour to the Earl. He treated Lord Elstow with a kind of scoffing affection, the derision shown by a younger brother to an elder who, though kind, is low in mental powers; rather, in fact, as Ned had behaved to his brother Tom. Lord Elstow, in his turn, submitted with unassuming mildness to this usage and seemed to defer to the Abbé's opinion in most matters.

It therefore came as a considerable surprise to Hatty when she heard the following exchange take place between the two men (Hatty was an unwilling auditor; she had been choosing a volume, concealed from view in one of the bays of the library when the two men walked into the room, unaware of her presence, and their conversation was in process before she could declare herself):

'Would you not think it an excellent thing, sir, if I were to marry your daughter Barbara?'

Lord Elstow in his reply sounded exceedingly startled. '*You?* Marry Barbara? My dear fellow, *no*. No, indeed. What can have put such an idea into your head?'

'It would be advisable for me to marry. To have a wife. Advantageous. And it would be an excellent thing for the young lady. Can you not see how unhappy she is here? She chafes. Married to me she would have more outlets. I know all her difficulties, I would be kind; I understand her very well. And her marriage to me would rid you of a problem.'

'She is no problem,' said Lord Elstow calmly. 'She may very well remain here for the rest of her life. As to her marrying you – my dear fellow, that is out of the question. You are quite ineligible – hopelessly ineligible. Your family have disowned you and your political reputation is doubtful. What sort of future would the girl have with you? No, no, that would not do at all. Not at all! Marry the governess if you feel it is necessary for you to have a wife – she is a decent sort of girl, not bad-looking and respectable as to family – her mother was a Wisbech—'

'The governess! I thank you, no! Besides, was there not some scandal with Camber?'

'Oh, nothing that is not readily forgotten—'

Hatty, trembling with rage and astonishment, here made her presence known by dropping a heavy volume loudly on the floor. There was an aghast silence and then the two men hastily left the library without waiting to see who their auditor had been. Hatty herself slipped away by the service door at the far end of the room, in order to avoid the possible awkwardness of meeting either of the men outside.

Later that day she was in the schoolroom (use of which for lessons had been resumed during the Earl's visit) when du Vallon came there, ostensibly to bring a map of the battle of Charlestown.

Hatty was alone in the room, for Drusilla had fallen asleep, after suffering a seizure, and Barbara was out trying the paces of the new mare.

Du Vallon came to the point at once. 'Miss Hatty, was that you in the library when Lord Elstow and I were talking?'

Hatty met his eye squarely. 'Yes, sir, it was.' She was interested to see that he looked extremely relieved at this information. 'I could not make my presence known in time to prevent your conversation,' she added.

'No, I appreciate your difficulty. We should have been more circumspect.'

'Yes, sir, you should,' said Hatty coldly.

'I am sorry if you were mortified. It was most unfortunate.'

'It was indeed.'

He surprised Hatty by saying, 'But still, as you have no great opinion of either myself or his Lordship, no bones are broken. What do *you* care for our disparagement?'

'Just the same, it is not very pleasant to hear oneself spoken of in such terms—'

'Oh, pfui! You are a clever girl. Within your secret self you believe that you have a better brain than either of us.'

'Not than you, Monsieur. I think you have a great deal of intelligence.'

'And you wonder that I waste my time here making lists of books.'

'That is not my affair.'

A slight frown crumpled his high bare brow. He said: 'I am not so sure about that. Now that I have given the matter some serious consideration, I believe that Lord Elstow may have been right. An alliance between the pair of us would be advantageous to both.'

'Advantageous, Monsieur?'

'You have bestowed your heart on Camber. Oh, do not stiffen your neck and raise up your chin at me – every time his name is mentioned, your eyes become as brilliant as carriage lamps – but Camber is no use to you. He will never make a *parti*. His head is always in the clouds. If he ever comes back from chasing wild geese in America – which is possible, for none of his designs have been successful hitherto and few of them last for more than a few months – if he should come back, do not deceive yourself that you will be able to pin him down to any connection, to any rapport. He will be off again on some new fool's errand.'

'You are entirely mistaken, Monsieur,' Hatty said with icy dignity. 'I had no such hope or intention as you seem to suggest. All I can claim – or would wish to – from Lord Camber, is friendship. I have no expectation of ever seeing him again. I have my own plans—'

'Which are?'

'My private business, Monsieur.'

He shook his head impatiently.

'What can you possibly achieve by yourself? You are young – friendless – female – lacking in birth and fortune, already your reputation somewhat tarnished—'

'Not unlike yourself,' she could not help saying.

'Yes! Except that I do not entirely lack for friends. Listen, Miss Ward. Do not immediately repudiate my offer. Take some days – weeks, months, if you will – to consider. I will ask you again. Rome was not built in a day. *Entendu?* I have a very considerable respect for you, Miss Ward.'

'Despite the fact that I am no more than decent, and have some scandal attached?'

The Abbé performed the flutter of his eyelids and twitch of the lips which passed with him for a laugh.

'No person of sense – such as yourself – cares a pinch of snuff for such trifling opinions. Forget Lord Elstow. He is of no consequence. He will never succeed in his aspirations, though he dangle round the fringes of the Whig party until he is in his dotage. But you, Miss Ward – I look at you, and I think to myself, That young lady has a future ahead of her. If someone – like myself – should take her in hand.'

'Perhaps,' she said thoughtfully. 'Perhaps I have. But I do not think my future contains you, Monsieur l'Abbé. Now I believe we had better end our conversation, for I see Barbara out there dismounting, and you know how angry she becomes if we confer too long together.'

'Very true.'

He left the room.

Well! thought Hatty, not without some complacency, for a friendless, middle-class disgraced governess in a secluded, tumbledown mansion in the middle of a wood, I have not done badly. Two proposals of marriage in the space of a few months. What next! (At least, I suppose that du Vallon's was a proposal of marriage?) Really, though, it is quite surprising. Why should Sydney, and now the Abbé, find me so captivating that they are impelled to propose? What makes them do so?

XX

THE EARL'S VISIT was not of long duration. He found it necessary to hurry back to London and test the political climate there. Unfortunately his hopes were due to be dashed: by March the King had recovered his wits, the Tories were triumphant and the Whigs disappointed yet again.

In March, Hatty had a letter from her sister Fanny begging for help. 'I suppose you are paid a decent salary for your teaching labours – which is more than I do, for I toil all day and receive nothing but hard words for my pains,' wrote poor Fanny. 'We are now remov'd to Portsmouth, but the house is small, dark, and inconvenient. Oh, Hatty! When I think of our pleasant childhood and the woods and meadows of Bythorn and the kindness of our dear Mother, my heart is like to Break. Never marry, Sister, marriage is but a trap, you are better by far with none but your own Self to care for and none but an Employer to please.'

That is as may be, thought Hatty; Lady Elstow had been somewhat bored and peevish since the departure of her husband and required to be played cribbage with for long hours each night, which duty fell mostly on Hatty as Barbara refused point blank, Drusilla was not capable of mastering the rules, and the Abbé now always pleaded writing work in the evenings. He must, thought Hatty, have very nearly completed his task of cataloguing; what would he do then? Would he devise some other pretext to keep him at Underwood? Or would he flit away as suddenly as he had arrived? She would miss his company, she thought, if he went, for he always had something lively to say, and the journals and newspapers he received were freely available to all the household and frequently referred to by Hatty in discussions with her pupils on contemporary history and current affairs. Drusilla made little of these but Barbara could at times be quite engaged, especially over such topics as the emancipation of women and the slave trade. During lessons she talked with reasonable civility to Hatty, but at other times the mantle of sullen antagonism drew down over her again and she could maintain a hostile silence for hours on end, particularly if Hatty and the Abbé fell into conversation, or seemed to be getting on well together. As April drew into May and May into June this antagonism became more pronounced, and Hatty sometimes wondered wearily how long she would be able to live and deal with such a continuous barrage of resentment and ill-will; trying to battle against it was like walking all the time through heavy, clogging sand. She thought it strange that two sisters out of a family of five should have such a capacity for enmity, and sometimes wondered what Mary and Anne, the two who had married, were like. And where was Lady Ursula all this time? After leaving Bythorn Lodge she had gone, Hatty knew, to the sister who had hired a house in town, and from there to Mansfield Park, but where had she gone after that?

When Hatty wrote to Fanny sending money (Lord Elstow had paid her a year's salary in arrear and six months in advance so she felt at last quite comfortable and beforehand with the world), she asked Fanny if she knew anything about the whereabouts of Lady Ursula, but had received no reply. This, for some reason, made Hatty anxious. Lady Ursula was such a powerful, unpredictable factor; she seemed like a loose cannon rolling about the deck of a ship (as described vividly by Ned in one of his letters); not to know where she had got to made life seem even more hazardous.

In June Lady Elstow required to visit a dentist in Bythorn. Haymaking was in process on the home farm, and neither of the girls wished to leave the cheerful scene and take a tedious drive into the town with their mother, so Hatty accompanied the Countess and took the chance to purchase herself some muslins and trimmings for new summer gowns. When, with the help of Bone and the advice of the Abbé, she had the muslins made up into simple but pleasing garments, she felt Barbara's hostility increase tenfold; the girl could hardly speak without letting fall some bitter, disparaging remark.

Unfortunately du Vallon was greatly preoccupied at this time. In part, this may have been the cause of Barbara's bad temper. Normally, he would have tried to mend matters and ameliorate her mood by his chat, inventing some lively absurdity, or relating some odd piece of information culled from his reading; but, at present, events across the Channel were absorbing most of his attention.

A National Assembly had been summoned in France, the States General were convened at Versailles, in order to try to solve, probably by means of a tax, the critical economic state of the country. Regrettably, no agreement had been reached among the three bodies that made up the States General, and, after six weeks' fruitless disputation, the King had called a halt to the proceedings and closed the hall in which the meetings had been held. Enraged by this high-handed action, the deputies had continued to meet in a tennis-court, where they took an oath not to break up their gathering until a constitution had been drawn up for France. The King, alarmed, ordered foreign troops into Paris under the command of Marshal Broglie.

'It is folly – suicidal folly,' said du Vallon one evening to Hatty. 'The Parisians are a volatile, unruly mass; threatened by foreign mercenaries, they will explode. Louis is like a man knocking away the props of a dam.'

He sounded disapproving, but his strange eyes were bright with excitement. Barbara, left out of this conversation, scowled and bit her fingernails – a habit which Hatty had managed to persuade her to leave off, after a long, hard-fought campaign, only two months ago. She then stood up and walked noisily out of the room, slamming the door.

'Barbara needs attention,' said Hatty sighing. 'She misses her father. Attention from me is no use to her.'

'*Dommage!*' said du Vallon, shrugging. 'She must learn to manage without – like the rest of us.' He returned to his journal.

Five minutes later Barbara opened the door again and put her head round it, keeping the rest of her body concealed.

'Marcel,' she said, in a charged, meaningful voice. 'Come out to the Pavilion. I have something to show you.'

Sighing in his turn, the Abbé folded the *Moniteur*, raised his brows ruefully at Hatty, and followed Barbara into the garden.

Lady Elstow had retired early, complaining of toothache, which made an excuse for a dose of laudanum. Drusilla, who needed a great deal of sleep, had long ago gone to bed.

Hatty, thankful for an interval of solitude, walked up to her own room. But she paused when she reached it, finding the door ajar. Puzzled by this – for the chambermaid never left it so – she went directly to the desk where she kept letters and papers. This had been ransacked. Letters lay strewn about, and a notebook was missing – the book in which she jotted down her current, unfinished work.

Without a moment's hesitation — her heart hot as a cannon-ball under her ribs — Hatty ran downstairs again and went out through the library french window, through the overgrown shrubbery, and across the unkempt lawn. Beyond it stood the building that was known as the Pavilion. This was an imitation Greek temple facing away from the house, embellished with four Corinthian columns. It had a floor of cracked tiles and a stone seat for those hardy enough to sit there and look at the encroaching woods.

As she approached, Hatty could hear a voice reading aloud — Barbara's loud, triumphant voice reading her own lines, recently written, the conclusion of a sonnet:

> 'The road leads on no farther than your gate
> Having come so far, one can only knock and wait.'

Hatty swung round the corner and into the Pavilion with the pace and mien of an avenging Fury. Barbara and du Vallon were sitting side by side on the seat, she reading from a thick notebook with brown marbled covers, he listening with an intent, critical expression on his face. Both looked up, startled, as Hatty confronted them; her approach in sandalled feet across the grass had been quite silent. Barbara's face turned a dark, dusky red; the Abbé's expression remained unchanged.

'*My* book, I thank you, Lady Barbara,' Hatty said quietly, and extended her hand. Barbara had now begun to grin: a broad, challenging smirk, as if to say, Well, all right, you have caught me, but who cares? Even so, *I* have made a greater fool of *you*. Still smirking, she handed the book to Hatty.

'Very nice poem, Miss Ward,' she said. 'Is it by any chance addressed to Lord Camber?'

Hatty had to battle with an almost ungovernable impulse to strike that red, grinning face — to slash at it with the heavy, thickly bound notebook. She did not do so. She clutched the book in her hand, took a long, steadying breath, repressing the shudder of rage that ran through her, and said, 'I shall leave this place tomorrow morning. I cannot stay in a house where my personal possessions are not secure.'

Barbara's face turned from red to white. Her mouth assumed an ugly twist.

The Abbé had sprung to his feet. '*Miss Ward*,' he said urgently. 'These are hasty words. Do – pray – take time to reflect.'

'Reflect? Why should I reflect? Why should I remain where I am of no value, where my pupils are detestable? Let their own sister come back and look after them.'

Hatty strode away and returned to her bedroom. Too angry to remain at rest, she packed up her belongings, then went out to the front of the house, to walk impatiently back and forth along the carriage-way and wait for the hours of darkness to pass.

It was a sultry July night, scarcely dark yet, though so late; by now the sky was overcast and a few drops of rain fell. A rumble of thunder sounded far away, in the distance. Hatty was reminded of the night, so long ago now, when she had dropped her sister Agnes's trayload of precious possessions down the stairs.

And that accident, she thought, has led me, step by step, to this place. And where will this night's events lead me?

An hour or so later the Abbé came out and found her there.

'Barbara is in bed,' he said in a low voice. 'Mrs Winship has given her some drops of Lady Elstow's tincture in hot milk to quiet her. She was greatly over-excited. And I have come to apologize. Had I known – had I only known what she was about to read to me, I would have stopped her. But, once she began, I confess I was too interested to interrupt.'

'Fine words,' said Hatty.

'Oh, I know, I know. Truly I have no excuse. But so it was: during my life I have read little verse, I have not the poetic ear, yet your lines, your images and ideas, impressed me greatly.'

'*Merci du cadeau, Monsieur.*'

'Listen,' he said. 'I am planning to leave this place.'

'I, too.'

'Folly, my dear Miss Ward! You have nowhere to go and nothing to live on. For you to storm away from here now, in a rage, with no security, no plans made, would be highly – *highly* – injudicious.

Suicidal, I might say! But come with me; and I will introduce you to a new life.'

'What can you *possibly* mean?' Despite her angry mood, her attention was caught.

'Pay attention! I have been watching affairs in France. I am about to return there.'

'But you were cast out? You are *persona non grata.*'

'Aha! All that is due to change. There will be a rising. And *my* friends, my sympathizers will be those who hold the power, who take command. Here we are, entering July – the change will take place at any moment now. It will have been precipitated by the King's stupidity, his drafting those foreign troops into Paris. The populace will not tolerate that. So: I am going to leave and return to Paris. Miss Ward, come with me! The new scenes, the new life and activity will change your whole way of thinking. No more drowsing in a damp grove with two stupid, ill-conditioned children! You are made for better things! You will meet politicians, men of letters, musicians, sculptors, painters. It is not unlikely that you will be a sensation. There are few English women in Paris at present. You may have a *salon* – you may command your own select circle.'

'But I do not wish to do any of those things.'

'*Why?* What *do* you wish?' he demanded impatiently.

'To write down my own thoughts, whatever they are.' And I *certainly* do not wish to spend all my days discussing politics with a lot of chattering French, she thought, and asked, 'How is it that you are so confident of all this, Monsieur? How can you be so well informed about what is going on in Paris?'

'Oh, I have correspondents who keep me *au fait* with what happens. And I, in my turn, keep them apprised about events in political circles in London.'

'I see. You have been a kind of spy.'

'Say, rather, a political analyst.'

'Well, it is obliging of you to invite me to accompany you, and I appreciate the offer – but that life would not suit me, not at all. I wish to read, to write, to reflect; to express myself; I certainly do not want to become involved in a whirlpool of political activity. That would not agree with me in the very least.'

'But you would see Paris! Paris is a magnificent city!'

'I prefer these woods. And I particularly would not wish to see Paris in the middle of a *coup d'état*.'

'Oh, that will soon be over,' he said.

'Well, I prefer to wait for that time, until affairs there have settled down.'

'Oh, you are besotted with that wretched man!' he exclaimed furiously.

'To what wretched man are you referring?' Hatty's tone was chilly.

'That Camber! "One can only knock and wait!" He has caused infinite trouble in this family and doubtless will cause more when he returns from his ill-conceived excursion. No wonder that Barbara has such a dislike of him. He turned her sister Ursula into a prematurely aged, sour, self-absorbed shrew and will probably do the same to you!'

'I am going back to the house, Monsieur. This conversation is unprofitable, and has lasted quite long enough.'

Hatty rose at six in the morning, after three hours of restless slumber. She knew that a butcher's cart called at Underwood before breakfast and then went on to Bythorn, taking in Wanmaulden Cross on its route.

She had left a letter for Lady Elstow, enclosing one month's unearned salary. She knew there was no point in attempting to speak to the Countess who would lie in a drugged slumber for many hours to come. She left a note explaining that she could not any longer tolerate her position in a house where her private possessions were subject to rifling and misuse and she herself to malevolence and gross insult. She bore no ill-will to Lady Elstow personally and apologized for the abruptness of her departure, but she felt that Barbara had by now become too advanced in years to profit from the company of a governess, and Drusilla, alas, though a sweet and friendly child, not capable of making further educational progress. Hatty gave as her direction her cousin Sydney's address at Bythorn Lodge (in case of any letters for her arriving subsequent to her departure) and concluded with her respectful regards and polite wishes.

She wondered, as she thumbed down the sealing-wax, whether Lady Elstow would even read through the letter.

Hatty had made her intentions known to Glastonbury on the previous evening, and he himself carried out her bags and gave instructions to the driver of the cart.

'We'll be right sorry to lose ye, miss; as far as a person can, ye've kept the young ladies in good order; better by far than that other poor lady. Lady Barbara's neither to hold nor to bind; we often ask ourselves what black misadventure will come *her* way, in days to come. Well, miss, we all wish ye well. Take a thought for us sometimes. And stand no undueness from that Lady Ursula.'

He raised his hand in greeting and the cart jogged on its way.

What in the world had he meant by his parting remark? Hatty wondered.

XXI

It was a most disagreeable shock to Hatty, on arriving at the Thatched Grotto, to find Lady Ursula installed there.

It was a close and sultry morning; last night's threatened storm had never come to pass. Lady Ursula was sitting outside the house in a basket chair (one from Lord Camber's attic study, Hatty recognized), sharply instructing Godwit in the correct procedure for planting leeks.

The Thatched Grotto did not boast a flower garden, but the grass close to the house was kept short, and there were vegetable-plots, bordered by pinks, marigolds and geraniums planted by Mrs Daizley.

'You should cut the tops back by at least a quarter of an inch, and the roots by half. No, *no*, do not plant them as close as *that*, you stupid man—!'

Both Lady Ursula and Godwit looked up simultaneously at the sound of Hatty's approach. Godwit had an air of mild harassment which did not diminish when he saw Hatty. He had been kneeling upon an old piece of straw mat; now he rose slowly to his feet and brushed his earthy hands together.

Lady Ursula lifted the lorgnette which hung round her neck on a velvet ribbon and stared at Hatty through it. She learned that trick from her mother, Hatty thought; Lady Elstow makes just the same gesture with her ear-trumpet. I suppose it is a means of keeping people at arm's length.

'*Harriet!* What in the world are you doing here? Have you taken leave of absence from your duties?'

Her tone did not suggest that this was an estimable thing to do.

'No,' said Hatty. 'I have left Underwood Priors.'

'*Left?* You have left Underwood Priors?'

'Yes.'

'Have you been dismissed from your post?'

'No, Cousin Ursula. I left of my own accord. I could not continue there any longer.'

'And may I ask why not?'

Hatty felt as if she were enmeshed in a horrible dream. The previous night she had slept little and very uneasily; painful thoughts followed and pounced and repeatedly woke her each time she sank into exhausted slumber; a miserable sense of failure kept scalding and stinging her into wakefulness; and the knowledge that she must rise very early kept her from real repose. The ride in the butcher's cart from Underwood to Wanmaulden Cross had been penitentially slow and jolting; during the two hours it lasted she had ample time to recapitulate, again and again, the scene in the Pavilion, and her last conversation with the Abbé. Was I unfair to Barbara? Hatty asked herself, over and over. She is a jealous, spiteful girl, but what chance has she had to be otherwise? Brought up in such dismal surroundings, with so little variety of company – one parent hardly ever at home, the other sunk in drugged apathy . . . Should I have, could I have taken more pains, found other means to rouse her interest, befriend her, improve her spirits?

I wish I could have had Lord Camber's advice!

When she had left the butcher's cart, depositing her bags at the Woodpecker Inn, and set off to walk through the woods, Hatty's own spirits had lifted immeasurably. At least now she was able to exert herself, and the path reminded her of the previous time when she had walked that way with Godwit, through the snow, wholly unaware of the happiness that lay ahead. The thought of the little house that awaited her in its clearing at the end of the path, and its simple, friendly inhabitants, wonderfully warmed and cheered her. *They* will not blame me for turning to them, she thought; indeed they invited me to come back again, that day when I called with Barbara; they made it quite plain that I would be welcome, that they were always happy to see me. It will be like coming home. Better than coming home.

After making her way through the woods at a quick pace, sped on by such thoughts, it was a strange and chilling rebuff for Hatty to arrive and find Lady Ursula established in her basket chair, giving orders to Godwit, as if she had always been mistress of the house. Hatty glanced at Godwit, hoping for guidance from him, but his expression remained studiously blank.

'Was it your intention to stay here? In this house? Was *that* what you proposed?' said Lady Ursula.

'Yes! It was.' Hatty drew her capacities together. It was ridiculous to be afraid of this pale, gaunt woman. What threat could she possibly offer? 'It *is* my intention to stay here. Lord Camber has given me permission to do so. I have his invitation. Mr Godwit knows that is so.'

'Yes, ma'am; I do,' said Godwit. 'Lord Camber left word that the young lady might come to reside here at any time she chose.'

'Well, I may remind you that *I* am the owner of this house now,' said Lady Ursula. 'I have the title-deeds, which Lord Camber relinquished into my care for the duration of his sojourn in the Americas. And it does not suit *my* convenience in the very least that you should come trespassing here. Not in the very least. Firstly, how can you maintain yourself?'

'Oh, I can do that for a year without any difficulty,' said Hatty with confidence. 'I have a year's wages saved ... And—' she broke off and went on firmly, 'I do not think, ma'am, that Lord Camber would be pleased if he should hear that I had been denied the hospitality of his house. I shall write to him directly and explain the matter to him, for he has repeated his kind offer several times. Mr Godwit knows this.'

'Yes, my Lady, that I do,' said Godwit again.

'Oh.' Lady Ursula paused; reflected. 'Well – I may say that it is in the highest degree inconvenient that you should come here at this juncture. I do not know how you are to be accommodated.'

'I reckon Mrs Daizley will see to that, ma'am,' said Godwit, his brow lightening a trifle. 'Did you leave your bags at the inn, Miss Hatty?'

'Yes.'

'I'll send the boy for them.'

Hatty was greatly relieved to hear Godwit allude to other members of the household; there had been such a dead silence about the place that she had begun to fear – in a mindless, superstitious terror – that the other inhabitants had all fled, or been driven away.

'I can sleep in a closet, anywhere,' she said gladly, remembering that, in fact, there were several small empty rooms under the thatch.

She walked briskly indoors, to be greeted with a throttling hug by Mrs Daizley. Lady Ursula had remained out of doors in her basket chair.

'Oh, Miss Hatty! Miss Hatty, dear! We've fell on hard times, we have indeed! But now you have come it will be better.'

'How long has she been here?' Hatty asked in an undertone.

'Nigh on six months, miss. We did think Mr Godwit should send ye a note, when she first come – but he's no great hand at the letter-writing as ye know – and we thought as how *That One* would likely send word, once she'd settled here, to let her ma, Lady Elstow, know she was so close to the Priors – but there's no denying they are a right queer family, the Fowldes, they don't seem to take much heed of each other ... Mr Godwit, he reckons she was obliged to come here because her own sisters wouldn't take her in, after Sir Thomas sent her packing from Mansfield Park.'

'Oh, did he so?'

'That's what they say about the country, miss.'

Hatty, looking round the kitchen, noticed some changes. A small table had been introduced and set by the window.

'At first, miss,' Mrs Daizley whispered, '*That One* wanted to have all her meals carried up to her in her bedchamber. But Godwit said we was not paid to do that, we was not her servants. So, in the end, she allowed she'd eat her dinner at that table there. I do take her breakfast up to her chamber, though, for by so doing she stays upstairs half the morning and that gives us some peace and quiet.'

'She brought her cat with her, I see.'

'Yes, she did! And the nasty, ill-conditioned brute drove poor Tib out of doors into the wood and we haven't seen a whisker of him since.' Mrs Daizley wiped her eyes. 'Oh, Miss Hatty, it *has* been hard. Little did his Lordship know what he'd laid on us. But you are a sight for sore eyes, Miss Hatty, *that* you are; maybe we shall all come about now. Maybe you'll sweeten the lady.'

'Where is Mrs Godwit?'

'Took to her bed, missy, when *That One* came, and she hasn't left it since.'

'Oh dear me . . .'

Mrs Daizley resumed her occupation of shelling peas, and Hatty helped her, and thought, as she did so, how frighteningly fast a household's peace and harmony could be shattered by the insertion of one unconformable element. This happy community, which before had positively hummed with kindliness and cooperation, was now silent, nervous, oppressed and low-spirited. When dinner-time came, and Lady Ursula ate her meal by the window, Hatty chose to sit with the others at the large kitchen table, assuming that Lady Ursula would not wish for her company. No comment was made on this by anybody. The meal was taken in silence.

Later in the evening, after Lady Ursula had retired, Hatty contrived to beckon Godwit away from the house, well out of earshot, in order to ask about Lady Ursula's arrival.

'Well, Miss Hatty, it was last autumn, just afore the weather turned wet, that she turned up here; she had paid two fellows from Bythorn to drive her nigh all the way in a little governess cart. Pity she wouldn't ha' waited a few weeks longer! The ground was still hard as a bone then. After the rains began she'd never ha' made it. And she showed me the title-deeds that she had come by, all parchment and lawyers' writing and a big seal, which was, as you may imagine, pretty fair Greek to me, as can read regular lettering but no more; but Miss Stornoway gave it as her opinion that it was all fair and square. And she was an educated lady as should know; and – more than that – there was a note writ from his Lordship to Lady Ursula which said, "Dear Cousin if you are ever in need of a place to stay, you know you may always rest your head at the Thatched Grotto. I do not doubt that little Miss Hatty, if she is there at the time, will make you welcome." So that was fair and square too, for we knew he'd told you that *you* was welcome whenever you chose to step this way and we'd always be happy to give you house-room.'

'Yes,' sighed Hatty. 'Lord Camber is very generous.'

If she thought that sometimes generosity was better diluted with discretion, she kept the thought to herself. 'So Lady Ursula just moved in, last autumn?'

'She did that, miss. Well – she was fair put out to find Miss Stornoway already living with us, so snug and friendly; I'm sorry to tell ye, miss, that from that day on she made the poor lady's life a burden.'

'How? Doing what?'

'Dropping hints: as how *she* – Miss S – hadn't a personal invite from Lord Camber's own self, but was asked only at second-hand, as it were; and how, being as this was the case, the sooner Miss S found new quarters, the better it would be.'

'Oh, good heavens,' Hatty said. 'Do you think – do you think that Lady Ursula drove poor Miss Stornoway to – to make away with herself? Do you think that?'

'No, I do not, Miss Hatty,' Godwit said sternly. They were walking along a woodland path, in a mild mixture of dusk and moonlight; he saw that Hatty was trembling; he took her arm and held it in a firm clasp. 'No, I don't think that, miss, dear, and nor must you either.

What I do think is that Lady Ursula so nagged and badgered the poor lady, always at her, that she started off with the intention to walk all the way to Underwood, wishing to see you and ask for your help or counsel. But she was getting on in years, and none too steady on her pins, and she slipped on the path's sliddery edge and tumbled down the slope. That's what I reckon happened.'

'So Lady Ursula did really drive her to her end.'

'Well – that is what it adds up to. And,' said Godwit, 'she will have to answer for that at the final reckoning. We'd best turn back now, miss, dear. It grows late. And you must be mortal tired.'

During the next few days Hatty felt mildly surprised that Lady Ursula did not interrogate her and comment on the circumstances which had caused her to quit her post at Underwood Priors. The matter was not alluded to at all. Lady Ursula, in fact, spoke very little. When she did, it was mostly to complain about the food, or the hardness of her bed, or the inadequacy of the services that were performed for her. This she did in a haughty but joking manner as if it were only a matter of oversight that everything done for her did not reach a standard of complete perfection. Hatty thought it singular that Ursula did not at any time inquire after her own mother, father or sisters at the Priors; she seemed to have expunged them from her mind, and to be existing in a vague, cloudy world of her own.

'Does she still have the title-deeds of the house in her keeping?' Hatty asked Godwit.

'She must have, Miss Hatty, for she's never left the place since she come here, nor sent anything away by the post. She must have them up in her chamber. No, she does not use Master Harry's study. I often ask myself what possessed Master Harry to entrust the deeds to her – 'twas a most ill-judged piece of work, to my way of thinking – but there! I daresay he had a lot on his mind at the last, before he went off. But those title-deeds she has got, certain sure.'

Perhaps, Hatty thought, Lord Camber made a last gesture, hoping, somehow, to re-cement their friendship – perhaps that was what he had in his mind. Had that gesture resulted in this curious state of cloudy vagueness which now enwrapped Lady Ursula and kept her at arm's-length from everyone around her?

The only character she addressed freely was her cat, to whom she poured out a continual string of endearments in a high, artificial fluting voice – these were of a most sentimental and sugary nature, entirely at odds from the lady's usual vinegared and astringent style. They embarrassed Hatty when she heard them – they seemed so incongruous – and the cat took no notice of them at all.

'*Tweedlums! Tweedlepussy!*' she would twitter in a high, piercing voice, and the cat would slink away with ears laid back and tail carried low, pointedly ignoring her.

'Reckon he knows his own mind,' Godwit would mutter. 'Can't say as I blame him.'

'*Was a, was a chucklepussums, then!*' But Chucklepussums took no notice. Hatty began to wonder, for the first time, whether Lady Ursula could be slightly astray in her wits; with what pertained to most daily affairs she seemed sensible enough, and well in control of anything that concerned her; but there was, all the time, this queer remoteness, as if daily affairs were hardly of importance to her. Had her rootless, homeless state, moving on from one unfriendly domicile to another, driven her over some mental precipice?

One day Godwit, who had ridden in to Bythorn on the cob to perform various domestic errands, returned with a budget of startling news. He had brought a newspaper with him, and displayed it to the household.

'First-off, there's the devil to pay over there in France! For those Frenchies have risen up, it seems, in Paris – it appears they didn't like their King fetching in foreign troops to keep order in the city – so a mighty crowd all banded together and went to beat down the door of that big prison they have – the Bastille, 'tis called – broke in the door and let out all the prisoners.'

'Good heavens!' said Hatty. She remembered du Vallon's confident prediction: 'The change will take place at any moment now.'

It seemed that he had been right in his information.

'But that's not all,' went on Godwit. 'Not all by any means. For that Frenchy fellow they've had at Underwood these last nine months, the one that's been making a list of all the books in the library there – he's took and skipped – shown a clean pair of heels – gone back to France by all accounts – and, not only that, but he've took Lady Barbara with him!'

'Oh, dear God!' Harriet stared at Godwit, transfixed.

Why, why did I not anticipate that? she asked herself. Of course! He planned to go to France, he wanted a companion – and no doubt he thinks that to elope with Barbara, to take her into that French hurly-burly, will be to hold a pistol to the Earl's head, will make him provide her with a dowry.

But will Lord Elstow give in and pay up? She very much doubted it.

She thought of that brief dialogue in the library. The Earl had sounded immovably opposed to du Vallon's offer. But perhaps the Abbé really has got important friends in the revolutionary movement, thought Hatty, perhaps Barbara will now have the chance, that he offered me, of an exciting new and active career in Jacobin circles? She could well imagine Barbara, clad in some flowing, dramatic attire, her thick black locks cascading over her shoulders, shouting exhortations to an enthusiastic crowd of followers. But what about that unfortunate habit of purloining other people's belongings? Well, perhaps she will not need to do that any more; or perhaps in a revolutionary setting, it will not be held to matter – they all do it . . .

'And,' went on Godwit, who had not concluded his tale yet, 'as you may suppose, Miss Hatty, there was a mighty to-do at the Priors, and his Lordship sent for from London; and then they find there's valuable books been took from the library, books worth hundreds of pounds, and a note found from Lady Barbara, saying they was took in exchange for her marriage portion, for well she knew she'd never see a penny of that.'

'No,' said Hatty thoughtfully, 'no, *that* she will not.'

'And *then*,' continued Godwit, 'to cap all – after there'd been a deal of welter and pelter in the library – his Lordship and a chap he brought down from London, a Mr Artingstall, trying to see what's missing, they go off and leave the youngest girl, Lady Drusilla, alone in the place, and what does *she* do but set fire to a lot of papers and nigh to burn the place down!'

'No!' exclaimed Hatty, aghast. 'She was always fascinated by fire. I was always afraid something like that would happen. Was she hurt?'

'No – Glastonbury saw the flames and fetched her away – but a deal of damage was done, and when the fire was put out they found Lady Elstow in a swound, for the smoke had risen up to her chamber and like to suffocated her. So Lord Elstow will have to stop at the Priors for a long time, till all's set to rights.'

'He will not like that,' commented Hatty.

Lady Ursula, sitting nearby in her basket chair, had been listening to all this narrative with a severe, remote expression, her upper lip drawn downwards over the lower, her eyes veiled behind their lids, her mouth pulled down at the corners.

Now she suddenly turned on Hatty.

'This is all *your* fault – you miserable, neglectful girl!' she said sharply. 'If you had remained at your post, as you should, and minded your charges, none of this would have occurred.'

Hatty had indeed been feeling considerable remorse over the chaos that had overwhelmed Underwood Priors after her own departure. Though would my presence, she wondered, have made any difference to the flight of Barbara and du Vallon? – I very much doubt it.

But this sudden attack stung her so much that she retorted: 'How can you say such a thing, Lady Ursula? When it was *you* who went off and left those poor girls to the care of governesses – in spite of Lord Camber telling you that it was your duty to stay at home and look after them!'

Godwit had tactfully gone off across the garden.

Lady Ursula started to speak, then apparently thought better of the impulse. A silence prevailed for some minutes. Then Hatty said: 'Would you care to look at the paper, Cousin Ursula?'

'Thank you.'

Hatty handed it over, glancing at it. There had been very few prisoners, it seemed, in the Bastille; storming it had hardly been worth the trouble, though it made a fine, symbolic gesture. And it must have seemed worthwhile to those poor souls who were released, thought Hatty. I could write a poem about that . . .

If such uprisings were to take place in *this* country, I suppose Underwood Priors and Bythorn Chase would be ransacked by angry mobs. I am sure Lord Elstow is a shockingly bad landlord – and I know the Duke is, for Camber said so. They would quite deserve to be disappropriated. But will such a thing ever happen in England? I hardly think so. I have read that the French peasants are miserably poor. Conditions are much better here.

Are they not?

She went quietly indoors and left Lady Ursula, who hardly seemed to be looking at the paper.

XXII

Letter from Lord Camber to Miss Hatty Ward:
My dear little Miss Hatty:
Those last two words might be found inscribed on my heart. I miss Hatty a great deal – how often do I find myself wishing for your discerning eye and your descriptive tongue! I wish so much that you could see Amity Valley, where the village begins to take on a charming appearance as the little wooden frame houses are given a coat of white paint by their proud occupiers, and a few creepers start to climb the walls and cottage flowers to blossom in the garden plots. A wooden bridge has been built over the river, so the ford is no longer used, and a stone grist mill has been erected. I wonder if you are now installed in the Thatched Grotto? Half of me hopes that you are there, conversing with your Muse; but half would still be glad to know that you remain at Underwood, opening the eyes

of my young Cousins to all the world's beauty. I must confess that I
— now that our little community here is in a prosperous way and
soon bids fair to be able to support itself — I now begin to fret and
hanker for fresh woods and pastures new; I have a mind to sling a
pack on my back and make off westwards, to unexplored ground. I
have met travellers who tramped off into the unknown land across
the Mahoning Creek in Eastern Pennsylvania and on to the
Muskingum River in Northern Ohio — this land is so vast and so
wonderful that it seems a waste not to adventure farther into its
mysteries and its wilderness. I have heard tales of the Dakota
Indians and of Assiniboia — savages dwell there, to be sure, and they
are said to be very ferocious, but I have never yet met the man — or
woman — whom I could not befriend (with the possible exception of
my Cousin Ursula — how is she, by the bye?) and I have a mind to
try my fortune in those western regions. You, meanwhile, are
exploring the realms of Faerie — and, I hope, finding plenteous
treasures. You wrote in your last that a volume of your writings had
been accepted for publication — I cannot begin to express how happy
this news makes me and how proud I shall be when I first peruse it.

Your friend H. C.

P.S. By the bye, did you ever receive a package which I ordered,
at my departure, to be sent to you in Bythorn Lodge?

Please give my best regards to my cousin Ursula, if you should be
in touch with her. It is my dearest hope that you two may become
good friends.

Letter from Lady Barbara Fowldes du Vallon to Miss Hatty Ward
Dear Miss Ward:
I daresay by this time the furore over my elopement with Marcel
has died down and I don't doubt you are now snugly establish'd at
Harry Camber's Grotto. I wish, when you have time, you will ride
over to Underwood and ask Winship to pack up my chemises and
send them to me here, to the address at the head of this paper,
which is in the Cordeliers' District of Paris, a most Quaint and
Picturesque neighbourhood, very ancient, with dark alleys and

crooked streets leading nowhere. My husband (Marcel and I were
married in a civil ceremony) is a friend of a surpassingly interesting
man, Jean-Paul Marat, a doctor who, however, has forsaken
medicine for politics. He considers that Lafayette, who is now in
charge of the National Guard, is a hopelessly ineffective and useless
figurehead, and writes many pamphlets about it. Marat is not
handsome in appearance, but has an intent and burning gaze, and
the most brilliant mind I have ever encountered. Please tell Winship
not to forget those chemises, and to mend a great rent in one of
them before she sends it.

    Yours,
    Barbara du Vallon.

Letter from Lieutenant Edward Ward to Miss Hatty Ward
Dear Cousin Hatty:
I have two weeks' shore leave coming soon & sh'd be happy to ride
north and spend a portion of it with you if convenient. Tom, who is
now an Ensign in General D——'s regiment, encamped at
Brighton, writes that our father has married Burnaby – did you
know this? So I have no great wish to spend more than a day or so
in Portsmouth – it will be cold cheer in Lombard Street from now
on I fear! And though I writ to my dear Nancy in London, I have
not yet received her answer, so cannot be sure of seeing her, tho'
confident in her loving constancy at all times. So no more now from
your affct. Cousin Ned.

    P.S. Tom writes that Burnaby is *increasing* – there's for you!
Ain't it horrid?

Letter from Mrs Agnes Norris to Lady Ursula Fowldes
My dear Lady Ursula:
I was more shock'd than I can say to learn that my inconsiderate &
flighty young sister had abandoned her responsibilities at
Underwood Priors & removed herself to the wholly undesirable
shelter of Lord Camber's abode. (The fact that Lord Camber is
himself at this time somewhere in the Americas makes no

difference at all to the gross impropriety of her action.) I was indeed distress'd to hear, also, of the other Unfortunate Occurrences at Underwood – the elopement of your sister Barbara with that ramshackle Frenchman whom your dear Father employ'd to index his library books (*I* could have told him that no good would come of *that*) – the theft of books by your sister Barbara, thus confirming what we already apprehended as to her predatory and untrustworthy nature; and the further Misfortune of your youngest sister Drusilla starting a Conflagration from which your dear Mama was drawn out only just in time to preserve her life. I am afraid these events will be injurious to the reputation and fortunes of your family in general, for who would wish to connect themselves with a group so signall'd out for scandal and misfortune? So I have said to everybody I know & they all agree with me. Rumour has it that you yourself are also install'd at Lord Camber's residence, which seems most strange, but I address this there, having no other direction for you. I do think it your duty, my dear Friend, to return without delay to your Paternal Home. It is your plain charge to set matters to rights there.

    I am, dear Cousin, with sympathy,

    Yours etc. A. Norris

'They do tell as how his Grace is very poorly,' said Godwit one day, happening upon one of Dickon's singing lessons.

These were held at a safe distance from the Thatched Grotto, for the mere proximity, within a hundred yards, of Lady Ursula frightened Dickon acutely, and rendered him not only dumb, but witless and shivering. Whereas, when well away from her, he was making excellent progress; the ground lost through his disappointment when Hatty went away to Underwood had been made up by Miss Stornoway, who continued with Hatty's letter-game until he was able to read for himself; and Hatty had now found that if she sang words and phrases to him at a certain pitch, he could hear them very well and understand them. So she was able to make use, with him, of various singing games which she had invented to bridge the gap between Drusilla's musical

genius and her total vacancy in all other departments. Dickon had a
good natural wit, she knew, and he could recognize a tune, and nod
his head in time to it.

They held their lessons walking about the woods, or in a keeper's
hut, if it rained.

> 'A noun is a thing like a ring,
> A verb is for doing, like baking and brewing'

Hatty was singing when Godwit came into the gamekeeper's hut with
the private smile he kept for her and his piece of news.

'Poor man,' said Hatty, who had never met the Duke, and had only
Lord Camber's descriptions to go on, which did not give her a very
high opinion of his Grace. 'Is he going to die?'

'They have recalled Colonel Wisbech from his regiment. But of
course the one they are really wishful to get hold of is Master Harry.
When did you last hear from him, Miss Hatty?'

She shook her head doubtfully.

'The last letter I had was a month ago. In that he announced his
intention of going off next week on a journey to explore the unknown
regions west of Ohio; but I noticed that, instead of the usual eight or
nine weeks, that letter had taken five months to reach me; it was dated
some time in last autumn. Plainly it had gone astray. So I do not know
whether he did take his journey and, if so, whether he is still away
from Amity Valley. I have not had any letter later than that one. But I
suppose the Duke's people will send an urgent message to recall him.
There is the postman on his pony now. Let us go and see what he has
brought.'

The postman had brought a letter from overseas, but it was for Lady
Ursula, and not in Lord Camber's writing. Mrs Daizley took it up to
Lady Ursula, as she was spending the wet afternoon in her own
chamber.

Hatty, meanwhile, had opened a letter which was addressed to her
from London.

'Oh!' she cried out joyfully. 'It is from my publishers – they say they

287

will very shortly be sending me copies of my book of poems. Oh, how I wish Lord Camber were here. I should so much like him to see it.'

'Well, let us hope that he will soon be back at home, dearie,' said Mrs Godwit. 'If his Grace is in such a sorry way as they say. Looks like Master Harry will soon be stepping into his Grace's shoes.'

'And a precious tight fit he's like to find them,' observed Godwit.

'I cannot imagine Lord Camber as a duke,' said Hatty. 'I do not think he will make a very good one.'

'Can't be worse—' began Godwit, but they were interrupted by a strange keening wail from upstairs.

'Dear gracious! What's amiss with Lady Ursula?' exclaimed Mrs Godwit, struggling to her feet. Mrs Daizley, who was halfway down the stair, turned and retraced her steps. Hatty ran up after her.

They found Lady Ursula in a very peculiar condition.

She had been seated in an oaken armchair in her bedroom. Now she was leaning back, with her legs stretched out stiffly in front of her, and her head twisted as far as it would go to one side. She looked as if she were trying to see some distant object, or catch some fleeting sound. But her eyes were closed, and her hands hung down limply on either side. A letter she had been reading had drifted down from her grasp and lay on the floor.

'We should get medical help,' said Hatty. 'She looks as if she has had some kind of seizure. Like her sister Drusilla. First we had best get her into bed.'

Hatty, Godwit and Mrs Daizley lifted her on to the bed and then he went off to fetch Mr Jones while the others undressed her. She remained unconscious or asleep. When nothing more could be done for her, Hatty read the letter to see if it could give them some clue as to the cause of her mysterious spasm.

'Ah, it is from Amity Valley; from a lady called Lucy Kittridge. I have heard Lord Camber refer to her brother Humphrey. She thanks Lady Ursula for her letter of last year – informs her that Lord Camber and her brother have gone off on a journey of exploration across the unknown western territories – she—' Hatty checked and looked back at the top of the sheet. 'This letter is quite recent, I see, it has taken only five weeks to get here – Miss Kittridge says they are all greatly concerned in Amity Valley because Lord Camber and her brother had promised to be back by Easter, which is long past, and there is grave reason to fear that some fatal accident has befallen the travellers. Oh, heavens!'

'Eh, dear, deary me!' lamented Mrs Daizley. 'No wonder Lady Ursula was took queer. If his Lordship's dead and gone, she'll never get over having behaved so harshly to him – that she won't! Never!'

Mrs Godwit nodded her head in gloomy concurrence.

'She'll feel it to her dying day. But it wasn't *she* who turned *him* down, Mrs D. It was his Lordship as begged off.'

'Really?' said Hatty. 'I thought she cried off because she wanted to marry Lord Fordingbridge.'

'Na. That was put about. The truth of what happened was that, over at Underwood my first cousin once removed, Prue Hedger, got dismissed for stealing a lady's reticule. (That was in the old days, when they used to have parties of guests at the Priors.) All the time it was not Prue what took the thing at all, but that Lady Barbara. And Lady Ursula knew that full well. And Lord Camber knew it too, for Prue told me, and I told him. He found Prue another place, at Lady Munster's, in London. It was not long after that that Lady Ursula made an end of their courting.'

'I think I begin to see ...' said Hatty slowly. 'That accounts for a great deal ...'

Godwit arrived back with the apothecary, who examined the unconscious lady. After careful inspection he gave it as his opinion that what afflicted the lady was a disorder of the heart, not a paralytic seizure, as they had feared, and that she would presently recover.

'For,' said he, 'she has naturally a very robust constitution.'

Hatty, remembering Aunt Polly, was not so sanguine, but in the event Mr Jones was proved right. Lady Ursula, after a day or so, began to move, moved a little more, opened her eyes ... and was then able to converse quite sensibly. The only odd thing was that she appeared to believe that she had been on a long journey, from which she was just returned. It was the Grand Tour, she explained.

'I said to my father, the Earl, "Sons go on the Grand Tour, why not daughters?" "Why not indeed?" said he, and sent me off with my tutor. It was most enjoyable and instructive. We met the Pope. But the fleas in the Appenines were very bad.'

Poor thing, thought Hatty. I suppose the Grand Tour was what she always longed for.

Another disconcerting feature of Lady Ursula's recovery was that she mistook Hatty for her mother, Isabel.

I daresay I may look very like Mama, Hatty concluded, at the age when she and Ursula became such good friends.

'Isabel!' Lady Ursula said, over and over. '*Don't* go away, Isabel. Never go away again! Stay near me.'

She was very much milder and more gentle in manner than she had been before the mysterious attack. When possible, she liked to hold Hatty's hand, and would lie, sometimes for an hour or more, trustfully, smiling at her, occasionally saying, 'It is so *good* to have you with me, Isabel. So good. You mean far more to me than anybody in my own family.'

'I am not Isabel, you know,' Hatty said. 'I am Hatty.'

'Yes, Isabel,' Lady Ursula said.

'Here is a letter from your father, Lord Elstow,' Hatty said one day. 'Shall I read it aloud?' Lady Ursula closed her eyes, as if she did not care, one way or the other.

Lord Elstow wrote urging Ursula to return to Underwood Priors as soon as she was back on her feet. 'Your Mother is sadly weakened by all the smoke she breathed in, and little Drusilla not in much better case. I would wish soon to return to town, but can hardly do so until there is some responsible body to keep an eye on all here. It is therefore your duty, Ursula, to come here as soon as you are able.'

'Should I go, Isabel?' asked Ursula.

'No, not until you are fully recovered,' said Hatty. 'And not then, unless you wish to. Let your father look after his own house.'

'Yes, Isabel. Unless you would come with me?'

'No. That I will not do,' said Hatty, who, these days, was heavy-eyed and pale. She lay awake at night, worrying about Lord Camber, imagining him lost in pathless wilderness, savaged by bears, captured by ferocious Indians. She had a superstitious belief that, only by staying in his house, under his roof, could she ensure his possible return. Which seemed a remote, forlorn chance.

She found the task of sitting by Lady Ursula's sick-bed heart-breakingly sad and tedious. The invalid would talk for hours on end about her clothes, listing bygone wardrobes in minute particulars; or she would recount in merciless, laborious detail portions of conversations held years past with individuals generally alluded to as 'the man' or 'the woman'. 'So I said to the man, my good man, I said, if you think I am prepared to accept these shoddy goods you offer you are wrong, very wrong indeed. Some of us, I said, *some* of us in this world were not born yesterday. Oh, said he, but you must remember the high price of raw materials. Oh *indeed*, said I, and what do you call raw materials . . .'

In these encounters, Lady Ursula always seemed to have come off best.

What a harrowingly dull life she has led, Hatty thought, in pity. She should have married Camber, I can see that. Life with him would have been the best choice for her.

The invalid would permit no other member of the household to sit with her. She would have only Hatty, and sometimes wept piteously if the latter remained away too long; or what was thought to be too long; her estimate of time was not reliable.

'Will she ever want to get up, do you suppose? Should we bring her downstairs?' Hatty said to Mrs Daizley.

'That one? Not until she choose to come of her own self. And you can't deny it's by far more peaceful when she's above stairs. Not but what it is hard on you, Miss Hatty, having to spend so much time with her. Lucky it is, she sleeps as much as she do.'

During these long interludes of slumber Hatty gave Dickon his lessons, wrote poems, and was learning cookery from Mrs Daizley.

'For it's odds that some day you will wish for a rest, or want to go on an outing. And at the present time I cannot even cook a cow-heel, let alone make curry or fry a bit of tripe.'

One day, when they were discussing wine-making, Mrs Daizley said,

'Did you not once tell me that your auntie had left you a receipt book in her Will, that your cousin brought you?'

'So she did! Sydney brought it, not long before I left Underwood, and I was so distracted, at that time, that I packed it away among my things and forgot all about it. I never even unwrapped it.'

Hatty fetched it from her room. It was a small volume, carefully bound up in brown paper to preserve it from grease and staining. Its title, found inside, was *The Art of Simple Cookery by a Lady*. Tucked in among the pages were about a dozen loose scraps of paper with recipes written on them in Aunt Polly's scrambling hand: Mrs Ashworth's Quince Jelly. A very good Orange pudding. A receipt for Solid Custard from Mrs Sawbridge. To pickle Mellons. Miss Thornhill's Green Gooseberry Wine.

'Here is the recipe for walnut-leaf wine. But it says "Pick the leaves in May". We must wait until next year. Why – good heavens! Here is a note in Lord Camber's writing!'

'Fancy that, now. Did he send your auntie a recipe, then?'

'No . . . it seems to be a letter. Aunt Polly must have tucked it into the book. I remember that was a habit she had, with letters she wished to keep – she would put them in books—'

Hatty moved to the window and read Lord Camber's letter to her aunt while Mrs Daizley went on placidly kneading her dough.

My dear Mrs Ward:
I was greatly grieved to hear that you had been laid low on a bed of sickness. I do hope that by this time you are restored to complete health and are as usual being the pillar of your household. I am writing to consult you in regard to my feelings for little Miss Hatty whom you must regard in some sort as your adopted daughter. It may not have escaped your observant eye that, over the last months, I have come to feel a strong admiration and tenderness for the young lady and I would, if circumstances were otherwise, wish to apply to her father for her hand in marriage. Circumstanc'd as I am, however, this at present cannot be; nor would I wish to lay any kind of constraint upon Miss Hatty who is, in any case, at present

far too young to consider matrimony. Do you think the age gap between us is too great a barrier? Supposing that I should come back in five years or so, from my American venture, and find her still unattach'd? I should be eternally grateful for your views on this matter.

I suppose I am writing to you, dear Mrs Ward, partly because I know that you are very fond of Hatty and it is such a gratification for me to be able to express my feelings of admiration and attachment to a sympathetic ear! I know that the child still feels in some degree an intruder in your house (not your fault, Mrs Ward, but that of other persons in the household) and I have heard her express a longing for 'a little house of her own' so I propose making over my cottage to her in the hope that she may there be able to pursue her literary career (in which I believe). I intend sending her the Title Deeds. I hope this will be a benefit and not a burden to her. I shall be looking forward to hearing your opinion on these matters in due course, dear Mrs Ward.

Your sincere friend,

H. C.

Hatty sat down abruptly at the little table on which Lady Ursula had been in the habit of eating her meals.

He loves me! thought Hatty. Lord Camber loves me! Oh, how can life hold so much happiness ...? But where is he? Shall I ever see him again? Will he ever come back? Oh, *why* could he not have said those things to *me*? Then I should have had all this time with that knowledge to uphold me ...

'Are you all right, dearie?' said Mrs Daizley. 'You look a bit queer-like.'

'I shall be all right in a minute.'

Did Aunt Polly ever answer this letter? If so, what did she say? Did she leave the letter in the book for me to find? Or did she forget about it when she was so ill? Will these questions ever be answered?

'Isabel! *Isabel!*' came a plaintive cry from upstairs.

XXIII

Mrs Godwit had risen from her bed with alacrity as soon as Lady Ursula was struck down, and resumed her place in the household. Also – now that Lady Ursula was in a milder, more approachable humour – the older woman was now sometimes acceptable to her, for short periods, as a companion. Mrs Godwit had been in service, years ago, at Underwood Priors and could remember the visits of Miss Isabel Wisbech, and how friendly the two cousins had been.

'She had a nonsensical, humorous way with her, Miss Isabel did in those days. Dear me! How she used to make you laugh, my Lady. Laugh! Times were you'd nigh split your sides. And Lord Francis – he was another one for a joke.'

'What was he like, Lord Francis Fordingbridge?' asked Hatty, who was dusting the bedroom while Mrs Godwit helped Lady Ursula with her hair, which was long, grey and lifeless and reached nearly down to her knees.

'Yes, it's true, Lord Francis used to make me laugh,' Lady Ursula said reminiscently, leaning forward to let Mrs Godwit get at the back of her head. 'He was such a light-hearted boy! He delighted in teasing and riddles. Of course he was in love with Harry, really. All the young men were in those days. It is queer how Harry always managed to command such devotion. And now there is nothing left of him ... Nothing in this world ...'

She sounds almost *glad* of it, thought Hatty in amazement. Almost as if she were relieved to be free of him – him and his troublesome conscience. 'We don't know for sure that anything bad has happened to him,' she said stubbornly. 'He may just be in some very remote place with no means of communication.'

Mrs Daizley called up the stairs.

'Miss Hatty! There's a young fellow to see ye. Says as how he's your cousin.'

'Ned!' exclaimed Hatty joyfully, and ran down.

But it was Sydney, plump and spruce; plumper and sprucer than ever. His face assumed an expression of total disapproval as he caught sight of Hatty, who had tied up her hair in a duster, and was wearing one of Mrs Daizley's sacking aprons over her muslin dress.

'My dear Cousin Harriet! I was told that you were here, but hardly thought it could be so. What can have possessed you to leave Underwood Priors? There, at least, it could be said that you were residing at a respectable address – but here! What are you *doing* here?'

'Just at the moment,' she said, 'taking care of Lady Ursula, who suffered some kind of seizure when she heard a piece of troubling news about Lord Camber. However I am happy to say she appears to be making a slow but steady recovery.'

'That evil woman – why should you take care of her?'

'Oh, evil? I doubt she is that! I thought you were used to admire her, Cousin Sydney? Just at the moment, in her present state, I feel much pity for her. She seems a sad, lost creature.'

'Do you know,' declared Sydney, 'that she stole the title-deeds of this house? Stole them!'

'No, did she do that? But how do you know such a thing?' said Hatty, showing much less surprise than Sydney had hoped for.

'Before his departure for America, Lord Camber wrote me a brief note, expressing his intention of bestowing the deeds on *you*. (A most injudicious step),' added Sydney irritably. 'But I was not able on that occasion to voice my disapproval or endeavour to dissuade him from his foolish intention because he had already taken his departure by the time his letter reached me. The deeds which previously had been deposited at Foale's Bank in Bythorn were to be despatched to you by messenger. But they never reached you – did they?'

'No. They did not. I suppose I had already left for Underwood when they were delivered at Bythorn Lodge.'

Hatty considered with wonder what a different course her life might have taken if she had known of Camber's gift at the time he bestowed it; instead of accepting the position at Underwood she would have returned directly to the Grotto; would that have been better? Then I

295

would never have met du Vallon, she thought – or Barbara or Drusilla – or Miss Stornoway. She would never have come to this place. Lord Camber must have thought it strange and uncivil of me not to have thanked him for his gift. He did write asking ...

'Why did you not tell me this before?' she asked.

Sydney chose not to answer that question. He said, 'Lady Ursula took possession of the deeds when the messenger delivered them at the Lodge; she never passed them on to you.'

'No ... she never did ...'

'She is evil!' Sydney repeated.

'Well – I suppose taking the deeds was an act of sudden impulse. If anybody asked her, she could say that she was holding them for me. Evil?' said Hatty doubtfully. What would Lord Camber think? she wondered. She went on, half to herself, 'Her usage of poor Miss Stornoway was certainly very bad. But I believe that her nature has been much altered since her illness. She seems so much easier and gentler now. For instance, she has never once complained, whereas before she did so continually. If a person's nature changes, can one blame them for acts performed before?'

'She is milder, I daresay, because she is not yet fully recovered. Wait until she is quite mended and you will soon see a different face! But Hatty, it is not right that you should stay here.'

'Why? And where else should I go?'

'Hatty! As I have said before, why do you not marry me and come back *home* – to your true home at Bythorn Lodge? That would be such a good – such a *right* solution to all your problems!'

'But living here is an even better solution to my problems, Cousin Sydney! Especially if I am the owner of the house. And – I have told you before – we should not suit. Not at all. I can only tell you again.'

They had left the house and were walking to and fro on the patch of grass in front. Hatty wished that Godwit would come back from his errand in Bythorn, or Mrs Daizley from picking blackberries in the wood. She wished this interview would end.

'We have had this conversation so often, Cousin Sydney. I am sorry. I cannot love you. How many times do I have to tell you that?'

'How old are you now, Hatty?' he surprised her by asking.

'Nineteen, cousin. Old enough to know my own mind.'

'Not at all!' he said sharply. 'Nineteen is by far too young to run off by yourself and live in this ramshackle way in the woods. There is already talk about you – about the sudden way in which you quitted Underwood just before that havey-cavey Frenchman eloped to France with Barbara Fowldes. (Paris! The Fowldes will be lucky if they ever see *her* again. Think of it! A member of the British aristocracy! The French will probably hang her from a lamp post.)'

'Oh, surely not? Du Vallon told me he has influential friends in the radical movement. More likely they will both become members of the Legislative Assembly.'

'I very much doubt that,' he said sourly. 'And, Cousin, as I said, I am sorry to have to tell you this, but unpleasant talk is percolating about the countryside – to the effect that the Frenchman had – had taken advantage of you while you were both at the Priors; and that, tiring of you, he asked Lord Elstow for his daughter's hand, and *that* being refused, he abducted her.'

'Well, the story is not true,' said Hatty, 'except the bit about asking Lord Elstow for Barbara's hand.' Then she wished she had not spoken, for Sydney at once looked very acute and demanded, 'How do you know that?'

'Never mind how I know.'

'Hatty – *Hatty*! Pray, pray consider my proposal. So much depends on it! More, much more than you suppose!'

'What *can* you mean?' she said wonderingly.

At this critical moment Lady Ursula came downstairs. This in itself was an event of considerable moment, since she had previously negatived any suggestion of leaving her couch. But now, here she was, a somewhat formidable figure in a long, trailing book-muslin bedgown, chambray gauze shift, Paisley shawl, and heavily be-ribboned French net nightcap, standing in the open door at the front of the house, between the pillars.

'Isabel!' she said plaintively. 'Why did you leave me for so long?'

'She takes me for my mother,' whispered Hatty.

Quickly she ran forward and clasped the lady's arm.

'Lady Ursula, it was very rash of you to come down the stairs alone. Why did you not ask Mrs Godwit to help you?'

'Ursie! Why will you not call me Ursie?'

Then her gaze fell on Sydney, and she said crossly, 'There is that tiresome young lawyer's clerk who insisted on escorting me back from church. Tell him to go away. He has been pestering me for ever about some documents. Tell him that I am not in the mood to answer his questions just now. Or ever.'

'Why did you take the deeds of this house, Lady Ursula? Did you not know that was a felony?' demanded Sydney. 'Where are they?'

Taking things, thought Hatty, is just a hereditary habit in the Fowldes family, perhaps. Perhaps they do not even know that it is wrong. It is a *droit de famille*. They also have the capacity to make one feel guilty just for being the owner of something they want for themselves.

'You need concern yourself in the matter no longer,' Lady Ursula told Sydney loftily. 'For Isabel has recently returned to me, and so she and I will be able to share the deeds.'

Sydney looked helplessly at Hatty, who raised her brows and said, 'I think that just now the matter is of no particular importance. Let us hope that Lord Camber will soon come home.' *Oh, let us hope so!* 'Then he can sort matters out for himself.'

'There is much reason to suppose that he will *never* come home. Or so I hear. But, cousin, those deeds must be found and put in a place of safety.'

'Well, I will try to do so. I believe they are in Lady Ursula's room. Ah, here come Godwit and Mrs Daizley. You had better take your leave, Cousin Sydney. You are tiring Lady Ursula.'

'I shall come back!' he said furiously. 'Very soon!'

It was only after his departure that Hatty thought: Good gracious! He never once mentioned his father's marriage to Burnaby! But perhaps he cannot bring himself to do so. It must have made him very angry . . .

Lady Ursula's humour changed for the worse after Sydney Ward's visit; he seemed to have recalled her mind in a sharper degree to her present circumstances. Her manner grew harsher, she became tetchy and irritable. The matter of the title-deeds had not been raised again. Hatty, indeed, returning some clean laundry to Lady Ursula's closet, had discovered the deeds, wrapped up in a Norwich shawl; they are as safe there as anywhere, she decided; let them remain there for the present. She did, however, send a note to her cousin Sydney at Bythorn assuring him of this fact.

Godwit and Mrs Daizley had heard the closing exchanges between Sydney Ward and Lady Ursula and were now clear that the deeds rightfully belonged to Hatty.

'—Which I always suspicioned was the case,' said Godwit, 'for that had been Master Harry's intention, I knew full well; he spoke of you often; and it seemed mighty strange that he should have changed his mind so sudden; but then Lady Ursula told us of the note she had from him – and she did have the deeds – and he is one to keep surprising us all – so what were we to think?'

'You could not think anything else,' Hatty agreed.

He shook his head.

'They are a freakish lot, those Fowldes, there's no denying,' he said. 'The last Earl, it's said, could not abear for any water to be thrown away, ever; he had great tanks and cisterns all round the garden and even in the house there was pots and pannikins of water everywhere you looked; frightened of drought, he was. Or fire.'

'How very strange. Why?'

'I dunno. Maybe he had his reasons. Went thirsty some time when he was a young lad, maybe.'

I could write a poem about that, thought Hatty.

'But, Miss Hatty, dear,' said Mrs Daizley – they were outside, winding up a pail of water from the well, safely out of earshot of the house – 'now we know *That One* don't own the deeds, and took them without a smidgeon of right to do so – could you not take it upon yourself to give her her marching orders? Tell her to walk her chalks and find some other place to perch. She's such a burden to us all – and most special to you, Miss Hatty! I know there's times ye're a-dying to go off to Master Harry's study and write one of your poems – and you have to sit listening to her and twiddling your thumbs—'

'Oh, darling Mrs Daizley, I know she's a burden – but Lord Camber did invite her after all—'

'Ye-es,' assented Mrs Daizley doubtfully, 'he did, there's no doubt of that – his Lordship is *that* good-hearted – special when it's no skin off *his* nose. But did he mean her to stop here for *ever* – surely not that?'

'Well,' said Hatty, 'I don't say I disagree with you – not at all – but since he did invite her – and more especially since we don't know where he is at this present – and since she can only go back to Underwood – and that is such a terribly sad place to live – I cannot find it in my heart to ask her to leave. Let us wait until we have more definite news of Lord Camber.'

'But perhaps we never shall,' Godwit pointed out.

'No. That I will not believe,' said Hatty.

Godwit gave her a long strange look – of pity, understanding, earnest desire to do all he could for her – and, after a moment, said, 'No. You are right, Miss Hatty. We must honour his Lordship's wishes – so far as we know what they are. We'll try to put up with the lady a while longer.'

Hatty smiled at him gratefully. He is such a good man, she thought. As good as Lord Camber, indeed. Perhaps even better. Because he takes a more realistic view of humanity – and adapts his behaviour accordingly.

She carried her pail of water indoors, while Godwit wound up another.

The hot summer drew on into a hot dry autumn.

The former Lord Elstow would have been in a dreadful state of worry, thought Hatty; he would have had basins of water all over the house.

A gipsy, selling clothes-pegs, came by and told them that the Duke of Dungeness continued to linger between life and death, that there was still no news of Lord Camber, that Colonel Wisbech remained at Bythorn Chase, making everybody's life a burden.

'Which you can't blame him,' said Godwit. 'He don't know will he inherit or not. Hard on anybody's disposition, that would be.'

That year there was a lavish crop of quinces, and Mrs Daizley, who had already made gooseberry and currant preserves, apple jelly and plum jam, now turned her hand to quince preserve. Hatty helped her carry baskets of the stone-hard russet and yellow fruit into the house and cut them into segments. Cauldrons of them simmered all day over the fire, and the whole house filled with their sharp, aromatic scent. Which also brought the wasps in their hundreds, hovering, humming and greedily immolating themselves in the tempting scarlet syrup.

'Plaguey things,' said Mrs Daizley. 'There must be a nest of them close by, don't ye think so, Eli?'

Lady Ursula was one of those who could not remain calm in the presence of a winged insect. She seemed to have a personal vendetta against them, cried out angrily, slashed at them with knife or spoon, behaved as if they had come with intent to attack her. Although the weather continued so torrid, she would hardly stir out of doors, and during Mrs Daizley's jam-making days, keeping well away from the kitchen, with its syrupy odours and myriad winged visitants, she remained upstairs, cloistered in her own chamber, with her cat, who was also terrified of wasps, probably because he had once been stung by one.

'Good riddance to both,' said Mrs Daizley, chopping quinces on a wooden board.

Godwit went hunting for the wasps' nest and found it, buried in the thatch at the end of the house.

'I'll put a brazier full of damp straw underneath, and smoke them out,' he said.

'Yes, do, Eli dear, for there's a squillion of them in my kitchen this minute,' said Mrs Daizley. 'I can hardly pour the jelly without them falling into it.'

When this was done, and the row of covered pots stood waiting to cool and set, Hatty went upstairs to read Law's *Remarks Upon the Fable of the Bees* to Lady Ursula.

'But do let us have the window open,' she pleaded. 'For it is terribly close in here.'

'Whose fault is that?' grumbled Lady Ursula. 'If Mrs Daizley did not keep that furnace roaring away in the kitchen—'

'We shall be glad of all her quince jelly next winter,' said Hatty, thinking of the cold weather ahead, wondering how long Lady Ursula intended to quarter herself on them. For ever? It was a daunting thought.

She opened the window and sat down to read aloud.

Two things then happened very suddenly. A black humming cloud, the size and shape of a hogshead of beer, boomed in through the open window and began to disintegrate into a million buzzing wasps. Lady Ursula's cat gave a yell, and leapt from the bed where he was lying. His moving shape attracted the swarm, which dropped on to him.

'Get him *out* of here!' shrieked Lady Ursula, and, springing from her chair, she seized a large shawl, bundled it round the shape of the cat, almost hidden by wasps, and flung shawl and cat together out of the window, just as Godwit entered the room with a pail of water in one hand, and a smoking brazier of straw in the other.

'Quick, Miss Hatty!' he said. 'Out of here. And you, too, my Lady!'

They needed no urging. Lady Ursula was out through the door in a flash, along the dark upstairs hallway, and had shut herself into one of the small, unused attic rooms before Hatty could follow. Hearing the slam of the door Hatty ran downstairs and went outside, taking up a pail of water as she went. Her pitying thought was all for the cat – a dismal, bad-tempered beast, to be sure, nobody in the household liked him, but something must be done to save him.

She found that Dickon had anticipated her: he had already flung a basin of water over the cat's body and was dispersing the wasps by knocking them off with a knotted towel.

But he spread his hands wide and shook his head.

'It is no good,' he said, in the sign language they had begun to use. 'The cat is dead.'

'Oh, poor thing! I wonder if it was the wasps that killed him, or the fall from the window. At least it was a quick end. But Lady Ursula will be very sorry . . .'

It took the household some considerable time to resume its normal tranquil activity after this dramatic disruption. First, all the dead wasps had to be swept out and incinerated. Lady Ursula insisted that her room must be fumigated and disinfected with carbolic acid, or that sulphur must be burned there.

'I refuse to occupy that room again until it has been thoroughly cleansed,' she said.

At that, Mr Godwit very deliberately laid down the broom he was wielding, and folded his arms.

'My Lady,' he said, 'it will not be convenient for you to continue residing in this house any longer.'

'You impertinent man! How *dare* you say such a thing! I shall reside here just as long as I please!'

'No, ma'am. I am Lord Camber's steward, and he gave me authority to say who should stay here, and who should not. Lord Camber is a gentleman of very high principles – as ye are no doubt aware, ma'am – and it would be flat against his wish that anybody should live under his roof who had killed a poor animal, *on purpose*, by flinging it out of a window. Lord Camber can't abide cruelty. As you well know, ma'am.'

Lady Ursula's gaze fell. After a moment, she faltered: 'Isabel! *Isabel!* You will not let this be done to me?'

'I am not Isabel,' said Hatty sadly. 'I am Hatty. Which you know quite well, Lady Ursula.'

'But where can I go? Who will have me?'

'You can go back to the Priors, ma'am – where you belong. And where there is work waiting for you to do,' said Godwit indisputably. 'The ladies will pack up for you now.'

'But how shall I go? I have no means of transport. It is impossible—'
'No, ma'am, it is quite simple.'

And, while Hatty and Mrs Daizley packed Lady Ursula's things, Godwit, with swift efficiency, arranged for a chaise to convey the lady from Wanmaulden Cross to Underwood, and for a sedan chair to carry her from the Grotto to Wanmaulden Cross. (It seemed they had a sedan chair mouldering in the stables of the Woodpecker Inn, and were only too pleased to fetch it out, dust it, and provide it for the lady's use at an exorbitant fee.) Two men from the inn, with Dickon and Godwit, carried her through the wood, Lady Ursula maintaining a grim silence all the way.

Godwit paid the fee. 'Which I am happy to,' he said, 'just to rid us of that bird of ill omen.'

Hatty was torn. She could not but remember Lord Camber's letter to his cousin, offering her the use of the house – she could not help but remember his own expressed wish to her that she and his cousin should be friends – but, in opposition to these thoughts, came the huge relief that Godwit had so firmly, so clear-sightedly taken matters into his own hands and sent the lady back where she belonged.

The matter of the title-deeds had not been raised. Hatty had quietly removed them and placed them among Lord Camber's papers.

'Poor Lady Ursula!' she sighed. 'I am afraid she will have a most dismal home-coming. But perhaps Drusilla will be happy to see her. Poor little Drusilla will have found life sadly tedious with only her piano and Winship for company. Perhaps she can teach Lady Ursula some battle games. And, who knows? Lady Elstow may be pleased to see her daughter again.'

XXIV

THE UNSEASONABLY WARM weather lasted for another three weeks, until well into October.

'When it breaks,' said Godwit, 'it will break sudden. There will be a bad storm, likely.'

In the meantime, the occupants of the Thatched Grotto rested, not unhappily, in a quiet frontier-land between grief and hope, between past and future. The relief and easement of not having Lady Ursula with them was very great. They hardly ever spoke of her; if they chanced to think of her they exchanged wordless smiles. Hatty remembered reading of some savage tribe who took pains to avoid treading on the shadow of an enemy or an accursed person; the Grotto family behaved in the same way over the name of Lady Ursula.

Perhaps she really is an ill-luck bringer, thought Hatty. At all events I am pleased that she left before the copies of my book arrived. I should not have liked her to set eyes on them.

They understood that the lady had arrived safely at Underwood Priors, for Godwit, buying a newspaper in Bythorn, had encountered Glastonbury, who inquired kindly after Miss Hatty, and said the repairs to the library at the Priors were taking a mighty long time, because Lady Ursula and his Lordship could never agree about a single thing. And his Grace the Duke, over at Bythorn Chase, had taken a turn for the better, and was now believed to be out of danger.

'So if Master Harry *was* to turn up unexpected,' said Mrs Daizley, 'he's like to find he's had his journey for nought.'

Hatty had a melancholy letter from Ned.

My dear Cousin Hatty:
When I rid to London, what did I find but that Miss Nancy Price whom I had always thought to be so Faithful, has play'd me False & now tells me that she has pledg'd her hand to Another, some older

fellow whom she has been meeting and entertaining these many weeks; she will not tell me his name or rank for fear that in my jealous rage I might Call him Out; but in any case I can see that she is now a Fine Lady of the town & would never consent to accept the hand of a poor naval lieut; her uncle died and left her 10,000 L., so she feels herself quite beyond my Touch. I am wholly quenched & cast down by this blow, dear Hatty, & do not after all plan to come to see you this leave, as it would waken too many painful memories of Portsmouth & our beloved Kingdom Tree. (Also my leave has been curtail'd from two weeks to one, so there would barely be time.) I heard a tale from Tom that our brother Sydney plans to marry you, but I am sure it is no such thing for I know you never could abide him. He (I hear) thrives apace and all the Nobs go to him. Just as well for Tom tells me that Burnaby had her child & it is a Boy. No doubt B will contrive that our Father leaves him all he has; I shall need to become an Admiral and Tom a General.

 With many kind remembrances,
 Yr affct Cousin Ned.

And then, on a sultry day of black-piled cloud and warm, dank air, who should come walking up to the Thatched Grotto but Lord Camber, with a thin, dark-skinned girl beside him. He wore a curious broad-brimmed hat, and she a magnificent mantle of dark furs.

Hatty was upstairs in Camber's study, working, at the time of this arrival; it was Mrs Daizley who opened the door to his knock, and let out an ecstatic shriek of surprise.

'My Lord! You are safe home again! Oh, what a joyful, joyful day! Just wait, just wait, till I call the others.'

But Godwit, outside collecting wood not far off, had seen his Lordship through the trees and came at a run, along with Dickon; and Mrs Godwit, who had been in the dairy, heard Mrs Daizley's cry and tottered along as fast as her aged limbs could carry her. There was a loud clamour of happy welcoming voices.

'My Lord! Your Lordship! Welcome home! This is a glad day indeed!'

Outside the house there came a sudden ear-splitting clap of thunder.

'We seem to have arrived not a moment too soon!' said Lord Camber laughing. 'Hark at the rain! How shall we ever be able to leave again? But now let me make this lady known to you – she is my wife and a long way from her home for she is from the Indian tribe of the Algonquins—'

A startled silence fell. Hatty, coming down the stairs, heard Lord Camber's words and was thereby given a moment to catch her breath. Then Lord Camber looked up and saw her; he broke off abruptly in what he was saying. He and Hatty stared at one another for a moment of silence that seemed to last a lifetime; then old Mrs Godwit ended the pause by saying comfortably, 'Eh, then you wed an Indian maid, did you, your Lordship? Fancy that, now! I never looked to see a real Indian lady, not in my whole lifetime. What may be your name, my dearie? (Does she speak our tongue, Master Harry?)'

'I speak a very little,' the girl said, smiling cautiously – she had seemed a little frightened at first, perhaps by the sight of so many strange faces. 'My name in your language is Changing Sky.'

'Changing Sky! Well! What next!'

'But *I* call her Anna,' Lord Camber said. 'It is quicker – and more friendly.'

He was regaining a minor portion of his old, easy, kindly manner; for a moment, before, he had turned perfectly white and seemed quite lost.

A sudden splash of lightning lit the room, which had grown oppressively dark, though it was only mid-afternoon. The women cried out in fright, and then Mrs Daizley said, 'I'll put on the kettle. Your Lordship and the lady will be glad of a hot drink I'll be bound – some of my camomile tea.'

They drew round the table, and amid the bustle of plates and cups, Lord Camber said quietly to Hatty: 'I am surprised to see you here. I had thought you would be at Bythorn.'

'At Bythorn? No. Where else should I be but here? Lord Camber, let me now thank you—'

'But,' he broke in, 'I understood that you were married? To your cousin. The lawyer.'

'To Sydney? Great heavens, *no*! What can have given you that notion?'

'It was in a letter. Not to me. From my cousin Ursula to Kittridge's sister Lucy—'

Their eyes met helplessly. Then old Mrs Godwit said, 'But tell us the tale, Master Harry. Tell us how you came to marry this handsome Indian lady.'

'Well,' he said, 'I found her on an island where she had been left to die.'

'Dear to goodness! Why?'

'She had broken a tribal law. By mistake. But they are very strict. The Indian tribes are governed by a hierarchy of *manido*, or spirits. Each tribe has its own totem animal or plant. Anna's tribal totem was the squirrel. She killed a squirrel, quite by accident, shooting an arrow at a woodchuck. And so she was left to starve on the island.'

'Could she not have escaped?' Hatty asked, caught, in spite of her own anguish, by such a strange, unexpected story.

Camber looked across the table at her. Each time their eyes met she felt pierced by a completely unfamiliar pain. But I shall get over it, she promised herself. I have survived other pains. I shall survive this one.

He said, 'Yes, she could have escaped, but she would not. She felt she deserved to die, for her transgression. And she would have stayed there and starved to death, and her bones would have remained unburied, and her spirit would have roamed as an exile for ever outside the Happy Hunting Grounds. It was a hard task for me to persuade her that she had a right to live – but in the end I managed it.'

He smiled affectionately at Changing Sky, and she smiled back at him with a look of such total devotion and trust that Hatty, clenching her hands under the table, thought: I do not even have the *right* to feel this pain. After all, he does not know that I read his letter to Aunt Polly.

He never committed himself to me in any way. Never.

'And will you never be able to go back to your tribe?' she asked the girl, who shook her head. 'That is very hard.'

'And she has an even harder task ahead of her here,' Lord Camber said. He laid a protective arm round Changing Sky. 'She has to learn to be a Duchess. For my poor old father died last night and it seems there is nothing for it now but for me to take his place.'

'Oh, bless me, my Lord – I mean, your Grace,' said Godwit. 'That *will* be a stony row for you to hoe. But I'm sure we all wish you and your lady the very best of good fortune.'

'Where did you get married?' Mrs Daizley asked.

'At a little mission church in the wilderness. And then, when we returned to Amity Valley, I found a message waiting that my father was gravely ill; and we were lucky enough to find a boat at Baltimore that was just due to sail. We had prosperous winds crossing the Atlantic, and I am glad to say that we arrived at the Chase in time for me to see my father before he died. Mrs Daizley, I have come to ask a very great kindness of you. And you are so good that I am sure I can rely upon you.'

'Oh, of course, Master Harry – I mean your Grace. Anything I can do!'

'Will you come back and be our housekeeper at the Chase? Just at present Anna finds it all rather frightening and huge there – but I am sure that with such a kind barrier as yourself against all the unknown and alarming people she will soon discover how to go on—'

'Bless her heart! Yes, of course I will come,' said Mrs Daizley. 'That is – I mean – if Miss Hatty can spare me—'

She glanced appealingly at Hatty, who was looking at Changing Sky. The girl cannot be more than sixteen, Hatty thought. She had a thin face with high cheekbones, a fine straight nose and soft night-black hair. She wore a beautiful cloak of soft dark fur and had gold rings in her ears. Nonetheless she looked young and vulnerable. Sixteen seemed a perilously young age to travel to a foreign land and be elevated to a duchess. Of a sudden she raised her eyes and gazed straight at Hatty, who said, 'Of course you must go to the Chase, Mrs Daizley. We shall manage very well here. After all, I can cook a cow-heel now, excellently well – or so Mr Godwit says!'

The thunder cracked again, and a new torrent of rain started beating down on the thatch and coursing over the windowpanes. Hatty was reminded of the untimely storm that had caused her to drop her sister Agnes's tray of toilet articles. She said, 'Excuse me. I should like to get something.' And went upstairs to Camber's study – now hers, she supposed, and looked lovingly about its disciplined untidiness. This is my place. Nonetheless she stood for a moment holding her head in her hands, as if it might suddenly rise and whirl away like a balloon.

Then she walked downstairs and handed Camber a pair of volumes bound in blue morocco leather.

'I do not know if this is your first wedding present,' she said, 'but I do know that you will not receive one that is given with warmer good wishes and friendship.'

He opened the cover and read: 'The Moon is Upside Down. A New Collection of Poems by Mr Anthony Bailiff. My dear Miss Hatty! I am overwhelmed! Am I the first recipient?'

'Yes! The books only arrived two days ago. I suppose I must send some copies to my sisters – but I received only five free sets, and I have such a large family,' said Hatty cheerfully, 'that I hardly know where to begin.'

'The rain is letting up,' said Lord Camber, looking out of the window. 'I fear that Anna and I must return to the Chase.'

XXV

THE MOMENT THE Duke and Duchess of Dungeness had left the house, Godwit exploded, 'Now isn't that just *like* Master Harry! Inconsiderate! Never thinks of anybody else!'

'Eli! How can you say such a wicked thing?' His grandmother was scandalized. 'When you know his Lordship fair *lives* for others, and gives away every penny he can to the poor – and – and is so easy and affable to his inferiors—'

'Yes! And look what comes of it! Look at the trouble he leaves behind him everywhere he goes. I wonder what kind of a hurrah's nest there is this day in Amity Valley – I'll wager he left all there at sixes and sevens—'

'But he saved the life of that poor young thing,' pointed out Mrs Daizley, dropping a sympathetic tear. 'Think of it! Left alone to starve!'

'That's as maybe,' said Godwit grimly. 'He saves her life – but she can never see her own folk again. Even if she went back, they'd not take her in. And what kind of life will she have here – as a *Duchess*, for pity's sake! I'll lay the gentry round about and Master Harry's kin give her a hard time – *they* won't want to know her. An Indian savage! They'd sooner he'd marry somebody with a bit of breeding who'd bring money into the family. Why, even—' He stopped abruptly.

''Tis true, she'll be *that* homesick, poor lassie,' ruminated Mrs Godwit. 'But what else could he have done with her? If her own kin had cast her out? She'd be no happier in an orphanage – let alone they probably don't have orphanages in those American lands. And he had to come home to his old Dad.'

'She'll be so lonely.'

'Miss Hatty will go and see her and be a sister to her – won't ye, Miss Hatty dear?'

'Of course I will,' said Hatty.

'*Miss Hatty!*' said Godwit indignantly. 'Miss Hatty ought to be getting on with her poetry-writing, not visiting Indian maidens and cooking cow-heels. How is Miss Hatty going to manage when you are off at the Chase, may I ask?'

Mrs Daizley looked stricken. 'I hadn't thought of that,' she said. 'His Lordship was so pressing—'

'But you'd *like* to go – wouldn't you?' said Hatty. 'You'd like to be back at the Chase?'

'I've a deal of old friends in the servants' hall,' admitted Mrs Daizley. 'And, Miss Hatty, I'm sure I could find ye a stout girl who'd come and do all ye need done about the place.'

'I'm sure you can. Thank you, Mrs Daizley. Though we shall miss you terribly.'

'That we shall!' said Mrs Godwit. 'Who's to rub me with camphor oil? And supposing I get sick?'

She stared at them fiercely. She was by now shrunken, wizened, lame – but still full of energy. She is eighty-nine, though, thought Hatty; how much longer can she go on? And she said, '*I* shall rub you, Mrs Godwit. I am an excellent sick-nurse. I have had a great deal of practice.'

Godwit's eye met that of Hatty.

It is very singular, thought Hatty. Harry Camber's eyes – no, I must learn to think of him as the Duke – his eyes each time they sought mine, were full of some terrible pleading question that I could not answer at all; but Godwit's angry harassed look is somehow *warming* – he has had to deal with difficulties caused by Harry Camber before, he is not unused to this kind of situation.

'I suppose there must be a grand funeral,' she said ponderingly.

'And quantities of relations invited from all over the country. And that poor girl will have to receive them all.'

I shall not be invited, she thought; but Lady Ursula and the rest of the Fowldes family will be there; gracious! what in the world will Lady Ursula make of Changing Sky? Now she has really lost Lord Camber, much more than if he had died in the wilderness. But perhaps she never really wanted him? What *did* she want? I shall never know. Why did she write to Lucy Kittridge and say that I was to marry Sydney? What did she hope to achieve by that?

Hatty recalled the last funeral she had attended, that of Lady Pentecost, and Lord Camber's warm, prompt, instinctive kindness with the poor hysterical daughter, and Lady Ursula's scathing comments afterwards. It is impossible to enter into the minds of other people, thought Hatty. We can make maps of them for ourselves, and the maps are about as illusory and deceptive as those of old cartographers with mermaids and monsters. 'Here be Dragons.' For a moment she longed to be back in the library at Underwood Priors, peacefully browsing amongst its contents. But Barbara stole some of those and little Drusilla set fire to the rest. I have no right to grumble, I am comfortably provided with books upstairs. But will Lord Camber want them? They are his books after all. Still, no doubt there is a handsome library at the Chase – now he has command of all that plenty. *Oh*, how sorry I am for that poor child . . .

Her thoughts ran about like ants.

'You are tired and moithered, Miss Hatty,' said Godwit kindly. 'And, lord knows, there's enough to bother ye. But, look, the storm is well ended now – why don't ye step outside for a breath of air?'

'A good idea,' sighed Hatty.

The Thatched Grotto was not restful just then: Mrs Daizley pottered about, murmuring to herself, concerned with the items she might want to take to the Chase, and those she must replace. 'And they have some grand big copper cauldrons in the kitchens there, but no proper pastry-room. I must talk to his Grace about that – and take my own rolling-pin, Godwit will have to make her another—' while Mrs Godwit could be heard disapprovingly listing the names of all the aunts and cousins, such as Lady Ursula Fowldes, who could be expected to darken the life of the new young duchess.

Hatty and Godwit strolled away from the house, up the long tree-bordered slowly ascending path which led to the top of the hill where she had once walked with Lord Camber.

No: twice. And the second time we saw my father out with the hunt. Poor Father. He never did get to be Master of Foxhounds, and that is all he ever really wished for. I have been far luckier than Father already, for my wish was granted: I have had a book published. And I am only nineteen! The pride and glow of that will never go away. When I was a child I thought that life went up continuously to a peak, getting better and better all the way. Now I know that was just a childish fancy. There are small peaks – that walk with Harry Camber was one – and then we come down from them again. But memories are like leaves – he said that once – they fertilize the ground on which they fall . . .

During this stroll – alongside of her thoughts – she had been discussing with Godwit various repairs that needed doing in the house.

'We must get Sid Thatcher to come and mend the hole those wasps made. And the rain barrel is beginning to rot.'

'I have the money from my publishers,' said Hatty. 'We are rich.'

'In the old days, Master Harry would have mended that hole,' grieved Godwit. 'He was a rare thatcher. But he'll be too busy now, clearing up all the old Duke's topsy-turveydom. Like father, like son.' Suddenly he chuckled. 'Fancy getting *paid* for writing poetry! You might as well pay birds for singing!'

Hatty laughed too.

'Aren't I lucky? Paid for what I like doing best.'

They came to the bench at the top of the hill.

'Too damp to sit on, after all that rain,' said Godwit. He took off his jacket and spread it, and they sat on that. After the rain the air was very clear and they could see Underwood Priors in its valley, and Bythorn Chase on its hill. I wonder what Harry Camber and Changing Sky are doing now, thought Hatty, and, far away, the spire of Mansfield church.

None of them will come to see us. How peaceful that will be.

Godwit said: 'I'm a bit bothered, Miss Hatty.'

'Why, Godwit?'

'With Mrs Daizley going – and my old gran not likely to last many winters longer – with just you and me in the Grotto, that's going to lead to talk. I'm afraid, Miss Hatty, it seems to me – that if you want to stay on here—'

'Which I most certainly do—'

'I can't see any other way out of it but for you and me to get married.'

'But, Godwit,' she said, 'there's nothing in the world I should like better.'

He laughed his soundless laugh, his eyes flitting from side to side.

'Then,' he said, 'you'll have to learn to call me Eli.'

'Nonsense! Godwit suits you perfectly well! I shall stick to that.'

XXVI

Letter from Lady Barbara du Vallon to Miss Hatty Ward
Dear Miss Ward:
Rumour has it (in a letter from Winship – nobody else writes to me
from the Priors) that you are now married most demeaningly to a
butler or valet or some such, but I daresay Winship has it wrong so
I shall continue to address you as Miss Ward. Our friend M. Marat
had a narrow escape recently when an army of three thousand men
was sent into the Cordeliers' district to arrest him for his critical
pamphlets against the government. Fortunately our other friend, a
Monsieur Danton, was able to delay the officers until Marat had
time to escape through the back door. So he is still at Liberty, I am
happy to say. Miss Ward I hear (through my husband, who still
reads the English Journals when he can get hold of them) that you
have had a book of poems published with great critical acclaim.
Although under a *nom de plume* he recognized some that he had
read before. He sends his congratulations and so do I. As you must
now be rich, I should be greatly oblig'd if you could send us a trifle
of money, since Marcel at present receives very little remuneration
for his revolutionary activities. 10 L. would be most acceptable.
Fortunately, living is cheap here, there is a restaurant not far from
our lodging where, for six sous, you can get a meal of roast lamb,
lentils, bacon, salad, cheese, and a carafe of red wine. So your 10 L.
will go a long way. Thank you for reminding Winship yet again
about the chemises which she has now sent.
　　Yours B du V.

Letter from Tom Ward to Ned Ward
Dear Brother:
It seems a long Time since word passed between us. I hope that you
are in Good health and well on the road to become a Captain. I

myself hope to be promoted Captain in a month or so; meanwhile the ———th has been drafted into Bedfordshire for the winter so, as the distance was not too great, I took the opportunity of riding over to visit our Cousin Hatty at Wanmaulden & can give you News of her. Well! She is married to a fellow called Godwit who used to be Lord Camber's batman or something of the sort. (Lord C is now Duke of Dungeness, I suppose you may know that.) Hatty and this Godwit seem to be happy together as the Day is Long, living in an amazingly ugly cottage in the midst of a forest. He told me he had always loved her since the day he first set eyes on her when she was sent from our home in Disgrace for conniving at your clandestine meetings with that Slut, Nancy Price. I suppose you know N.P. is now married to our Brother Sydney? It seems S. went to see her in London to caution her against any Hopes she might have of marrying *you*, and she contriv'd to get her claws into him. I know she came into 10,000 L. when her uncle died & Sydney got wind of that no doubt. Brother, you are well quit of that designing Hussy and our brother Sydney will doubtless be well served for his interference. Talking of Legacies I will tell you a Joke. You know our great-aunt Winchilsea died two years ago and left us each a Bible. Well it seems she also left a Fortune and Sydney's partner Saul Brabham had the handling of it. Well, it seems the old girl had took a fancy to our Cousin Hatty (who put a posy by her bedside or some such Token at Maria's wedding when H was but a little thing). The old Girl never forgot, and left her fortune to Hatty, but only on condition that she got wed before the age of 21 – it seems Aunt W was in favour of girls marrying before they grow too opinionated. *But Hatty was not to know about this*. If she did, or if she failed to marry, the cash was to go to a Sailors' home. Sydney knew about the Bequest but he never told us for fear we should make up to Hatty and snatch the prize which he had marked for himself. So is he not well paid in his own coin? There's for you! He told me none of this until news came of Hatty's marriage – he was in a rare Tweak about it. I am happy for our Cousin, who *still* does not know her Good Fortune since she will not be 21 until next year.

She is a Good Girl and always used to help me with my Euclid and Latin irregular verbs. Well Adieu my dear brother and send me a line when convenient. Here's Hoping our paths may cross before too long.

Lt Thos Ward.

Letter from Mrs Fanny Price to Mrs Harriet Godwit
Dear Sister:

This comes to thank you for the 10 L. but pray do not send *any more*, as Sister Agnes says I am not to accept any more gifts from you since you have disgraced the name of our family by your Shocking Misalliance and Mrs Norris has told me that your name is never to be mentioned by us *ever* again. My daughter Fanny, who had Harriet as her middle name, is not to use it & I grieve to say that Mrs Norris has forbidden me even to speak of you to the children. So no more now & this is to say Goodbye from your sister Frances Price.

Letter from Sir Nicholas Bertram to Miss Sarah Ward
Dear Sal:

Laid up for a week with a sprained ankle (squash) I've been amusing myself delving about in boxes of papers which Henshawe brought down for me from the Mansfield Park attics. Came upon a most interesting trove. Did you know that our great-great-aunt Harriet Ward was the poet Anthony Bailiff (the one that the B.B.C. Third Programme did weekly readings from a couple of months ago)? What an interesting ancestor we have! I am going to try to find out more about her life. She died, it seems, at an early age. What a pity! Maybe there would be the makings of a T.V. programme, what do you think?

Best to you and Pete, love Nick.